Crinoline Cowboys

A Cowboy of Her Own © 2019 by Patty Smith Hall
Josephine's Dream © 2019 by Cynthia Hickey
Love's Cookin' at the Cowboy Café © 2019 by Marilyn Turk
Bea Mine © 2019 by Kathleen Y'Barbo

Print ISBN 978-1-64352-241-8

eBook Editions:
Adobe Digital Edition (.epub) 978-1-64352-243-2
Kindle and MobiPocket Edition (.prc) 978-1-64352-242-5

All scripture quotations are taken from the King James Version of the Bible.

This book is a work of fiction. Names, characters, places, and incidents are either products of the author's imagination or used fictitiously. Any similarity to actual people, organizations, and/or events is purely coincidental.

Cover Image: Magdalena Russocka / Trevillion Images

Published by Barbour Books, an imprint of Barbour Publishing, Inc., 1810 Barbour Drive, Uhrichsville, Ohio 44683, www.barbourbooks.com

Our mission is to inspire the world with the life-changing message of the Bible.

ецра Member of the
Evangelical Christian
Publishers Association

Printed in Canada.

Crinoline Cowboys

4 Southern Women Head West to Crinoline Creek, Texas

Patty Smith Hall
Cynthia Hickey
Marilyn Turk
Kathleen Y'Barbo

BARBOUR BOOKS
An Imprint of Barbour Publishing, Inc.

A Cowboy of Her Own

by Patty Smith Hall

Chapter 1

Crinoline Creek, Texas
Spring 1868

Carter Wilbanks grabbed his younger sister and tossed her over his shoulder like a sack of cornmeal. An eleven-year-old girl spitting with the cowhands and beating them, if their long faces were anything to go by. Goodness gracious, Ma would be spinning in her grave if she could see the mess he'd made with Cassie.

"Carter!" Cassie squirmed as he turned toward the ranch house. "Why'd you take me away like that? I wasn't doin' nothin' wrong!"

The fact she didn't see the harm in what she was doing was just another example of how he'd failed her. He should have taken more time with the girl. But he'd been too busy getting the ranch on solid footing, growing the dream his parents had shared with him when they left Kentucky ten years ago. Still, that was no reason to neglect his duties as an older brother.

"I bet I could outspit you!"

"Probably," Carter answered, walking across the yard. "From what I can tell, you've had a lot of practice at that disgusting habit."

"The boys do it. Big John says I'm the best he's ever seen." Excitement crept into her voice. "Said I might be the best in all of Crinoline Creek."

He'd have to have a word with his cook when he got back to the house. The man knew how much the girl looked up to him. Carter shifted her weight on his shoulder. "Just because you can do it doesn't mean you should."

"Are you mad at me?" Cassie's girlish whisper curled its way around his heart.

"No," he answered softly. It wasn't her fault she'd grown up wild and untethered as an unbroken mustang. No, he laid the blame solely at his own feet. It'd been easier to outfit her in dungarees and cowboy boots than the frills and laces girls seemed to enjoy. What did he know about raising a child?

Nothing, but it was time he took responsibility and helped his sister become the lady their parents would have wanted her to be. "I don't want to see you spitting with the hands again. Is that clear?"

"But we were only playing around." She pressed her hand against his shoulder and leaned back so she could see him. "It was only a game."

"I don't care if it was a game, Cassie. This stops now."

"Why?"

The whiny note in her question set Carter's teeth on edge.

"Because it's not proper for a young lady to be spitting with the help, Cassie. That's why."

She was quiet for a second. "Then it's okay if I do it with the boys at school?"

Lord Almighty, help me here. Please. "You don't go around spitting with anyone, you hear me?"

She blew air between her lips, making an unladylike noise. "Don't sound like ladies have much fun."

"They do." At least, he hoped they did. Ranching hadn't left him any time to know much about the fairer sex. "It's just a different kind of fun. Don't you want to be a lady like Ma was?"

"Ma would have let me finish the game."

Carter started to speak, then stopped. Cassie didn't know what Ma would have done. She'd barely been in leading strings when first Papa then Ma had been taken by the fever. Carter had been little more than a boy himself, but at seventeen, he'd been left with a toddler and a hundred head of the finest cattle this side of the Mississippi. He'd almost worked himself to death in those early days, building a home for Cassie, proving himself to men nearly twice his age. But it had paid off. The Double C provided beef to the men building the railroad east of the Rockies. He carried a nice sum at the bank, and he'd even managed to set some aside for Cassie when she married.

Which would never happen if Cassie didn't tame her wild ways.

The question was how, when she lived among crotchety old cowboys and young bucks trying to prove themselves. He needed a lady, someone who could take Cassie in hand and show her the ropes. But who?

Carter climbed the steps to the wraparound front porch and

set Cassie on her feet. "Now, go upstairs and take those pants off. Young ladies don't go gallivanting around in jeans."

Her blue eyes widened, and for a moment, he was struck by her resemblance to their mother. A teasing smile lifted a corner of her mouth. "So you want me to run around the house in my long johns?"

Carter pinched the bridge of his nose. He might not know much about women, but he was fairly certain they didn't talk about men's unmentionables, much less wear them. Another mistake he'd have to correct. He drew in a calming breath. "Go upstairs and change into a dress."

"The only one I have is my Sunday-go-to-meetin' dress." She smiled up at him. "You wouldn't want me to get that all dirty, would you?"

He glared down at her. "I'll ride into town and get you a new one, and some underclothes and boots too."

Her lips tightened into a scowl. "I can't wear a dress. I'm supposed to go fishing with Tommy Snow this afternoon, and I won't be able to climb down to our favorite fishing hole in skirts."

Carter walked over, opened the door, then gently pushed her inside. "Then you can stay at home and help Big John fix supper."

He could feel anger vibrate through her small body. Without another word, she stomped her way upstairs like a prisoner being sent to the gallows. The door slammed, the noise echoing through the house.

Stubborn as a mule, that girl. Another trait that ran in the family. Once Cassie made up her mind, nothing and nobody would change it.

Well, he could be stubborn too. He'd turn that child into a

young lady or die trying. But he'd need help. Big John knew most of the folks in town. Maybe he knew a lady or two that could tutor Cassie without breaking her spirit. Carter headed down the hall toward the kitchen.

The smell of fresh beef frying met Carter at the kitchen door, the succulent combination of steak and butter reminding him of his rushed breakfast. On the table, slices of fresh bread were stacked beside a platter of fried potatoes. They ate well on the Double C. Paid well too. But it would all be for nothing if he failed his little sister.

Hopefully, his cook could help. His mentor from the early days, John Fricks had been a fixture in these parts since Sam Houston was a babe. Surely he knew someone who could help with Cassie.

"Smells good in here."

The older man turned, his hunched body barely taller than the stove he cooked on. "Nothing fancy. Just plain food and a lot of it." He studied Carter for a moment then forked the sizzling steak onto a plate and lifted the pan off the stove. "You didn't come in here to talk about food though, did you?"

John may have been with him since the early days, but it still surprised him that the man could read him so well. "I'm worried about Cassie."

That got his attention. It was no secret Cassie had the old man wrapped around her little finger. "What has that little firecracker done now?"

Carter drew in a deep breath. "I found her in a spitting contest with the younger hands behind the barn."

The old man made the same unladylike noise Cassie had not five minutes earlier. Well, at least Carter knew where she got that habit. "Is that all? I figured from the sour look on your face you'd caught her skipping school again."

Blood pounded in Carter's ears. "She's skipping school? When?"

"Only once or twice." The wrinkles around John's eyes deepened as he laid out the jelly and butter. "That Satterfield girl has been giving her trouble."

"The Satterfields are always causing trouble." It was just the way they were. Mean as a snake, all of them. The folks of Crinoline Creek had learned to deal with them without riling them up. Cassie needed to learn to do the same.

Still, that wasn't an excuse to skip school. "Why didn't you tell me?"

"Because it was only those couple of times." His wrinkled face turned sober. "She was crying her poor little eyes out, and you know how I feel about that young'un. So I gave her some sugar cookies and a glass of milk, then sat with her until she calmed down." His pale gray eyes turned watery. "It almost broke my heart."

Carter's heart ached for his sister. If only Ma had lived, she would have taught Cassie how to handle people like the Satterfields. "She has to learn how to get along with these folks, and the only way to do that is be around them."

"And you're a good example of that, aren't you?"

Carter glared at the man. "I get along with most people."

"When you're around them," John retorted, grasping the coffeepot with a dish towel. "You don't go into town unless you hain't got a choice, and you leave church before the last hymn is barely finished. You hain't got a friend outside of me."

"Running this ranch takes up most of my time. You know that."

John poured him a cup. "Still, if you'd had a woman in your life,

Cassie wouldn't be as wild as she is."

"Are you talking marriage again?" Carter sat down at the table, picked up his coffee, and blew on it. "Because if you are, I'm not listening."

John threw the towel down then cocked his fists on his hips. "You should be. You've built a legacy in this ranch. Don't you want to have children to pass it down to?"

Carter stared into his cup. "I always thought I'd leave it to Cassie."

"She ain't goin' to want it once she gets married and has a family of her own."

"Maybe not, but it would be here for her just the same." Carter reached for a slice of bread, only to get his hand swatted. "I'm hungry, old man."

"Not too old to knock you on your backside, boy." John grimaced, then his wrinkled face softened. "I'm sorry, I just worry about you. Your ma and pa would have wanted you to be settled down by now with a couple of little ones and a woman who loves you." His gray eyes twinkled. "And Cassie would have someone to help her."

Carter nabbed a piece of bread and slathered it in butter. There was some truth to what John said. He'd like to have a wife and children someday. But there was still a lot he had to do to get the ranch on better footing and Cassie to think about.

He finished off the bread then reached for another. "All I need right now is to find someone to teach Cassie how to be a young lady."

John leaned back against the counter as if the discussion had taken the fight out of him. "Who do you have in mind?"

"I was hoping you had some ideas."

"Let's see." The old man glanced up as if picking answers out of the air. "There's Widow Handley. She's got four daughters, the last one just married. She might trade lessons for some help around her place. Or Ellen Brunner, though I don't know how much time she has, working in the hotel restaurant like she does."

Carter shook his head. "Ellen was just promoted to manager, and Widow Handley is looking for a husband, not a trade."

"All right, all right." John walked over to the table, pulled a chair out, and sat down. "There's Miss Turner. She moved in next door a few months ago. Cassie says they seem nice enough."

Carter had seen the freshly mended fence when he'd been out checking for new calves, but he'd never met the family. "What do you know about them?"

"From what I've heard, they're from Georgia, moved out here after the war ended. The young'uns look to be around Cassie's age, but Miss Turner..." He thought for a moment then shook his head. "I can't remember her name right now, but she's a proper little Southern belle. Maybe she could help you."

Pampered and spoiled, more than likely. Probably never done a hard day's work in her life. Perfect for what he needed if she'd take Cassie on. "You think her parents would approve?"

"Hain't no parents. From what I hear, their daddy died during the war. But Miss Turner's a fine lady." John gave him a crooked smile. "Quite the looker too."

Carter didn't care what she looked like as long as she could help Cassie. Southern ladies were known for their impeccable manners. Maybe he could work something out with her. Trade a couple of cows for lessons in etiquette. Carter pushed back from the table and stood. "I think I'll ride over and introduce myself."

"You'll want to go into town then."

Town. He'd waste half the day doing that. "Why? What's she doing there? Doesn't she have a ranch to run?"

"Because she's interviewing cowhands at the restaurant this afternoon." John gave him a crooked smile. "I saw an advertisement she put on the board in the mercantile a few days ago."

An odd place to be talking to a bunch of cowpokes. The dirt and mud they dragged in would keep Ellen Brunner cleaning for a week. Inconsiderate of the Turner woman if you asked him. Probably used to having people pick up after her.

Still, if she could teach Cassie how to be a proper lady, he'd ignore it. "Save me a plate. I've got an appointment in town."

Chapter 2

She missed her mountains.

Madalyn Turner took another sip of her coffee as she stared out the picture window of the Crinoline Creek Hotel & Restaurant. Oh, Texas had its own beauty—a field of cheery bluebonnets swaying gently in the late afternoon sun, the feel of the sunshine on her face as she fed the chickens. The fresh start they needed. Still, she missed the gentle slopes and lush foliage of her beloved Blue Ridge Mountains.

Home. A sense of sadness settled over her. No, not home, not anymore. More like a memory of a life once lived. Home was the ranch, a place she shared with her younger sister and their patchwork family of war orphans. It had been hard leaving Marietta, but after the carpetbaggers descended on them, there had been nothing left to keep them there. With Mama and Papa gone, it was left to Maddie to make a home for her little family and to keep them safe.

Yes, Texas had its beauty. Like the herd of prime cattle ready for branding at her ranch. Her own cattle ranch. It was all she'd ever dreamed of, ever since she'd read an article in the *Atlanta Journal and Constitution* about the early settlers of the West. She'd devoured every book on the subject, even earmarked a few, hoping that one day her dream of becoming a cowboy would come true.

Not that anyone back home believed in her. How many men had suddenly changed their minds about courting her when she shared her hopes of owning a cattle ranch? And their sisters had been even worse, shunning her and her crazy ideas. Maybe they were right. Doubt lodged itself deep in her chest. Daddy always said she could do anything she put her mind to, but even he might question her abilities if he could see her now.

Which was the reason she was in town today rather than repairing the fence in the southern pasture.

"No luck?"

Maddie glanced up to find Ellen Brunner standing beside her, coffeepot in hand. Another Southerner who had moved west after Appomattox, she'd worked her way from waitress to manager of the hotel restaurant here in Crinoline Creek soon after Maddie arrived. A friendship had blossomed over their shared goal of being working women.

Maddie pushed her coffee cup toward Ellen. "This is harder than I expected."

"It's always hard to find good help." The older woman refreshed Maddie's coffee. "Though I imagine looking for a man to work for a woman would be a mite difficult."

"It's not like I'm the first woman to own a ranch."

"I don't think many of the ranch hands have read your book about women ranchers." Ellen smiled as she pulled out the chair opposite Maddie's and sat down. "And to be the first in a place like Crinoline Creek. The men are none too happy about it. They say the Steele place is too fine a place for a Southerner, let alone a lady."

"I don't care two figs what the men think. They started a war they had no business fighting, then left us to clean up their mess," Maddie replied. If she closed her eyes, she could still feel the house shake as cannons exploded around her. Well, the Lord had pulled her through the war. Running a ranch couldn't be any harder than what she'd already survived. Still, she was curious. "What do the women say?"

"There are a few who don't approve, but most think it's wonderful what you're doing for those children, bringing them out here, giving them a home."

"Why shouldn't I? After all, I'm an orphan myself." She gave a little sigh. "But it won't be so great if I don't hire a decent hand to help us out." She needed more than a cowhand really, but Ellen didn't need to know that.

"What happened with the man you interviewed earlier?" Ellen poured herself a cup of coffee. "He seemed very interested in the position."

"Oh, he was." The muscles in her shoulders tightened at the memory of the man's lewd suggestions. "But only if the job included me."

"Oh dear. Why didn't you say something? I would have tossed him out of here." Ellen reached across the table and covered

Maddie's hand. "What happened?"

"I set him straight." Maddie leaned back in her chair, all of her mother's careful training going right out the window. "When he realized I wasn't about to change my mind, he told me no man would be caught dead working for a woman, much less a rebel." Even now, her cheeks heated with anger. "Honestly, Ellen, it took every ounce of my patience not to lean across the table and smack him good."

Her friend laughed. "You're not the first woman in town to have to deal with Jessop's attentions."

"Oh dear. Not you too?"

"I'd barely gotten off the stagecoach before he started in on me," she said over the rim of her cup. "But he changed his mind when he got a glimpse of the pistol I carry in my skirt pocket."

"I wish I could have seen that. I might just have to go to the mercantile and order me a gun." Maddie giggled softly. "But really, aren't there any cowboys like the ones I read about in my book? Someone who's gallant and forthright. You know, a real man."

"Does your book have a chapter on fisticuffs and brawling in the streets?" Ellen took a sip then replaced her cup on its saucer. "Because they're good at that."

"They can't all be like that." Maddie sighed again. "I want to hire a man who respects women and reads his Bible. Someone who will be a good role model for the children. Someone who will teach me the basics of ranching without squawking about it."

"In other words," Ellen answered, "you're looking for a needle in a haystack."

The memory of her interview with Jessop weighed on her. Was she looking for the impossible? Surely there was a cowboy out there who could teach her the ropes. Someone who would understand and respect her dream of being an honest-to-goodness cowboy. Well, God had given her this dream, so she'd just have to pray and wait on Him to fulfill it. "I guess I am. It just seems to me that there's a reason the men I've interviewed aren't employed."

"Mr. Barrett doesn't seem to have any problems finding good ones."

Maddie followed Ellen's gaze to a tall, rugged man in the corner. "I noticed him when I walked in. How many days has he been in here this week? Three? Four?"

"Six days. I was off on Sunday." A smile lit Ellen's face. She took another sip. "That's only because his cook is caring for his mother in Houston."

"If the man's expression every time he glances at you is anything to go by, his cook might not have a job when he comes back."

A blush rose in Ellen's cheeks. "Stop it. He just enjoys the food here."

Maddie smiled over the rim of her cup. "I can see."

Ellen's eyes widened. "Maddie."

"I shouldn't tease you. Your Mr. Barrett has one of the largest cattle ranches in the state." But not for long, if Maddie had anything to say about it. Give her a few years and a few good hands, and she'd give any rancher around a run for his money.

She just needed someone to teach her how to be a cowboy first.

The bell over the door tinkled. Maddie and Ellen turned toward the door in time to see a man step inside and remove his hat, revealing a mop of dark hair that looked as untamed as himself. He was tall and lean, muscled with broad shoulders that filled out his cotton shirt. Maddie shifted her gaze to his face, her breath catching in her throat. Mercy sakes, he was handsome, with cheekbones cut from granite and a slash of a nose.

And he was walking toward her. From the expression on his face, he'd found her. . .

Lacking?

Irritation pressed her back into the wooden chair. How dare he judge her without knowing the first thing about her? A true gentleman didn't look at a lady in such a way, but as she was quickly learning, the usual rules of etiquette didn't apply out here. Still, his assumption smarted more than she cared to admit.

By the time he stood next to their table, she'd calmed down a bit.

He tipped his hat to her friend. "How are you doing, Ellen?"

"Doing well, Carter," Ellen replied. "And you? How are things out at the Double C going?"

"We're doing good. Had a bumper year for new calves."

"That's good." Ellen shifted her attention to Maddie. "Have you met my friend here? Maddie Turner, this is Carter Wilbanks. He owns the ranch just west of you."

Maddie held out her hand. "Mr. Wilbanks."

"Miss Turner." The man glanced at her hand, then back at her. "You're just the person I came to see."

Pushing away from the table, Ellen rose from her seat. "Let me get you a cup of coffee, Carter. Is there anything else you might want? We've got a peach cobbler in the back."

"I'll take some," the man replied as he took the seat Ellen vacated.

"Coming right up." Ellen bustled toward the kitchen.

What a rude man! First he stared at her like she was a cow pie on his shoe, then he ran her friend off. If she could she'd ignore him, but that would just cause a scene. Maddie lifted her chin and stared down her nose at him. "You came to see me."

"I need to talk to you."

That was an odd way to ask for an interview, but then again, he owned his own ranch. Why would he be interested in working for her? She folded her hands in her lap. "You could have waited until after I'd finished speaking to my friend."

The man looked surprised by her rebuke. Well, if he intended to work for her, he'd better get used to it. Ellen gave her a comical look as she came back with a cup and two pieces of cobbler. "Anything else I can get for you?"

"Maybe the recipe to your apple pie so I can give it to Big John. You know how much I like it."

"You know I can't do that." Ellen laughed, then gave Maddie a knowing look as she turned toward the kitchen. What was that all about? What did her friend know that she didn't? Probably nothing she wouldn't find out during the interview.

When she turned her attention back to the man, her breath caught. He was doing it again, studying her as if trying to measure her worth. Well, if he thought for one moment she was someone who could be pushed around, he was sadly mistaken. Picking up her pencil, she met his dark blue gaze. "Your name again, please?"

"Carter Wilbanks."

Wilbanks. Why did that name sound so familiar? Maybe one of Papa's associates back home? "And how long have you been a cowboy?"

"Ten years," he answered with a ghost of a smile.

He was laughing at her. Maddie set her pencil down then glared across the table at him. "Is something funny, Mr. Wilbanks?"

The corner of his mouth tilted up in a lazy smile. "Yeah."

Her lips tightened. He probably thought a woman running a cattle ranch was humorous. What would he think if he knew everything she knew about ranching and cows she'd learned from a book? "I always enjoy a good laugh. Why don't you tell me what's so funny?"

He thought for a moment. "Miss Turner, I didn't come here to apply for a job."

"You didn't?" For some strange reason, she felt slightly disappointed.

"No." His expression grew serious. "I came here to offer you one."

Chapter 3

"ut I'm the one with a job to offer."

Carter glanced across the table at the woman, his palms breaking out in a sweat. Big John hadn't done her justice. Maddie Turner wasn't just pretty in the usual sort of way like he'd been led to believe. Her golden-blond curls were piled low at her long slender neck, the errant strands reminding him of sunlight dancing along waves in the stream. Her eyes were a color he couldn't decipher, an interesting mix of blues and purples that a man could get lost in. And she smelled of warm baked cookies, or at least, he thought she did, but they were in a restaurant, so he could be mistaken.

The job.

Carter cleared his throat. "Maybe we could help each other out. What is this job you need done? Help with branding? Mending a fence or two? I can spare a day or two to do odd jobs around your place. I'll even arrange to drive your herd to market if that's what you need."

"Yes."

Carter didn't understand her answer. "Yes to what part?"

"To all of it, of course."

"I don't understand."

She took a deep breath, almost as if to get her courage up. "I need a cowboy who can show me the ropes. Branding, calving, everything I need to know to run a successful cattle ranch."

Carter wasn't completely certain what she meant. "You mean you need help finding a ranch foreman to take care of those things?"

"No." She hesitated a moment then lowered her voice. "I don't intend to hire someone to do all those things. I need someone to teach me how to do them."

Carter blinked. It sounded almost like she. . . "You want to be a cowboy?"

She nodded. "That is my intention. I've wanted to be a cowboy since I read an article about them in the local newspaper back home when I was ten years old. Of course, women couldn't be cowboys back in those days, but then I read this book." She pulled a small well-worn copy from her reticule and placed it on the table between them. "It gave me hope enough to follow my dream. All I need now is a few lessons, and the book should tell me the rest."

Of all the cockamamie. . . He barked with laughter.

She stiffened. "I don't see what's so funny."

No, she wouldn't. Carter rubbed his eyes with the back of his hand. "I'm sorry. It's just most of the cowboys I know didn't learn their trade from some silly book."

"Yes, well." Her cheeks had turned a becoming shade of pink, and Carter regretted his words instantly. Still, she didn't seem to be giving up. "That's why I need you to teach me what the book doesn't."

Which would be everything. Really, the government ought to outlaw that kind of rubbish for the ideas they put into gullible people's minds. "Ma'am, it would take years to teach you everything you need to know. Besides, I've got my own ranch to tend to."

"Don't you have a ranch foreman?"

"Of course I do." What an odd question to ask. A ranch his size couldn't do without one.

She stared at him with wide-eyed innocence that stole the breath from his lungs. "Then you're not really running the ranch, are you?"

The wily woman had him there. She sounded so earnest, almost as if it meant the world to her to achieve her goal. But this woman, a cowboy? It would be best to let her down easy. "Do you know the hours you have to put into your place every day? You're up before daybreak, and most nights you drag in just in time to eat supper and go to bed. It's backbreaking work for a man, but for a woman. . ." He shook his head.

She lifted her chin at a stubborn angle. "I'm not afraid of hard work."

Of course she wasn't. She'd probably never worked a lick in her life. "This isn't your father's plantation with you as lady of the manor."

"Mr. Wilbanks." There was a steely edge to her voice, as if she'd had enough of his nonsense. "We didn't own a plantation, nor did we partake in the vile practice of enslaving people. We had a farm that I ran after Papa joined the Union army. Everyone who worked for us earned a good wage." She took a deep breath. "I worked along-side our employees in the fields because that's what was needed to be done to survive the war going on around us."

Carter felt like the lowest worm. He'd misjudged her, and badly at that. "I'm sorry, Miss Turner. I shouldn't have insulted you like that."

"I accept your apology. It's a common misconception." Staring at the tablecloth, she drew in a shaky breath. "What's done is done, and we must move on, mustn't we?"

Miss Turner was gracious as well as ladylike, even if she was outspoken. She would have been the perfect example for Cassie to follow, but he'd ruined the chance for that. "I'm sorry for interrupting your interviews. I just thought we might be able to help each other."

She glanced at him. "How can I help you?"

"Are you sure you want to know? From where I'm sitting, I just made a hash of things."

"And you've apologized for it." Miss Turner gave him a kind smile that made his heart race. "So, would you give me some lessons in ranching?"

He took a bite of peach cobbler to give him time to think. She was stubborn, and she wasn't afraid of hard work. If any woman could run a ranch, he had a feeling this one could. "It won't hurt to give you a few pointers. Maybe teach you some of the basics."

Her expression brightened, and Carter felt it all the way down to his toes. "Will you let me practice on the cows?"

He didn't understand her. "Practice what on them?"

"You know." Her voice dropped a degree as though she didn't

want anyone else to hear them. "Roping, branding, riding."

His ears perked up. "You don't know how to ride?"

"Of course I do." She glanced around then shifted her attention back to him. "Sidesaddle."

"Of course." Carter pinched the bridge of his nose. How could she run a ranch if she didn't know how to ride properly? This might be worse than dealing with Cassie.

Cassie.

He'd almost forgotten what he'd come to town for. "You haven't heard my terms yet."

She sat back, eyeing him suspiciously. "What kind of terms?"

Smart woman. Maybe she could be a cattle rancher if she wasn't so. . .womanly. He cleared his throat. "I have a younger sister."

"I do too." She gave him an encouraging smile. "Her name is Shelby."

So Cassie would get two Southern belles for the price of one. This trade was looking better by the moment. "Our parents died when Cassie was barely a year old, so she hasn't had much in the way of a female influence." He hesitated, not sure how much to reveal. "She's a bit of a tomboy."

"How old is she?"

"She's ten."

Miss Turner's smile tied his stomach in knots. "Most girls are tomboys at that age. At least, I was."

He didn't know why, but her words gave him comfort. "She's never been one to wear dresses or play like other little girls. She likes to be outdoors, tending to the animals or fishing." He left out the spitting for now.

"Sounds like you've given her a wonderful childhood."

He hadn't expected her compliment or the way it warmed some place deep down inside him. Carter cleared his throat. "Cassie has been raised around men all her life, and because of that, she's a little rough around the edges." He glanced at her. "That's where you come in."

"Wait a minute." Miss Turner glanced around the café then leaned toward him. Yes, she definitely smelled of fresh baked cookies. His mouth watered. "Is she the one who broke Wendall Loudermilk's nose during recess last week?"

He jerked back in his seat. "Cassie broke a kid's nose?"

"That's what Robin told me. She's one of the orphans we brought with us when we left Marietta," Miss Turner explained. "Robin also said Wendall deserved it."

"Did she tell you why Cassie hit the boy?"

"No, but Robin's usually a fair judge of a situation." Miss Turner pressed her lips together. "What exactly is it that you want for your sister, Mr. Wilbanks?"

"I want Cassie to be a lady." He traced the outline of his spoon with his finger. Carter had never asked for a lick of help his entire life, but for Cassie, he would. "I can't teach her what she needs to know, but you and your sister can. Ranching lessons in exchange for teaching my sister how to be a lady. Is it a deal or not?"

She seemed to consider it, a mite too long in his opinion. What would he do if she turned him down? There weren't too many women in town who would take on his sister.

Miss Turner held her hand out. "We have a deal."

"Deal." Carter grasped her hand, the shock of soft skin against his calloused fingers pulling the air out of his lungs. Shaking to the core, he let go, the warmth of her fingers etched against his palm.

He glanced up at her. Her cheeks had gone pink again, and there was a confusion in her eyes that matched his own. So she had felt it too. For some strange reason, he sat up a little straighter at the thought.

❧ *Chapter 4* ❧

$\mathcal{A}$unt Maddie, I'm telling you. Cassie Wilbanks is mean as a snake."

Maddie handed Robin a washed dish, then dunked the roasting pan in the soapy water and let it sit. "Why do you say that?" Robin opened her mouth, but before she could speak, she added, "Besides the incident with the Loudermilk boy, what else has she done to make you think that way?"

"Well, I. . ." Robin stopped drying the dish she was holding and thought for a moment, her eyes lighting up when she finally came up with an example. "Melanie Waters said Cassie put salt in Miss Worth's tea the first day of school."

Melanie Waters also told the occasional tall tale. Besides, most children pulled pranks in school. Both Maddie and Shelby had done their fair share. "Did Melanie actually see Cassie do it?"

Robin shook her head. "Another kid told her about it."

"Then you mustn't hold that against Cassie. Anything else?"

Robin looked up at her, wide-eyed. As if she'd saved the best for last. "She spits."

Maddie wasn't expecting that answer. "What do you mean, 'she spits'?"

Robin wiped the dish dry and placed it on the stack with the others. "With the boys. Sometimes they bet their lunch pails on who can spit the furthest." She pressed her lips into a disapproving line. "Cassie's actually won a couple of times."

"Oh dear." That was disconcerting. Maddie's heart went out to the poor motherless girl. "Not mean, but not exactly ladylike. Maybe she doesn't know any better."

"And she wears jeans to school." Robin's braids swished from side to side. "Just like the boys."

Maddie scooped up a bubble and put it on the girl's nose. "I wear jeans when I work on the ranch."

"That's not the same thing." She giggled then lifted her gaze to meet Maddie's. "Is it?"

It wasn't, but Maddie didn't want to give the girl any reason to dislike Cassie. "Maybe Cassie feels more comfortable in jeans."

"Maybe." Robin considered that for a moment. "But that doesn't mean she should do it. Girls are supposed to wear dresses. That's the way it is."

Of course she thought that way. Robin was raised in a home where women were considered gentle creatures without a worry in the world. The war had changed that, driving people to do the unthinkable just to survive. More so for her family. Papa's decision to spy for the Union had Maddie walking on pins and needles for fear she'd let something slip and put Papa in danger. She'd handled their small farm while caring for her younger sister, always fearful word of Papa's work would get out. Only with God's help had she managed, and it made her stronger in her faith and in her abilities.

But was it enough to run a cattle ranch? She'd soon find out. After much discussion, it was decided that Carter Wilbanks would come to her ranch and give her lessons. Her first would be bright and early tomorrow morning.

"Maybe I should be nicer to Cassie," Robin whispered softly.

"That would be nice of you." Maddie smiled, her heart light from pride in the child. "And you can begin tomorrow morning. Her brother is going to help me out around the ranch for the next few weeks, so he's bringing Cassie with him."

"That girl is coming here?" Robin exclaimed, a grief-stricken look worrying her expression. "I figured I'd start out by saying hello at school or offering to eat lunch with her, not have her at my house!"

"Don't look like I've thrown you into a pit of copperheads. You're just going to have breakfast, then walk to school with her."

The girl's blue eyes widened in panic. "But everyone will see us!"

Maddie wrung out her dishrag, then folded it and hung it on the sink. "Have you ever thought that if you're kind to Cassie, maybe others will be too?"

"Or maybe she'll put a mouse in my desk. I've heard she's done that before too."

"Or maybe she won't."

"Or maybe she will. It's just that. . ." Robin hesitated. "She always seems so mad, and nobody knows why."

Maddie understood that feeling. After they'd lost Mama the

summer before she turned fifteen, she'd railed at everyone. It had taken time for her to realize she'd really been angry at God. Once she asked Him to forgive her, the anger had faded like sun-bleached cloth.

How much more difficult it must be for Cassie, growing into a young woman without a mother to guide her?

"You know, you and Cassie have a lot in common," Maddie said, thinking Robin might understand the girl if she knew a bit more about her. "Did you know Cassie lost her mama and papa when she was just a baby?"

"I didn't know that." Robin's lips quivered as tears pooled in her eyes. "That's hard."

Reaching out for her, Maddie drew her into her arms. "Oh, sweet girl, I didn't mean to make you cry."

"I miss Mama and Papa so much sometimes, it's hard to breathe." Her voice cracked. "I wish that old war had never happened."

"Me too." Maddie kissed the child's head then snuggled her closer.

"I only saw Papa twice, and once was when I was born." Robin leaned her head back, her eyes as blue as the cornflowers blossoming along the ridge. "Do you think Cassie feels the same way I do?"

Maddie cupped the girl's face in her hands. "Probably."

Robin thought for a moment then nodded decisively. "Then I won't just be nice to her. I'll try to be her friend if she'll let me, Aunt Maddie."

"Good girl!" Maddie kissed Robin's head. "You've always had the kindest heart. Just like your sweet mama."

"Which is why you were best friends."

Maddie nodded. Her heart ached just thinking about her

childhood friend. Robin was barely walking when Lillian had become pregnant with her second child. The death of her husband at Bull Run had sent her into a tailspin until she died in a cholera outbreak less than two months later. But Maddie knew the truth. Her dearest friend had died of a broken heart.

Which is why Maddie was in no hurry to fall in love. She knew herself well enough to know that when she fell in love, it would be with her whole heart, and after witnessing first her pa's loss then Lillian's, seeing the pain they experienced, she wasn't certain she could survive such heartache.

She gave Robin another kiss, this time on her cheek, then turned her toward the door. "You've got an early day tomorrow. Best get ready for bed."

"All right." She headed toward the door then turned back. "I love you, Aunt Maddie."

"I love you too, baby girl."

As Robin reached the door, it swung open. "Aunt Shelby." Robin ran up and kissed her. "Did you hear Aunt Maddie is taking cowboy lessons?"

"I know. Isn't it exciting?" Shelby gave Robin a hug then gently pushed her toward the door. "The boys are already asleep, so be quiet when you go up."

"Yes, ma'am."

Shelby waited until the door swung shut behind Robin before pulling out a chair and sitting down. "Are you sure about this? And I don't mean the cowboy part."

"What's there to be sure about?" Maddie grabbed two cups and placed them on the table. "It's just a little girl."

Shelby picked up Robin's discarded dish towel. "It's just I don't want her bullying the children. You know what they've had to deal with. Why, Robin has just begun sleeping through the night this last week." She shook her head. "I don't want them to be terrorized in their own home."

Maddie scraped the last plate into the bin then dunked it in the soapy water. Maybe if Shelby knew a little about Cassie she'd be more understanding. "Cassie's been raised around cowhands all her life. She doesn't know any other way."

"She lost her mother?"

Maddie nodded. "And her father when she was barely a year old. So you can't blame the girl for the way she acts." Her lips tightened as she scrubbed the last dish. "You can blame her brother for that."

"Why would you say that?" Shelby pried the plate from Maddie's hands and dunked it in clean water. "It was his loss too."

In her heart, Maddie knew her sister was right. She even felt kind of sorry for the man. He couldn't have been—what? seventeen or eighteen?—when he'd taken over the ranch after his parents had passed. But if he was anything like the confident man she'd met today, he knew better than to neglect his baby sister as he had over the years. "I just think he could have done better by her."

"Well, he's doing that now, isn't he?" Shelby stacked the last plate on the counter then folded the dish towel. "It's like that saying 'better late than never.' And he's agreed to teach you how to be a cowboy. That should make you happy."

"It does." Or it did until Carter had taken her hand. Even now, hours later, she could still feel the rough calluses of his fingers scrape gently against her palm. Just a simple touch, but as his hand had closed around hers, she'd felt closer to home than she had in years.

Maddie shook her head at the silly thought. "So is there another reason you asked me if I was sure about Cassie?"

"The whole deal you've made." Shelby let out a heavy sigh. "Sometimes you're as thick as a brick."

Maddie let that insult slide off her as she picked up the coffeepot and headed for the table. "I've always dreamed of being a cowboy, so why shouldn't I try?"

Shelby took the pot from her and poured them each a cup. "Because you don't know the first thing about ranching."

"I do too." Maddie heaped a tablespoon of sugar in her cup then added another. "I've read Miss Johnson's book and every article about ranching I could find."

Shelby shook her head. "Books aren't the same as real experience, and you know it."

They'd had this discussion a dozen times before. Still, Shelby couldn't understand this desire Maddie had to be out in the fresh air, working the rope and raising cattle to feed this growing country. She blew on the hot liquid. "Mr. Wilbanks will teach me what I need to know."

"Papa wouldn't approve."

Maddie took a small sip. Papa hadn't approved of the idea of women doing "men's work" at first, but once he'd gone to war and seen firsthand the accomplishments of the women who'd worked for both sides, he'd slowly changed his mind. "You're forgetting he bought this place for us before he passed. He'd want us to make the most of this opportunity."

Shelby rolled her eyes. "I don't know why I'm arguing with you about this. You made up your mind a long time ago."

Shelby was right. Ever since the day Maddie had read about ranching, she'd known this was her life's calling. The newspaper's description of a cattle drive had infused her with excitement, making her wonder what it would be like to own a ranch. It wasn't until she'd read the writings of Elizabeth Johnson about her own ranching experience that Maddie began to hope.

"Did you see anyone else in town today?"

That was an odd question. Shelby knew exactly what she'd been doing in town today. "Of course I did. I interviewed ranch hands."

"Anyone in particular stand out?" Shelby's expression was blank as she lifted her coffee cup to her lips.

Which meant she was up to something. Maddie placed her cup back on the table. "What's going on, Shelby?"

"Nothing." She took another sip. "I just heard Bennett Marshall was looking for a new situation."

Now it all made sense. "You mean that good-for-nothing cowboy who works for Clyde Muster?" Maddie scoffed. "I wouldn't hire him if he was the last cowhand in Texas."

Coffee sloshed onto the table as Shelby slammed her cup down. "You don't even know him. He's sweet and funny. The best man I've ever met in my life."

"Then you haven't met enough men to know the difference."

Shelby drew in a sharp breath. "That's a horrible thing to say!"

"He works for the man who would like nothing better than for us to give up this property." Maddie pulled the sugar bowl to herself and spooned some more into her coffee. "That's all I need to know."

"You'd fault a man for taking work?"

"Working for that man, I do," Maddie retorted. "Why are you so interested in him anyway?"

Shelby folded her arms across her chest. "If you got to know Bennett, you'd know he's a good man. He goes to church every time the circuit preacher comes around, and he sends home part of his earnings to his mama back in Kentucky."

"Sends home part of his. . ." Maddie felt her temper rise. "How would you know all of this?"

Her sister stared down into her coffee. "I see him in town on occasion, and I might have run into him when I'm taking my evening walk."

So that's where her sister had been! Maddie fought to keep quiet—after all, at eighteen, Shelby was a grown woman. Still, she had put herself in a perilous situation. "You know better than to go off alone with a man you hardly know."

"I know Bennett well enough." Shelby stiffened. "I'm in love with him."

In love! Shock ran through Maddie. "How can you love him? You barely know the man!"

"I know enough about him to know I love him. He wants to court me real proper-like, Maddie, and he was going to ask you for your permission today." Her sister's expression turned stormy. "You must have done something to scare him off."

"Doesn't say much for a man who'd turn tail and run so easily," Maddie muttered under her breath.

Shelby pushed her chair back and stood. "He's not afraid. Probably saw you and figured it just wasn't the right moment to be asking for my hand."

"Your hand? I thought he was going to court you."

"He is. I mean, yes, we've talked about getting married but. . ." Shelby let out a tiny grunt. "I swear, Maddie, you'd irritate the bark off a tree."

Not as much as you would, Maddie thought. And all this talk

39

about marriage to a man she didn't even know! Closing her eyes, she drew in a steadying breath. *Dear Lord, please give me the words to say, because my own will just anger her more.* She lifted her gaze to meet Shelby's. "I think we need to sleep on this before either of us says something we might regret."

Shelby gave her a stiff nod. "I agree, but understand me, Maddie. I'm going to marry Bennett whether you give us your blessing or not."

❧ Chapter 5 ❧

"Are you sure this lady wants to be a cowboy?" Cassie glanced around as they rode up to the front yard of Miss Turner's place. "It sure looks like a mess around here."

Carter couldn't argue with his sister there. Though the house had a fresh coat of paint, the yard around it made him groan. Several boards were missing from the fence around the barnyard, and a broken gate hung at an angle close to the ground. Weeds as tall as Cassie swayed side to side in the early morning breeze. Even the water trough for the horses looked to be in disrepair.

Climbing off his horse, Carter yanked his hat off and slapped it against his thigh. The woman had bitten off more than she could chew. But that wasn't his problem.

Or maybe it was.

He turned to Cassie as she climbed down from the saddle. "You just listen to everything Miss Maddie says about being a lady, you hear?"

"Yes, sir." Cassie grabbed the painted horse's reins then glanced around. "I don't see a hitching post."

Carter looked around. His sister was right. No hitching post. Taking the reins from her, he led the horses over to the front porch. "We'll just have to use this for now."

Cassie came up alongside him, giving the place a dubious glance. "This woman hain't no cowboy."

"I'm not one yet," a feminine voice responded from somewhere near the front door. "But I'm hoping your brother will show me how to become a good one."

Carter lifted his gaze, his mouth going dry at the sight of Miss Maddie Turner standing in the doorway. Mercy sakes, she was wearing blue jeans, not the frilly shirt and split skirt he'd expected. Not that he minded. He'd just never seen a woman look so right in them, as if they'd been made for just her. Her hair lay in a braided rope over her shoulder, stopping just short of the soft indention of her waist.

She was prettier than any cowpoke he'd ever seen.

"You look just like a bull when we put him in the field with the heifers," Cassie whispered beside him.

"Shh," Carter admonished, heat burning a path up the back of his neck. Miss Turner walked toward them, her boots making soft clicks against the hardwood floor. She stopped at the top of the stairs, then gave them a welcoming smile that Carter felt clear down to his toes.

Her attention shifted to his sister. "You must be Cassandra."

"Nobody calls me that." Cassie snorted, kicking a pile of dried grass with her boot.

Before he could correct his sister, Miss Turner laughed. "Nobody calls me by my first name either, not unless I'm in trouble." She held her hand out to the girl. "I go by Maddie."

"Cassie, ma'am." Cassie took her hand and gave it a firm shake before releasing it.

"That's a lovely nickname, so unique." She gave her another smile. "Just like you."

His sister eyed Miss Turner for a long moment then glanced at him. "What does she mean by that?"

Carter tugged gently on his sister's braid. "It means you're one of a kind."

Cassie perked up for a moment, then eyed Miss Turner. "Then why do you two want to change me?"

Leave it to his sister to see it that way. He beat his hat against his leg out of frustration. "I just want you to blend in more with the other girls at school."

"But then I won't be unique."

Cassie was messing with him now, waiting for him to make a mistake. Well, he'd made enough mistakes to last a lifetime. He only prayed he hadn't waited too long to help his sister. "Cassie. . ."

"Mr. Wilbanks, I do believe your sister is teasing you." Miss Turner came down the steps and crouched in front of Cassie. "Your brother didn't tell me how smart you are."

Cassie's eyes lit up. "No one's ever said that about me before."

Miss Turner seemed surprised to hear that. "Not even Miss Worth?"

"Especially not her!" The corners of Cassie's mouth curled

43

upward into a wide grin. "She says I'm too much of a troublemaker to amount to anything."

Carter felt his temper rise. That skinny old spinster woman, telling Cassie something like that. Who does that to a child? He rested a hand on his sister's slender shoulder. "You know that's not true, don't you? You can grow up to be anything you want."

Cassie's eyes lit up. "Even a cowboy like Big John?"

"That's not what I—" Carter started to explain.

"Of course," Miss Turner piped in. "That's part of the reason your brother brought you here. He wants to help you learn how to be a lady so that everyone can discover what a wonderfully unique cowboy you're going to be."

Carter wasn't sure why, but Miss Turner's answer satisfied any lingering doubts he might have had about her. He didn't want to break Cassie's spirit. He just wanted other folks to give her a chance.

His sister must have realized that too, because her smile had turned genuine. "I don't rightly know what to say, except I'm sorry."

Miss Turner glanced up at him, but all he could do was shrug. His sister's mind worked differently than his. Miss Turner finally turned back to Cassie. "Why do you feel you need to apologize?"

Cassie lifted contrite eyes to her. "Because I was planning on putting a spider in your bed."

"Cassandra!" He glared down at the girl. Poor woman. Probably regretting what she'd gotten herself into, teaching this one. Well, he'd better grovel if he wanted Miss Turner to train Cassie now. "I'm so sorry, ma'am."

Maddie Turner did the most amazing thing. She laughed, a low throaty sound that bubbled from her like a spring after the winter thaw. "At least you're honest about it. But, for the record, I'm not afraid of spiders or snakes, and sometimes I take the occasional salt in my tea."

Cassie giggled. "I'll keep that in mind."

Miss Turner touched her fingertip to the tip of Cassie's nose and smiled. "I will too."

Carter stood speechless, shaking his head. For the life of him, he'd never understand how a woman's mind worked. Yet he was sure of one thing. Maddie Turner could help his little sister become less of an outcast and more of a lady.

At least, he hoped so.

"First thing we need to do is cut down some of this grass."

Cut the grass? Maddie gave the man an incredulous look as they headed to the barn to start their day. "There's nothing about that in my book on ranching."

"Probably because it's just good old common sense to cut the yard around your house." He held the barn door open for her then followed her inside. He made a quick sweep of the area before turning back to her. "At least this place looks decent."

"Now, just a minute." She dug her heels in, fisting her hands on her hips. "I keep a clean barn, well, as clean as you can keep one with all the livestock we have."

Throwing a look over his shoulder, he replied, "I wouldn't have known that by the look of your yard."

She took a deep breath to calm herself. "There's a reason I'm letting the grass grow out."

Mr. Wilbanks spun around to face her. "That reason being?"

Maddie started to say something then stopped, noting how his

45

broad shoulders filled out his flannel shirt. Heat flared in her cheeks, and she dropped her gaze. This was ridiculous. He was just a man.

She cleared her throat. "I was saving it for the cows."

"The cows." There was a hint of laughter in his voice.

Maddie stomped over to where he stood, glaring at him. "I read in an article that cows like sweet grass. So I thought once I got the fence fixed I'd let them have dinner in the front yard."

His lips twitched, but at least he had the decency not to laugh out loud. "You're right. Cows do enjoy sweet grass. But I don't think you'd like having them this close to the house, especially with the children around."

She was confused. The man was talking in circles. "Why is that, Mr. Wilbanks?"

"It's Carter."

A strong name just like the man. Still, it was much too early for such informalities. Maddie straightened. "We don't know each other well enough to—"

"It's a cowboy thing."

Maddie eyed him suspiciously. "I've never come across that in any of my reading."

"And you won't." He pulled his hat off and slapped it against his thigh. "Look, all my cowhands call me by my first name. That's just how it is."

What could she say? Mr. Wilbanks—Carter—was doing her a favor, teaching her how to take care of this place. The least she could do was abide by his wishes. "All right, Carter. You may call me Maddie."

"Good." He grabbed a sickle from its place on the wall and handed it to her.

"You never answered my question. Why is it a bad idea to let the cows graze around the house?"

"Well, there's a couple of reasons." He grabbed the other sickle and held it as if weighing it in his hands. "There's the smell."

"I happen to like the smell of cow flesh." She leaned on the sickle as he handed her a pair of leather gloves. "I don't know why, exactly. It just makes me happy."

"I wasn't referring to the cows."

Maddie stared at him. Then what in blue blazes was he. . . . Her face went hot. "Oh, you're thinking about what happens after they eat all that sweet grass."

He gave her a knowing nod. "It starts a good fire on a cold day, but a fresh cow patty on a July day. . ." His nose crinkled.

How stupid of her not to think about that. She dropped her hands to her side. "And the second reason?"

He hesitated. "Snakes."

"Snakes?" she squealed, glancing around her feet, expecting to find a cottonmouth within striking distance.

"You told Cassie you weren't afraid of snakes." His eyes had taken on a hard glint. "You didn't lie to her, did you?"

That he was concerned about his sister touched her for some odd reason. Maybe it was because she was the oldest and had always been expected to take care of her younger sibling. Maddie shook her head. "I'm not afraid of snakes, at least, not the ones I can see. But I've heard of enough people who were bitten by copperheads or water moccasins to be leery of them."

He seemed satisfied with her answer. "Rattlesnakes are the problem out here, to be precise. Tall grass gives them a great place to hide, particularly on hot days."

"The children play outside every day after school," she whispered. What if one of them had been bitten? She wouldn't be able to live with herself if her ignorance caused something to happen to one of the children. "I thought the cattle needed more grass."

"It was an honest mistake." Carter took the sickle from her and walked out of the barn. "Don't beat yourself up over it."

She followed him out into the sunlight, waiting as he locked the barn door. "I bet you wouldn't make that kind of mistake."

He chuckled, and somehow that made her feel better. "I wasn't born into ranching like most of the folks out here. I had to learn like you, through experience and practice."

"And books?"

"Didn't have time to read them after I got out of school." He shook the barn doors to make sure they were secured, then as if making a mental list, cut across the drive to the front yard. "Been too busy getting the ranch on good footing and raising Cassie since then."

Soon they stood at the edge of the yard. Waves of grass shifted from side to side making distinct patterns as drops of dew caught the sunlight. For a brief moment, the urge to run through the tall grass, to feel it whip against her legs and smell the clean scent of earth and sky, was overwhelming. To stretch out her bare hands and feel the water against her fingertips and thank God once more for providing for them.

Instead, she pushed her hat further down on her head and grasped the sickle. "We'd best get to work."

Before Carter could answer, she marched toward one corner of the yard, high-stepping in case she came down on a rattler. A tremor slid up her spine at the thought. Then she squared her shoulders. A little old snake wasn't going to scare her away from her dream.

"Do you know how to use a sickle?" Carter called out behind her.

She swung around to find him gaping at her. "Of course I know how to use a sickle. Why wouldn't I?"

He glanced around, then stared back at her. "It's an honest question."

"Yes, I know how it works," Maddie replied, a bit testy from his sarcastic reply. "Remember, I worked our farm back in Georgia."

"I remember. Your family didn't own a plantation. Correct?"

He remembered their conversation from yesterday, almost word for word. A first for any man in her recollection. "Now, can we get to work?"

"Yes, ma'am." A faint smile on his lips, he tipped his hat, then started off in the opposite direction.

Maddie pressed her lips together. This day wasn't starting out as she had hoped. She'd barely slept last night, thinking about roping and wrangling, about becoming the rancher she'd always dreamed of being. Cutting the grass hadn't even entered into her thoughts. Yet she understood why Carter had started with this job. If it kept the children safe, that was all that mattered.

She glanced over her shoulder. Carter had his back turned to her, but she sensed the tension in his muscles in every swing of the blade.

"We've both got a day's work ahead of us, Maddie."

She twisted back around, heat crawling up her neck into her cheeks. How did he know she'd been watching him? The man had to have eyes in the back of his head!

But he was right. They did have a full day's work ahead of them, and she'd spent the last few moments gawking at him like some cow-eyed miss.

She tugged on her leather gloves, and then grasping the sickle's handle, she took her first swing. The blade flew through the air as she found a rhythm to each swipe. The grass fell in small heaps around her, and she couldn't help but smile in satisfaction. This was the start of her dream, the only thing that had kept her sane as she'd lain in bed at night, gunfire in the distance.

The air grew hot, drops of sweat beading along her hairline until finally tracking down the length of her spine. But she wouldn't stop. Call it pride or just plain stupidity, but she'd prove herself worthy of this beautiful, untamed land.

A hand came down on her shoulder, and Maddie dropped the sickle to the ground.

Whirling around, she found Carter standing there, holding a water bucket and a cup. "Why did you stop me?"

He held the cup out to her. "Here, you need some water."

"I'm perfectly capable—"

"I'm sure you are." He gave her a lazy smile that made her heart flutter. "Still, you don't want to have heatstroke, do you?"

"I doubt it would have come to that." Maddie drew a clean handkerchief from her pocket and blotted her drenched face.

"Here." Carter took the piece of cloth from her and poured water on it before handing it back. "This will cool you down a bit."

The cloth felt heavenly against the back of her neck, cool like it had been dipped in a sparkling brook rather than their well.

Carter dipped the cup into the water and handed it to her. "Drink this."

Maddie took a sip, then another before finally guzzling down the rest.

"Guess I'll have to make another trip to the well."

She felt herself blush at his amused words, then registered their meaning. "Why didn't you stop me from drinking all of it?"

His lips quirked in amusement. "You were kind of thirsty."

"Yes." Truth be told, she could have drunk the well dry. And now she'd left him without water. "I'll get another bucketful."

"You don't have to do that."

She couldn't leave him thirsting to death after the work he'd done. "It will only take a—"

His hand came to rest on her shoulder, a gentle touch that made her breath lodge in her lungs. "I drank my fill before bringing you some water. Though after watching you guzzle that down, I should have brought another bucket."

Was he teasing her? Whatever it was, she rather liked this side of him. "Maybe we need to build a movable horse trough just for me."

He chuckled then, a low masculine sound that drew a smile from her. Carter studied her for a long moment then straightened. "You're still as red as a beet." He glanced around then took her arm in a gentle grip. "Here, let's sit for a little while. We could both use a break."

Maddie gave a thought to protesting—there was so much work to be done. Calves needed branding; fences needed repair.

Yet, as Carter led her into the cool shadow of a nearby oak, the thought of a short break didn't seem so bad. She slid down the trunk of the tree then glanced up at him. "Five minutes. That's all."

"Yes, ma'am." He sat down beside her, stretching his long legs out in front of him. They sat quietly until Carter finally spoke.

"What made you want to be a cowboy?"

Should she tell him the truth? Or would he laugh at her like everyone else? For some reason, she thought this man might understand.

"I always...," she started, but the words stuck in her throat. "It was an article I read."

"A magazine article brought you to Texas?"

"Not a magazine," Maddie corrected him. "An article in the *Atlanta Journal and Constitution*. It was by Miss Elizabeth Johnson. She was a teacher who took in extra work balancing accounting books for several different ranchers. She talked about investing her savings into the Chicago Cattle Company, then using the profit to start her own ranch."

Carter nodded. "Every cattleman in Texas knows of Miss Johnson. She's a savvy businesswoman, and one whale of a rancher. She's richer than Midas too."

"The money wasn't what got me excited, though it would be nice to earn a living." She rested her head back against the tree. "It was the peace she spoke about. The fact that you could ride for days and never see another person. No cannon fire or people running you out of the only home you've ever known. Just—" Maddie startled. She barely knew this man, yet here she was, laying out her deepest thoughts. He'd probably laugh at her silliness, but was it wrong to hope he'd understand?

"I know what you mean."

Maddie glanced at him. "You do?"

He nodded, staring out at the half-cut yard. "I feel closer to God when I'm out riding my land. It's just so peaceful." He ducked his head, but she caught the ghost of a smile on his face. "I catch myself praying on my rides sometimes. It's just too beautiful not to praise Him for His creation."

Unable to find the words, she nodded. That he'd taken her seriously, even understood her reasons, lifted the weight from her heavily burdened shoulders. Despite their bumpy start, Carter Wilbanks was the right man to teach her what she needed to run her ranch.

"Thank you," Maddie finally managed.

Carter chuckled. "Don't thank me yet. We've still got a lot of work to do."

We. The way he said it made her feel as if she wasn't alone in this anymore. Maddie lifted her gaze to meet his. "Yes, but now I trust you to help me with it."

It was his turn to blush.

❧ Chapter 6 ❧

"You may sit down."

Chairs scraped the hardwood floor as the children scrambled into their seats around the dining room table. The boys fell into their seats, unfolded their napkins, then shoved one end into their shirt collars.

Carter felt much like the boys did. After a hard day of patching up the livestock pen, he could scarf down a cow by himself. He looked down the table to where Maddie sat. No one would ever suspect she'd helped him repair the holding pen this afternoon. It had been hard work, pulling out nails and hammering new boards into place, yet Maddie was there, right alongside him, working harder than most men he knew. Since their first lesson almost two weeks ago, his respect for her and what she hoped to achieve had grown.

And now, in a pretty blue gown that matched her eyes, she sat at the head of the table, a ready smile on her lips. "Boys, napkins in your laps, please."

"Why?"

He should have figured it would be Cassie doing the asking. This dinner was her first lesson in table manners, and as usual, his sister was already questioning everything. Maddie encouraged her, telling Carter she felt it was important that his sister learn how to express her curiosity in a socially acceptable way.

"Very good question, Cassie. We don't tuck our napkins under our chins because it would look like we're eating from a pig's trough." Maddie's eyes sparkled with humor as she glanced at the boys. "Isn't that right, gentlemen?"

"Yes, ma'am," they replied in unison, pulling their napkins from their collars and laying them across their laps.

Maddie gave them an approving smile. "Thank you."

Cassie glanced at the boys then back at Maddie. "I still don't see what the problem is."

"Cassandra. . . ," Carter started but fell silent as he looked to Maddie for support. Understanding danced in her eyes as she cut into a large roast with carrots, onions, and small red potatoes then laid the utensils aside.

She shifted toward his sister, giving Cassie her full attention. "The truth is I don't know the reason why people do it that way. It's just considered proper." Maddie unfolded her napkin and placed it in her lap, her expression kind as she continued. "It's how my mama was taught, and her mother before her."

Cassie considered that for a moment. "Then why do it at all?"

"As clumsy as I am at times, I'd have food all over my clothes, and that wouldn't do." Maddie laughed, a lovely light sound that made his heart beat a bit faster. "Then again, I would be feeding the mice."

"I don't like mice," the older girl—Robin?—said with a grimace. She turned to Cassie. "Do you?"

His sister shook her head as she slipped the cloth on her lap without another question.

"I don't know what all the bother's about," the youngest boy, Luke, piped in, grabbing a biscuit from the plate in front of him. "A little mouse can't hurt you."

"Do we have to talk about vermin at the dinner table?" Maddie's sister, Shelby, glared at the little boy. "Every time we eat, someone brings up something disgusting."

"I think our talks have been interesting," Luke retorted.

"Children, please." Maddie glanced from one child to the next until her gaze met his. "Mr. Wilbanks, will you please bless the food?"

Why she'd slipped back to his formal name he didn't know. Maybe for the children's sake? Well, that was a ridiculous reason when she'd been calling him Carter for almost two weeks now. "It's Carter, remember?"

"Of course I remember." Her cheeks turned a rosy shade of pink as her attention shifted to the children before coming back to him. She bowed her head, and the children followed suit.

Carter lowered his head. "Dear Lord, bless this food to the nourishment of our bodies. In Christ's name we humbly pray, amen."

As he lifted his head, he caught Luke grinning at him. "What?"

"Straight to the point, just like I like it." The boy gave him an approving nod.

"Well, thank you." He leaned toward Luke. "And you're wrong about vermin, son. Mice and rats can be dangerous."

Seven pairs of eyes shifted their attention to him. John, the middle boy, finally spoke up. "What do you mean?"

Carter glanced down the table to Maddie, who gave him a brief nod. "Well. . ." He hesitated as he reached for the green beans. "Many years ago, in merry old England, people got sick and died, yet no one understood why. They didn't know what was causing it until a doctor noticed that almost all of the victims had rat bites. He figured that the rats were spreading the disease."

"Ewww." Robin sank back in her chair, her round face a bit pale.

"Is that true?" Luke asked, an impish gleam in his eyes. "I sure would like to know where I could find me one of those rats."

"Why would you want such a thing?" Maddie asked, passing the plate of roast to John.

Luke shrugged. "I don't know. It would just be fun to have."

"No, it wouldn't," Shelby exclaimed, reaching for a piece of bread and slathering it with butter. "If that thing got loose, it would kill us all."

"I'd put him in a cage," Luke answered back then added, "unless you make me clean up the pigpen again."

"Aunt Maddie, make them—" Robin started.

Maddie cut her off, giving Luke her sternest look. "No more talk about vermin. Is that clear?" Her face softened as she turned to the young girl. "Are you all right, sweet girl?"

"Of course she's all right," Luke answered, talking around the food in his mouth. "It's not like a rat bit her or something."

A chair fell to the floor as Cassie stood up. "Stop it! She said she didn't like mice, but y'all keep going on and on about them."

The situation was escalating out of control. One more minute, and he'd be breaking up a brawl. Carter slammed his open palm on the table, the wood vibrating beneath his touch as all eyes suddenly turned on him.

He met Robin's gaze. "I'm sorry I shared that story at the dinner table. I should have minded my manners better."

The girl gave him a weak smile. "That's all right."

"I won't do it again." Carter turned his attention to the boys. "If I hear another word about this, I'm certain Miss Maddie can find some extra chores to keep you out of trouble. Is that understood?"

Each boy nodded reluctantly. "Yes, sir."

Carter met his sister's dark brown eyes. "And you shouldn't have jumped out of your chair like that, looking for a brawl. Ladies don't do that."

"I don't know about that."

Carter met Maddie's gaze over the table. If the woman had something to say, she should have said it before a fight broke out. "Excuse me?"

She gave him a pointed look then turned to Cassie. "Your brother is partly right. You shouldn't have knocked over your chair. But you did it for a good reason. You considered Robin's feelings above your own. That says quite a bit about the tender heart that you have."

"You think I have a tender heart?" Cassie asked in a quiet voice.

"Yes, I do, but there's a better way to handle the boys instead of fighting with them."

Cassie glanced at him then back at Maddie. "What would that be?"

Maddie leaned forward as if ready to share a dangerous secret. "Ignore them."

"Ignore us?" Luke asked, frowning.

"Are you serious, Aunt Maddie? Would you really ignore us?" John asked, a hint of worry in his young voice.

Maddie smiled at the boy. "That depends. Are you going to behave?"

John nodded furiously. "Yes, ma'am."

She looked at his partners in crime. "What about you two?"

Sheepishly, Matthew responded. "Yes, ma'am."

"Luke?"

The boy huffed. "I'm thinking."

"Then you can think about it while you sit on your bed." Picking up a steaming bowl, Maddie took a spoonful of green beans. "Dinner is getting cold."

"I've thought about it." He glared across the table at Robin. "I'm sorry."

Conversation around the table turned to more suitable topics after that. One by one, the children shared what they had done at school that day. Robin crowed about the A she'd received on the spelling test while the boys described a game of stickball they'd played during recess. Throughout the dinner Maddie listened to each child, asking well-thought-out questions and giving words of encouragement when needed.

When Carter turned to Cassie, she kept eating, her eyes fixed on her plate. "How about you, Cassie? What did you do at school today?"

"Nothing much."

The other children stole glances at each other but continued eating. Carter tried again. "Did something happen at school today, Cassie?"

Covering his mouth with his napkin, Luke chuckled. "Something happened, all right."

That didn't sound promising. Carter wanted his sister to feel like she could share anything with him, the good and the bad. "You want to tell me what happened?"

Cassie slouched in her chair. "It wasn't my fault."

Carter closed his eyes. What had she gotten herself into this time? Another fight? Or was she spitting with the boys again? "Cassie, I need you to tell me what happened."

"Mr. Wilbanks, it wasn't her fault," Robin declared. "Well, not all of it."

"She poked Billy Satterfield with a broomstick," Matthew exclaimed. "And right when we were coming up to bat."

"Only after he was nasty to her." Robin reached out and took Cassie's hand. "I would have done the same thing."

Cassie jerked her head up. "You would have?"

Robin nodded. "Yes, and I would have told his mother what he said too."

He exchanged a look with Maddie before turning to his sister again. "What did he say?"

Cassie looked at him then shook her head. "Nothing."

"Cassie?"

Instead of answering, she went back to staring at her plate, moving food around with her fork.

His spirits fell. What had the boy said to her that had upset her so much? If only she'd tell him, then maybe he would know how to ease her pain. He started to ask her again, but Maddie caught his eye. She gave him a simple shake of her head then went back to her dinner. Maybe she was right. Maybe he shouldn't push Cassie for answers, at least not now in front of the other children. Hopefully, she'd open up when they rode home tonight.

The meal was a quiet affair after that. Maddie and Shelby had put a lot of work into the meal, but to him it tasted like sawdust. Five hundred head of cattle, nine men working underneath him, and he was still brought low by his sister's problems.

Mercifully, Maddie called an end to the meal a few minutes later, instructing the children to carry their empty plates into the kitchen.

Carter took one last sip of water as Maddie picked up his half-eaten plate. "I thought dinner went rather well."

Was she funning him? He glanced up at her and realized she was serious. "They almost broke out in a war right in the middle of supper."

"I know." Maddie smiled. "Did you see how Cassie took up for Robin? That girl has a good heart."

Carter knew that. Anyone who'd ever taken the time to know Cassie could profess to her kindness. Except for maybe the Loudermilk boy and Billy Jo Satterfield. "She still has a lot of work to do."

"Yes." Maddie placed her slender hand on his arm. "But remember, manners don't win friends. Actions do."

❧ Chapter 7 ❧

*H*e looked so discouraged.

Maddie pulled out the chair next to him and sat down. "It's hard to think about anything else when someone you love is in such pain."

Carter didn't look up at her but stared into his coffee cup as if he might find the solution to his problem there. "I haven't done right by Cassie. I know that. I just didn't know she was going to have all this trouble growing up."

"Every child comes with their own unique set of problems." She wondered if she should tell him, then thought it might lighten his mood. "Do you know what I used to do when I was a little girl?"

He lifted his gaze to meet hers. "What?"

Folding her arms on the edge of the table, she leaned forward.

"I told everyone in church every time my parents had an argument."

"I bet they loved that."

"Oh yes, particularly when the preacher came to talk to them about their 'rocky marriage.'" She mashed her lips together to keep from laughing. "Did I forget to mention Papa was a deacon in the church?"

Carter broke out into a smile. "I hate to ask how they managed to get you to stop."

"Oh, I was punished, many times over. But Mama and Papa didn't take it too seriously." She moved closer to him. "One time, when they thought Shelby and I were asleep, I overheard them laughing about it. They knew I'd stop doing it eventually."

"You think Cassie will grow out of this?"

"Yes." She reached out to touch him, give him comfort in some way, then thought better of it. "Like I told her at dinner. She's a good girl."

"But she doesn't know how to act like one."

"Neither do most girls at that age." Maddie chuckled. "Do you know I climbed a tree faster than a gray-tailed squirrel?"

He glanced up at her then. "You're making that up."

She shook her head. "I was the only girl my age in school, so I played with the boys."

A smile pulled at his lips. "Lucky boys."

She ignored the blush that rose in her cheeks. "I could spit too, probably not as well as Cassie. Did she really beat all the boys at school?"

Carter glared at her, though there was a hint of merriment in his eyes. "Are you impressed by that?"

"It is difficult to do."

Rubbing his forehead, he closed his eyes. "And you're supposed to teach her how to act like a lady."

"I will, but it takes time and patience." Folding her hands in her lap, Maddie gave him what she hoped was an encouraging smile. "Cassie is going to be just fine. Trust me."

"I do."

For some odd reason, her heart fluttered at his answer. She'd not expected to like this man as much as she did, yet how could she not when it was clear how much he wanted to help Cassie? Maybe, if he knew he wasn't the only one dealing with a problem, he might feel better. "You know, it only gets worse as they grow up."

Carter studied her. "Are the children giving you problems?"

"Not so much the younger ones." She glanced toward the kitchen door. Last thing she needed was for her sister to walk in on the conversation. "Shelby's not too happy with me right now."

"She seemed all right at dinner."

"A young lady never airs dirty laundry in front of company." Maddie sank back in her chair. "Anyway, she's upset that I won't let some cowboy who works for Mr. Muster court her."

Leaning forward, Carter rested on his elbows. "Who is it?"

"Bennett Marshall."

"He's a nice enough fellow. I almost hired him for the Double C, but Muster beat me to it." He paused for a moment. "What are your objections?"

She pressed her lips together, not sure if she should divulge the extent of her problems with Clyde Muster. Then again, maybe Carter could help. "The truth is I don't know Mr. Marshall, only who he works for. Mr. Muster made it very clear to me a woman shouldn't be ranching. Even went so far as to offer me a price below the ranch's value so that 'a little lady' like me could settle in town and focus my attentions on catching a husband."

Leaning back in his chair, Carter laughed. "I hate to tell you this, but there's a lot of men who think like Muster."

"You don't!" Uncertainty coursed through her. "Do you?"

"How can you ask me that?"

"You didn't answer the question." She rested her chin in the palm of her hand, anxious for his reply. It shouldn't matter what he thought—she'd keep working her ranch no matter what he said. Yet she wanted to know what Carter thought of her. It mattered to her very much.

"Maddie." His voice rumpled through her, drawing her attention to his eyes. There, she saw it. Respect. "If anyone, man or woman, can make this ranch profitable, it would be you."

"Thank you." Her heart burst with joy at the confidence in his words. He truly believed she could do this, just like she believed in him. "I owe you an apology."

He turned his head to meet her gaze. "What for?"

Maddie was almost too ashamed to admit it. "When you first came to me about lessons for Cassie, I thought you the worst kind of brother. But now. . ." She swallowed. "I think you've done a fine job of raising her."

Relief shone in his eyes. "When Ma and Pa died, I thought about giving up and taking Cassie back home to Kentucky. But that wasn't what our parents wanted for us, so in the end, we stuck it out."

"I hope I feel that way in a couple of years. That is, if Muster doesn't run us off this place first."

Carter leaned closer. "Just because you heard him say that

doesn't mean he'll really try to do it." He must have read something in her expression, because he took her hand between his. "What else has he said?"

She leaned forward, comforted by the warmth of his touch. "A couple of months ago I was in the mercantile when Mr. Muster came in. He must not have seen me, because he was talking to someone, loud enough for me to hear. He said he'd be buying another two hundred head of cattle once he claimed the Steele ranch." A knot formed in her throat just thinking about what she'd heard. "When the man asked how he planned to do that when I'd already claimed the place, Muster told him all I needed was a little push." She closed her eyes against the memory. "Then he laughed."

"Maddie, look at me." He tightened his hold on her hand until she opened her eyes. Goodness, he was close, so close she could see the tiny threads of silver in the dark depths of his eyes. "Old man Muster shoots off his mouth like that to everyone. He doesn't mean anything by it."

Jerking her hand away, she straightened, disappointed by his reaction. "He sounded very serious to me."

"He's always been like that." Carter fell back in his seat. "A blowhard who thinks he's gonna be the next big cattle baron, that's all."

Maddie wasn't so sure. Still, if Muster acted like this toward all of his competition, she shouldn't worry about it. "Maybe I'm just borrowing trouble, and as Papa used to say, ain't no sense borrowing it because trouble finds you soon enough."

❧ Chapter 8 ❧

A day like today, when the air was filled with the scent of wildflowers and the sky was a perfect shade of blue, usually filled Carter with a sense of purpose, of belonging. But not today. Sleep had evaded him again last night.

All because of Maddie.

Carter clicked his tongue against his teeth and tugged on Malcom's reins, turning them west toward Maddie's place. Their lessons had become much more than simply teaching her about ranching. She was someone he could talk to, who understood the problems of raising a child alone, who knew the heartache of losing your parents. He'd never laughed with another person as much as he did with Maddie. He'd never had many friends—he'd always been too busy running the ranch—but he considered her one.

The evenings spent dining with her and the children were what he enjoyed the most. He'd forgotten what it was like, the feeling of family. Even in the months before their parents died, the unending work of the ranch hadn't allowed for his family to have a meal together. Maddie had given that back to him and Cassie.

Cassie seemed to be more settled too. The friendship between her and Robin had grown over the last week, and Carter had to admit it felt good to see his sister happy for a change.

Yet, Carter knew Maddie still worried about Muster. Maybe she had cause to. Yesterday, while checking for new calves, they'd come across the carcass of a dead cow. He didn't think much of it until he saw the knife marks on the cow's underbelly. Someone had cut the calf out of its body.

What if he'd been wrong about the rancher? The man had made his opinion of women ranchers known all over town, but he was always spouting off about one thing or another. Muster might bark, but he'd never bit before. Still, the thought of Maddie worried and scared kept Carter up at night. He'd just have to reassure her that she and the rest of her brood were safe from any of Muster's possible shenanigans. That and Carter would keep an eye on her.

Which wouldn't be difficult to do. Carter smiled at the thought. Whether in jeans or the dresses she wore to dinner, Maddie was a fine figure of a woman. Beautiful without all the fuss and bother he'd heard most women went through. She was knowledgeable, yet confident enough to ask questions if she didn't know something. And she worked hard at making her ranching dream come true.

Maybe Maddie *was* cut out to be a cowboy. He should tell her that. Maybe she'd grace him with another one of her beautiful smiles.

The horse neighed softly, drawing Carter out of his thoughts. Best to keep his mind on the work ahead, counting Maddie's herd. She had a good idea of the number, but he wanted to make sure after the incident with the calf. Rustlers thinned out one or two cows at a time so that by the time a rancher notices, he's out hundreds of dollars. It was a hard lesson for a new rancher to learn, and one he hoped to keep Maddie from experiencing.

Turning off the main road, he headed toward the pasture where they'd agreed to meet, nudging his horse forward. "Come on, boy. Maddie's waiting."

But the stallion stopped in his tracks, his nostrils flaring. That's when Carter felt it. The ground rumbling beneath them. He held the reins tightly to keep the horse from bolting. To his left, a great cloud of dust and debris rose in the air, the pounding of hooves matching the frantic beat of his heart.

Stampede!

He glanced toward the pasture where Maddie waited. Even from this distance, he could tell she was unaware of the herd of hoofs barreling toward her. If he hurried, he might reach her. But if he didn't. . .

He kicked Malcom into action then slapped him on the rump with the reins. "Come on, boy! Maddie needs us!"

He tore off across a grassy area toward the tree line. He would make it to her. He had to. The children needed her, Cassie too. *And me?* Yes, he needed Maddie, more than he'd ever needed anyone else in his life.

Branches slammed into him as he reached the trees, pulling at his shirt and scratching his arms. Malcom slowed slightly, and Carter flicked the reins against the horse's hindquarters. The stomping and snorting echoed in the air around him as he drew in a lungful of dusty air. He pulled up his kerchief over his nose and mouth, breathing easier as he pushed the horse hard.

Please, God, let me get to her in time!

The Lord must have heard him. As they burst out of the trees, Malcom sprinted toward the fence line where Maddie was supposed to meet him.

Only she wasn't there.

Carter followed the line of the fence. There, running for the gate, Maddie glanced back at them, the terrified expression on her face twisting his gut.

Hooves chewing up the ground behind him, Carter pushed the horse harder. Just a few more strides, and he'd reach her. "Maddie!"

She stopped and turned, frozen in place as if mesmerized by the horrific scene of a herd coming straight at her.

Carter's chest constricted. Riding as hard as he could, he prayed he'd make it in time.

If she could make it to the gate. . .

The earth moved beneath her feet, almost knocking her to the ground. Each breath became more difficult, dirt drying out her mouth, debris swirling around her like a spring tornado.

Lord, please save me!

A strong arm came around her, pulling her up. She moved to

gain her seat on the horse, then the arm tightened around her, pulling her snug.

"I've got you."

Carter! She relaxed back against him, resting her arms on top of the one he had wrapped around her waist, trusting that he would keep her safe.

He made a sharp left, forcing her to grab his thigh. Hard as granite, the muscles flexed with each movement, sending little sparks of warmth through her fingertips and up her arms.

"Hang on!" His breath was warm, his lips brushing against the shell of her ear as he spoke. "I'm going to try and make it to the gate."

Closing her eyes, she hung on for dear life. She would have died if Carter hadn't been nearby to save her. Still could if they didn't make it through the gate. The thought of what that would do to her sister and the children after all they'd lost in the war sobered her.

Thank You, Father, for sending Carter to me.

Seconds later, Carter led his horse through the open gate, grabbing the rope attached to the handle and pulling it closed behind them.

He walked them farther into the woods, then stopped, jumped off his horse, and reached for her. "Are you all right?"

"Yes." His hands slid around her waist, holding her steady as he lifted her to the ground. Her feet had barely touched the ground when he wrapped his arms around her and pulled her trembling body against his. She slumped against him, drawing on his strength. If Carter hadn't come. If he hadn't been there to save her. . .

Maddie yanked free of his embrace, stumbling on wobbly legs.

She yanked off her hat and smacked him in the chest. "What were you thinking, putting yourself in danger like that? You could have been killed!"

He blinked, then with the lift of one brow, gave her a sarcastic smile. "You're welcome."

"How would I. . ." Maddie caught herself. How would she survive if something had happened to Carter? He'd become as much a part of her world as Shelby and the children. She ground her teeth together. "How could I face Cassie if I got you killed?"

Carter stepped toward her, their noses almost touching. "You wouldn't tell Cassie anything. You'd be too busy being dead yourself."

"I could have made it to the gate," she countered, knowing the instant she spoke it was the wrong thing to say.

His dark eyes held her captive. "Have you ever seen a stampede? I have, and let me tell you, you'd have never made it to the gate before you were crushed to death."

Carter was right, of course. If he hadn't risked his life, she would have been stomped into the dust. "I'm sorry," she whispered. "I wasn't thinking. I just. . ." The terror of the last few minutes lodged in her throat. "I just didn't know what to do."

"Shh." Taking her hat from her, Carter dropped it to the ground, then gently tugged her back into his arms. Maddie buried her face in his chest, the emotions she'd never allowed herself to feel bursting to the surface. Tears burned her eyes, and she finally wept for everything she'd lost, all the hardships she'd endured over the last ten years.

"You have a good cry," Carter whispered in her ear, his fingers drawing calming circles on her back. "I'm here for you."

After she'd cried herself out, Maddie lifted her head to meet his gaze. "I'm sorry."

"Nothing to be sorry for." Carter touched her wet cheek, smoothing a tear away. "Everyone needs a good cry now and then."

She sniffled. "Do you?"

"Do I what?"

"Do you. . .cry?"

"Once, about a year after Ma and Pa died." Still holding her close, he reached into his pocket and pulled out a clean handkerchief. "I was about to lose the ranch, and then Cassie got sick. She got so bad, the doc wasn't sure she'd make it. I never felt like such a failure in my life."

She understood that feeling. It was how she'd felt in the first months after the war. "But you managed to make it through."

"Only by the grace of God." He smiled. "I learned a lot about leaning on the Lord then."

"I'm still learning that lesson." She blotted her face, then wiped her nose before folding the handkerchief.

"I'm of the belief it takes a lifetime."

She gave a watery chuckle. "Wonderful, just what I wanted to hear."

Laughter rumbled beneath her fingertips. He stepped back then, holding her at arm's length as he stared intently into her eyes. "You feel better?"

"Yes." It felt good, the way he worried about her as if she mattered to him. She'd never had that before, at least, not since Mama had passed. Papa had relied on her for everything after that. But then Carter always made her feel special. . .

She couldn't think about that right now. Stepping away from him, she snatched her hat off the ground and jammed it on her head. "The herd came from the northeast, from the direction of Muster's ranch."

"We don't know that for sure."

"But I have a pretty good idea he's behind it." She walked over to where Carter's horse stood grazing. "I should dam up that stream that feeds into his water supply just to spite him."

Carter snagged her by the arm and whirled her around. "You're too good to do something like that. Too kind and compassionate."

She wasn't so sure about that. But the fact that Carter believed those things about her sent warmth deep to the very core of her being.

Since when has Carter's good opinion mattered so much to me?

"Why don't I drop you off at the ranch, then head back out to see if I can locate where the stampede started?" Carter shortened his stride to match hers. "You can rest before the children get home from school."

Rest? When there was work to do? She shook her head. "I'm not going to let a little stampede get in the way of caring for my herd."

"We only have Malcom here," he said, his voice ripe with laugher. "Not that I mind you sitting on my lap."

Maddie stopped and searched the woods. "Gilly must have got spooked when the stampede—" She swallowed the rest of the sentence, then continued. "She's probably back at the barn by now."

Carter stepped in front of her, his gaze trained on her. "I can take care of this, Maddie."

"I know you can, and I appreciate the offer." She touched his arm, not realizing until that moment how much she'd enjoyed being held by him. "But cowboys don't turn tail and run at every little thing. Besides, I want to know if someone started the stampede on purpose, and why."

❧ Chapter 9 ❧

There was no talking Maddie out of this, the stubborn woman.

Carter walked toward his horse, Maddie at his heels. Why couldn't she just go home and rest like he'd suggested? She could use it after what she'd been through. But he should have known better. Maddie wasn't the type of woman to let someone else do her work, and she was determined to figure out who started the stampede.

What if they discovered Muster was behind the stampede? What then? They couldn't just march up to the man's front door and accuse him of trying to kill her.

If Maddie rode with him, there'd have to be some rules. He turned to face her. "You can go with me as long as you understand we're only going to find out where the stampede started. I'll handle it after that."

"What? No!" She glared up at him, her chin at that stubborn angle he'd come to recognize. "Someone tried to kill us! You bet I'm going to talk to him about it."

"What good would that do, except to get us both shot for trespassing?" He'd about lost his patience with her. "You will accept my terms, or I'm taking you home."

"Hmm," she snorted, her arms wound tightly around her waist.

Carter grabbed the reins and led his horse alongside a downed tree. "You can huff all you want to, but I'm doing this for both our sakes. Do you understand?"

She climbed onto the fallen tree and stood. "I don't like it."

"I didn't expect you would." He vaulted into the saddle, then he leaned down and caught her by the arm. Putting her boot in the stirrup, she threw one slender leg over the back of the horse. The air in his lungs caught as she settled in behind him, wrapping her arms around his waist.

How was he supposed to ride with Maddie plastered against him? He was still contemplating that question when she broke the silence. "Are we just going to stand here all day?"

"No." Carter kicked the horse into movement, walking him toward the gate. Once through, they settled into a silent ride, following the trail of trodden grass and broken tree limbs across Maddie's land.

They'd been riding for twenty minutes when they found where the stampede began. Divots chewed up the once grassy pasture, and the faint smell of cow flesh and dust still hung in the air. It was as Maddie predicted, at the boundary line between her place and Muster's.

As they neared the fence that separated the two parcels, Carter sat up in his saddle, his attention drawn to the railing. Something was odd, though he couldn't quite put his finger on what it was.

Holding on to him, Maddie rose and looked over his shoulder. "What is it?"

"I'm not sure." He rode closer, coming up alongside the wood railing. It looked much like it had when they had ridden out to check the property lines a few days ago. He tilted his head back to tell her as much, when the sun winked off one of the wooden rails.

"Did you see that?" Maddie asked. "Something is catching the sunlight."

Tossing the reins over the railing, Carter climbed down, then helped Maddie. As soon as her feet touched the ground, she hurried to the fence, rubbing her gloved hand over the rough surface of a post.

"Maybe your cattle got spooked."

She shook her head. "My cows were in the south pasture when I came through there this morning."

It didn't make sense. "Muster wouldn't have his own herd stampede on your land for fear you'd claim them for yourself."

"If he scared me off the land, he wouldn't have a problem reclaiming them." Maddie focused on a section of the fence, then glanced at him. "Come here."

"What are you looking at?" Joining her, he looked where she pointed. "The stake?"

"The shiny new stake."

The shiny new stake? Carter examined it closer. "But you said none of these fences had been repaired in the last couple of years."

"Which means the stakes should be rusted over. Yet this one looks brand-new." She glanced down the fence line. "I bet if we looked at the rest of our fence, we'd find more new ones."

Our fence. Carter liked the way that sounded, as if they were in this together, partners in life as well as business. He cleared his throat as he studied the ground around the posts. "If he's behind it, he's been planning this for a while."

Maddie gave him a quizzical look. "What do you mean?"

Carter stepped up on the lowest rail then held his hand out to her. "Look at Muster's land. It's not broken up like your side is. I think Muster had this portion of the fence removed, then transferred his cattle to your land over the last few days. Then when the time was right. . ."

"He started the stampede." She studied the ground below them, then glanced up. "But what made him decide on today? How did he know you were going to meet me in the north pasture? You and I were the only ones who knew we'd be there today."

That was a puzzle. "Maybe the children told someone."

She shook her head. "The only person who knew was. . ." Her face went pale. "But she wouldn't. . ."

Of course. Shelby. "Has she seen her cowboy recently?"

"I don't know." Maddie pinched the bridge of her nose. "She was sneaking out to see him, but I thought she'd stopped that." Her shoulders slumped. "I guess she hasn't."

Carter couldn't stand seeing her upset. Maddie worked so hard to provide for Shelby and the children, gave them the love they needed, someone they could always count on. Surely Shelby understood that. He had the sudden urge to talk some sense into the girl.

But that wouldn't solve their problem. "She didn't do it to hurt you."

"Whether she did it on purpose or not, she managed to do just that." Maddie took a deep breath before continuing. "Anyway, what are we going to do about it?"

"If Shelby told Marshall where we were going to be, and that's a big if, then it's time to discuss this with Mr. Muster."

"We can go there right now."

He knew he was in for an argument, but he intended to stick to his guns. "We've already talked about this, Maddie. I'm not putting you in danger."

"But I already am," she growled. "It's my land he's trying to run me off of."

"Maybe it's as simple as that, but I'm not taking any chances." He caught her chin in his hand and lifted her gaze to meet his. "I couldn't live with myself if something happened to you that I could have prevented. And what about the children? What would happen to them?"

"All right," she answered reluctantly, then added, "I don't want you going out there alone."

He gave her a teasing smile. "Afraid Muster will try something with me?"

Worry clouded her blue eyes. "I mean it, Carter. Please don't go see Muster alone."

It had been a long time since he'd had anyone care about him. Yet Maddie did, even if it was only because they were friends. "I'll get Big John to go out there with me."

That seemed to settle her mind. "Well then, I guess we should get back to work."

He helped her down from the fence, steadying her as they walked over the rough terrain. "Are you sure there isn't something we could do closer to home? Maybe fix the hitching post?"

"We have cattle to count."

We again. He could grow accustomed to hearing that all the time. He helped her onto Malcom then climbed into the saddle. "The cows will still be there tomorrow, Maddie."

She pressed her head against his shoulder blades, her body vibrating with tension. "I won't let that man bully me off my land. I just can't. And we won't be doing work around the house, not when my herd needs to be counted."

Heavens, but she had a fire in her, one that drew him closer with every passing day. There was a strength in her he'd never seen in other women of his acquaintance, a backbone made of iron. Yet the navy ribbon holding back her hair and the cotton shirt she wore with buckskins reminded him of the lady she was.

If Maddie wanted to count cows, he wouldn't stand in her way. "We'd better get moving if we want to get finished before supper."

She tightened her grip on him, and he could feel her smile against the muscles in his shoulders. "Thank you."

❧ Chapter 10 ❧

Maddie sat on the front porch swing, lazily pushing it from side to side. The sun had sunk behind the trees, leaving in its wake a cool evening breeze, the light notes of the mockingbird singing in the distance. The faint scent of wildflowers lingered in the air.

Today had almost been more than she could bear. The stampede and the knowledge that Mr. Muster had started it might have broken most people, but she'd witnessed the flames of Yankee torches, watched as they laid siege to everything they owned, leaving them to starve.

It would take more than a greedy old man to scare her off her land.

But this morning, watching Carter race toward her, a thundering herd threatening to stomp him underfoot, had terrified her more than anything Sherman could have done to her.

She pushed the swing into a slow, steady rhythm. Was this how it felt to be in love? She didn't know. The war had stolen any suitors she might have had, not that she'd had many. Most men didn't appreciate her plans.

Maddie had always dreamed of running a profitable ranch on her own, but now she wasn't so sure. She liked having someone to bounce her crazy ideas off of, someone who took her seriously, who made her feel like her thoughts mattered.

Someone like Carter.

The screen door opened then slammed shut as Shelby joined her. "I thought you might be out here."

"Are the children in bed?"

The swing dipped slightly as her sister sat down next to her. "Robin is reading. But the boys are already asleep, which is a minor miracle."

Maddie chuckled. "Don't count your chickens too fast. The evening is still young."

They fell into a compatible silence. Leaning her head back, Maddie closed her eyes, the steady to and fro of the swing lulling her into a comfortable peace. Carter's arms made her feel the same way, as if there were only the two of them in the whole world.

"What happened today?"

Maddie stole a glimpse of her sister through her lashes. "Why do you ask that?"

"You were quiet at the supper table as if you have something on your mind. And Carter. . ." She mashed her lips together. "He looked concerned when he dropped you off this afternoon."

Maddie didn't want to worry her, even though she couldn't forget her suspicions about Shelby's involvement. Could her sister have inadvertently helped Muster plan the stampede?

"Why won't you tell me?"

"I don't want you to be concerned." Maddie shifted toward her sister. "But I was caught in a stampede this morning."

"Are you all right?" Shelby raked her gaze over her. "You're not hurt or anything, are you?"

Maddie shook her head. "Carter pulled me away before the cattle could reach me."

"How did it happen? Did some of our cows—"

"Our cattle weren't involved." Maddie swallowed hard against the memory. "We were going to count the cattle in the large pasture, so I told Carter I'd meet him there. I hadn't been there for long when I heard it. If Carter hadn't gotten to me when he did, I probably wouldn't be here tonight."

"Thank God for Carter," Shelby breathed out on a whisper. "Do you know what caused it?"

Ask her if she's seen Bennett Marshall in the last few days. Maddie sat up. "We have a theory. We found new stakes in the fence bordering Mr. Muster's property even though those railings hadn't been repaired in years. We think—"

Shelby interrupted. "You and Carter?"

"Yes," Maddie went on. "We think Muster intentionally planned it to scare us off the property."

The poor girl looked befuddled. "Why would he do that? You own this land, free and clear."

Maddie sighed. Shelby had never been one to see the bad in people, or maybe she'd done too good a job keeping her sister away from evil. Just one of the reasons why she refused Bennett's suit on Shelby's behalf.

She took her sister's hand in hers. "Our land has plenty of sweet grass and a good water supply. Everything you'd need to become a cattle baron."

Shelby thought for a moment, then shook her head. "From everything I've heard about Mr. Muster, I can't believe he'd do this."

Maddie didn't have time to be hurt by her sister's words; she was too angry. "How would you know what he's capable of doing? You've never met him."

Shelby raised an eyebrow. "Neither have you."

There was an ache starting behind her eyes. Maddie rubbed her forehead. "I saw him once in the mercantile. He was talking to someone about buying this place after we abandoned it."

Shelby's curls bounced wildly as she shook her head. "But Bennett said—"

"Bennett!" Maddie interrupted, grabbing her sister by the arm. "Are you still sneaking around with that cowboy after I told you to stay away from him?"

Shelby jerked her arm out of Maddie's clasp. "I wouldn't have to if you'd give him permission to court me properly."

"The man he works for almost got me and Carter killed this morning," Maddie spat out, the urge to shake her sister until her teeth rattled growing stronger. Not that it would help. Shelby could be as stubborn as a mule when she set her mind to it. "Did you tell Bennett we would be in the small pasture today?"

Shelby's back stiffened. "We have more important things to talk about than your silly ranch. We talk about how much we love each other and where we're going to live after we get married."

Married? What had Shelby done? Maddie slammed her eyes closed. "You didn't make any promises to this man, did you?"

Shelby chuckled. "Of course I did. That's what people do when they're in love."

Dear heavens, this was worse than she could have imagined. With her sister bound to this Bennett, Muster would have access to her every move. "You have to break it off, Shelby."

Putting her feet down, the girl jerked the swing to a stop. "I will do no such thing."

"Shelby?" Maddie reached for her, but her sister jumped up, just out of her grasp.

"I have no intention of being an old maid just like—" She clamped her mouth shut, but Maddie knew how she wanted to finish the sentence. *Just like you.*

The air left her lungs as if Shelby had punched her in the gut. She couldn't mean what she was implying. "There was a war going on."

"Oh please." Shelby leaned forward, shaking her finger at her. "You've never even had a suitor, because everybody in town knew you were a strange bird. What kind of woman wants to own her own ranch?"

"It wasn't like that, Shelby," Maddie said, feeling the need to set her straight. "The war started when I was barely sixteen years old. All the men worth marrying had gone off to fight."

"Yes, I know, but the war's been over for four years." She blew out a huff. "But instead of finding a husband and settling down, you dragged us out here where we knew no one without thinking how I might feel about it."

Maddie tried to explain. "The bank took our home. We had nowhere else to go."

"You could have tried harder to save our place. Or sold the ranch to pay the back taxes. But you didn't even consider it, did you?" Her slender jaw tightened. "You knew I had several gentlemen interested in courting me before you packed me off and moved us out here."

Broken men who didn't have a way to support her. Maddie sighed. There was no way to win this argument. "If I thought any of them were good enough for you, I would have given my blessing in a heartbeat. But there was nothing left for us in Marietta, Shelby. I did the best I could do."

When her sister didn't answer immediately, Maddie's spirits lifted slightly. Had she somehow gotten through to her little sister?

Shelby's next words dashed her hopes. "It doesn't matter if you give us your blessing or not. I'm marrying Bennett."

"What would Papa say, Shelby? How do you think he'd feel if you married someone he didn't approve of?"

The question caught her off guard. Good. Shelby needed to think about what she was doing. Then she straightened, her face expressionless. "He wouldn't want me to be unhappy, and Bennett makes me happy."

"No, Papa wouldn't want us unhappy." Yet their father wouldn't favor one daughter's happiness over the other. She had to stall her sister, put off the marriage until they figured out what Muster was doing. By then, Shelby might have come to her senses. "I'll think about it."

Shelby blinked. "You'll think about giving us your blessing?"

"You may say you don't want it, but I know you." Maddie tried to work up a convincing smile. "I'd like to get to know Bennett before you make any announcements."

Shelby beamed as she flung her arms around Maddie and squeezed her. "All I've ever wanted was for you to give Bennett a chance." She kissed her on the cheek then retook her seat on the swing. Pushing it into motion, she said, "Now we can enjoy this lovely evening."

Maddie nodded, her thoughts a jumbled mess. So much for finding out any information about Shelby's part in the stampede. And now she'd promised to consider her sister's future with a man she didn't trust.

Breathing a quiet prayer, Maddie hoped Carter had a better night.

Chapter 11

The Dry Gulch was one of the largest and most profitable cattle ranches in all of Texas, and Clyde Muster would go to any lengths to keep that reputation. A quiet man, he was ruthless in his business dealings, acquiring property and cutting down competitors with the precision of the gunfighter Robert Clay Allison.

And now, his sights were on Maddie.

Big John leaned up in his saddle. "It might have been better for us to come tomorrow morning."

"And worry about what might be happening at Maddie's tonight?" Carter shook his head. "I want answers about the stampede, and I want them tonight."

"Even if you get shot for your trouble?"

Carter didn't answer, just led Malcom onto the path that led to Muster's main house. Maddie hadn't been far from his thoughts since he'd left her this afternoon. She plowed through their work, stiff lipped and stubborn, but every once in a while he'd catch a glazed look, as if she were reliving those moments when the herd hurtled toward her. He understood. The thought of losing her before he'd had a chance to explore these feelings he had for her had sent him to Muster's doorstep tonight.

John came up alongside him. "I hope she's worth it."

"She is." A smile pulled on Carter's mouth as he thought about the way he'd held her in his arms. He wanted more of those moments, a lifetime of laughter and family, a partner in work and in life. "I love her, John."

"I figured as much." The older man chuckled. "She must be a fine woman for you and Cassie to care so much about her."

He stole a glance at John. "Cassie likes her?"

"Quite a bit, it seems." John's eyes crinkled in the corners as he smiled. "She told me she wished you would marry Miss Maddie so y'all could be a real family."

Carter chuckled. "I don't know if we're ready for a parson just yet. I'm not even sure how Maddie feels about me."

Big John scoffed. "She'd be a durn fool not to see what a good man you are."

"Yeah, well, we'll just have to see."

A few moments later, they broke through the trees into Muster's front yard. Carter led Malcom over to the hitching post, tying the reins loosely around the cedar post.

The Muster place was the kind of place he'd like to build Maddie someday. The walls to the two-story building looked freshly painted, the shutters an emerald green against pale yellow. As they drew nearer to the house, the air was heavy with the scent of an assortment of flowers that lined the large front porch.

When they took the first step up to the porch, the hammer of a rifle clicked.

The two men stopped and held their hands up. "It's Carter Wilbanks. I'm here to pay a call."

"Clyde, put that gun down. We've got company." A woman stood to the side of the porch, her silver-blond hair cascading over her shoulders like a waterfall he'd seen in a newspaper in Houston. She smiled as she came to the railing. "I'm sorry about that, Carter. Clyde wouldn't hurt a fly."

"Flossie Dewberry," John called out. "What are you doing here? I didn't know you knew Clyde."

Her laughter set Carter on edge. "Of course I know him. It's my business to be acquainted with all the men in Crinoline Creek." She gave Carter a sarcastic smile. "Well, most of them."

Best to get this meeting over with. Carter tipped his hat to her. "I'm sorry to interrupt your evening, but I'd like a quick word with Clyde. It will only take a few minutes."

"As long as you keep it short so I can get back to enjoying my wife's company." A rocking chair squealed as the man stood and lumbered over to the railing. Clyde towered over most men in these parts, and the scars he'd accumulated over the years were enough to scare the meanest snake of a man. Yet, as he turned to his wife, there was a softness about him.

He bent to kiss Flossie on the head. "Go on inside, darling. I don't want you to catch a chill."

"All right, sugar." She gave him a peck on the lips then turned to them. "Nice to see you."

"Same here, ma'am," Carter answered.

Once Flossie was safely inside, Clyde turned to him. "She's somethin', ain't she?"

John gave Carter a dubious look. "She's something, all right."

Carter turned back to Clyde. "I didn't know you and Flossie were married."

Clyde grinned from ear to ear. "Almost two months now. I'd wanted to marry her for years, but you know how it is. She's very independent and wanted to make her own way in the world." He smiled. "I convinced her she could be married and still own a business in town."

"So, you don't mind that she runs—" John started, the disbelief on his face almost comical.

Clyde interrupted, his voice rumbling with irritation. "A boardinghouse of sorts."

John's bushy gray eyebrows shot up. "Is that what they're calling it these days?"

Before Clyde could answer, Carter jumped in. "There's something I need to discuss with you concerning Maddie Turner."

The man scoffed. "Why? I barely know the woman."

Maddie had told him as much, yet she still had her concerns about him. "There was a stampede near your north pasture today, and Miss Turner was caught in it."

Clyde leaned forward on the railing, his face suddenly pale. "She didn't get hurt, did she?"

The note of concern in his voice was unexpected. Carter continued, "She's fine. Just spooked us a little."

"I'm glad to hear it." Clyde drew in a deep breath almost as if he'd been holding it. "Did you figure out how it happened?"

"We have our theories." Carter explained finding new stakes in the fence. "What I'd like to know is if you know anything about it?"

Clyde blinked as if he hadn't expected the question. "Why would I know anything?"

Carter felt his temper climb. "Most of Crinoline Creek knows you want the Turner land."

The man nodded. "I did once, I'm ashamed to say. Even thought of some ways to get that Turner woman off the property. But after I got married I realized there was only so much one man needed." He smiled. "I have all I need right here."

Carter glanced at John, who shrugged. This didn't sound like the Clyde Muster he'd known for the past ten years, yet he seemed sincere. "Do you know anything about the repaired fence?"

Clyde shook his head. "I've been leaving those kinds of chores to my foreman."

"Then can I talk to him?"

Clyde shook his head. "I sent him to Houston on business a week ago. He should be back next week."

None of this made sense. Muster was being honest with him. Carter could feel it in his bones. Still, someone who worked for Muster had to know who repaired that fence. Once he found him, Carter would have the culprit. "Thank you, Clyde. I won't keep you any longer."

"If you want to see if my boys know anything about it, you're welcome to come and question them."

It was a kind gesture, certainly not one Carter had expected. He tipped his hat. "Thank you. I might just take you up on that offer."

"Anything to help." Clyde nodded. "And tell Miss Turner I hope she enjoys ranching as much as I do." He smiled again. "I didn't understand until I married Flossie how important owning your own business was to some ladies."

"I'll tell her that," Carter replied. Whether she believed him, that was anyone's guess. One thing he knew was that Clyde Muster wasn't behind the stampede.

Then who was?

🌿

"It's one, two, three. One, two, three."

Cassie pushed out of Matthew's grip and spun toward Maddie, scowling. "Exactly why do I have to do this?"

"Because young ladies must know how to dance," Luke answered in a high-pitched voice. Tilting his head back, he stared down his nose at the two older children. "Not that I see a lady anywhere."

Cassie stalked toward the younger boy, her fists tightly knotted by her side. "I ought to—"

Maddie jumped in front of her before she could do any damage. "Luke's just trying to get your goat, but you're above that."

"But he's. . ." The girl clamped her lips together. "Mean."

"Sweetheart," Maddie cooed, sliding her arm around the girl's shoulders and leading her back to where Matthew stood. "Don't you know when boys like Luke tease you, it's because they secretly like you?"

"I do not!" Luke jumped out of his seat. "I'd like a rattlesnake better than her!"

Matthew smiled from his place on the dance floor. "Is that why you're always staring at Cassie when we're in school?" He laughed.

"Maybe you'd rather be dancing with her."

"I'd rather dance with the pigs," Luke grunted, folding his arms over his chest. "They'd smell a sight better."

"Enough!" Maddie cried out. Why she'd thought teaching the children to dance would be easier than dealing with Shelby, she wasn't sure. All she truly wanted was some peace and quiet so she could think.

There was one way to get some peace. "Luke, I'm sure there are some chores out in the barn that could use your attention."

"But I've done all my chores."

"Well, until you can learn to be respectful of ladies, you'll just have to do some more." She pointed toward the door. "Go. Now."

When the door closed behind the boy, Cassie rushed over to Maddie, her smile uncertain. "Do you really think he likes me?"

Before Maddie could answer, Matthew piped in. "Remember when your chalk went missing last week, and you had to ask Miss Worth for a new piece?"

Cassie nodded.

"Luke took it. It's sitting on his nightstand."

"He did?" Cassie's eyes widened as if she'd just discovered a new and exciting part of her world. She glanced up at Maddie. "Has a boy ever done that to you?"

Maddie tugged gently on her braid. "Once, a boy I knew found a glove I'd lost and kept it. Papa told me it was amongst his belongings when he died in the Battle of Kolb Farm."

"That's so sweet," Cassie replied, slipping her hand in hers. "He must have really liked you."

"Yes, I guess he did." She hadn't thought about the shy young man she'd grown up with in years, but then, they were barely out of the schoolroom when the war started. She gave the children a smile. "I didn't even know he had my glove."

Cassie tugged at her hand. "I don't mind if Luke keeps my chalk. Maybe under all that meanness, there's a nice boy."

"Don't tell him that," Matthew said. "He'd do everything he can think of to prove you wrong."

Maddie didn't want to think about it. "Why don't you two go out in the kitchen for some milk? Shelby's been baking cookies all morning."

"I love Miss Shelby's tea cookies." Matthew grabbed Cassie's arm. "Come on!"

Maddie watched as the two walked out of the room, chatting like a pair of magpies. Ah, to be young again, before war, hunger, and need stripped your innocence away, leaving you in a world you didn't recognize anymore.

Maybe Shelby was right about one thing. She didn't want to be an old maid. But marriage had to be more than just being some-one's wife.

Not just someone's wife. Carter's.

He was everything she'd ever hoped for in a husband, some-one who respected her opinions and supported her dreams for the ranch, a partner in the true sense of the word.

But could he love her?

Maddie shook her head. Didn't she have enough on her mind to worry about? They were friends, nothing more. End of story.

Then why did her heart ache at the thought?

"What are you thinking about so hard?"

Maddie jerked around to find Carter in the doorway, one boot crossed over the other as he leaned against the frame. Her heart fluttered at the sight of him until she realized he'd asked her a question.

She blurted out the first word that came to mind. "Cows."

"Cows." One dark brow lifted. "In the middle of the parlor."

"Yes, well." The scent of fresh air, horse flesh, and Carter sent her pulse racing. She stepped deeper into the room, aware he was right behind her. "You know me. I'm always thinking about cows."

He didn't answer right away, just studied her for a long moment, something unsettling in his gaze. "Where are the children?"

"In the kitchen. We've spent the afternoon learning how to dance, and I thought they could use a break."

"Dancing, huh?" The corner of his mouth lifted in a soft smile. "It's been so long since I've been to a barn dance, I might need you to remind me how." He stepped closer until he stood in front of her, every breath he exhaled a warm caress against her cheek. "How about it, Maddie? Could you teach me? Right now?"

She stepped into his outstretched arms, lightly placing one hand on his shoulder while he took her other hand in his. He pulled her close, and she forgot to breathe.

She tipped her head back to meet his gaze. "I don't remember any dances where a man held me so close."

His smile curled around her heart. "You've never danced in Texas."

"Oh, it's a Texas thing, is it?" She swayed from side to side along with him, relaxing into his embrace, the peace she'd sought all day found here in his arms.

Carter hummed a few broken chords of a song.

"I've never heard that tune before." She inhaled, the fragrance of flannel and sunshine filling her lungs.

"It's something my pa used to play on his fiddle for Ma sometimes." He smiled against her hair. "She seemed to like it."

"Papa played the fiddle too, but he gave it up after Mama died." She wound her arm around his shoulder, tucking herself beneath his chin. "He didn't have a heart for it after that."

His arms tightened around her. "I can understand that."

He understood. Did that mean he'd been in love? Hot coals came to life in her stomach. Who was this woman? Was he still in love with her?

Pulling away from him, Maddie tilted her head back to meet his gaze. "I don't recognize this dance step. What's it called?"

His lips spread into a warm smile. "I made it up."

"You what?"

"I made it up." His dark eyes twinkled with mischief that made her heart beat faster. "Don't give me that look."

"Do you know how scandalous we look standing here like this?" Maddie gave him a gentle push, and though he relaxed his hold, he didn't let her out of his arms. "Both our reputations would be ruined."

He lowered his head, his breath mingling with hers. "That wouldn't be good."

"No, it wouldn't," she whispered, closing her eyes as he kissed her forehead. "It wouldn't be good at all."

"Let's find out." He lowered his lips to hers.

Maddie had always been taught that a proper young lady would push out of a man's arms and slap him for taking such liberties. But that young lady must have never been kissed by Carter Wilbanks. She twined her arms around his neck and gave herself over to the kiss.

And it was wonderful. Everything she dreamed her first kiss would be, tender yet fierce, like the man himself.

Too soon, he lifted his head, staring at her, his dark eyes warm and vulnerable. "Maddie—"

She didn't give him a chance to finish his thought, instead pulling his head down to hers. She brushed her mouth against his, her world teetering on the brink of wonderful when his lips caught hers in another searing kiss.

Maddie's knees had gone weak by the time Carter broke the kiss. He leaned his forehead against hers. "Maddie, I'm. . .sorry."

Sorry? For what? Maddie pushed away from him, and this time, he let her go. She took a deep breath then straightened, meeting his gaze. "What's there to be sorry about? It was nothing."

"Nothing?" Carter looked into her eyes, and for one brief moment, Maddie thought he might haul her back into his arms and show her exactly how wonderful their kisses had been.

"Unless you want it to be something?" What on earth was she thinking, asking him something like that? Maddie blamed it on him. He'd muddled her thoughts.

"Not right now," Carter finally said, raking a hand through his mussed hair. "We've got enough problems as it is."

Maddie pressed her lips together and nodded. Was that how Carter thought of her, just another problem? Then again, she almost did get him killed yesterday. But really, that wasn't something to say to a woman after you'd just kissed her senseless.

Maddie schooled her features, praying he couldn't see the turmoil raging inside her.

"What problem are we going to discuss now?"

He took her arm and led her to the love seat. "I talked to Clyde Muster yesterday."

"And?"

"It's not him."

Maddie blinked. It had to be Muster. He was the only one who stood to gain if she abandoned the ranch. Still, Carter had to have his reasons for believing the man was innocent. "Why do you think that?"

"He denied it, of course." Carter rubbed the back of his neck. "But it was his responses, as if he were surprised by the whole thing, like he'd never think to take such action."

Maddie sank back against the cushions. "I only met him once, but he seemed the type of person who would crow about his involvement in such a scheme."

Carter nodded. "I wonder if marriage has softened him up."

"Muster's married? To whom?"

He gave her an uncertain glance. "The former Flossie Dewberry."

Maddie shot up in her seat. "You mean that woman who ran the. . ." She choked on the word. "That place!"

"She still does, and with Muster's blessing, it seems."

"But—" she sputtered. "How can she. . .?" She finally gave up on her questions. "I've never heard of such a thing."

"You're not the only one. Big John went on about it all the way home. I thought he'd never shut up."

She chuckled. "Well, it does take the cake."

"At any rate, I think we can clear Muster from planning the stampede."

She'd forgotten about that. "So who started it?"

"I don't know. It could be anyone."

Her stomach churned, the taste of bile sour in her mouth. She'd lived through four years of war, gone without food so Shelby and the children could eat, lived in terror as the cannon balls rained down on them. All she wanted was a piece of land to raise her little makeshift family in peace.

"I'm staying here until we figure out who's after you."

She shifted her gaze back to Carter. "You can't do that. You have your own ranch to run."

There was a slight tremor in his hand when he took hers. He feared for her safety. "I've got good people who'll run it in my absence."

She had to talk him out of this before he got himself killed. "People in town will talk."

"That's not my concern right now." He gave her a ghost of a smile. "Besides, people will always talk."

"But—"

He pressed a calloused finger to her lips. "No more buts, Maddie. The only thing that matters is finding out who did this. Until then, I'm staying right here."

She couldn't argue with him. Truth be known, she found comfort in knowing he'd be just a few steps away. "All right then. I'll double some of the children up."

"And where will I be?"

He was teasing her again. Well, she could give as good as she took. "There's a nice cot out in the barn with your name on it."

He laughed. "That's all right. I'm going to bunk down on the front porch."

The porch? "But it still gets cold at night. I don't want you to catch a chill or anything."

He cupped her chin, his expression unreadable. "I've spent many nights out in the elements. Don't give me a thought."

But she would, and not just tonight, but every moment for the rest of her life.

That's what you did when you loved someone.

Chapter 12

Carter burrowed into the mountain of quilts Maddie had given him, then threw the last one over him. The calendar may read spring, but there was still a bite in the air after the sun set.

Folding his arms over his chest, he remembered Maddie's words. *"I don't want you to catch a chill or anything."* Almost the same words Clyde Muster had said to his bride earlier in the day. Did that mean Maddie cared a little bit about him? Did she love him as he'd realized he loved her?

Carter closed his eyes, the memory of their kisses playing through his thoughts. It had started out so sweet, her first, if he wasn't mistaken. But when she'd tugged him down for a second one. . .goodness gracious! The woman almost blew his boots off!

He drew in a deep breath, his thoughts shifting to the stampede.

If Muster didn't want Maddie out of the picture, then who? With Clyde ruled out, he wasn't sure where to look. The only thing he could do for now was keep Maddie safe.

Which was why he was lying here, freezing on her front porch. But he'd do anything for Maddie, even give his life if it kept her safe.

He closed his eyes again, willing himself to sleep. Had she locked the back door as well as the windows like he'd told her? The upstairs windows had been open earlier—he'd noticed when he'd ridden up this evening. Had she closed them for the night?

He couldn't take a chance. Shoving the quilt aside, Carter pulled on his boots, then stood, reaching for the gun resting nearby. He barely made any noise as he tiptoed across the wooden floor, checking one window then another.

After checking the front door, he made his way down the porch stairs and around the corner of the house. In the moonlight, he could see that the window to the room Cassie shared with Robin was closed. But the window next to it—Maddie's room, he'd been told—was cracked an inch or two. So she liked the night air. Carter smiled as he filed away that intimate little tidbit about her, then proceeded toward the back of the house.

After checking the kitchen door and all the windows, he started around the corner.

Omph!

What in blue blazes? Carter stepped back. How had a ladder gotten here? His gaze shot up to the second story.

Curtains fluttered from an open window.

For Pete's sake, how. . . ? He didn't have time to think on that now. His heart pounding, Carter ran back to the front porch, threw open the screened door, and beat his fist against the wooden door. "Maddie! Wake up! There's someone in the house!"

Agonizing seconds passed slowly as he waited for some kind of response. At the end of his rope, Carter took several steps back, then rammed his shoulder against the wood. The door cracked but didn't give. He stepped back again, but before he could move, it opened.

"Carter, what's wrong?"

Holding a lit candle, Maddie looked like a sleepy angel, her lovely golden curls falling down over her shoulders, ending at the knot in her robe. Carter's mouth went dry. "Someone's in the house."

Her eyes flew open. "An intruder?"

He snapped to his senses then, gently pushing her aside as he walked through the parlor. "There's a ladder against the house near an open window."

"I'm the only one who sleeps with the window cracked." She made a startled noise. "Shelby."

Carter turned to find Maddie, her shoulders hunched, her face twisted in pain. He rushed to her. "What is it?"

"She told me she would do it, but I didn't believe her." Moisture glimmered in her eyes. "I should have known better."

"You think she ran off to get married?"

She sniffed. "She's been threatening to for weeks. I even told her that if she let me get to know the man, I'd reconsider giving my consent." Her face crumbled. "I guess she couldn't wait."

Resting his hands on her shoulders, he met her watery gaze. "We don't know that for certain. For all we know, they just went out for a moonlit walk."

"You think so?" Her voice wobbled.

"Sure I do." He coaxed her into his arms. "She'll probably be back any minute."

Movement by the door caught Carter's attention. The children crowded into the hallway. "It's all right. Everyone go back to bed."

Luke rubbed his eyes with his fists. "Y'all are sure noisy tonight. I just got back to sleep after all that banging."

Maddie jerked around. "What banging?"

"I don't know," the boy answered sleepily. "It sounded like someone was hammering nails into the wall."

"How long ago was that?" Carter asked.

He shrugged. "I don't know. It woke me up and I saw a light under the door."

But it was the middle of the night. If Shelby did leave with Bennett, the young couple could be anywhere by now. Tracking them in the dead of night would be next to impossible. He glanced down at Maddie. "We need to know what all she took. That might give us an idea of how long she intends to stay gone."

She nodded. "I'll check her room."

As they neared the hallway, Carter heard whispers.

"Did Shelby run away?" John asked his older brothers.

"Grown-ups don't run away, stupid." Luke hoisted the younger boy.

"No, but they die sometimes like my ma and pa." Cassie's voice trembled as she spoke. "They didn't love me enough to stay."

Is that what his little sister thought? True, he never talked much about their parents. It had been too hard at first, then growing the ranch and just getting by had occupied much of his mind. All this time, poor Cassie had thought their parents didn't love her.

Letting Maddie go, Carter walked over to his sister and

crouched down in front of her. "That's just not so, baby girl."

"It isn't?"

He shook his head. "Ma and Pa loved you so much. Ma used to say you were God's gift to her to keep her young. And Pa. . ." He stroked the girl's cheek. "He used to carry you around wherever he went just because he couldn't stand being apart from you."

Blue eyes so like their mother's looked back at him. "So they loved me?"

"Yes, honey. If they could have stayed they would have, because they loved us so much."

Cassie threw her arms around him. "I love you, Carter."

"I love you too, Butterbean." Carter squeezed her close, then let go. Glancing over to the boys and Robin, he stood, catching Maddie swiping at her cheek. "Let's get you kids back into bed, then we'll worry about Shelby."

"Good," Luke mumbled, taking the stairs two at a time. "All this mushy stuff has worn me out."

Fifteen minutes later, Carter stood at the stove waiting for the coffee to boil when Maddie finally joined him. Her face still pale, she'd changed into a simple blue calico dress and wore her hair braided in a single plait down her back. Leaving his post, he grabbed two mugs from the sideboard and placed them on the table.

"I checked her room." Maddie pulled out a chair and slumped into it. "It's a mess. Hair ribbons everywhere. Hats and bonnets scattered all over her bed."

"Sounds like an elopement." Using a dish towel, he carried the pot to the table. "Did she have any pin money?"

"I didn't check, not that I'd be able to tell amongst everything thrown about."

He glanced down at her. "Cream and sugar?"

She reached for a mug. "Cream is in the cold box."

"I take mine black." He joined her at the table as she poured. "Did she take all of her dresses?"

"I would think so." Maddie wrapped her hands around the mug as if drawing comfort from its warmth. "Knowing Shelby, though, she'd get married in her night rail."

"Still got your sense of humor, I see."

One blond brow rose. "It's not the worst thing that's happened to me this week." Her face fell. "At least, I hope not."

Poor darling. He wished he could find a way to make it all better. "Drink. It might help."

Maddie shook her head. "I should have taken her seriously when she said she wanted to marry him. I just hoped—"

"Are you absolutely sure she's with Bennett?"

"Who else would she be with?" Maddie lowered her mug. "There's something you should know. I haven't told you because, well, Papa always said family business needs to stay in the family." She swallowed hard. "Shelby has been sneaking out with Bennett for weeks."

"Then you're probably right. She's with him." He thought for a moment. "I'd still like to see her room. It might give us a clue if she'll be back." He stood and held out his hand to her.

She hesitated, then slid her hand into his, her fingers cool to the touch. He rubbed the pad of his thumb across her knuckles in small circles, wanting to comfort her any way he could. She stood but didn't let go, as if she were tied to him, anchored in the storm.

They climbed the steps until they reached the narrow hallway. Maddie stepped ahead of him then, leading him to an opened door. "This is her room."

He followed her inside. Holding up the lantern, he surveyed the room. It was a mess, just like Maddie described. Ribbons tossed across a dressing room table, bonnets strewn across the floor. It was as if she'd left in a hurry instead of for a planned elopement.

He hurried to the closet and opened the door. "How many dresses does Shelby have?"

"Three." Maddie sat down on the mussed bed and started folding clothes. "We sold the rest when we came west."

"Maddie, there are three dresses in the closet."

"What?" Jumping up, she hurried to his side. "That can't be."

"Maybe she wore something else," he suggested. "Maybe one of those skirts you go riding in."

She shook her head. "Shelby thinks split skirts aren't feminine enough for her. Is there anything else missing?"

They searched in earnest then, opening dresser drawers and hat boxes. Maddie finally stared at him across Shelby's unmade bed. "The only thing missing is the night rail she was wearing."

"Which means this wasn't an elopement," Carter said, dread flowing through him. "This was a kidnapping."

✤ Chapter 13 ✤

Carter thought it would be best to wait until first light before they searched for Shelby, but for Maddie, another minute was too long. The girl only had her nightgown, robe, and slippers to keep her warm. And who would have taken her if not Bennett? There were tales back home of women being snatched from their beds only to end up in houses of ill repute. Maddie had never believed them, but now, she could only pray they weren't true.

Carter's hand covered hers as they sat at the kitchen table. "I'll find her. I promise."

She glanced up at him. He exuded such confidence, as if only he could slay her dragons. She couldn't help but believe him. "How can you be so sure?"

He rubbed a calloused thumb across the back of her hand.

A Cowboy of Her Own

"Because I won't stop until I do." He glanced toward the window, then stood, letting go of her hand. "The sun will be up any minute now, then I'll go get Sheriff Hollis. We'll stop by the ranch and get Big John and the boys before we head over to Muster's."

"You think Shelby is there?"

"I'm not sure, but seeing how Bennett works for him, it's a good place to start."

Maddie stood with him. "Thank you, Carter. I don't know what I'd do without you."

Pulling her into his arms, he cradled her against him. "I promise you. This will all work out."

Knowing Carter, the type of man he was, she believed every word. "I trust you."

He pressed his lips against her forehead, lingering as if he never wanted to let her go. Then suddenly, he released her. He grabbed his hat and headed toward the door, turning when he reached it. "Put your rifles next to the doors and keep them locked. You and the children stay inside until I get back. Okay?"

Maddie nodded, uncertain what to say. Carter could be walking into danger. He could be wounded or killed if things turned ugly. The pain that sliced through her at the thought left no doubt in her mind about her feelings toward the cowboy. "Carter?"

"What is it, sweetheart?"

"I love you."

He gave her a smile, then opened the door and left.

Maddie slid into her chair, her legs suddenly wobbly. What had she done, telling Carter that she loved him? And why hadn't he answered her back when she'd worn her heart on her sleeve like she had? Had she embarrassed him with her declaration?

III

Or maybe he didn't feel the same way about her.

She covered her face with her hands. There were more important things to be thinking about right now than Carter's feelings toward her. Like following his directions. Maddie stood up and walked into the parlor, to the front closet where she stored her rifles. Pulling two out, she checked the barrels then snapped them into place. She put one next to the front door, checking the lock before she headed to the kitchen with the other one.

As she entered the room, a knock at the door jarred her composure. Carter hadn't had enough time to get Sheriff Hollis, much less return. What if the kidnapper hoped to gain another hostage as a bargaining tool? One of the children perhaps? Leveling her gun at the door, Maddie quietly slid over to the window. Heart pounding, she glanced outside.

Shelby!

Laying her rifle on the table, Maddie hurried to the door, hesitating before she opened it. What if it was a trap? "Shelby, are you alone?"

"Yes," her sister cried. "I made sure no one followed me."

Maddie opened the door cautiously. Shelby threw herself at Maddie, knocking the air out of her lungs. "Oh Maddie, I've never been so scared in my life." She crumpled against her like a wounded child. "Thank God, I was able to get away."

Maddie tried to pull back, but Shelby just tightened her grip. "Honey, I need to lock the door just in case—"

The girl released her immediately. "Yes, lock everything. Don't let those two anywhere near me again!"

Maddie hurried and locked the door then turned around, her heart plunging into her stomach as she caught her first glimpse of her sister. Twigs hung in Shelby's bed-ragged hair, and there were tears in her robe. Her face held streaks of dirt, and there was a bruise over her left eye. Her shoes missing, her feet were covered in bloody scratches and dirt.

Touching Shelby's arm, she led her to a chair, then bent to get a closer look at the bruise. "Did Bennett hit you?"

Shelby shook her head on a sniffle. "Bennett didn't lay a hand on me except when we rode together."

So, Bennett was involved. Maddie had known not to trust the cowhand, but there was no sense holding that over Shelby's head now, not when the girl had learned such a hard lesson. "What happened?"

It was several long moments before Shelby finally spoke. "I was almost asleep when I heard a stone against my window." She chanced a glance at Maddie, shame in her eyes. "It's how Bennett always lets me know he's here. Anyway, he said if we wanted to get married, it would have to be right away. His mother was with him, and he wanted her to witness the vows. He didn't want to wait for me to pack or even get dressed. He said his mother would understand. We were in love." Her voice broke on the word. "I thought it was romantic."

"Of course you did." Maddie rose, went over to the counter where the water bucket was, and poured out a dishpan full. Returning to the table, she lowered it to the floor and helped Shelby place her feet in the water.

"But we didn't go to the justice of the peace. He took me to some ranch not far from here." The tears started again. "That's when I realized he had no intention of marrying me."

Poor Shelby! She'd been so sure of Bennett's love. "He didn't—"

She shook her head violently. "It was all a lie. He'd only courted me to get you to turn over the ranch to him and his mother. They thought you'd sign the ranch over to them if they held me hostage."

They were right, of course. She would have given up everything to get Shelby back. Still, Maddie was confused. "But Muster was the one who wanted us off this place."

"No," Shelby whimpered, her face crumbling. "Mr. Muster is dead. At least, I think he is. I overheard Bennett's mother say that she'd poisoned him last night before they went to bed." She looked at Maddie. "I didn't even know Mr. Muster was married."

Bennett's mother was Mr. Muster's new wife, Flossie? It was beginning to make sense now. Maddie cupped her sister's face in her hands. "It's over now, dearest. You're safe."

"You warned me about Bennett, but I wouldn't listen. I thought I knew better." She swiped at her wet face. "I'm sorry I didn't believe you."

"Oh Shelby." Maddie took the edge of her apron and wiped her sister's cheeks. "Sometimes our brains don't listen, particularly when we fall in love."

"You found yourself a good man in Carter." She gave Maddie a watery smile. "I saw the two of you dancing in the parlor."

Letting go of her, Maddie walked to the counter and grabbed a clean towel. "It was that obvious how I felt about him?"

"No," she replied, flinching as she touched her bruised eye. "But Carter was obvious. The way he looked at you. Like you were the most precious thing in the world to him."

"I don't know about that." She knelt down to dry Shelby's battered feet. "I told him I loved him, but he. . ." His silence afterward sliced through her again.

"Maddie, knowing you, you probably told him in the middle of branding calves or mucking out the barn."

Or when he was heading out the door to save her sister. She blushed. "Maybe it wasn't the right time."

Shelby took the towel from her and finished drying her ankles. "Wait until it's the right time, then tell him again. I'll bet his response will be different."

When had her baby sister become so wise? "That's good advice."

Shelby leaned down and gave her a kiss on the cheek. "Well, I learned from the best."

Once she got Shelby settled into bed, Maddie made breakfast for the children. Of course, they were excited about a day off from school, though staying inside was not their idea of fun. Nervous that Bennett and Flossie might return, Maddie kept busy giving the house a good cleaning and occasionally glancing down the road. All morning long she kept an ear out for Carter.

It was early afternoon before there was a knock at the kitchen door. Brushing the wrinkles out of her skirts, Maddie drew in a deep breath as she peeked out the window. Seeing him, standing hat in hand outside her kitchen door, was too much, and she launched herself into his arms.

Thank You for bringing him back to me, Lord!

"Are you all right?" she asked against his shoulder.

He chuckled softly into her ear. "I'm fine, sweetheart. Not even a scratch for all my trouble."

"I'm glad." Maddie let go of him, heat racing up her neck into her cheeks. She walked over to the warmer where she'd saved lunch for him. "I guess you know Shelby's here."

Hanging his hat on a nail, Carter followed her into the kitchen. "Bennett said he let her escape. Said his mother wanted to get rid of her, but he just couldn't do it."

"Maybe there's some hope for the boy."

"Not for at least a few years. Maybe less, if he turns evidence against his mother. It appears Mrs. Muster was the mastermind behind the stampede. Bennett simply followed her instructions."

"Shelby said Flossie was after my place, not Muster." Maddie set the food on the table, remembering what her sister had said about the poisoning. "Is he really dead?"

Grabbing a clean towel from the table, Carter wiped his hands. "Flossie poisoned him just enough to make him sick as a dog, but Doc says he should pull through."

"I was worried." And she had been. She may have disliked what she thought he'd done, but she would never wish him ill. "I owe him an apology for suspecting him of trying to take our ranch."

"I'm sure he feels he's the one who owes you an apology for what Flossie and her son put you through." He watched her as she poured a cup of coffee. "He feels mighty stupid about being taken in by Flossie like that."

"It wasn't his fault." She set the coffeepot on the table. "A person does foolish things when they fall in love."

"While we're on the subject." Taking her hand, he tugged her onto his lap. "You said something mighty sweet before I left this morning."

Was this the perfect time Shelby talked about? Uncertain, she glanced down at her hands in her lap. "Yes, well. . ."

Cupping her cheek in his hand, he turned her face until their gazes met. "Say it again, please."

She couldn't refuse him. "I love you."

A wondrous smile spread across his features. "I love you too."

It was her time to grin like a silly fool. "You do?"

"With all my heart."

"Oh Carter." She flung her arms around his neck, raining kisses on his cheeks, his hair, his forehead. "I was so scared something would happen to you when you left here this morning. I had to tell you how much I loved you in case I never got the chance again."

"I couldn't wait to get back to you so I could tell you how much you mean to me." He leaned toward her, kissing her cheeks and the tip of her nose before his lips closed over hers. It was a wondrous kiss full of desire and love and promises of the years to come. When he broke off the kiss, they were both breathless.

Carter recovered first. "Marry me? Please?"

Maddie's heart sang at his question. "We'll need to talk to the children."

"I think we can convince them." He leaned his head against hers as if soaking in her warmth. "Don't you?"

She nodded. "Without a doubt."

Lifting his head, he met her gaze. "So, will you marry me, and soon?"

Staring into his dark eyes, Maddie found what she'd been looking for. A home, and the man she loved to share it with, living the life she'd always wanted. God truly had bigger dreams for her than she'd had for herself. She chuckled at a thought.

"What's so funny?" Carter asked, brushing a kiss across her forehead.

She leaned back, just enough to see his wonderfully handsome face. "I was just thinking. I'm getting a cowboy of my own."

Carter smiled up at her, his eyes twinkling with love and respect. "Me too, little cowgirl. Me too."

Patty Smith Hall

A multipublished author with Love Inspired Historical and Barbour, Patty lives in north Georgia with her husband of over thirty years, Danny, two gorgeous daughters, her son-in-love, and a grandboy who has her wrapped around his tiny finger. When she's not writing on her back porch, she's spending time with her family or reading on her front porch swing.

Josephine's Dream

by Cynthia Hickey

Chapter 1

Texas, 1868

Josephine Montgomery, dressed in what used to be her third-best dress and now was her first best, stared once again at the crumpled sheet of paper in her hand. The stagecoach had dropped her off in Crinoline Creek almost an hour ago. Where was her new employer?

After the loss of her family's land and her parents' deaths, she vowed—no, dreamed—of being a self-sufficient woman. One day, she'd own something of her own that could never be taken away from her. This place, this town, was her hope for the beginning of that dream.

A commotion across the street drew her attention. A small boy darted from the café into the street. A tall man chased after him, three more children on his heels, scooped the runaway, and carried him under his arm like a sack of flour. As Josephine stared, the group tromped her way and stopped in front of her. Five pairs of blue eyes stared.

"Hello," she said. Heavens. Four children under the age of ten. "I'm Josephine Montgomery. Are you Mr. Owens and family?"

The man set the little boy on his feet but kept a firm grip on the collar of his nut-brown shirt. "I am. This rascal is Ben; he's nine. Sadie is seven, Robbie is five, and this scalawag is Luke, age four. We've supper ordered at the café so we can get acquainted." He peered around her. "Your things?"

"Inside the office. They can wait." She swallowed against the cotton in her throat. What in the world possessed her to come to Crinoline Creek, Texas, as a nanny-housekeeper? Mr. Owens would see through her lie in seconds. Still. She tightened her grip on her reticule, lifted her chin, and stepped off the wooden sidewalk. Her foot sank into something soft.

"You stepped in dung, Miss Montgomery." Ben slapped his hat against his thigh.

"That's enough." Mr. Owens's attempt at a straight face failed. Soon the entire family was laughing at Josie's expense.

She scraped the bottom of her shoe against the sidewalk and marched toward the café. If she had any other recourse, any other way of making a living, she'd plant her petticoated self in the stage-coach office until another arrived to take her back to Georgia. As it was, she was penniless and had sold most of her clothes, as evidenced by the out-of-date traveling suit she now wore. She had to stay and make the best of things.

She stopped in front of the café and waited for Mr. Owens to open the door for her. He must have said something to the little ruffians, because not one word was spoken as they entered and took their seats.

"I do apologize, Miss Montgomery," Mr. Owens said, pulling

out her chair. "I'm not making excuses, but my brood have been without a mother for four years. They could use the influence of an educated lady such as yourself."

Josie took her seat and stared at her lap, trying to come up with a suitable response. "I. . .will do my best." She met his gaze and lost her nerve at the warm look in his sky-blue eyes and spilled out the fact she'd never worked as a nanny or a housekeeper. Her family used to be plantation owners before the war. She badly needed a job. After much prayer for the right opportunity to come along, she sincerely hoped she'd found it.

Her employer took a seat across the table from her. "You do know children though, right? How to run a house? Aren't Southern ladies taught these things?"

"I know how to embroider, paint, and press flowers." Tears stung her eyes. The things she'd once enjoyed seemed so frivolous now. She glanced up and squared her shoulders. "I'm willing to learn anything, Mr. Owens."

He sighed. "Might as well call me Parker. We'll discuss your duties on the ride home. Best eat fast. It's a good ride from town." He motioned to a young girl who set plates of stew in front of each of them.

"Call me Josie, please." Her stomach rumbled. Peeling off her gloves, she set them inside her reticule and lifted her spoon.

"You sound like a bear," Luke said.

"I must confess to being as hungry as one," she replied, taking her first bite. Oh my. She glanced at the kitchen. Would the cook offer to teach her how to create such delicious fare?

Luke's statement seemed to have opened the dam, and the children fired Josie with questions. "What do we call you?"

"Can you read?"

"Are you old?"

"You ain't bigger than a minute."

They kept on until she set down her spoon. Glancing from one to the other, finally settling on their father, who watched the proceedings with amusement, she held up her right index finger and returned her attention to the younger Owenses. "First of all, one at a time. Second, you may call me Miss Josie. Third, yes, I can read, and I am nineteen. Please do not comment on a woman's size or age; it is not proper." She lifted her chin. Perhaps she could be of use to these children after all. She cut a glance to their father. "Well?"

"What?" His spoon paused on its way to his mouth.

"You obviously allowed this type of behavior as some sort of test. Did I pass?"

He chuckled. "With flying colors, Miss Josie." He removed his napkin from his lap and placed it on the table. "Children, let's get Miss Josie home before dark." He led the way, and Josie followed. When she glanced back, she saw the children falling into line youngest to oldest, like an adorable bunch of little ducklings.

The little girl stepped out of line and slipped her hand into Josie's. "Thank you for being a girl."

Josie fell in love.

***

If Parker had any second thoughts about the hiring of a woman who reached to midchest while wearing boots, they fled with the simple statement from his little girl. He'd never realized how much she needed a womanly influence in her life. Whether she was experienced or not, they'd have to manage with the new nanny.

"This is our wagon." He patted the neck of one of the bay horses. "We've a fine ranch of Texas cattle, a comfortable home, and ten ranch hands." He helped Miss Josie onto the seat while the children climbed in back with the supplies. Two trunks he'd never seen before had been placed among the sacks of feed and other household necessities. Obviously, someone had figured out Miss Josie would be leaving with him.

Sadie, staying as close to her nanny as possible, leaned over the seat and fingered the lace around the brim of the woman's hat. Silly thing. Wouldn't keep the sun out of a person's eyes. He eyed the dress she wore. Not fitting either, especially with all those layers. Hopefully, she'd brought more sensible clothing. If not, some of his late wife's things might fit. No, they'd be too big. The woman would have to make do.

He swung onto the buckboard and clicked his tongue. The horses headed east, then south out of town.

"My duties?"

"Pardon?" He glanced her way.

"You said once we headed for the ranch, you would list my duties."

"Oh, right. Well." He tugged his hat lower over his eyes. "You'll be responsible for the children, first and foremost, feeding, learning, that sort of thing. We have a cook, Mrs. Davis; she'll need help feeding the hired hands. You'll have some light chores around the place. Not too much."

"Heavens, are there enough hours in the day?" She paled, her dark eyes flashing.

"That's why we hired you. Mrs. Davis is as old as the dirt itself and wants to spend the rest of her days in leisure with her sister in Oklahoma. She needs to teach someone else to take over, and you're young enough to fit the requirements."

She fiddled with the lace around her throat. "To take over," she whispered.

"Well, Sadie does what she can, but she's a child." What was the woman's problem? She looked as if he'd asked her to kiss a snake. "What did you think a nanny and housekeeper did?"

"I really wasn't sure." She faced away from him. "How much time do I have before she leaves?"

"One week from today."

She gasped and turned wide eyes on him. "You cannot be serious."

"Yes, ma'am. It isn't my fault you weren't truthful in your letters. You managed the children just fine in the café. You'll do the same with everything else."

Well, that hushed her up. She huffed and turned away from him.

No matter. He preferred the drive through the prairie full of waving grasses and wildflowers, listening to nothing more than the breeze and the chattering of his children. The sun began its descent and kissed the tops of trees with rays of light. God's creation. Nothing better. He clicked his tongue for the horses to increase their speed.

When he'd first bought his land, he and Leah had had stars in their eyes and dreams as big as the sky. Then she'd fallen ill shortly after giving birth to Luke. Having no other choice, Parker had worked overtime keeping up the ranch and raising his children, but things were now at the point he needed help. Hopefully, the pretty little thing next to him would be that help. At least until

Sadie was a few years older.

"Oh." Miss Josie straightened as they rode under the sign to the Tilted O. "I didn't expect something so grand."

Pride swelled as he parked in front of the sprawling ranch house. Shaped like an L, with a second floor over the longer section, in his mind it looked like a jewel set among the Texas prairie grasses. In the distance, the Davis Mountains sat as the crowning touch to the picture.

"Took me years, but I finished the house last year. The front room is the original house, and I built from there as time and money allowed." He hopped down and moved to help her out. "Welcome home, Miss Josie."

With one hand holding her hat, she tilted her head back to follow the lines of the roof, then turned toward the barn and bunkhouse. "You, sir, have managed to pull out of the devastation left behind from the war."

"It didn't touch us much here."

Her eyes widened. "You didn't fight?"

He shook his head. "I couldn't leave the children alone." He hefted one of her trunks on his shoulder. "Let me show you to your room."

He led her to a small room at the back of the house. Once used for sewing and set away from the children's rooms, it would afford Miss Josie a small measure of privacy. He'd left Leah's sewing things in the corner and brought in a small bed and dresser. A chipped pitcher and bowl sat on top of the pine dresser. A rocking chair with a crocheted afghan draped over the back nestled against a small window. Mrs. Davis had donated a mirror that hung over the water pitcher, saying a woman of her age no longer needed to worry about her looks.

He set the trunk at the foot of the bed. "It isn't much, but you should be comfortable here. Feel free to make it yours."

"It will suit me fine. I've a few things in my trunk to make the room personal." She clasped her hands in front of her. "What time shall I start my duties in the morning?"

"Sunup." He grinned. "When Red, the rooster, crows, you'll have just enough time for your morning ministrations before Mrs. Davis will expect you in the kitchen. Good night, Miss Josie."

"Josie, please." She turned to the window. "I no longer have need of formalities in my life. I'll see you in the morning."

He smiled and went to fetch her other trunk. It would take her a few days to adjust, but he felt confident God had sent the very woman his family needed.

Chapter 2

A rooster crowed from her windowsill. Josie bolted upright in bed. No way she'd miss hearing the bird when he sat right outside her window. His name was Red? Right then, she wished he were dead. Didn't he have a coop to be in? Anywhere other than close to her head? She shoved her hair out of her face and climbed from under her grandmother's quilt. After a night spent tossing and turning, fear stirring in her heart like a wooden spoon in stew, her eyes were gritty and her skin clammy.

She splashed her face with water from the porcelain bowl, donned a day dress of yellow over several petticoats, and tied her hair back with a ribbon the same shade as the dress. After a quick peek in the mirror, she deemed herself ready to face the day and left her room, pulling the door closed behind her. Now, to find the kitchen. There were enough odds stacked against her, she didn't need being late added to the list.

She followed the banging of pots and pans to the opposite side of the house where a wizened old woman bent over a stove. "Stubborn thing." Without turning around, she stuck out her hand. "A match, girl."

Josie retrieved one from a tin on a side table and peered over the woman's shoulder. "What's the problem?"

"No fire."

Josie blinked and straightened. She'd expected a larger problem, something the mere striking of a match couldn't fix. "What would you have me do?"

"Fetch a pail of water from the pump outside." Mrs. Davis struck the match and held it to a piece of kindling. A small spark ignited. "Now we've a fire for cooking. Go on, girl. No time for dawdling. We've hardworking men to feed."

Josie grabbed a pail from near the door and stepped into dawn. A few feet from the back steps she spotted the pump and hurried toward it. As she filled the pail, she took a moment to take in her surroundings.

The ranch seemed to stretch for miles in every direction, the expanse broken by the occasional outbuilding, horse, or cow. A bird trilled from a nearby tree. It might not be her lovely home of Georgia, but this section of Texas held a beauty all its own.

When she'd filled the pail as full as she could and still be able to carry it, she moved back to the house and set the bucket on the counter. Mrs. Davis rolled dough for biscuits, motioning Josie over.

"Boss said you can't cook. No time like the present to learn." Her dark eyes roamed up and down Josie's gown. "Just as soon as you remove most of the petticoats. Those are dangerous in here and could catch on fire."

"A lady wears her. . .underthings, Mrs. Davis."

"Not all at once and not in Texas. We've more sense. Wear only what is necessary." She stretched her arm in the direction Josie's room lay. "Go. Save the fripperies for church."

Josie quickly removed two of her three petticoats, hung them on pegs, and rushed back to the kitchen where Mrs. Davis set her to work cutting biscuits. By the time the men gathered in the dining room, she felt as if she'd already put in a full day. She hadn't been in the kitchen long before her hair no longer hung down her back but sat pinned on top of her head. Still, tendrils stuck to skin damp with perspiration. She planted her palms flat on the counter and hung her head for a moment's rest.

"Are you all right?" Parker leaned back against the counter.

"I'm exhausted, and we've only prepared one of three meals." She narrowed her eyes at him. "Then we have to clean up, I'll have an hour to teach the children, then be back in the kitchen, then another hour with the children, then back in the kitchen, and that isn't counting the laundry, housecleaning, gardening. . .the list is massive." She planted her fists on her hips. "May I ask what *you* do all day?" The man looked freshly washed, his wheat-colored hair combed and in place.

"Not much." The corner of his mouth quirked. "Branding, feeding, roping, breaking horses, riding the fence line—"

"Riding? That isn't hard. Go sit down so we can serve you *hardworking* men." Was it the same everywhere? Women worked from sunup to sundown doing a million and one things while the men worked with the animals and went for rides?

"It isn't a competition, Josie," he said. "I work plenty hard."

She was a fool. Comparing her job to her boss's? She thought she'd left behind her spoiled ways. Obviously not. She had a lot to learn. "I apologize," she said as he turned to go.

"Apology accepted." He paused in the doorway. "You'll get the hang of things. You aren't alone."

She nodded. God would give her the strength she needed to do all that needed doing. She lifted a heavy coffeepot and moved to the dining room.

Ten men sat around the table. All conversation stopped when she entered, and they stood, gazes on her. She smiled. Similar enough to the dinner parties her parents used to throw that she felt some of the tension leave her neck and shoulders. With a grateful look at Parker, she started pouring.

Thank-you after thank-you was sent her way as she rounded the table. Once the coffee was poured, she set a platter of biscuits in the center of the table along with butter and jam. Then followed it with a mound of eggs and bacon. Once the table was laden, she turned toward the kitchen.

"Where are you going?" Parker asked.

"To have my breakfast."

"Here, Josie. We all eat together in this house. There is no separation between family and staff."

She sat as the children thundered into the room and took their seats around her.

※

Josie seemed to brighten a bit as the children sat around her. She might claim not to know much about young'uns, but her smile said otherwise. She was no stranger to them.

Parker buttered a biscuit and watched as she served his children, giving each of them a warm smile and a kind word. He didn't put much stock in her tirade in the kitchen, but he would keep as close an eye on her as possible to make sure she didn't overdo the physical aspect of her job. She'd need time to adjust. In fact, he should have insisted she spend her first day not working but getting adjusted.

He'd need to find her a suitable hat too, although it would be a shame to cover up that silken mass of deep mahogany. Her pale skin would burn easily under the Texas sun.

"She's something to look at," Mrs. Davis, who was seated beside him, said. "Even if she don't know much about hard work. I'll whip her into shape in no time."

He chuckled. "I'm sure you will. Just make sure I still have a nanny for my children when you leave next week. Take it easy on her today. Let her settle in."

"Don't worry about a thing. I know how to handle city gals." She smiled, sending her face into a layer of wrinkles, then stood and began clearing off the table as the workers filed from the room.

Sadie jumped up to help while Ben followed Parker outside, leaving the younger boys to wait for Josie. He'd tried giving them chores, but rambunctious Luke only caused more work and kept Parker hopping to keep the boy out of harm's way.

"Take care of the pigs, Son. I'll meet you by the corral in a bit." Parker ruffled Ben's hair and grabbed a bridle from a hook on the barn wall.

A while later, as he led a yearling in a circle to get it acclimated to a bit in its mouth, he glanced up to see Josie, basket swinging from one arm, stroll through the meadow with his four children following like little ducks. The sun shone on the nanny's upswept mane, kissing it with touches of gold. A picnic sounded like a wonderful idea and something he hadn't enjoyed since courting Leah.

He grinned and removed the bit from the horse's mouth. It wouldn't hurt for him to spend an hour with his children and a pretty woman from Georgia.

By the time he caught up to them, they'd spread an old quilt on the grass next to a stream and nibbled on tiny sandwiches. Parker hung back for a moment and watched from the shade of a tree.

"A lady balances her tray, Sadie. She does not set it on the ground to invite insects. Gentlemen regale the lady with tales to keep her entertained during their time together. Why don't you try, Ben?"

Parker's mouth fell open. She used their lunchtime as a lesson in etiquette? Clever, but what good would fancy manners do on the Texas prairie? Still, his children didn't seem to mind, so he felt it wise to keep his mouth shut. He could speak with Josie later about putting reading, writing, and arithmetic as priorities.

He moved closer as his son told of the time the sow got loose and pulled Mrs. Davis's favorite quilt into her pen and proceeded to have her piglets on it. Josie's laughter reminded him of the babbling of a brook as it trickled over rocks.

"Mr. Owens, I mean, Parker, please join us." She motioned her head to a corner of the quilt. "Your son is quite the storyteller. May I presume we sit on the infamous quilt?"

"You may." He smiled. "It's the only way you got it from Mrs. Davis without a fight. She refuses to put the quilt back on a bed or sleep on a blanket the pig did." He snagged a sandwich from the basket and peered between the slices of bread. Good. Ham and cheese. Something he recognized, although it would take a goodly amount to fill his belly.

"You should see the books Miss Josie brought," Sadie said. "Patterns of pretty dresses, manners, stories. . ."

"Anything on schoolwork?" He raised his eyebrows at Josie.

"Of course." High spots of color appeared on her cheeks. "I've kept mine from when I was a child. You did specify in your letter of employment you wanted the children to have lessons. Deportment is just as important if they are to grow and be successful."

"I didn't have fancy teaching, and I've done just fine."

"That's debatable." She set her empty plate on the quilt and crossed her arms. "Children, please excuse us. You may wade in the creek while I discuss something with your father."

With shouts of glee, they pulled off their shoes and raced for the water.

Josie narrowed her eyes. "I must insist, Parker, that if you have further problems with my methods that you not bring them up in front of the children. I need their respect in order to teach them. Before lunch, I had them practice writing their letters and numbers to see where their education levels might be. Luke is quite smart for one so young, and he is eager to learn. I felt mealtimes better suited for manners as I caught Ben sticking his finger in the butter dish and licking it off as he ran outside. Your daughter hungers for gentility. I can give her some of that. Perhaps I shall give you a written report each evening of what we did that day?" She started packing the dishes into the basket.

Parker felt like an idiot. He'd assumed much and knew little. He should have stayed with the horses.

Leaving Josie to the task of ignoring him, he joined his children. With careful questioning he discovered he didn't mind the lessons in manners because, as Ben pointed out, "It's different from what we usually do and seems to make Miss Josie happy."

All four children were of one accord in wanting to make their pretty nanny happy. Parker agreed. Maybe he needed to take a lesson or two from the young'uns.

☙ Chapter 3 ❧

Josie's eyes still burned the next morning from crying herself to sleep. Her first day working on the ranch, and she'd failed. Oh, maybe not in the kitchen, because she'd had the guidance of Mrs. Davis, but as a nanny to the children. Things that had been drilled into her all her life as important were deemed nonsense by Mr. Owens.

First, she'd been instructed to put away her petticoats—her petticoats with ribbon and lace and things that made her feel pretty—then she'd been bossed around by an old woman, then ridiculed in front of the children. Today had to be better. All she wanted was a place to call home, to belong, a small piece of what she'd once had. *Is that too much to ask, Lord?*

She sighed and splashed water on her face. From luxury to

virtually penniless, all before the age of twenty. *Stop it, Josephine Montgomery. You are a Southern lady with a spine of steel. Act like one.* There was no room in life for self-pity. God would bring her circumstances to good. All she needed to do was hold on to her faith.

With a firm nod at her reflection in the mirror, she squared her shoulders and marched to the kitchen. "Good morning, Mrs. Davis."

The woman peered up from where she stoked the stove. "I reckon. Glad to see you survived your first day."

"Famously." Josie tied a faded yellow apron around her waist. "Shall I cook the bacon?"

"I've already done that." Mrs. Davis straightened. "Why are you so chipper?"

"I enjoy facing each day with optimism."

Mrs. Davis narrowed her eyes. "I hope that still holds true when I leave next week."

"It will." If only Josie's insides didn't quake at the thought of the other woman's leaving. "What jobs are on our list this morning?"

"Laundry and weeding. Sadie helps in the garden. I don't see how you'll do it all, Miss Josie." She shook her head. "You're young and optimistic, but you have the duty of caring for the children right along with the house. I do believe I'll speak to the boss about hiring you some help."

"You do all right."

"I've been doing this sort of thing since I was Ben's age, and I don't teach the children their schooling." She thrust a stack of bowls into Josie's hands. "Maybe we can get you some part-time help."

Josie shrugged and set the table. Sadie raced into the room, her brothers on her heels. Josie put her hands on her hips. "What did I tell you, missy, about running in the house?"

"Not to." Sadie flashed a grin. "Notice anything?"

"You're missing your two front teeth." Josie returned her smile. "How marvelous. Now, you three go back out and enter properly. I'll give each of you a slice of bacon hot off the stove."

They thundered out of the room and re-entered at a more sedate pace. Their father moved into view, his head cocked. "That in itself is a miracle. I didn't think the word *walk* was in their vocabulary."

"They learn quickly." She finished setting the table. "I've a promise to fulfill."

"One moment, please." He took a deep breath and cleared his throat. "I need to apologize for my behavior yesterday at the creek. You are doing a fine job, Josie."

"Well then." She folded her hands in her apron.

"Well, what?" His brow furrowed.

"Apologize."

"I just did."

"No, sir, you did not." She raised her eyebrows. "You said you needed to, but you have not yet done so."

He exhaled heavily. "I apologize for my behavior. It was uncalled for. Satisfied?"

"Very." She smiled. "Apology accepted. Please have a seat. Breakfast is ready." She turned and entered the kitchen, retrieving the bacon Mrs. Davis had set aside. Then, on her way to taking her seat in the dining room, she handed each child their extra slice of bacon. "Lessons will commence after laundry. I expect you children to help in the garden." If work was going to cut into teaching time, she'd turn chores into a lesson. She might not know how to boil water, sew a gown, or hoe a garden, but she did know schooling.

After the backbreaking task of laundry, the workers fended for themselves, thank goodness, and a weary Josie led four children to the garden and surveyed the row of carrots. "Ben, please count the green stalks you see."

"All of them?"

"Yes, sir."

He groaned and walked up and down the row. "Thirty-one, but they aren't all carrots. Some are weeds."

Josie smiled. "Robbie, please pull five weeds."

Ben frowned. "You having us do your work?"

"Just follow my instructions, please." Josie's gaze flicked to him and back to his brother.

Robbie handed her four weeds and one carrot. "Sorry."

"Not a problem. It looks ready to be picked. Luke, how many carrots are in my hand?"

"One?"

"Very good. Sadie, if Ben counted thirty-one plants, and Robbie pulled five, how many are left?"

The little girl tapped a finger on her lips. "Twenty-six?"

"Yes. Very good. Now, how many carrots does Mrs. Davis need for her stew?"

"She said several," Ben said, crossing his arms. "How many is that?"

Josie laughed. "I have no idea. Let's take her ten. Pull the weeds as you go. I'll work on the... Where are the potatoes?" She could see the orange ends of the carrots, but so many of the other rows looked the same. Her confidence slipped. Give her something familiar and she could soar with the eagles. Give her something unfamiliar and she scratched for grubs like the chickens.

She glanced up to see Parker leaning on the fence railing. "Did you need something, or are you making sure I'm following orders?"

"I found myself intrigued with your arithmetic lesson." He grinned and tossed her a wink. "Clever way of lessening your workload too. I applaud ingenuity." With a touch of his fingers to the brim of his hat, he headed for the corral.

Josie's face heated. She wasn't unaccustomed to teasing from gentlemen, but she wasn't quite sure how to respond when said gentleman was her employer.

🌿

"Hiring another hand doesn't make sense to me." Parker frowned at Mrs. Davis. "Josie managed to teach and weed the garden. She'll manage the other chores in the same manner."

"She hasn't built calluses on her hands yet and you're expecting her to do the work I'm accustomed to. You'll work her to the point of exhaustion. She's not much bigger than your children. I've a niece that is used to the labor. I'll send her over for a few weeks. When you're confident Josie is competent, then send my niece home." She stared up at him, not stepping down from her decision. "I heard the girl crying last night."

"Josie?"

"Well, I didn't hear anyone else, now did I?"

He sagged into a kitchen chair. "She acts as if she has it all under control."

Mrs. Davis put a hand on his shoulder. "She needs to be eased into this life, and I've no desire to stay longer. I'm an old woman. I want to spend what time I have left knitting in a rocking chair on the front porch."

He sighed. "Send your niece." He rubbed his hands down his face as the older woman left.

The last thing he needed was another young gal to distract the workers. Already heads turned every time Josie stepped outside. Last night he'd had to step between two of the men fighting over who would have the right to court her. Parker had managed to get them to let her have time to settle in before sniffing around her skirts, but now. . .well, they'd have someone else to chase. He didn't like it a bit.

Footsteps behind him alerted him to the fact he wasn't alone. "She has no faith in my abilities." Josie stepped in front of him. "I'm doing fine. I've been taught how to run a household."

"With servants." He stood. "You aren't used to doing it all yourself. My guess is you've not worked a day in your life until the war."

"You would be right, but I've learned along the way." Pain shadowed her eyes. "I can't tell you what to do with your ranch, but another girl is not needed. I am not a fragile flower. Women have been doing what you've hired me to do for centuries. Let me prove to you that I'm capable. Give me two days of Mrs. Davis not helping me. If I can't do it, then have her send the girl."

He thrust out his hand. "Deal. Starting tomorrow."

She slipped her hand in his. "Deal."

Mrs. Davis was wrong. A callus rubbed against his palm. He turned Josie's hand over and winced at the sight of the open blister. "Let me tend to this." He sat her in the chair he'd vacated and pulled a jar of salve from the kitchen shelf. He pulled up a chair and sat facing her. "Hold still. This might sting a little." He spread the salve across the blister, then lifted the hand to his lips and blew.

"Oh." Josie gasped and lunged to her feet. Eyes wide, face pale, she gathered her skirt in her hands and bolted from the kitchen.

"For mercy's sake, Parker." Mrs. Davis passed through, her arms full of folded towels. "If you want to give the poor thing a heart attack, then bend her over your arm and kiss her. It'd have the same effect." She laughed and climbed the stairs.

The blood drained to his feet. Again, he was an idiot. He'd been responsible for nursing every little cut and scrape of his children's, and he hadn't thought twice of doing the same with Josie. He'd overstepped the boundaries of what was proper and embarrassed her in the process. Another thing he needed to apologize for. Saying he was sorry was quickly becoming a habit where she was concerned.

He smiled. Her hand had felt mighty fine in his though. Maybe he wasn't sorry after all. And she'd smelled nice. Not like the lye soap that permeated Mrs. Davis, but something soft and flowery.

Whistling, he slapped his hat on his head and headed for the barn. Chores never went away. He understood Josie's insistence on doing it all, but Mrs. Davis was right. She shouldn't have to. Not with all the hired hands eating the meals she prepared and tracking dirt into a house she'd just cleaned. No, hiring some help for the kitchen seemed the smart thing to do after all. If Parker wanted to be a big-time rancher, then he needed to act like one. That meant hiring the necessary help. Mrs. Davis might have put her foot down years ago about not wanting another woman in her kitchen, but he wouldn't allow the same of Josie. If he thought another worker was needed, he'd hire one.

He switched direction toward the herb garden where Josie cut snips of mint. "I'll give you the two days, but I'm still set on hiring you help. You'll also have Saturday afternoons and Sundays off." She blinked up at him like a startled kitten. "The new girl will have different days off, but also Sunday mornings. Mrs. Davis worked hard all her life and it aged her beyond her years. I won't have it said that I'm a harsh taskmaster."

She set her basket on the ground with slow deliberation. "Sir, the men will still need feeding. You may give me those days off, but I'll still help prepare the meals." Her eyes flashed. "I appreciate the time off, as I yearn to explore the meadow and paint the mountains in the distance, but I refuse to be pampered like a kept woman. If that is how you view me, I will pack and leave at once."

A kept woman? "What are you spouting off about?"

Tears welled in eyes the color of walnuts. "I will earn my keep by working. If you've lured me here for any other means—"

Land's sakes. He swallowed against a suddenly dry throat and rushed to the barn as fast as his legs would carry him. What a mess he'd created.

Chapter 4

Josie stared at the cold stove. In one hand she clutched a match, in the other the scrawled note from Mrs. Davis informing her she would be in her room today and not to bother her unless an emergency arose.

All right. Josie had seen this done a few times. One needed kindling, correct? A basketful sat a few feet away next to a small pile of wood, which Ben stocked each evening. She could use the note in her hand to light the kindling. She piled the necessary items in the burning box and lit the match. After several attempts, it occurred to her she'd done something wrong. The fire would not stay lit.

"You need to move the slide," Sadie said, hopping onto a chair. "It's in the back."

"Oh. Thank you." Josie fumbled around until she located a small flap. Soon, a fire burned hot. Wonderful, except for the smoke filling the room.

"You got to put the slide back." Sadie coughed. "You really are pretty but don't know much about cooking."

Tears welled in Josie's eyes. The child was right. What an utter failure. She fixed the flap and opened the kitchen door. "Wave the smoke outside while I try to get breakfast going, please." She handed Sadie an apron. Her first chore of the day and, left to her own devices, Josie was not off to a good start.

She burned the bacon, the eggs were overcooked, the biscuits soggy in the middle, but the food was on the table in time for the workers. Josie twisted her hands in her apron and watched their stoic expressions.

Parker glanced up once after biting into a biscuit but wisely held his tongue. Josie couldn't be certain, but she thought he muttered that her cooking could only get better with practice. She huffed and stomped back to the kitchen, her appetite gone after the morning's cooking battle.

Her mood did not improve when Sadie announced that the list Mrs. Davis left said they needed to make soap. "I've never made soap in my life." Josie took a deep breath and braced for the worst.

"I got something." Sadie raced from the room and returned minutes later with a leather-bound book tied with twine. "My ma left this for me for when I grew up."

Josie flipped through the handwritten pages. Note after note on how to do anything that needed doing on the ranch. Josie placed a kiss on the child's forehead. "You are an angel. Let's go make some soap."

By lunchtime, Josie's confidence had returned, and she strolled across the lawn with a basket of sandwiches on her arm. The men were busy branding, something she'd never witnessed firsthand. She'd volunteered to bring their meal to them.

"You're awfully chipper," Parker said with a smile.

"I made soap." Her face heated. The man kept her unbalanced for sure with his smiles and admiring glances. He was much too handsome and charming for his own good, and she refused to be swayed into making a ninny of herself.

She wouldn't mention how the lye burned her hands or made her eyes water because she'd gotten a little careless. Nor did he need to know about the stove lighting struggle that morning. The man had made up his mind to hire kitchen help, and Josie was determined that she would rule the roost, not some younger upstart. Keeping a smile on her face, she moved from worker to worker serving lunch.

"I didn't mind the breakfast," one man with a scruffy beard said. "You're pretty enough to eat dirt for."

Josie jerked to a stop. "The men were talking about my cooking?"

"There ain't much else to talk about but the food and how pretty you are." He winked and accepted a sandwich from the basket.

She had no idea what to say. She finished serving the men and found a spot to watch them work while she ate.

Two men threw a rope around a calf's head, then wrestled the poor thing to the ground. Josie's hand froze partway to her mouth when a third man took a glowing red iron from a fire and pressed it against the animal's hip. The calf bawled in pain as the stench of singed hair filled the air.

Josie tossed aside her sandwich, grabbed the handle of the lunch basket, and darted for the house as laughter rang out. Branding was not for her.

Trying to dispel the unpleasantness of the branding, she called the children to the kitchen table and started their afternoon lessons. "Please practice your writing for ten minutes, then we'll move on to reading."

Mrs. Davis passed through with a cup of tea. She glanced at Josie and laughed. "Stomach can't take branding? You've been green in the face since you returned to the house."

"I managed." Josie narrowed her eyes.

"You and my Lucy will find a routine and get twice the work done with half the effort. Someday, if you marry a Texan, you'll be prepared. For now, accept the help offered and let go of your pride."

Josie sighed. The woman was right. She did need help. She went to bed each night exhausted, her body aching, her mind racing lest she'd forgotten to do something. To let her pride prevent her from a job well done was probably the most foolish thing she'd ever done. "Thank you, Mrs. Davis. I needed your advice."

"You're welcome, child." She stopped in the doorway. "Maybe you should set your cap for the boss. He needs a new wife."

Parker froze in the doorway to the kitchen after overhearing Mrs. Davis's statement. He thought for a moment that maybe that's why Josie applied for the job, but then dismissed the idea. No woman with a goal of snaring a husband would run off in embarrassment or turn pink at a wink. Maybe he should ask her what, exactly, she wanted from her employment. If it *was* marriage she wanted, she'd be sorely disappointed. He had no time for another wife. The ranch took up all his time, thus the reason he'd hired a nanny.

He backed toward the door leading outside. His gaze fell on his wife's book on the counter. Ah, yes. Josie would have all the information she needed. He brushed his hand over the book.

Leah had had the foresight to write down everything her daughter would need one day. Thankfully, she'd taken the time to list step-by-step instructions, never knowing how soon she'd be gone. She'd died with fever shortly after birthing Luke. The book had passed to the daughter God had blessed them with. Parker was glad to see it being put to good use.

He closed the door carefully behind him, not wanting to alert Josie to his presence or disturb his children's lessons. Mrs. Davis's niece would arrive in the morning. Parker would send one of the men to fetch her. He needed to update the financial books and would rather do that than pick up some young woman from town. Unless. . . He ducked back into the kitchen. "Josie, do you need anything from town?"

She glanced up, a pleased expression flickering across her face. "I do need a few things. Are we going?"

"Right after breakfast tomorrow. I've got to pick up Lucy. We can make a stop at the mercantile."

His children's shouts of joys echoed. A trip to town was always something to look forward to. The finances could wait. Seeing the pleasure on his children's and Josie's faces was worth putting off work. "Make a list, Josie. I'll take care of the cost." Whistling, he headed for the corral to supervise the rest of the branding. It wasn't until he arrived that he remembered why he'd gone to the house in the first place.

Glancing down at the rip in his shirt, he hurried back. "Don't mind me." He darted past his children and to his room, discarding the torn shirt and donning a fresh one. He tossed the shirt he'd ripped on a loose nail in the barn into a pile of other things that needed mending. He really needed to let Mrs. Davis know. The shirt he now wore was his last one. No, he needed to let Josie know. The job was hers now.

He scooped the mending into his arms and headed back to the kitchen. "These items need mending. Where shall I put them?"

"Mending?" Her eyes widened.

"You do know how, don't you?" Not if the look on her stricken face was any indication. "I thought you said you embroidered."

"I don't think it's the same thing." She pointed to the table. "I'll figure it out. Put them there, please."

"Maybe I should give them to Mrs. Davis."

Josie stood and narrowed her eyes. "She will be leaving soon. I'm certain I can handle mending. I tackled the stove, didn't I?"

He met her stern look with one of his own. "There's no need to be upset. Wouldn't it be easier for you to accept the help and stop being so stubborn?"

"Children, please give your father and me a few minutes of privacy." She lifted her chin. She sure looked pretty when anger kissed her cheeks with red and sparks flew from her dark eyes. When his children filed from the room, she turned her attention fully on him.

Taking a step back, he said, "I mean no offense, Josie, but you've a chip on your shoulder the size of Davis Mountain. May I ask you something?"

"What?" She crossed her arms.

He dropped the shirts on the table. "Why did you apply for this job? You skirted the truth about your qualifications, and while you are very good at schooling the children, you know little about what it takes to run a household."

"I know how to run a household, but as you so eloquently put it before, I'm used to supervising servants. If you are unhappy with my abilities, then I will pack my things and you may leave me in town tomorrow."

"I didn't say that. I'm only asking why."

She fell into a chair. "Because I am penniless. I have a dream of making something out of nothing. Of rising from the ashes, so to speak." She leaned her head in the palm of her hand. "I am absolutely alone in the world, Parker. My parents are in heaven, I have no siblings, no land, no prospects. A fresh start in Texas seemed just the thing."

"A lovely, educated woman such as yourself should have had men lined up for her hand." He sat down across from her.

"I did, until I no longer had anything to offer." She ducked her head, but not before he saw the sheen of tears in her eyes. "Are you dismissing me?"

"Of course not." Nothing in the world could make him send her away after hearing her explanation. He'd be as patient as Job while she learned what needed doing. "At least the children behave for you," he said in an attempt to lighten the mood.

"Let's hope they continue to." Her smile trembled. "Luke seems like a barrel filled too full and ready to burst. I fear they're in a honeymoon period and will break loose like a herd of wild horses when I least expect it."

She could very well be right.

✤ Chapter 5 ✤

Before breakfast the next morning, after flipping through Parker's late wife's book and not finding what she needed, Josie located Mrs. Davis in the parlor. "I need you to show me how to mend." She held up the load of clothing.

"I can teach you in the time it takes to thread a needle."

After poking herself several times, Josie got a needle threaded and watched as Mrs. Davis showed her how to sew on a button or a hook and how to mend a tear or a seam. "That isn't too far from embroidery."

"No, but I suggest you see if the mercantile has a book on sewing." Mrs. Davis tied off the end of the thread. "Those children grow out of their clothes very quickly. In fact, Sadie could use a new nightgown. You might be able to put one of those silly petticoats to good use."

"I've some muslin I could use, Mrs. Davis. Someday, I might return to civilization." Josie collected the mending and went to prepare a quick breakfast. What was it with Mrs. Davis's aversion to petticoats? Josie had caught a glimpse of a faded green one, with a rip near the hem, under the older woman's skirts. Surely she did nothing more than jest about Josie having too much of a particular item. She laughed. She did possess too many frilly things with lace and ribbons.

She was still smiling as she set biscuits and gravy on the table. "I do believe I'm onto you, Mrs. Davis," she called. "You may have your pick of any of my petticoats."

"I want the one with the blue ribbons!"

Of course she did. That was Josie's favorite.

"I don't want to know about my sons wearing women's undergarments as shirts," Parker said, taking his seat. "But we're taking Mrs. Davis to town with us. We'll leave her and bring back Lucy."

Josie's smile faded. "I thought she was staying until next week."

"She sees no sense in staying when you are managing and help is coming." He slathered butter on a biscuit as the workers barged into the room. "You'll be fine."

"I know." She frowned. *God, let Lucy be sweet and accommodating.*

An hour later—the wagon crowded in back with Josie and the children, and Mrs. Davis riding up front with Parker—they started the journey to town. When they arrived, Josie clutched her reticule and jumped from the wagon to the road without waiting for Parker's assistance. The constant chatter of the four children caused a headache to throb behind her left eye.

"Lucy will meet you at the café at noon," Mrs. Davis said.

Parker nodded. "That works perfectly. Mrs. Davis, I'll escort you to the boardinghouse while Josie and the children head to the mercantile."

"All right." Josie collected the children close to her, holding tightly to Luke's hand, and headed for the mercantile.

Inside, the aroma of pickles, cinnamon, and crackers greeted them. "If you four behave, I'll buy you a peppermint stick," she said. "Do not leave the store." Heaven help her if she lost one of them and had to hunt them down through a strange town.

She stepped up to the counter and placed the list Parker had given her onto the polished top. "I also need these items on a separate bill, please. Do you have a how-to book on sewing clothing?"

The plump woman behind the counter nodded. "We also have patterns, if you know sizes." She puffed up like a chicken. "We are quite up with the times despite being a small town."

"I can see that." Josie smiled. "I would love to browse your patterns while you fill my order." She headed for a wall of brightly colored fabrics. A hook on the wall held several pattern books of simple, serviceable clothing. No more party dresses for her, it seemed.

A crash sounded behind her, then the sound of running feet. Josie turned just in time to see Luke dart out the door, Robbie on his heels. Sadie, her hands over her mouth, stared at an overturned pickle barrel.

Heavens. Josie moved the child from where the juice pooled around her shoes, set her on a stool, and took off after the two younger boys. "Ben, watch your sister," she called over her shoulder. "Sorry, miss. I'll pay for the damages."

On the sidewalk, she glanced up and down the street for a sign of the wayward boys. Oh, when she got her hands on them! She hitched her skirts to her ankles and sprinted around the corner.

A broad chest stopped her forward pursuit. Her nose smashed against a flannel shirt right before she fell back and landed on her backside in a puddle of mud. Oomph. Water soaked through her skirt.

Her gaze rose and settled on Parker's face. "Luke and Robbie took off."

He held out a hand to help her to her feet. "Are you all right?"

"Yes, if not a bit. . .damp. Have you seen them?"

"They're most likely at the stable." His gaze hardened.

Josie didn't know if he was angry at her or his sons. "They knocked over an entire barrel of pickles."

"What were you doing while this happened?"

"Browsing clothing patterns."

"Don't you have enough clothes? Didn't you say yourself that my children's good behavior wouldn't last? The safety of my children is of top priority. You cannot let them roam the streets without supervision." He glared down at her.

She planted dripping fists on her hips. "Rather than stand here and badger me, shouldn't you be searching for your children? Also, the patterns I looked at were for your children. Sadie has outgrown several things, and Ben's pants only come to his ankles. It is not my fault that your boys are undisciplined."

"It is your job to make them disciplined."

"Ah!" She lifted her chin and set off for the livery. She wanted to box not only the two younger boys' ears but their father's. Discipline, her foot. She'd show them discipline. The two would regret misbehaving.

They were indeed at the livery, jumping from stall walls into piles of hay. Josie glowered, arms crossed, while their father stood behind her. "Boys," she said in her sternest voice, "you will follow me this instant." Without waiting for a reply, she turned, daring them to disobey. She'd show their father what happened to unruly children.

Parker regretted scolding Josie the moment the words left his mouth. Still, he had hired her to watch his children, and the very first time they left the ranch, the two youngest got away from her. When she ordered the boys to follow her, he motioned his head for them to do as they were told and prepared himself to watch how the story played out.

She marched back to the mercantile and set the boys to work cleaning up the mess. "If you wouldn't mind, Parker, please go on and take Sadie and Ben to the café to meet Lucy. These two rascals will not enjoy the same meal but will greatly appreciate the pickle and crackers they'll receive for lunch."

"What about you?" He bit back a grin at the shocked expressions on his sons' faces.

"I would appreciate a simple sandwich at your convenience."

"Yes, ma'am. We'll fetch you three here when we're finished." With a hand on Sadie's shoulder and another on Ben's, he walked to the café, where they were directed to a table with a curvy little blond already seated there.

She batted long lashes over bright blue eyes up at Parker. "I'm Lucy. Mrs. Davis is my aunt."

"Parker Owens. Nice to make your acquaintance." He sat the children between them. He recognized the hungry look in the girl's eyes. Josie might not be on the lookout for a husband, but this one sure was. He'd do his best to steer as clear of her as possible.

"Do you have a fine ranch, Mr. Owens?" Lucy spread her napkin on her lap. "I do yearn for a fine place to live. Will I be working in the kitchen?"

"You'll be doing whatever Miss Josie requires of you."

"Who's that?"

"Our nanny and housekeeper," Sadie explained. "She's real pretty, and smart too. Right now, she's covered in mud and smells like pickles, but usually she smells like flowers. It's the soap she uses." She grabbed a square of corn bread from a basket in the center of the table.

Parker agreed. Josie did indeed smell like flowers. "With your aunt leaving us, and the ranch employing ten full-time hands, we've need of someone to help around the house."

Lucy's smile had slipped a bit at Sadie's glowing description of her nanny, but she recovered. "Sounds fascinating. Ten hired hands. You must be quite successful."

"Our pa has the finest ranch this side of the Mississippi," Ben said. "It'll be mine someday."

"Aren't you just the luckiest little boy." She reached over and pinched his cheek.

After a trying, long lunch, seeing Josie and the two youngest waiting by the wagon had to be the best sight Parker had seen all day. He stepped forward to help Josie into the seat but watched in dismay as Lucy clambered up first and firmly planted herself next to where he'd sit.

"I'll sit in the middle, since I'm smaller than you," she said, smiling at Josie.

Josie's brows rose. "I'll sit in the back with the children. I wouldn't want to get your dress dirty."

"She isn't smaller than you," Parker whispered, helping Josie into the back. "A strong wind would blow you away while it would take a team of oxen to move her."

She giggled. "A gentleman never remarks on a woman's weight."

"Right. I'd forgotten." He winked, delighted to see the familiar flush spread across her face. Then, squaring his shoulders, he climbed into the driver's seat. It would be a long ride home.

By the time they arrived, he'd wanted to turn around and drop Lucy off with Mrs. Davis no less than five times. The girl's unending prattle grated on his nerves to the point he declined eating supper and headed for the barn.

Josie, a plate in one hand and a coffee mug in the other, joined him an hour later. "I brought you something to eat. Not to mention I needed a break from the chatter."

"She does go on. Thank you." Parker took the food and sat on an overturned barrel.

Josie leaned against a stall. "I've set the two youngest to doing dishes, then shine my shoes, and all the while have Lucy talk to them." She grinned. "It's part of their discipline."

"Brilliant. They should lock prisoners in the same room as her, forgive my unkindness." He spooned stew into his mouth. "This is rather good."

"I found the recipe in Leah's book. Your wife cared about her daughter very much to leave such a gift behind. I'm blessed to be able to use it."

"Leah would be happy to see it used." He made short work of

his dinner. "Call me a coward, but I'll turn in once I'm certain Lucy has gone to bed."

Josie laughed. "She does look on you like a prime piece of beef." She waggled her finger. "Be careful, Mr. Owens, or you'll find yourself married."

He shuddered. "No, thank you." He watched, admiring the view, as Josie strolled back to the house. If he were in the market for a wife, which he wasn't, he'd want a kindhearted, stubborn, hardworking one like her. Not a silly little thing with too much space between her ears.

Pulling his gaze away from where Josie had disappeared into the shadows, he picked up the harness he'd been repairing earlier and bent over the worn leather. He wouldn't be idle while he waited for the house to grow dark and quiet. There was always work to be done.

As he worked, he realized he hadn't apologized for his behavior in town. How many things did he owe Josie an apology for? He'd lost count. He glanced up as a shadow blocked the moonlight.

His heart stopped.

Lucy, wrapped in a blanket, the hem of her nightgown peeking out from under, smiled at him from the doorway.

Chapter 6

Josie banged a pot onto the stove. Was Parker toying with her? She thought they'd shared a moment in the barn, but when she'd gone to the outhouse before retiring, she hadn't missed Lucy's silhouette in the barn door.

She cut the other woman a sharp glance. "Sleep well?"

"Like a dream." Lucy actually purred.

Josie wanted to yank her blond hair. Instead, she'd take out her anger on the stove. Why should she care what Parker did with the new girl? She was his hired nanny-housekeeper, nothing more. "The bread needs kneading. Breakfast is oats this morning, but we need to think ahead to the noon meal."

She glanced out the open kitchen door in time to see Parker stroll by. He smiled into the kitchen. She scowled and returned to the task of stirring the vast pot of oatmeal.

Behind her, Lucy giggled and waved.

Parker increased his pace. Most likely to avoid Josie's condescending glare, the scoundrel.

"My aunt told me what a fine-looking man Mr. Owens is, but I never imagined he could be this fine." Lucy sighed. "Don't you think so, Josie?"

"Yes, very fine, now focus on your work." Did the girl ever hush?

The men trooped in and sat, every eye on the new girl who fluttered her lashes and twittered like a silly bird. She might be only two years younger than Josie, but Lucy's actions made Josie feel decades older.

Josie set the bowl of oatmeal in the center of the table and called the children down. After breakfast, she'd leave the cleanup to Lucy and take the children on a walk while discussing the various plants growing around the property. She looked forward to time away from the chattering Lucy. She glanced over at Parker. Even if it meant leaving her boss in Lucy's clutches.

A dull ache started in her stomach and rose to her heart. She hadn't come to Crinoline Creek with any aspirations for love or romance, but despite it all, a few moments' conversation had left her vulnerable. She needed to guard her heart and prevent any further damage to her emotions and focus on what was really important. Working until she could move into a better future forged by her own hands, maybe a business of her own somewhere. A place no one could take away from her. Love did not enter into that dream.

She turned her head as Parker smiled in her direction, then stood and cleared away her dishes. As she passed through the dining room, she motioned for the children to follow her and led them outside.

"As we walk today, I'd like for you to tell me the names of the plants we pass. If you don't know them, we'll take notes so we can ask someone who does." She took Luke's hand to make sure he stayed with them. "It's important to know your surroundings."

The children pointed out sagebrush, desert roses, and field grass as they moved past the corral. Josie did her best not to notice Parker working with a young horse. Still, her gaze drifted that way like the ocean tide, unstoppable and fixed on one destination. When Robbie asked to stop and watch for a moment, she knew all hope of passing unnoticed had vanished.

The children clambered to the top rail and perched like birds. Josie crossed her arms and leaned against the fence.

Parker jogged around the corral and held the end of a rope. A shiny black horse trotted on the other end. Josie had never seen anything more beautiful. Man and horse moved as one, muscles rippling. It was no wonder Lucy was stricken. Josie too was in danger of forgetting her dream for the future.

"Come, children." Amid protests, she led them away from the enticing vision of their father and into the woods.

"I want to watch Pa." Luke stomped his foot. "Lessons are boring."

"Yeah," Robbie added. "We need to know how to train horses and rope cattle, not name plants."

"Your father hired me to make sure you are ready to face whatever life throws at you." She knelt to make herself eye level with the boy. "What if you were lost? Would you know which plants you could eat and which could harm you? I have a book in my room we can go through and read about the ones you've identified today."

"She's right, Son." Parker grinned at them from a few feet away. "To run a ranch you need to know the land as well as your letters and numbers."

While she appreciated his help, Josie refused to give in to his charm. His words might be directed toward the children, but his warm gaze settled on her. The man was a scoundrel of the highest order. "Thank you for your input, Parker. If you'll excuse us, we'll continue with our lessons."

His smile faded. Confusion etched across his features. With a nod, he backed away, then turned and marched to the corral.

Josie sighed and led her charges deeper into the woods. "Let's continue our lesson, shall we?"

🌿

She'd dismissed him like an unruly child. Parker kicked a rock, sending it scuttling into the brush. What had he done to vex her? He palmed his forehead. Apologies! He owed her several. He could think of no other reason for her cold shoulder. He'd remedy the situation immediately after dinner.

"Hey, boss." His youngest hand, Barney Calhoun, approached him shortly before lunch. "Mind if I court Lucy? She's something, isn't she?"

"She's something, all right." Parker grabbed a wheelbarrow and headed for the barn. Normally, he'd set Ben to work on shoveling manure, but Josie and the children hadn't returned from their hike. "Feel free, and good luck." The lad would need all the help he could get cornering that little wildcat. Maybe if Barney spent time with her, she'd leave Parker alone.

As the lunch bell clanged, he glanced toward where he'd parted ways from his children. Perhaps he'd simply missed their return. Then why had his heart lodged in his throat? When he entered the kitchen to the sight of a frazzled, irritated Lucy, dread became fear. He whirled and raced for the woods.

He located their tracks near the creek, then again heading upstream, and then the trail grew cold. "Josie! Benjamin!" His cries did nothing but startle a bird from a nearby tree.

How in tarnation could someone get lost on ground that stretched forever? It wasn't like the trees were thick where they lived. It wouldn't take more than a few minutes for a person to step into the open and see the house from any direction.

This time the pretty little teacher had gone too far. Literally. He called their names again and continued following the stream.

"Pa." He turned to see Ben dashing toward him. "Miss Josie is hurt."

Parker sprinted after his son to where Josie, surrounded by the children, sat in a puddle of navy wool and sagebrush. Pain radiated across her face as she held her ankle. Parker fell to his knees and frowned at the silly heeled boots she wore.

"I tripped and sprained my ankle," she said. "You needn't look so cross about it."

"You shouldn't have gone so far without proper shoes." He gently took her foot in his hand. At some point, she'd untied the laces. Her ankle swelled against the leather.

"It's my fault." Luke tapped him on the shoulder. "I chased a rabbit and fell. She came running after me." Tears had left tracks down his dirty cheeks.

"We'll discuss this later, Son." Again, Parker had something to apologize for. "Josie." He took a deep breath. "I cannot wait until this evening to settle some things between us. I have a very poor habit of jumping to conclusions where my children are concerned." He locked gazes with her. "Once again I am apologizing to you. For my behavior yesterday in town, and for now."

"You do tend to assume things, sir. Apology accepted. May we go home now?" Her smile didn't quite reach her eyes. "I'm sorry to be a burden, but I fear I won't be able to walk the distance."

"Then I will carry you." Without further words, he scooped her into his arms and headed home, grateful she weighed so little. Still, by the time they reached the house, his arms ached.

Pushing past Lucy, he plopped Josie on the counter. "Cold water and something to wrap the ankle, Lucy."

She glared at Josie but did as he said, returning with strips of cotton and a basin of water from the well. When Parker started to remove Josie's boot, Lucy shoved him away. "I'll do it. You shouldn't touch a lady."

Josie's eyes widened. She opened her mouth to say something, then clamped her lips shut, hissing as Lucy tugged off her boot.

"You're hurting her." Parker tried to step back into place.

"No, I'm not. Get back."

"Stop it." Josie hopped off the counter onto one foot. "Ben, your assistance, please." Leaning heavily on the boy's shoulder, she hopped toward her room.

Looking quite pleased with herself, Lucy handed Parker a plate. "I kept it warm for you."

He fought back the desire to slap the food from her hand. "I'm not hungry."

She pouted. "But you carried her all that way." She put a

hand on his arm. "She must have been heavy. What an evil trick to play."

"What do you mean?"

"It's quite obvious she faked an injury. After all, she made her way to her room easily enough."

The girl was delusional. Parker shook his head and stormed outside.

He caught sight of Barney chopping wood and made a beeline for the young man. "Have you started courting Lucy yet?"

"No, sir. She says I'm not a big enough fish." He set the ax firmly in the stump. "I think her eyes are set on you."

"Change her mind. Soon." Parker marched for the barn and, he hoped, peace. He glanced back at the house. Sadie waved from Josie's window. The nanny would be fine with his children helping her. She didn't need him. Her cold reception to his apology showed him as much. She couldn't even tolerate his touch when she injured herself.

One of the bay horses stuck its head over the stall door. Parker pressed his forehead against the horse's. "I might have been wed once, my friend, but I know very little about women."

The horse nickered.

Parker chuckled. "Are you laughing at me? Well. . ." He stepped back and patted the horse's neck. "It is rather humorous. I'm the father of four and can't get a pretty young woman to stay in the same room as me." He sighed and grabbed a pitchfork.

Since losing Leah, he'd vowed to focus on the ranch and the children. Having a pretty woman in the house again made him rethink things. He rather enjoyed seeing her when he woke in the morning and before retiring at night.

He stepped into the shadows as Lucy exited the house. Standing on the porch, she searched the yard. Not seeing anyone, she moved back inside, and Parker released the breath he hadn't noticed he'd held.

❧ Chapter 7 ❧

*N*ot being able to help Lucy in the kitchen due to her ankle needing rest, Josie cut up one of her remaining petticoats into a nightgown for Sadie and shirts for the boys. She smiled, knowing their reaction if they discovered what fabric she'd used. The pattern she'd purchased from the mercantile seemed easy enough, and she'd taken the children's measurements the night before.

Mrs. Davis had been right. Josie didn't need multiple petticoats. They were best put to use somewhere else. When and if she left the ranch someday to pursue a different future, she would buy new petticoats. In the meantime, she didn't need them.

Parker passed by the parlor, slowed, stared, then shrugged and continued moving. "I don't want to know."

Chuckling, Josie continued to crawl around the floor making

her cuts. Perhaps she'd embroider flowers along the hem of Sadie's gown. Even on the prairie a little girl would enjoy something pretty. She hummed "Amazing Grace" as she worked, trying to ignore the banging from the kitchen.

Lucy had not been pleased to hear Josie would not be helping with the meals for the next two days. All for the best in Josie's opinion, since she still wasn't the best of cooks. That was one area the younger girl exceeded her.

Finished cutting, Josie scooped the pieces into her arms and headed to the front porch where she'd asked the children to meet her after breakfast. Not surprisingly, Sadie was the only one in sight. The honeymoon period was definitely over, and the three boys tried her patience on a regular basis.

She set the fabric on a rocker. "Where are your brothers?"

Sadie shrugged. "They said they'd be back, but since they took their poles, I'm guessing they're at the creek. Want me to fetch your crutch?"

"Yes, please." It wouldn't do for Parker to find out she'd let his children out of her sight again. She sat while Sadie went to fetch the crude crutch, and tried to figure out a way to turn fishing into a school lesson or a lesson in discipline.

When it became obvious that Sadie too had disappeared, tears sprang to her eyes. She'd really thought she had connected with the children, especially Sadie. She stared across the expanse of field rolling with tall grasses and thought, not for the first time, that she didn't belong there. Perhaps she should have sought work in the city.

"What's wrong?" Parker, his arms full of wood for the kitchen, stopped in front of her.

"You'll be sorely disappointed to discover that your boys are fishing at the creek, and I have no idea where Sadie has gone to." She heaved a sigh.

"Isn't today Saturday, or am I mistaken?"

She straightened. "Yes, it is." She smiled. "It's my day off. Although, I do still need to keep an eye on the children, Parker."

"They're fine, and I will speak with them. The boys will be back by lunch, I guarantee it." He dropped the wood into the box that allowed anyone in the kitchen easy access. Then he sat on the steps next to Josie. "As long as they keep you aware of where they go, and they stay together, they'll be fine. No need to worry unless they miss a meal."

He leaned back against the top step and stretched his long legs in front of him. "You've come a long way since your arrival, Josie. Don't second-guess your accomplishments."

"I don't."

He glanced over his shoulder. "I can see it written on your face and in the glimmer of tears in your eyes. You doubt your abilities. Keep in mind that you gained four children overnight with no time to work up to it as a mother would, nor have you had much experience."

"You're right." Her spirits brightened. "It's natural they would test me to see how I react to their misbehaving. I'll make sure I set boundaries."

"Good girl." He patted her knee, sending her heart stuttering and her stomach fluttering. "What were you working on in the parlor?"

"Shirts for the boys and a nightgown for Sadie. I'm using one of my useless petticoats."

He doubled over in laughter. When he could speak he said, "That right there will be enough punishment for the boys. Oh Josie, you are good for me. I haven't laughed like this in years." He pushed to his feet. "My advice would be to keep that a secret. Also, I can afford fabric for my children's clothes. You don't need to use your own things."

"They're going unused. Might as well." She held up a hand for him to help her to her feet. "Sadie was to bring me the crutch, but I see she's forgotten."

"Shall I carry you?" His eyes twinkled.

"Heavens, no." Her face heated. "Just give me an arm to lean on."

"My pleasure." He crooked his arm so she could slip hers through.

She let him help her into a chair in the kitchen so she could plan the next week's meals. After which, she intended to find someone to carry her watercolors to the porch. The ranch provided many beautiful landscapes to keep her entertained on her precious day off.

Lucy narrowed her eyes as Parker fetched a pencil and sheet of paper. "What have you two been up to?"

"Parker has helped me into the house, that is all." She smiled up at him. "Would you fetch the fabric from the porch and set it in my room? I'd planned on sewing today but have something I'd like to do more."

He nodded. "I'll fetch your crutch while I'm at it. Anything else before I head to the fields?"

"There is a black satchel and easel behind the door. I'd be most grateful if you'd put those on the porch."

"Only if you promise to paint something to hang over the mantel."

She smiled and ducked her head, not wanting to put too much stock into the warmth she saw in his eyes. The man was only being friendly, and she could certainly use a friend.

The second Parker left the room, Lucy stormed to the table. "I think it is shameless the way you fake an injury in order to gain his attention."

"I'm not faking anything." Josie leaned back to put a few more inches between her and the delusional girl.

"He's mine," Lucy hissed, all prettiness gone from her face, replaced by jealousy and desperation. "Why else would I leave a farm in Missouri and come to the middle of nowhere if not to wed and live a fine life?" She laughed without humor. "Don't worry. I'll keep you on as the children's nanny. I have no desire to be saddled with brats."

Josie pushed to her feet, being careful not to put too much weight on her sore ankle. "I have no worries where you're concerned. If anyone is a brat here, it would be you. I do believe you should worry about being found out."

Not that Josie would run tattling to the boss, but she couldn't help but enjoy the flicker of alarm in the little rascal's eyes, nor could she squelch the feeling of hope in her heart. If Lucy was worried about Parker's affections, then he must not care for her in the way she hoped.

✿

After taking care of Josie's needs, Parker found his daughter in the barn where a stray cat had a litter of kittens. "You were to take Miss Josie her crutch."

Sadie shrugged. "I wanted to play with the kittens." She picked up a fluffy gray-and-white one. "Do you think she would like this one? The boys are mean to her sometimes, and I really want Miss Josie to stay."

He lowered to his daughter's level. "You want to give her a kitten?"

"Can I?" She smiled, melting his heart. "I like Miss Josie."

"Yes, you may give her the kitten." He ruffled her hair. "Off with you now. I'm sure she can use your help while I hunt down your brothers." Mean, were they? He almost asked Sadie how but thought it better to hear it from the boys' mouths.

He headed for the creek while Sadie dashed for the house, a mewling kitten cradled in her arms. If his sons were overstepping the lines, why hadn't Josie said anything? He shared Sadie's sentiment in wanting the nanny to stay, and three little rascals would not jeopardize it.

The boys fished in a widened part of the creek, each holding a cane pole, their bare feet covered with mud. If Parker didn't feel annoyed, he'd have thought the sight endearing. Instead, he crossed his arms and cleared his throat.

Three tousled, blond heads turned. "Howdy, Pa," Ben said, grinning. "Come to fish with us?"

"No, Son, I'm here to talk. Please set down your poles and gather around." Parker perched on a sawed-off stump as the three boys moved reluctantly in front of him and sat on the ground.

Once settled, Parker took a deep breath. "It has come to my attention that the three of you have been mischievous toward Miss Josie." He held up a hand at their protests. "No, she did not snitch on you."

"Then it was Sadie." Ben glowered.

"I didn't say that." His son's unruliness bruised his heart. "I'm concerned with your behavior, Son. I thought you liked Miss Josie."

"I do, but I don't like schooling."

The other two echoed his sentiments.

"We've been over this. You need to be learned to succeed in life."

Luke shook his head. "All we need is God and the Bible. You said so yourself."

Parker rubbed his hands down his face. "I did say that, and you do need those things above all else, but a man needs to know how to write, add, and think logically to take care of his family."

Robbie frowned. "I ain't having a family."

"Don't you want to get married someday?"

"Nope." He picked up a twig and snapped it in two. "I don't like girls."

Parker laughed. "You will someday, Son, I guarantee. Now, listen up." Three faces peered at him. "No more tormenting Miss Josie, or there will be consequences. Understood?"

The boys nodded.

"Good. Catch us enough fish for supper. Remember, I'm headed off on a drive tomorrow. I need to know that I can trust you three to do the right thing." He patted each head and headed back to his chores, pleased with the conversation. They were good boys, if not a little rambunctious sometimes.

Catching sight of Josie and Sadie on the porch, he changed direction and stopped to watch. Josie dangled a length of ribbon in front of the kitten, laughing at its antics. "Thank you, Parker. Little Cloud is simply adorable."

"Cloud suits him." He propped one foot on the step. "I've spoken to the boys about their behavior."

She jerked in surprise. "I, how—"

"Let's just say a little birdie told me. Next time, I'd like to hear it from your lips." His gaze dropped to her mouth. Bad move. His breath caught. Why hadn't he noticed how kissable they were? His gaze lifted to see her cheeks tinted with a rosy sheen. "Uh, yeah." He turned and headed for the barn as fast as his legs would take him.

He liked Josie, he wanted her to stay, but romantic feelings? No, it had to be the talk with his boys about marriage that had him acting addlebrained. Still. . . He glanced back toward the house. Would it be such a terrible thing to consider getting hitched again?

❧ Chapter 8 ❧

Why hadn't Parker mentioned to her he would be gone for three days? Josie stared out the back door. Every time they shared what she thought to be a step toward a closer relationship, the man scurried off like a frightened rabbit. He couldn't be afraid of women, could he? He'd once been married and had four children. So it had to be that he could only tolerate Josie in small doses. But the look in his eyes...

With a sigh, she turned back to look into the faces of four children. Mischief lit up the boys' countenances, filling Josie with trepidation. Without their father here to intervene, she feared the next few days would be most trying. She cut a quick glance to where Lucy hummed while drying dishes. Especially with a snooty, evil-minded girl in the house.

"All right, children, please take a seat at the table. The two older will recite their multiplication tables as they write them. Robbie, you will do addition, and Luke will count and subtract beans. The one who gets the most correct answers by the time our sand runs out of the glass will earn a peppermint stick."

"Bribery?" Lucy raised her eyebrows. "How unconventional." She dried a dish with a muslin towel. "Did you know Barney asked me to marry him?"

Oh, if only she would. Maybe they'd move and get her out from under Josie's skin. "That's wonderful news."

"I turned him down." She grinned. "I told you, I'm after much bigger game."

"Good luck, Lucy." Josie bent over Sadie's work and made a few corrections. She refused to get into a debate with the other woman.

"Hmm." Lucy turned back to the sink.

Josie could almost see the wheels turning in the woman's head. Wheels that would devise ways to make Josie miserable.

After arithmetic, she moved the children into reading and picked up a basket of mending from the floor. While Ben read out loud, the other three following along, she could catch up on some work, adding the pink ribbons she wanted on Sadie's new nightgown.

Before he'd read a full page, Ben stood, motioned for his brothers to follow, and led them out of the house and in the direction of the creek. Josie called after them, then turned and frowned, glancing at Sadie when the boys ignored her. "What is going on here? We have not finished our lessons."

Sadie shrugged. "I heard them whispering last night when they thought I was sleeping that they were going to take over running the ranch when they grow up. They don't think they need schooling, Miss Josie." She cut a glance in Lucy's direction and lowered her voice. "She gives them cookies and tells them what to do. It usually means doing what you tell them not to do."

"Really?" And the woman condemned Josie for resorting to bribery.

She set down her mending. The cattiness of some women was not lost on Josie. She'd been to her share of tea parties and soirees and witnessed much of it firsthand, although she'd never participated. She now found herself at a loss how to respond. The children's lessons and protection were her responsibility. Josie also held the title of housekeeper. Lucy worked under her.

She drummed her fingers on the table. She had no idea how to keep the boys around during lesson time or how to put Lucy in her place without sounding like a shrew. *Lord, I need some guidance.*

Thinking back on her conversation with Parker and what he said about how well she did made her feel a bit better, but with him gone, she still felt outnumbered. "Sadie, what is the thing your brothers most like to do?"

"Fish, and swim without any clothes on."

"Oh." Josie blinked. She couldn't do anything about the swimming, but perhaps... She grabbed her crutch from next to the table. "Come along, Sadie. We're going to the bunkhouse."

"Pa won't let me go in there." Sadie kept her pace with Josie's limping one.

"Most of the men are gone." If she was correct, only the wizened, grumpy man who went by the name of Badger would be there. Too old to go on three-day drives, he'd been left behind to oversee the ranch. He'd not spoken one word to Josie, ever, but she hoped he'd help her now.

"Stay here." She motioned for Sadie to stay outside, then pushed open the door to the bunkhouse. "Mr. Badger?" She stepped into a dim room lit only by what little sunlight squeezed through the dusty fabric hanging on the window. "Hello?"

"I'm here, miss." He stepped from a back room, wiping his hands on a stained piece of calico. "Everything all right?"

"I'm wondering if you could help me with something." She explained the boys running off and her suspicions of Lucy pitting them against her.

"Want me to whomp on 'em?" His eyes widened.

"Of course not!" She stiffened. "I need your advice."

"Alrighty, then. Shoot." He kicked a straight-backed chair in her direction and glanced toward Sadie by the door. "Might as well sit. Come on in, girl."

Sadie peered through the open door. "Pa said no."

"He ain't here. I'm in charge. Come in and sit."

Grinning and looking as if she was getting away with something, Sadie darted in and sat on the floor next to Josie. Badger pulled up another chair.

Josie folded her hands in her lap. "I've discovered that the boys love fishing."

"And swimming as naked as the day they were born," Sadie added.

"Yes, well." Josie breathed deeply through her nose. "I'd like to know how Sadie and I can be guaranteed to catch more fish than the boys."

Badger stared at her for a moment. "You'd have to know where a really good hole is that they don't."

"Do you?"

"I reckon. You aiming to make a wager with those boys?"

"I prefer to call it a contest, but yes, sir, I am." She smiled. "If you would be so kind as to give me directions."

He explained how to get to his secret fishing spot, told her a good place to dig for grubs, and handed her his best fishing pole. "Good luck, gals."

"Thank you, sir." Josie shook his hand. Feeling optimistic about her plan, she hobbled for the creek to find three naughty boys.

They were stripped as bare as the day they came into the world. Josie turned her back and cleared her throat. "Gentlemen."

Shrieks and splashing followed her greeting. A few minutes later, a grumpy Ben spoke. "You can turn around now."

She did, keeping a smile on her face. "I have a proposition for you three."

"Yeah?" He tilted his head.

"As you know, I believe in schooling, same as your pa, yet you boys take every opportunity to thwart me. Because of cookies, I believe." She set a stern glance on each of them before continuing. "So, I'd like to make a deal with you. On Saturday, we have a fishing competition. The three of you against Sadie and me. Whoever has the most fish by dinnertime wins. If the girls win, you must attend all lessons without question."

"We'll win."

"That confident, are you?"

"Yes, ma'am." He thrust out his hand. "And if we win, we'll get no more lessons. We'll oblige you for this week, but no more, just to keep the peace."

She took his hand and gave a firm shake. "Deal." *Oh Lord, please let me catch the most fish.* Or Parker just might toss her in the creek.

Parker tugged against the loose barbed wire, feeling it cut into his hands despite the heavy gloves he wore. When he caught the scoundrel cutting his fences, he'd skin him and hang him up for the coyotes.

"This is the third time this week," Barney said. "I did some temporary repairs, but it's more than I can keep up with."

"We'll have to patrol the fence line. Any cattle missing?"

"Yes, sir. Thirty head at last count."

"Why am I just now hearing about this?" He secured the fence and wiped his sleeve across his perspiring forehead.

"I've tried twice during supper, but you've been preoccupied." Barney dragged the length of wire behind him as he headed for the next cut in the fence.

This was why Parker didn't need the distraction of a woman. He needed to keep his mind on the ranch and his children's future. Immediately, Josie's face popped into his head. He growled and shook his head to erase her image, then jogged to catch up with Barney.

A drive to mend fences and round up calves to be castrated and branded could turn into more than three days away. If so, he'd have to send some of the men back. The ranch couldn't be shorthanded if rustlers were on the prowl.

He and his men worked as long as the day's light allowed, then crashed exhausted onto bunk rolls and started all over again the next day. Not even the bitter coffee could wake him fast enough. His body protested, and amid the groans of his men as they got to their feet, he tossed the dregs into the bushes, mounted his horse, and got them to start their day. "Keep your rifles handy, boys. We're not taking any chances. Let's get the job done and get home."

The men split into teams and headed in different directions. Parker and Barney continued their patrol of the fence line, stopping to reinforce here, replace there, and study the area for signs of rustlers.

"Boss." Barney's warning almost came too late.

Parker glanced up, caught a glint of the sun on something through the trees, and rolled from his saddle, taking his rifle down with him as a shot rang out. His horse thundered away.

Barney belly-crawled to his side. "I make out three of 'em. There." He pointed. "They look to have been headed this way when we rode up."

"Yep." Parker peered through his rifle scope, counting three men on horseback galloping in the opposite direction. "They're leaving, but my guess is they'll be back with reinforcements at sundown."

"What're we going to do?"

"Be ready for them." He stood and brushed the grass from his pants, then marched away to fetch his horse.

By nightfall, they'd rounded up as many of the cattle as they could and put them into a makeshift corral. Ten men, counting Parker, stationed themselves around the corral, doing their best to stay out of sight. All they could do now was wait.

Shortly after sundown, the snap of a twig drew Parker's attention. He rolled to his back and slowly scooted against his saddle. Not a lot of protection, but better than nothing. Rifle in hand, he stared in the direction of the noise until he could make out the shape of a man, crouched and heading for what he thought to be an unprotected corner of the corral.

"Not so fast, buddy." Parker unfolded himself and stood, keeping his rifle on the stranger. "Drop your gun."

The man cursed and turned to fire.

Parker hadn't seen the pistol in his hand, only the outline of his rifle. The man's shot took him in the side, spreading fire across his skin. The night exploded in gunfire.

From the ground, Parker fired, taking the man down. With no further danger coming from the man, Parker untied his bandanna from around his neck and pressed it against the wound in his side, trying to determine friend from foe from those around him.

Several minutes later, the gunfire ceased. "Call out, men!" Parker sat up.

They had three wounded, plus Parker, and two of the four rustlers escaped. The others lay in the dirt in danger of their lifeless bodies being trampled by the very animals they tried to steal. Using his rifle, Parker got to his feet.

"You're shot, boss." Barney crawled from behind a boulder.

"Not fatally. Rest until morning, boys. Then we clean up and ride home. Somebody bring me a canteen and a clean rag." He'd do the best doctoring he could, then let the women take over when he got home.

He grimaced through his pain, imagining Josie's dark head bent over as she tended to his wound. He could already smell the fragrance of roses from her hair.

❧ Chapter 9 ❧

With her ankle much better, Josie left the crutch at home. She barely limped and, if she walked slowly toward the creek, would be just fine. Waving to the boys, who headed in one direction, she took Sadie's hand to lead her in the opposite. She looked forward to winning the fishing challenge and having cooperative children at the table for lessons.

Her optimism dimmed at the sight of a grub worm. "I'm supposed to pick that up?"

Sadie nodded, holding out the bucket. "And put it on a hook."

Josie shuddered. She picked up the squirming thing with the tips of her finger and thumb and dropped it in the bucket. It landed with a plop. Another shovelful of dirt uncovered a handful more. Was fishing going to be as disgusting as digging for grubs?

More so, it turned out. Her stomach churned as she tried to thread the worm onto a hook.

Sadie giggled and tossed her line into the small pool. "You're funny."

"I'm pleased to provide you entertainment." There. Worm on. Grimacing, Josie washed her hand in the creek, then tossed out her line. She really should have accompanied her father on a few fishing expeditions as a child.

Her line jerked. "Oh. What do I do?"

"Yank it up and let the fish fall on the bank." Sadie looked at her as if she'd sprouted horns. "If you leave it in the water, it'll get away."

"Right." Josie moved back, dragging the fish from the water where it flopped on the bank. "All right," she said to the fish. "Get off now."

"You have to remove the hook from its mouth." Sadie snatched the pole from her hand and gave her the one she held. "Here. I'll do it."

"You're a gem." Josie grinned. She had no problem turning over the unpleasant tasks of fishing to someone more experienced.

Sadie strung a length of twine through the gills of the fish and tied the other end to a low-hanging branch, letting the fish slip into the water. "That will keep it alive until we gut it later."

"I think we'll leave that task to Lucy." Josie bobbed her pole up and down.

They stopped for lunch when the sun hung high in the sky. Although she couldn't see them, Josie glanced up the creek and wondered how the boys fared. A string of ten fish promised the likelihood of her and Sadie coming out the victors, but there were still hours in the day.

"Pa should have been back yesterday," Sadie said, taking a bite of her biscuit.

"Well, maybe there was more work than he thought." Josie had felt the same niggle of worry when she'd awakened that morning and he hadn't arrived home. "Or, he could be at home right now anxiously awaiting his meal of fish."

Sadie's face brightened. "Won't he be pleased with our catch? I bet the boys haven't got near as much." She quickly finished eating and jumped to her feet. "I'm going to get more." She dashed to the water's edge and prepared the two poles.

While the thrill of a fish's pull on her pole sent a surge of joy through her, Josie determined that there were more unpleasant things about fishing than there were pleasant. She sighed and cleaned up from their meal, then joined Sadie.

By the time they headed home, twelve fish hung from their strings. They met up with the boys halfway across the meadow.

"Eight." Ben proudly held up their string.

"Twelve." Sadie grinned, holding up hers and pointing to Josie's. "See you boys at lessons."

The boys stared wide-eyed at the fish on Sadie's and Josie's strings. They grumbled about losing but were generous in their congratulations. Josie glanced up as the ranch hands rode into the yard. "Perfect timing," she said. "We'll get one of them to clean the fish."

"I'll do it," Ben said.

Smiling, Josie marched toward the ranch hands, her smile fading and her steps faltering as she saw Parker being helped from his saddle. Blood stained his shirt. She raced toward him, Sadie on her heels. "What happened?"

"Rustler," Barney explained. "He needs stitched up."

"Sadie, fetch the medicine box." Josie propped her shoulder under Parker's other arm. The paleness of his features alarmed her. "Lay him on the kitchen table and get that shirt off him." As soon as they stepped into the kitchen, she gathered the things on the table into her arms and thrust them at a wide-eyed Lucy. "Boil water."

Barney helped Parker lie on the table, then stepped back. "I'll take care of the horses." He flicked a glance at Lucy. "Let us know when dinner's ready. Looking forward to fish." He rushed out the door.

Josie smoothed Parker's hair away from his face. "You foolish man."

"Didn't. . .do it. . .on purpose." A corner of his mouth quirked.

She shook her head and removed the strip of shirt he'd bound around his waist. She was no doctor, but it didn't look like more than a deep gash. No penetration or exit wound. She could do this. She'd watched someone stitch her father's arm. He cut himself on a piece of fencing when he'd insisted on helping one of the hired hands. He'd ended up losing his arm to infection, but she wouldn't think about that right now.

"Just be still and bite on this." She slipped a strap of leather between his teeth. "It's going to hurt."

He closed his eyes and gripped the edges of the table. A moan escaped him and his knuckles turned white as Josie poured whiskey on the wound, then washed it with hot water, then more whiskey.

Parker spit out the leather. "Tarnation, woman, are you trying to drive me mad?"

"It has to be cleaned well. I'm sorry." She dipped a string and needle into the whiskey.

The four children thundered into the room. "You may watch,

but stand back. You might learn something." She held up the needle. "Cleanliness is the cure for most infections, which is why I flushed the wound with whiskey, then scrubbed it with a clean rag and hot water, and then used more whiskey. I also sterilized the needle and thread. I learned these things"—she narrowed her eyes at the boys—"by reading."

"Stop the school lesson and get on with it," Parker snapped.

"We made a deal, Pa," Ben said. "She caught more fish, so now we have to learn."

Josie smiled down at Parker. "We'll explain later." She replaced the leather strap in his mouth.

His skin resisted the puncture of the needle at first then gave under the point. Trying not to focus on his erratic breathing, she counted stitches, making them as small and even as possible. When she finished, she patted his chest. "There. Six stitches."

The woman took pleasure in torturing him. Ignoring her offer to help him sit up, Parker rolled from the table, reaching for the clean shirt Robbie held out to him.

Lucy rushed forward to help him, and he waved her off. "Cook the fish." Donning the shirt, he stormed outside.

Josie raced after him. "You should be lying down. You'll pull the stitches and reopen the wound."

"I have a ranch to run and cattle to protect." He marched toward the corral where the herd mingled and bawled, not pleased to be kept in a pen. He pressed a hand to his side and approached his men. "What did you do with the bodies?"

"Buried them where they fell, boss. While you slept." Barney hooked a leather circle over the post that kept the gate closed. "Badger is tending to the wounded."

"I'll go help." Josie darted for the bunkhouse.

Parker leaned heavily against the corral. "We need to send a group to find out where the rustlers are hiding."

"Not you." Badger approached from behind. "Your face is as pale as Miss Josie's blouse. Let me ride to town and get the sheriff to form a posse."

Parker nodded. "Good idea. Sheriff Hollis will find them for us and cart their sorry carcasses to jail."

"You need to go lay down," Badger said. "Get one of them pretty gals to wait on you."

The idea of rest sounded mighty good. Parker didn't lie down, but he did settle himself on a rocker on the front porch and close his eyes.

A hand gently shook him awake. He opened his eyes to see Josie smiling down at him.

"Shall I bring your food out here or will you come in?"

"I'll come in."

She hooked her arm to give him something to grab hold of.

He took her arm and tried to stand. Weighing much more than she did, all he succeeded in doing was pulling her onto his lap. He grinned, despite the sharp pain the action caused. "This is nice."

"You're incorrigible." She jumped to her feet, her face red. "I'll get one of the men from the dining room to help you." She darted into the house.

Barney came out. "You sure got her all flustered." He laughed. "Give me some tips. Lucy still won't give me the time of day."

"You'd best give up on her, son." Parker let the younger man help him to his feet. "Find a woman like Josie, settled and learned. Not a flighty thing who flits from one man to another."

Barney shrugged. "I like her the way she is. It'll keep me on my toes. All I got to do is get her focus off you and onto me."

Parker wished him luck. He'd like nothing more than to get the girl's hungry eyes off him.

He took his seat at the table and grinned at the mound of fish in the center. "This is fit for a king."

Ben explained the contest Josie had cooked up. "I can't believe we got beat by a couple of girls."

"Badger told us where to go," Sadie said.

"No fair." Robbie's eyes widened.

"It's fair, Son. You could have asked someone with experience, just the same as Miss Josie did." Parker slid several pieces of crappie onto his plate. "That's what learning will do for someone. Teach them to find ways to make their life easier. Get more done with less work." He smiled at Josie, pleased to see a tint of pink still on her cheeks.

Lucy scowled and plopped a mug of coffee in front of him. "You should be in bed getting tended to."

"I'll retire early."

"I can help you."

"Ben will help me." He didn't meet the girl's gaze nor did he glance up at Josie, but he could feel both of them looking at him and didn't want to know what he'd see in the eyes of either one.

When he finished eating he told Ben to meet him in his room in a few minutes. He made a slow walk around the ranch, then made his way to his room. Sitting on the bed, he toed off his boots. "What I'd like to know is why the need for the fishing contest in the first place." He locked gazes with his son. "I expect the truth."

Ben hung his head.

"Look at me. Don't hang your head when someone asks you to explain yourself."

"Me and the other boys left in the middle of lessons to go fishing. Miss Josie came up with the idea of a contest." He squared his small shoulders. "We have to attend her lessons without argument now."

"Good." Parker winced and stretched out on his bed. "What part did Lucy play in all this?"

"How did you know?" Ben's mouth fell open.

"Just a hunch. Thanks for confirming." He grinned. "So?"

"She bribed us with cookies. I don't think she likes Miss Josie and wants her to look bad in front of you. You aren't going to marry Miss Lucy, are you?"

"Not a chance."

"Good." Ben headed for the door, then stopped and turned back. "Because if you marry anyone, I want it to be Miss Josie." He left and closed the door behind him.

Parker stared at the ceiling. Maybe the children did need a mother.

Chapter 10

The next morning, Josie watched as a sullen Lucy and a stoic-faced Barney rode for town. Parker hadn't offered any explanation other than that the girl wasn't working out. She hadn't taken her things, and if a trip to the mercantile was the reason behind her leaving, Josie could have placed an order. But that didn't explain the comment about the girl not working out.

Josie had heard Parker's loud voice outside the kitchen that morning from the direction of the front porch, then a red-eyed Lucy had stormed inside. Now, this. None of it made any sense. She shrugged and grabbed a broom to sweep the porch. The pieces would fall into place soon enough.

"You're choking me to death with the dust," Parker complained, waving his hand in front of his face as he sat in one of the rocking chairs. "If you wanted to kill me, you could have let me bleed to death."

"There are chores to be done and only me to do them." She hit his foot with the broom. "Lift."

He sighed. "I know about her bribing the boys with cookies to make your life harder. I confronted her, found out she is with child and wanting a husband. I have no desire to be that husband, but Barney has had an eye on the girl since she arrived. They went to town to get hitched. You'll have your help back."

She leaned on the broom handle. "Why didn't you say so in the first place?"

"Wasn't my right to." He propped his feet on the porch railing. "I am disappointed in Mrs. Davis though. Do you think she knew?"

"Probably not. Lucy is very devious." A trickle of pleasure at knowing Parker could no longer be Lucy's goal swept over her. He grew more dear to Josie every day, as did his children. If he were to marry, she'd most likely have to leave, and she was nowhere ready to make that decision. The more she stayed on the ranch, the less city life appealed to her.

"What's going through that pretty head of yours?"

He thought she was pretty? A flush infused her cheeks. "I like it here."

"A lot different than your first few days, isn't it?"

"Very. At least I know how to boil water, light the stove, and put a disgusting worm on a hook now."

"Your cooking still needs work." He grinned.

She sighed. "I know. I may never be a very good cook." Her meals were edible, but Lucy's cooking was much better. "When will Lucy and Barney return?"

"This evening, but I've given her off until the weekend. There's a trapper's cabin not too far away that I told them they could fix up and live in. As a married couple, they'll need privacy." He chuckled. "We'll have to make do with your cooking."

"You'll live." A few blessed days without Lucy's mood swings. Sounded heavenly.

"To give you the time for your household chores, and since I'm taking it easy on my stitches until the sheriff arrives, I'll take over the children's lessons today."

"Wonderful. I do have laundry and baking to do." His offer lifted a weight from her shoulders. If she ever had to do it all herself, she'd need some sort of a schedule in order to get it all done. Perhaps she could come up with one for the week. When Lucy's child came, she'd need time off for that as well.

Propping the broom against the wall, Josie checked Parker's wound, carefully lifting the bandage. His breath tickled the hair around her ears. With her heart in her throat, she turned her head and found his lips inches from hers.

His eyelids lowered as he claimed her lips in a kiss. "I've been wanting to do that for a long time," he whispered when he pulled back. Then, before she could step away, he cupped his hand on the back of her head and kissed her again.

"Now you have to get married."

Heavens. Josie jumped back as if scalded and saw Sadie standing nearby with a grin on her face. Josie sprinted past the girl to the pump to prepare the large vat she used for laundry. When the shock of Parker's kiss faded, a grin grew. He kissed her! And it had been marvelous.

Could she dare hope that with Lucy gone perhaps something

more than friendship toward Josie would grow in his heart? Or had her reluctance to set aside her dreams of being self-sufficient created a chasm between them that could not be breached?

She filled bucket after bucket with water, then lit a fire under the copper vat. While the water heated, she returned to the house to collect Sadie and the clothes. While Parker did lessons with the boys, she could work with Sadie on measuring soap to use in the wash. Her very own nanny had told her once that life always held a lesson to be learned if you paid attention, and a woman's job left many things to be discovered.

As she passed through the kitchen, her heart skipped a beat at the sight of four blond Owens males bent over a ledger. Parker held their attention as he explained the ins and outs of keeping books for the ranch.

Sadie tossed a load of dirty clothes down the stairs, landing them on Josie's head. "Sorry." She ducked back out of sight, then slid down the banister, her pantaloons showing as her dress rode up.

Josie sighed. "Ladies do not slide down banisters."

"I'm not a lady today. I'm a child." She thundered through the kitchen, snatching a leftover biscuit from a plate on the cupboard, then raced outside.

Gathering up the dirty clothes, Josie followed at a more sedate pace, ignoring the amused look on Parker's face. Let him laugh. She'd turn his children into well-mannered adults if it took the rest of her life.

Whoops. He'd done something to erase the pleasure of his kiss from her face and replace it with annoyance. Women were very moody creatures. It might be wiser to teach his sons the fact they could never figure out the fairer sex rather than focus on a ledger of addition and subtraction.

The pounding of hooves drew him outside. The sheriff and Badger halted in front of the house and slid from their horses.

"Rustlers?" Sheriff Hollis propped a booted foot on the step. "You sure?"

Parker nodded. "One of my men said we had about thirty head missing. I'm pretty sure it wasn't upstanding citizens that shot at us under the cover of darkness."

"You got injured?"

"Yes, sir. Just a graze, but could have been worse."

The sheriff nodded. "Let's ride out and see if we can't find those scoundrels. We will not engage. If we find them, I'll put together a posse."

"Let me get my guns." Parker headed back into the house to see a red-faced Josie standing by the table.

"You're leaving, injured as you are?"

"It's my ranch, Josie. I have to go."

"You've men to go in your place."

"They're needed here." He buckled his gun belt around his waist and did his best not to show how much the action pulled at his side.

"If you rip out your stitches, don't come crying to me." She stomped out the back door.

He glanced at his wide-eyed sons. Yep, someday he'd have to try to explain the mystery of women. "Go muck out the barn, boys. Figure out a way of turning it into a lesson and report back to me when I return." He tousled their hair. "See you when I get back."

"When?" Luke pouted.

"Tonight or tomorrow, God willing. Take care of the women. You're the men of the house while I'm gone." *Lord, let me return home.* It hadn't occurred to him until he'd gotten shot that someday he could leave his children orphans.

He glanced toward Josie and Sadie on his way to saddle his horse. It was time to get a wife. His children needed a mother in case something happened to him. All he needed to do was make sure nothing happened until then.

The boys followed him to the barn and sat on the walls of a stall while he saddled his horse. "Badger, watch out for my family, please."

"You got it, boss. Good luck."

Once he'd climbed into the saddle, he tipped his hat to them and galloped off to join the sheriff.

At the sheriff's side, Parker pointed the way to the place where they'd had their run-in with the rustlers. Two fresh mounds marred the tree line where his men had buried the shooters. Dead men with no names. He couldn't think of anything sadder. *Lord, have mercy on their souls.*

"The survivor took off that way." Parker pointed.

"Any place out there where cattle could be hidden?"

"Not many. The ground's pretty flat around here, but there's a canyon in the mountains that might work."

"How far?"

"A day's ride, maybe a little less." It would be a long day. Already Parker's side protested the ride.

They headed for the mountain in the distance, taking the pace slow and steady. As they rode, Parker alternated between studying the ground for signs of anyone passing that way and thinking how good Josie's lips had felt against his. There were worse things in life to give up than a man's freedom if he were handing that freedom over to a good woman.

He spent some time in prayer, feeling confident when he'd finished that God would clarify whether it was His will for Parker to ask Josie for her hand. When he started the ranch, he'd had Leah at his side. They'd started with one bull and three cows and two pregnant mares, building up from there. What made him think he couldn't use a wife by his side now that things were better?

Leah had helped him build the ranch. Josie could help him sustain it and keep him company as he grew older. Even if she didn't love him as a wife should love a husband, she would make a nice companion for him and a wonderful mother to his children.

Sheriff Hollis held up his hand for Parker to stop. "Take a short break. You're bobbing in your saddle."

As much as he regretted admitting he needed one, Parker was grateful. "Thanks. My mind was whirling, but it wasn't enough to keep my body from screaming." Holding tightly to the saddle horn, he slid to the ground. His knees buckled, but he kept himself from falling.

Josie had packed them a lunch, and he dug it from his bags, tossing a sandwich to Hollis. "Might want to save some in case we aren't back by dinner."

"I've some jerky in my pack."

After a quickly eaten lunch and a short break, they were back in the saddle and headed for the canyon. They reached where a little-used path wound its way up as the sun started its descent. Not wanting to risk heading into dangerous territory in the dark, they decided to call it a night and find a place to camp until morning. It wouldn't be wise to stumble across armed men in the dark, if they found them. On the other hand, the rustlers could be long gone.

"Get some sleep, Parker," Hollis said. "I'll take first watch. Can't risk a fire." He tossed Parker a strip of jerky. "Eat up."

"Thanks." Parker checked his stitches. A small drop of blood stained his bandage. He lay down, using his saddle as a pillow. Josie was going to kill him when he got back.

Chapter 11

The rattle of the buckboard pulled Josie from the kitchen the next morning. Rather than return on their wedding night, Lucy and Barney had elected to stay in town. Now they'd arrived back on the ranch. Despite not getting the groom she wanted, Lucy smiled and waved as they passed the main house on their way to their smaller home.

Josie waved back. While the day before had been long, she preferred doing the work alone rather than be alongside someone as unhappy as Lucy had been. Hopefully, things had changed and the two could coexist peacefully. Only time would tell.

She moved back to the stove and stirred the pot of oatmeal, then kneaded the dough for the day's meals. She might not be the best cook, but she had settled into a routine of sorts and got the meals served on time.

Her gaze settled on the children seated at the table. They'd held to their promise of attending the lessons. Their father would be proud when he returned. She frowned out the window, hoping for a sign of him and the sheriff returning whole and unharmed. How did ranchers' wives handle the worry of their husbands being gone?

"He'll be back, miss." Badger dropped an armload of wood into the box. "God's with them."

"I know, and thank you for the reminder." She smiled and poured him a cup of coffee. "How are our injured men?"

"Fine. They'll be doing chores today, but a little slower than usual. It could have been worse."

True. After one more glance out the window, she set the dishes on the table and asked Ben to go ring the bell. Since he was the only child tall enough, the job helped him feel special, and he banged the cowbell with great enthusiasm.

When breakfast was served and cleaned up, she settled the children on the porch with their chalk and tablets while she stared into the distance waiting for a sign of Parker returning. As the hours passed, she grew more fretful. The children fed off her anxiety and bickered at each other rather than copying their spelling words.

Robbie threw chalk at Sadie, Luke raced around the porch after Cloud, while Ben yelled at them to behave. Josie sighed and clapped her hands three times. "Enough. No more lessons today. Instead, let's surprise your father by cleaning the barn."

She might as well have told them they were going to eat manure the way they grumbled. "Come along. It's not the first time you've had a shovel in your hand."

"I bet it's the first time you have." Ben grinned and darted for the barn, his younger siblings on his heels.

He was correct. Josie had never done physical labor of that kind before, but no one could say she wasn't willing to try.

"Are you going to marry my pa?" Sadie slipped her hand in Josie's. "I'd like you to be my ma."

Josie's words stuck in her throat. She'd come to Crinoline Creek with no intention of romance, but God had other plans. Day by day these children and their father grew more precious to her. She'd been foolish to doubt the warm look in Parker's eyes and think him interested in Lucy. "I, uh, we haven't discussed that, your father and I."

"I'll talk to him." She released Josie's hand and skipped into the barn.

Heavens. Josie leaned against the corral. She couldn't stop a smile from spreading as she envisioned the sweet little girl playing matchmaker.

A scream from inside the barn rent the air.

Josie whirled and dashed inside.

Something splatted her in the chest. A foul odor burned her nose. She glanced down to see a smear of manure across her shirtwaist. She stared at equally manure-covered children.

Sadie cried, clearly disgusted, but the boys merely looked shocked at hitting Josie rather than each other in what was obviously a battle of some sort.

"Hush, Sadie. It'll wash off." Josie wrinkled her nose. "But I do believe the chore of cleaning the barn will be left to you three boys. Benjamin, keep an eye on the younger two. I'll be back to inspect your progress before dinnertime, and I expect to see a barn your father will be proud of." She took the little girl by the hand and marched to the house, ignoring the laughter of the ranch hands they passed.

By the time she had water hauled and heated for bathing, her eyes were watering. She stripped Sadie down, cleaned her, then told her to play with her doll in the kitchen while Josie soaked. And she did intend to soak. She dumped the tub of water, dragged it to her room, then started the whole process of heating water and filling the tub. When she'd finished, she dropped the last sliver of her rose-scented soap into the water and undressed.

She stepped into the water and sank into its warmth, closing her eyes. Drat those rascals. Her mother would have a conniption if she knew Josie relaxed in a tub in the middle of the day when there was work to be done. Knowing that, she groaned, lathered, rinsed, and got out, retrieving what little of the soap she could. She'd enjoy a soak later.

With the afternoon wasted with the unplanned chore of hauling water, dinner loomed. She hadn't baked the risen bread yet or cut up the vegetables for the stew. Not to mention she needed to check on the boys, who most likely continued with their manure battle in her absence. If it wasn't so much work, she'd insist on nightly bathing as their punishment. As it was, the once a week she enforced caused enough grumbling that a person would think the world was coming to an end.

Passing the kitchen, Josie called out, "Sadie, sweetie, stay here while I check on the boys. I'll be right back." She pushed the front door open and stepped onto the front porch to see Sadie, not safely playing in the kitchen, but clutched in the arms of a stranger. His dirty hand covered her mouth.

"Scream and I'll wring her neck," he said.

Not a sign of cattle or rustlers. Parker sat in his saddle and stared over the canyon. They'd been here, as evidenced by the prints of hooves milling around, but they weren't now. His side felt as if someone held a branding iron to it. And now he'd wasted a day and a night.

"Where do you think they got off to?" the sheriff asked. "Could we be lucky enough to think they've headed somewhere else?"

"Maybe." Parker turned his horse toward home. "Easier rustling somewhere else, perhaps."

Sheriff Hollis narrowed his eyes. "You don't look so good."

"Not feeling very good, that's for sure. I'll settle into bed when I get home and let my pretty housekeeper take care of me." Parker grinned.

"You gonna marry her?"

"I've been mulling it over. The young'uns need a ma, and I like having Josie around. Nothing beats a woman's touch around a place." He could no longer remember what it was like with her gone. In just a few weeks, she'd integrated herself into the household like glue. The boys might run her ragged, but he knew they cared deeply for their nanny.

They spent the next few hours riding in silence, stopping at the creek so Parker could clean himself up and not send Josie into a fit at the sight of him bleeding through his bandages. Not to mention he feared a fever coming on.

He splashed his face with cold water. After soaking his bandanna in the creek, he wrapped it around his neck, almost sighing with the pleasure of the coolness against his hot skin. He needed his bed in the worst way.

By the time they arrived home, the sun had started its descent. Parker set his horse free in the corral, leaving the saddle in place in case he had to leave in a hurry, and made his way to the house. He needed rest. Everything else could wait.

He sat on the edge of the bed and started to remove his boots. Wait a minute. He rubbed his hands over his face. He should have heard the shouting of his children. It was late, but not late enough for them to already be in bed. Nor should the lanterns not be lit in the house.

He stood and set off for the barn. If they weren't there, maybe Josie had taken them to the creek for a picnic. He stopped one of the hands coming from the bunkhouse. "Where's Josie and the children?"

The man shrugged. "Ain't seen 'em. Badger told me to stay and him and some of the others went looking for you."

Parker pushed open the barn door, ordering the hand not to unsaddle his horse. In the far stall, he found his three sleeping sons, covered with manure, gags in their mouths and hands and feet bound, propped against each other. Where were Sadie and Josie?

"Get Lucy and Barney," he said to the ranch hand. He shook Ben awake and quickly untied the boys. "What happened? Why are you covered in horse dung?"

"We was throwing it at each other. We hit Miss Josie smack in the chest and she told us to clean the barn." He got to his feet. "We were, really, we were, but then these two men came in and told us to go into the stall. They tied us up, and the next thing I heard was horses going away."

"Did they take Miss Josie and your sister?" He put a hand on

Ben's shoulder and peered into his eyes.

"I don't know. I couldn't see." Tears welled in his eyes. "You told us to take care of them, and we played instead. Now they might get kilt."

"Nobody is getting killed. Go to the house, get cleaned up, and stay there." Parker grabbed a lantern and lit it. He'd have to look for tracks in the dark.

He found horse prints outside the barn door. Next to the porch, he spotted a man's footprints and a child's. Sadie's? Near those, he found Josie's. He had no doubt his girls had been taken by the rustlers he'd sought earlier that day.

Which way would they have gone? He turned in a slow circle, his gaze straining to see further signs.

"This way, boss." Badger ran toward him. "Two horses headed away from here in the opposite direction of town."

"Not toward the mountain?"

"Not unless they double back, but to my thinking they wouldn't take the females unless they wanted to be followed."

Parker agreed. "They'll want something for their return. My guess is they'll want cattle."

"Do we wait?"

"We do not. Gather up any man able to ride. Where is Lucy?"

"Here." She rushed toward them, Barney at her side. "I'll care for the boys."

"Thank you." He continued to bark orders until five armed men stood with him.

"You don't look good, boss," Badger said. "We can go without you."

"I'm fine. Send someone for Sheriff Hollis. The rest of you come with me." He clapped Ben on the shoulder. "It isn't your fault. Stay here with Lucy and watch your brothers. Understand?"

He nodded. "I won't let you down this time, Pa."

"You could never let me down." He accepted a filled canteen from Robbie, then climbed painfully into the saddle. "Say a prayer, boys." With a flick of his reins, he set off at a gallop in the direction Josie and Sadie had gone.

⚘ *Chapter 12* ⚘

G̶od, where are You? I thought You sent me to Parker, that You'd found me a home.

Josie's dream of a home of her own, with no fear of it being taken away, did not include being kidnapped. Now, not only was she in danger of losing a home, but her life and possibly Sadie's. "Strange way to fulfill a dream, God," she muttered.

"No talking." She got a jab in the back with a gun for her trouble.

Sadie sniffled from the back of a horse next to them, her small arms wrapped around the waist of her captor. Even if it meant her own demise, Josie would find a way to get the little girl free.

"What did you do to the three boys?" She tried looking over her shoulder, but the man behind her forced her to face forward.

"Tied 'em up. You two are all we'll need to convince that rancher to turn over his cattle."

This was about cattle? A chill ran down her spine. Their kidnappers were the rustlers Parker had gone searching for. Despite her fear, hope sprang in her heart. Taking her and Sadie meant Parker was alive. You couldn't bargain with a dead man.

They continued riding into the night, not stopping until the moon hung high over the mountain. Then the men had them dismount and walked them through a crevice in a cliff to a cave barely big enough for the four of them.

"Get some rest. We'll leave before daylight. Can't risk that rancher finding us until we're ready." He tossed her and Sadie a piece of jerky each.

"Can you at least untie our hands?"

"Nope." He propped himself against the wall and pulled his hat low over his eyes while the other man went outside to keep watch.

Sadie scooted up next to Josie and buried her face in Josie's chest. "I'm scared."

"It'll be fine. Your father will find us." Josie failed at keeping her voice from trembling and tried to mask it by clearing her throat. How would Parker find them in a cave? The rustlers would prevent him or any of his men from getting anywhere close to their hiding place.

Why didn't the rustlers just take the cattle? It didn't make any sense. Unless. . . She stiffened. It wasn't only about the cattle. She and Sadie were being held for ransom because Parker and the sheriff had foiled the rustling attempt.

She peered through the dark, barely making out the man's form in the corner. Did Parker have ready funds? She doubted he did. No, she'd have to find a way to rescue herself and Sadie before the rustlers came to the same conclusion.

Snores emanated from their captor. Placing her finger across Sadie's lips, Josie motioned for her to follow. Crawling wasn't easy with her hands tied, and movement had to be slow in order not to alert their guard, but inch by inch they reached the mouth of the cave.

A full moon lit up the area around them. There wouldn't be many places to hide, but staying put would get them killed. After a glance around to make sure the other man wasn't in sight, Josie led Sadie along the route they'd taken to reach the cave. A clump of bushes provided a bit of cover and they stopped.

Josie tore at the rope around her wrists with her teeth until she got free. She untied Sadie, then gripped her hand. "Be as quiet as possible."

A shout of alarm came from behind them.

All pretense of silence fled. Josie tore through the brush, dragging Sadie along with her. Thorny branches tore at their clothing and skin, but still they ran. Stopping was not an option.

Which way? She turned, aware they could be running in circles or farther from the ranch. Still, movement seemed the only chance they had of surviving the night.

The sound of cattle came from her left. Slowing her pace, she moved in that direction. Held in a makeshift corral stood cattle wearing the brand of the Tilted O. Josie told Sadie to climb on top of a boulder, then moved at a crouch toward the corral. Nothing seemed like a better diversion than a cattle stampede. It might be just what they needed to get away.

She lifted the leather strap keeping a flimsy gate in place, then gave a shout. The cattle lifted their heads. Cries of alarm came from the man set in place to keep a lookout. Desperate, Josie lifted her skirt and flapped it while giving the most primal scream she could drum up. It didn't take much. She put all her fear and frustration into it.

The cattle lunged as one. She dove to the side to avoid being trampled as they rushed through the gate.

Curses filled the air as the man raced for his horse.

Josie hurried to Sadie and commenced their wild dash to freedom. The rustlers would be torn between hunting down the cattle or chasing their captives. She prayed they'd choose the cattle. There weren't enough of them to split up and go after both.

In the distance, a light drew them like bugs to a lantern. As they moved closer, Josie made out the outline of a cabin. The light she'd seen was the moon shining off a glass panel. They were saved.

With tears streaming down her face, she darted forward and banged on the door. "Help us. Please."

The door opened. A large man sporting several days of beard growth stared down at them. He lifted his hand and waved the pistol he held. "Nice of you to join me. Come on in. There's no telling how long it will take my men to figure out you came here."

Josie's heart plummeted. She'd led Sadie straight to the lion's den. Their race for freedom had been a waste.

The man grinned, showing several missing teeth. "You'll be more comfortable here, ma'am. I won't invite you a second time. Whether you're dead or alive, Owens won't know."

She pulled Sadie into the cabin and glanced around. The glass pane she'd seen was the only window. The door they'd entered through, the only exit.

The stranger moved a chair in front of the door and sat. Josie gathered Sadie close and faced him, chin up, eyes shimmering, back ramrod straight. She would not beg or plead. The man would do what he would do.

Parker led his men toward the mountain for lack of anywhere else to search. With the moon high in the sky, they traveled up the mountain to the canyon. Not finding Josie and his daughter there, they headed down the other side. Josie and Sadie didn't just disappear into thin air. "Who lives around here?"

"Might be a couple of squatters," Badger replied, "but I ain't seen 'em. I heard tell of a hunter's cabin out that away. Might be a good place to hole up."

"Lead the way."

Once they were off the mountain, they caught sight of several head of cattle thundering toward them. Parker sighed with relief. They had to be his, which meant they were getting close to finding out where the woman he loved and his daughter were being held.

It felt good to say it to himself. He loved Josephine Montgomery and planned on telling her the moment he saw her. Not only did his children need a mother, but he wanted her for his wife. Someone to spend the evenings with, grow old with, maybe have a few more young'uns with. He dreamed of a future with her as he rode, doing his best to focus on the memory of her face and not the fever starting to burn through him.

Badger moved his horse closer to Parker. "You don't look good, boss."

"I'm fine. Keep leading me to this cabin."

Badger's eyes glinted in the moonlight. "If you die out here..."

"I won't. Shut your mouth and keep looking."

"Yeah, that's the Parker Owens I know. A real hard nose." Badger shook his head and motioned for one of the men to pull up on the other side of Parker.

They were going to treat him like an invalid. He wouldn't have it. He clicked his tongue, urging his horse to go faster. He'd worry about the infection in his side when Josie and Sadie were safe at home.

A gunshot rang out, and Parker slid from his horse, pulling his rifle from the scabbard as he hit the ground. The cattle switched direction, now heading away from the ranch instead of toward home.

Parker and his men returned fire. A few minutes later, only one of the two rustlers remained alive. Parker bent over him. "Where's my family?"

"I don't know. They run off, scattered the cattle, and disappeared. Get me some help, man." He clutched his shoulder.

"You aren't going to die unless you bleed to death. Where could they hide out here? Answer my questions, and I'll have one of my men bind your wound."

The man groaned. "Maybe the boss found 'em. He stayed at the cabin."

Parker hauled the man to his feet. "Show us to this cabin."

"My wound?"

Parker told Badger to wrap the man's gunshot. One of his other men brought a spare horse. Twenty minutes later, they galloped toward the hunter's cabin, stopping a few yards away and once again dismounting.

Keeping low, Parker dashed to the only window, in the back wall. Plastering his back against the logs, he peered into the house.

Josie and Sadie sat on two straight-backed chairs. Across from them, and blocking the front door, sat a large, bearded man. He held a rifle across his lap. A holster on his hip held a pistol. One man against Parker and his five.

"Hey, boss, they've come for you!" the wounded rustler cried out before Badger knocked him unconscious with the butt of his gun.

The man inside lunged to his feet, grabbed Josie, and held her in front of him. "Come on in, fellas."

"None of your men are here other than the loudmouth," Parker said. "He's out of commission at the moment."

The man squeezed Josie until she squealed. "Here's what we're going to do," he said. "I'm guessing you found your cattle, so I'm going to need to be paid for all my hard work. You pay me one thousand dollars in return for this woman and little girl. You have twenty-four hours."

"No rancher in Texas can get his hands on that amount of cash in such a short time." Parker motioned for Badger to take one of the men around to the front of the house and told him in a low voice, "If you get the opportunity, take him out. Wait for my signal. I've got to get him to let go of Josie before we start shooting." They needed to hurry. Parker's strength ebbed at an alarming rate.

Perspiration ran down his face and into his eyes. He rubbed his arm across his face in an attempt to see more clearly. Everything in front of him rippled.

He stumbled into the wall.

Josie and Sadie screamed.

A gunshot blew out the window.

Parker fell.

The world grew dark. His last thought was that he hadn't had the chance to tell Josie he loved her.

Chapter 13

When a loud thump sounded outside, Josie stomped on her captor's foot, then dropped to the floor, taking Sadie with her. Gunfire rang out.

Sadie screamed and covered her ears. Josie closed her eyes as bullets riddled the cabin. Her eyes popped open as the man fell to his knees, his gaze locking with hers before he fell prostrate and breathed no more.

Once upon a time, the most dangerous thing Josie had done was burn her hair with curling tongs. Now she cowered over a child to protect her from bullets. Life in Texas was not a sitting room in Georgia.

"Miss Josie." Badger helped her to her feet. "The boss is needing you mighty bad. Take the child and go. We'll clean up here."

Parker? Josie raced out the door.

One of the hands had Parker in the saddle in front of him, one hand on the reins, the other wrapped around his boss's waist. "We need to go, ma'am."

Josie helped Sadie onto a horse before climbing on behind her. "Make haste." She had so many questions but didn't want to waste a single second asking them.

Sadie, exhausted from their ordeal, fell asleep in the saddle. If not for worry over Parker, Josie would have done the same. But her thoughts, racing with every conceivable bad thing that could happen, kept her alert.

They arrived at the house by midday. Barney rushed forward to help Parker from the back of the horse. While the men helped their boss inside, Josie raced forward to pull down the blankets on his bed.

"What should I do?" Lucy asked.

"I don't know yet. Be ready for anything." She stood aside as Parker was placed on his bed, then stepped forward and placed the back of her hand across his forehead. "He's burning up."

"I'll fetch some cold well water." Lucy bustled away, calling for Ben and Robbie to help.

Josie ripped open Parker's shirt. He'd pulled several stitches, and pus oozed from the wound. "He's infected. Send someone for the doctor."

"I'll go." Badger thundered from the house. Seconds later the sound of pounding hooves reached those inside the house.

Josie had never been more frightened in her life. People died of infection. The doctor was hours away. "Hot water and clean rags, please. Oh, and whiskey." She'd clean it the best she could, pull out the rest of the stitches if possible, and let the wound remain open until the doctor arrived. Maybe. Oh, she didn't know. What should she do?

She put her hands on her cheeks. Her brain was so tired, her heart so full of dread. *Think, Josie.*

When Lucy returned with a pot of boiling water and Ben with a pail of well water, Josie rolled up her sleeves. *God, help me.*

She laid cool rags across Parker's face and neck, under his arms, and anywhere else she could think of that might bring down his fever. Then she plunged her hands into the hot water and scrubbed the wound.

Parker groaned and bucked under her hands but didn't open his eyes. Silly, beautiful, strong, stupid man. He shouldn't have gone looking for her in this condition. He should have sent someone in his place. She loved him all the more for endangering himself but would scold him soundly when he was out of harm's way.

When she'd cleaned the wound the best she could, she spent the rest of the day replacing warm rags with cool ones and praying, *Lord, don't let him die. Forget all those silly dreams that once filled my head. The only dream I have now is lying in front of me. Spare him, please.*

"Go rest, Josie." Lucy pushed her hands away. "Right there in the rocker. I'll take over for a bit."

"No. You're married and. . ."

"Happily." She gave a sad smile. "I'm sorry for being such a shrew before. I, uh, needed a father for my child, and who better than the boss? Will you forgive me?"

"Yes." Although, in Josie's exhausted state, she couldn't dwell on how long it would take for her to trust the other woman. "I'll sit right here in case I'm needed."

"I'll wake you the moment the doctor arrives." Lucy turned and took a tray from Sadie. "Eat this bit of stew. You need your strength."

Like an obedient child, Josie forced a few spoonfuls of stew down her throat, then pushed the tray away and leaned her head against the seat back. She started to close her eyes but caught sight of four worried children hovering in the doorway. Waving them forward, she wrapped her arms around them. "We're doing everything we can. It's up to God. Why don't the four of you go draw your father some pictures we can hang around the room. They'll be the first things he sees when he opens his eyes."

They shuffled off, the worry not eased from their eyes. Poor Luke's cheeks bore tear tracks through the dirt he'd been playing in. Josie sighed and started to get to her feet.

"No, ma'am. The children are fine. I've fed them. Stay in your chair and rest." Lucy frowned. "You'll be of no use to Mr. Owens if you fall ill."

"You're right." With one last glance toward the door, Josie sat back down and closed her eyes.

The doctor's arrival woke her, and she sprang to her feet. He took one look at her and told her to sit back down. "I'll tend to that cut on your head in a minute."

"Cut?" She put a hand to her head. A knot poked up from her hairline. Her fingers came in contact with clotted blood. She must have hit her head when she tackled Sadie to the floor. She grew woozy.

"Ma'am, I cannot tend to you right now."

She waved a hand to show him she was fine. She was fine, just surprised to know she'd been wounded. Colored dots swam in front of her eyes. Funny how Parker's blood hadn't made her want to faint.

"You did a good job cleaning the wound and keeping his fever from becoming dangerously high. I don't think he'll wake until at least morning." The doctor handed her a bottle of laudanum. "He'll be hurting when he wakes. Now, let me look at that head." He poked and prodded at her head until she wanted to slap him. "Not bad. Won't require stitches. I advise you to take a long bath and get some rest. Here's a packet to add to the water to help with any headache. Mr. Owens will be here when you get back."

Josie thanked him and left Lucy to watch Parker. After checking on the children and getting them settled into the boys' room since Sadie refused to sleep alone in hers after their ordeal, she turned to go to her room.

Sadie stopped her. "Is Pa going to be all right?"

"I think so." Josie stopped and faced the children. "He's strong, and God is with him. Let's pray he's awake in the morning." She went back and gave each of them a good-night kiss. "Such brave children. I'm blessed to be your nanny."

"You'll be our ma soon," Ben said. "I'd bet my hat."

"No betting." Josie smiled and headed to her room. A hot bath sounded heavenly. Barney and Lucy hauled and heated the water for her, and she soaked until the water grew cold, then dressed in a clean dress and grabbed a blanket from her bed. She had no intention of sleeping in her room. The rocking chair in Parker's would do just fine. She wanted to be there when he woke.

Parker groaned and shifted, trying to grow comfortable on sheets cool with dampness. He must have sweated buckets. He opened his eyes to see four crude drawings tacked on the wall. In each a stick man held hands with a stick woman and four little stick people surrounded them. His family.

He turned his head and smiled at the sight of a sleeping Josie curled up in his rocking chair. He'd literally gone into a dark and dangerous place and back to make sure she was safe. Her and his little girl. *Thank You, God, for giving me another chance to tell Josie how much I love her.*

He must have made a louder noise, because her beautiful dark eyes popped open. "Parker." She rushed to his side, dropping the blanket to the floor. She knelt next to his bed and lifted his hand to her cheek. "You had me so frightened."

"I couldn't breathe for fear I wouldn't rescue you in time. And I thought I'd never have the chance to tell you I love you." His gaze locked with her teary one. "When I get out of this bed, I want to marry you, Josephine Montgomery."

Four shouts rang out from the doorway. Josie smiled, nodding. "I will most definitely marry you. Right here if you want."

"No, I want to be standing. I want to watch you walk toward me. Do you love me, Josie?" His heart skipped a beat waiting for her answer.

"Oh. I did leave that part out, didn't I?" She laughed. "I do love you, you silly man. Are you going to kiss me?"

"As soon as the children give us some privacy." He smiled and motioned for them to leave. When they did—reluctantly, if the looks on their faces were any indication—he tugged her down so he could reach her lips. He pressed his lips against hers and closed his eyes. When they pulled apart, he whispered, "You're a dream come true."

"Oh Parker. Let me tell you about dreams." She laid her head on his chest. "When I accepted your job offer, my dream was to have a place of my own. One that couldn't be taken away in the ravages of war or because of death. I wanted to be self-sufficient."

"And now?"

She raised her head to look at him. "I still want those things, but I want them with you. God sure has a way of changing our dreams for the better. I'll be forever grateful."

"Kiss me again." Parker cupped her face and drew her close.

Cynthia Hickey

Cynthia Hickey grew up in a family of storytellers and moved around the country a lot as an army brat. Her desire is to write about real but flawed characters in a wholesome way that her seven children and nine grandchildren can all be proud of. She and her husband live in Arizona where Cynthia is a full-time writer.

*Love's Cookin' at
the Cowboy Café*

by Marilyn Turk

Chapter 1

Crinoline Creek, Texas
March 1868

Whump! The trunk landed on the dusty street.

Sarah Beth Taylor planted her hands on her hips and shot an angry glance up at the driver who tossed the luggage off the top of the stagecoach.

"Well, I never. Sir! Could you be more careful with my things?"

"Could you pack a lighter trunk? You must have an anvil in that thing!"

"Hmmph!" Sarah Beth brushed the dust off her traveling suit and adjusted her hat. What a miserable experience the trip had been from Georgia—a crowded conveyance with complete strangers and a bumpy ride with a rude driver. Thank God she didn't have to travel any farther.

She picked up her reticule and looked around. Crinoline Creek,

Texas, wasn't much of a town. Apparently, the people here had no concept of refined taste. Why, most of the buildings weren't even whitewashed! Well, she could help bring some gentility to the town once she opened her café.

But where was Mr. Wright? She'd wired the banker ahead of time to inform him of her arrival. Why wasn't he here to meet her?

The stagecoach pulled away, leaving her alone in the street. A man walking on the boardwalk glanced her way.

"Sir? Do you know where Emery Wright is?"

The scruffy-looking man stopped and pushed back his dusty hat. Skimming her with his eyes, he replied with a smug grin. "The banker? I s'pose he's at the bank."

Heat flushed Sarah Beth's face. "Well, I. . .then would you mind pointing me in the direction of the bank?" Ordinarily, she'd request the man to escort her, but the way this man leered at her prickled her spine.

He hooked his fingers in his belt and nodded toward the opposite side of the street. "Over yonder. That there building that says 'Bank' on it." He gave her a wink.

Her temper flared. She turned and saw the building that had been hidden by the stagecoach. The man must think her a complete ninny. Well, she didn't need any more of his help, even though she wanted her trunk moved onto the boardwalk. But since he didn't offer, she wouldn't lower herself to let him insult her one more time.

"Thank you, kind sir." She offered a mock curtsy and spun around. Lifting her skirts to avoid the unpleasant filth scattered on the street, she picked her way toward the bank. Behind her, the man guffawed.

Sarah Beth stepped up on the boardwalk in front of the bank, then grabbed the doorknob and pushed the door open. Customers stood in front of the lone man behind the teller's cage. Sarah Beth strode to the cage, wedging herself between the customers and the teller, receiving surprised looks from all of them.

She offered an apologetic smile to the other patrons. "I'll just be a minute." Then she turned around and addressed the teller. "Sugar, would you please tell Mr. Emery Wright that Sarah Beth Taylor is here?"

The bespectacled gentleman blushed. "I'm sorry, ma'am, but these customers were here first."

Sarah Beth gave her sweetest smile to the man and woman waiting in line. "I'm sure these fine people wouldn't mind if you helped a lady out." She put a hand to her forehead and closed her eyes for a moment. "Especially after such an arduous and dangerous journey!"

The woman's annoyance changed to concern. "Did you say *dangerous*?"

"Oh my stars, you just wouldn't believe how terrible it was!"

The woman leaned in. "What happened?"

Sarah Beth was about to give a detailed account of her trip when a door in the back of the room opened and a gentleman walked out. The strikingly handsome man with impeccably combed coal-black hair wore a fine suit with a starched white shirt and a perfectly tied cravat. Well, someone in this town had good taste after all. He strode across the room toward her with a raised eyebrow.

"Can I help you, ma'am? I'm Emery Wright, president of this bank."

"Mr. Wright? Oh my goodness, I expected someone much

older!" Sarah Beth smiled and curtsied, then extended her gloved hand. "I'm Sarah Beth Taylor."

"Miss Taylor? Nice to make your acquaintance. Why did you expect someone older?"

"Well, I thought the reason you didn't greet me when I arrived was because you forgot." Sarah Beth found herself captured by his eyes. Were they truly gray or light blue?

Emery Wright reached for the pocket watch in his vest, opened it and checked the time, then clasped it shut. "I apologize, Miss Taylor. I have to admit I did forget the time."

"You are forgiven. Now, let's get down to business, shall we?"

"Excuse me? Oh yes, you want the title to your establishment."

"Why, of course. I can't wait to open my own business!"

Mr. Wright gave her a puzzled look, then glanced at the other people in the room who watched and appeared very interested in their conversation. He motioned toward the back of the room. "Let's go to my office where we can talk privately."

"Certainly." She lifted her chin and headed for the office he'd indicated. She was now an important person in this town, a business owner. She'd spent her entire trip out west thinking about how she'd decorate her café and what wonderful meals she'd serve. In fact, it was the sheer excitement of her future that had made the journey bearable.

"Please have a seat." Mr. Wright motioned to the chair in front of his desk as he closed the door. He sat down behind his desk, then reached into a drawer and pulled out an envelope. "Your uncle, Homer Taylor, left you the building and everything in it. He said he wanted to help his niece out since the war had taken away so much from you."

Sarah Beth choked back tears. She couldn't break down in front of this man. The war, her parents' deaths, then the loss of their family plantation to carpetbaggers—she'd reached the point of desperation when her uncle's letter arrived giving her a chance at a new start.

"I am very grateful to Uncle Homer. His gift is an answer to prayer."

"He also left you some money to help you get started." Mr. Wright's eyes softened as they gazed into hers. "He said he wouldn't need it once he struck gold."

"How kind of him." A weight lifted off her shoulders. She had some money from the sale of the plantation but wasn't sure how long it'd last. "Of course, once the café opens, I'll have plenty of money."

Mr. Wright quirked a brow. "Well, here's your deed." He handed her the envelope.

Sarah Beth tried not to show how nervous and anxious she was and hoped her hands wouldn't shake. The envelope contained a key and a document. She withdrew the document and scanned it.

"The Thirsty Spur? What an odd name for a café."

Mr. Wright opened his mouth as if to say something, then closed it.

"Well? Aren't you going to show me my new business?"

He looked startled. "Oh, yes, of course. But surely, you don't want to see it now? Perhaps you'd prefer going to the hotel to freshen up first. I know it's been a long day, and you must be tired."

"Hmm." She tapped her chin. "Maybe I should. But I need someone to fetch my trunk. That rude stagecoach driver left it in the street instead of carrying it to the boardwalk. I need a strong man to tote it for me." From the looks of the banker's shoulders, he might qualify.

He pushed his chair back and stood. "I'll see what I can do. The hotel is around the corner, and I'll show you to it. They can send someone for the trunk."

Sarah Beth tucked the deed into her reticule then stood. "Very well." At least he would take care of the matter for her. She walked through the door he held open, then followed him out of the bank.

Emery didn't know what to think of Sarah Beth Taylor. It'd been a while since he'd seen such a refined Southern lady. The last time he'd seen one was during the war when his troops had ravaged the land as they crossed through the state of Georgia. Seeing this woman in his bank and hearing her Southern drawl brought back memories, not all good. But Miss Taylor was quite lovely, a welcome sight in this drab town. Her delicate appearance, with her blond ringlets and ivory complexion that had never seen sunlight, belied her feisty attitude. She wore her form-fitting purple traveling suit and matching hat perched high on her head like a queen and a woman of means. Obviously, she'd come from a pampered home and was used to getting her way. She might be disappointed if her Southern charm didn't work as well out here.

Why had she come out west if she had means? Her uncle had mentioned the loss of her family and hinted at bad times, but Emery could only surmise what that meant. Was she that desperate? One wouldn't get that opinion of her.

But how would she survive in this rough environment? This town was no place for the fainthearted. No doubt she'd be surprised, if not shocked, to find Crinoline Creek didn't offer the luxuries she'd enjoyed previously. As they walked down the sidewalk to the hotel, three cowboys galloped into town, stirring up the dust. She waved her hand in front of her face.

"My stars, shouldn't they be more careful?"

He kept quiet. If she only knew how rowdy cowboys could be.

They entered the hotel and walked to the front desk. "Yes sir, Mr. Wright, can I help you?" the clerk asked, offering a smile.

But before Emery could answer, the cowboys stormed into the hotel.

"Where's the saloon?" they shouted.

"Sorry, sir. It's closed," the clerk said.

"Closed? What on earth for?" The tallest cowboy took off his hat and slapped his thigh with it, creating a cloud of dust.

"Yes, sir. The Thirsty Spur closed about a month ago. The owner went out to California to strike it rich."

Sarah Beth Taylor jerked her head toward Emery. "The Thirsty Spur is a saloon?"

Chapter 2

She owned a saloon? Mother would roll over in her grave. Why didn't Uncle Homer tell her his establishment was a saloon? His letter said he had regular customers who enjoyed the refreshments he served. But liquor? My word! And Mr. Emery Wright hadn't had the backbone to tell her the truth when he'd handed her the deed. Her first impression of him as a gentleman had taken a step down.

Sarah Beth splashed her face from the basin in her room, shocked to see the dirty water she created. She'd love to take a real bath, but this primitive hotel didn't supply rooms with tubs. Once she got her own home she wouldn't have to worry about that. She studied her image in the mirror of the washstand. *Well, Sarah Beth Taylor, you've got your work cut out for you. That saloon of Uncle*

Homer's is going to be the nicest café in Crinoline Creek, maybe the only café in town, but it would definitely be the best in this part of Texas. So help me, God.

Tomorrow, she'd inspect her new establishment and get to work changing it into a café. Thirsty Spur indeed. That was no name for her place of business. It needed a special name. Perhaps the Southern Charm Café. Now that sounded much better.

"Mother, the woman has no place in this town." Emery poured himself a cup of coffee then brought it to the breakfast table and sat down. "I'm afraid she's going to have a rude awakening."

"Where did you say she's from?" Mother sipped tea from her rose-covered china cup.

"Somewhere near Savannah. Homer said they'd had a fine plantation before the war. It may have been one of the ones the Union troops burned on the way to the sea."

"I'm sure that was quite a shock to her." She set her cup down on the saucer and brushed a crumb from the lace tablecloth. "Her parents—they're deceased?"

Emery nodded. "According to Homer, she has no other family left."

"That poor child. She must be terrified being all alone out here in this strange place."

"If she is, she sure doesn't show it." He chuckled. "She acts like she's ready to take on whatever comes her way. But of course, she can't."

"Why not?" Mother's clear blue eyes studied him. "Aren't you selling her short? She hasn't even had a chance."

Emery shook his head. "Mother, this woman is used to telling people what to do, and they do it." He forked a bite of pie. "She has no one to boss around here."

"Doesn't the woman have a name? You keep calling her 'this woman.'"

"Sarah Beth Taylor."

"So Miss Taylor inherited Homer's saloon? My, my. It'll take some work to change it into a café."

"A lot of work. Especially a fancy one like she described to me."

"Who's going to help her?"

"I have no idea. Maybe her Southern charm will persuade someone."

"Emery, you can find someone to help her, can't you?"

Emery held his hands up in front of him. "I really don't want to get involved, Mother. I can't take on everyone else's problems. The military broke me of that."

Mother pointed her spoon at him. "Emery Wright. You've been raised better than that. You know people in this town, and she doesn't. The very least you can do is find someone to help her."

"All right, Mother, I will. But that's all I'm going to do. Miss Taylor made it clear she wants to do things for herself, and I'm willing to let her. I've got enough to concern myself with at the bank." He checked his watch. "Speaking of which, I better go to work." He pushed away from the table and stood, then leaned over and kissed his mother on the cheek. As he grabbed his hat from the hall tree, he paused.

"What is it, Son? You forget something?"

He nodded. "I'm afraid I told Miss Taylor I'd take her to her saloon. She's probably waiting for me at the hotel, and she was pretty miffed that I forgot to meet her at the stagecoach yesterday."

Mother waved her hand toward him. "Then hurry up. Don't keep the young lady waiting."

As Emery hurried down the boardwalk, he pictured Sarah Beth Taylor in all her finery, expecting to find a look of annoyance on her face when he arrived. But when he stepped into the hotel lobby, he was taken aback.

"Good morning, Mr. Wright! I've been talking to this nice man. Judd, isn't it?" She smiled in her sweet Southern manner and tilted her head at Judd Barton, an overgrown boy who helped tidy the hotel. Judd leaned on a broom, the tips of his ears red as he returned her smile. "Judd said he'd be happy to help me clean up my establishment. Isn't that so, Judd?" She batted her long eyelashes at him.

"Yes'm, if the boss don't need me here."

So she'd already found help. Obviously, she didn't need *his* anymore. Emery would deliver her to her place then get to work as he'd planned.

"That's good. I'm sure Judd can be a lot of help to you." The boy had plenty of brawn to make up for his lack of brains. "Are you ready to go see your, er, business?"

"I've been ready since I arrived in town!" She pulled on her gloves, stood, and took Emery's arm. "Judd, you come on down when you can. I'm sure you know where it is."

"Yes, ma'am. I'll be there quicker than a jackrabbit, if'n it's all right."

Miss Taylor gave him another coy smile, then turned and accompanied Emery out the door. She wasn't wearing the fine suit from yesterday. Instead, she wore a simple white blouse tucked into a gray skirt that accentuated her tiny waist. The black ribbon of her straw bonnet was tied under her chin. Even in plain clothes, the woman put on airs like royalty.

"Did you rest well, Miss Taylor?" She certainly looked refreshed.

"Yes, quite, although I could hear people in other rooms. I'm looking forward to having my own house here."

Emery lifted an eyebrow. "Homer lived up above the saloon. Will you be living there as well?"

"Above the sa. . .café? Why, I never considered the possibility. But maybe it would be better than the hotel, at least temporarily."

Emery wasn't so sure it would be better than the hotel. He hadn't seen Homer's room, but he knew Homer and doubted the room was up to Miss Taylor's standards. But that was none of his business. She could fix it up to suit herself.

They walked back down the street and turned at the corner, stopping in front of the door to the saloon. The glass in the door was covered with dust, as were the windows on either side, making it near to impossible to see inside. A faded sign that said SALOON hung loosely above the door. Miss Taylor eyed the sign.

"Well, that needs to come down first!"

He agreed but realized she couldn't reach it without a ladder, so he stretched up and grabbed the sign, jerking it free. "Here you go." He offered the sign to her.

She frowned and shook her head. "I don't want that thing. Please throw it away."

He dropped the sign beside the door. Her ladyship could ask Judd to take care of that chore for her.

She pulled the key from her skirt pocket and tried it in the door. But no matter how she twisted and turned it, she couldn't get the door open.

"May I?" He extended his hand, and she dropped the key in it.

He wiggled the key and doorknob just right, and the lock gave way. He turned the knob and pushed, gesturing for her to go inside. "Welcome to your new establishment."

Sarah Beth stifled the gasp that tried to escape her mouth. She waved the dust motes floating through the dim light of the window away from her face. What a dismal place. Dark, dusty, and disarrayed, the room was filled with tables and chairs scattered haphazardly throughout. A long counter ran in front of the shelf-lined back wall, and the odor of stale smoke and spilled liquor filled the room. It truly was a saloon. How on earth could she turn this place into the café she envisioned? The enormity of the task threatened to overwhelm her, and she wanted to cry and run back home. But there was no home to go back to, and she'd learned that crying wouldn't solve any problems. She certainly wouldn't let Mr. Wright see her cry.

Daddy had always told her a Taylor never runs from a challenge. So she wouldn't. Daddy also told her she could do anything she made up her mind to do. She just had to set her mind on it.

Mr. Wright watched her. "Is it what you expected?"

"Well, since I've never been in a saloon, I didn't know what to expect." She glanced around the room. "Is there a kitchen anywhere?"

He nodded. "Back through that door. Homer usually offered something, usually stew or soup."

She headed for the door he'd indicated and shoved it open. In a small room she found a stove and a table. A large skillet and big pot sat on the stove—not much of a kitchen. Pushing open a door in the wall, she found a small storage room. She pointed to another door in the back. "Where does that go?"

"Outside. That's where the pump is."

"Oh. How convenient." She spun and strode out of the room and back into the main room. "Would you show me the living quarters now, please?"

Mr. Wright followed her and pointed to stairs going up one end of the room. "Up there."

She strode to the stairs and stepped up one creaking board at a time. At the top, there was a door partially ajar. Sarah Beth steeled herself to go in, wishing Mr. Wright would go first.

"Shall I lead the way?" He walked ahead of her and pushed the door all the way open, then went inside while she waited, looking in past him. He poked his head back out. "You can come in. It appears safe."

Sarah Beth stepped inside and scanned the room. At one end was a simple iron bed. Beside it was a chest of drawers and a washstand. On the other side was a sofa and small round table. Two windows allowed light to seep through. The room was simple, more like the hotel room she was staying in now, but it wasn't clean, and it reeked of stale odor. She couldn't imagine calling that one room home, but she couldn't afford to stay at the hotel forever. No, this would have to do, but not in its present condition. Holding her breath, she strode to the windows and forced them open, then exhaled and brushed her hands off. At least she could get some fresh air in here.

She walked back out of the room and hurried past Mr. Wright and down the stairs.

"Are you all right?" Mr. Wright followed her.

She rushed to the front door and threw it open, sucking in the outside air.

"Miss Taylor?" Mr. Wright's look of concern was genuine. "Have you changed your mind about the place? Would you like me to find a buyer, and you can go back to Georgia?"

She fired a glance at him. "Change my mind? Of course not. I just needed some fresh air." She removed her bonnet and fanned herself with it. "Mr. Wright, there is no going back. My daddy always said, 'Never look back at where you've been. Keep your eyes straight ahead so you can see where you're going.'"

"Wise man."

"Yes, the wisest." She surveyed the inside of the saloon again. "Well, I better get to work. There's much to be done. Thank you for accompanying me. I'm sure you need to get to the bank now."

He arched his eyebrows. "Yes, I do. I'll leave you to your work." He tipped his hat as he started out the door, almost running into Judd Barton. "Excuse me, Judd. I was just leaving."

Judd nodded at him as he blew past to get inside, his eyes fixed on Sarah Beth Taylor.

"I'm so happy to see you, Judd! We have so much to do. First, let's air this place out. Can you raise all the windows down here? When you get finished with that, help me fill a bucket and find something to clean this place with." Sarah Beth's enthusiasm took over her initial disappointment in the place.

Mr. Wright stood just outside the door. "Good day, Mr. Wright." She turned to Judd. "Let's get to work, Judd!"

The banker seemed to be in a hurry to leave. Sarah Beth couldn't figure him out. He obviously was too fine a gentleman to get dirty cleaning her establishment, yet he didn't hesitate to go inside before she did. However, it was clear he was too nicely dressed for this place, at least for the time being. One of these days, her café would attract all the nicely dressed and well-to-do. She was sure of it. She had to be.

❧ Chapter 3 ❧

*E*mery glanced back over his shoulder, surprised to have been dismissed so easily by Miss Taylor. She seemed more excited to have Judd there than himself. Well, he'd done his charitable duty as Mother suggested and shown Miss Taylor her establishment. She didn't need his help anymore. Judd was strong, a good worker, and didn't mind being bossed around, as he often was. From the look on his face when he glanced at Miss Taylor, he would do whatever she wanted him to do. Well, good for her.

The bank was just around the corner and across the street from the saloon. Close enough if she needed anything. Not that he wanted to be bothered. After all, he'd done his part as far as Sarah Beth Taylor was concerned. He unlocked the bank and let the teller in who waited for him by the door.

"Good morning, Mr. Wright."

"Good morning, George."

George followed Emery to the safe. Emery opened it, pulled out some money, and handed it to the teller. As George went behind the teller's window, Emery opened the shutters on the windows and door to signify the bank was open for business. He paused to stare across the street.

"She's right pretty, ain't she?" George said.

"Hmm?" Emery turned to look at the teller, heat rushing to his face. "You mean Miss Taylor? Yes, I suppose she is."

Emery went to his office and tried to do some work, pushing papers around his desk, but the image of Sarah Beth Taylor's face kept getting in the way of his focus. He checked his watch several times to see if it was time for the midday meal, wondering why the watch was so slow. Finally, at eleven o'clock, he stood and grabbed his hat off the hat rack, then walked into the main lobby. He waved to George, who had a customer in front of him, and George nodded.

He planned to eat in the hotel dining room, the only place besides the boardinghouse to eat these days unless he went home. The town could certainly use a café, the way it was growing. Speaking of cafés, how was Miss Taylor's coming along? Perhaps he should stop by and check on her, maybe even invite her to lunch. She must be hungry after working all morning.

When he stepped through the doors of the former saloon, he halted, shocked by the change. The floor had been swept, and all the tables and chairs had been cleaned and polished. He glanced around at the clear windows and at the mirror reflecting behind the bar. Someone had worked hard. Had Judd done all this? A clinking noise came from behind the bar.

"Hello? Anyone here?" Could there be rats back there? Where was Miss Taylor? "Hello?"

Blond hair popped up from behind the bar, then the rest of Miss Taylor followed. "I'm back here." Then she disappeared again.

Emery sauntered to the bar and peered over the top. "What are you doing down there?"

"Finding glasses."

He tried not to laugh at the dust smudged on her pretty face and streaked on her blouse sleeves. "To see out of or to drink out of?"

She stood up and twisted her lips, hair tendrils hanging loose from her coiffure. "Why, Mr. Wright, I do believe you have a sense of humor. To drink from, of course. There's a bunch of glasses up under here. Most of them are those short, squatty ones men drink whiskey from, but I'm sure there must be some decent iced tea glasses here somewhere."

Iced tea? He'd never known of anyone ordering iced tea in a saloon before. And ice was a rare commodity around here. Miss Taylor wore a stained apron that swallowed her, almost reaching the floor and tied several times around her waist. She lifted the apron to pat the perspiration on her face.

"Where'd you get the apron?"

She glanced down at herself. "Back in that room." She pointed toward the kitchen. "It's a little big but serviceable."

"I see." He glanced around the room. "Looks like you've made a lot of progress toward getting this place clean. Guess Judd's a good helper."

"He sure is, and a sweet boy too. Why, he even offered to go fetch us something to eat from the hotel. Isn't that sweet?"

Sweet? Judd? "I thought you might want to take a break, so I was going to ask if you wanted to accompany me there for some lunch. But I see that won't be necessary."

She gave an endearing smile. "Well, aren't you thoughtful, Mr. Wright! However, I can't afford to waste time now. I've got to get this place ready for customers!"

"Yes, of course. Then I'll let you get back to work."

She grabbed his wrist, her touch sending a warm jolt up his arm. "Oh, please stay a few minutes. I'm fixing to make a list of things to get from the mercantile and hope you can help me figure out what I need." She came around the bar, removed the apron, laying it on top, then walked to the nearest table and patted it. "Come over here and sit down. Do you have anything to write with or on?"

"A banker always has both." He followed her to the table and sat beside her, reaching into his pocket for a pencil and small, leather-bound notebook. Opening it, he poised the pencil. "So what's first? Dishes? Cooking utensils?"

She tapped her chin. "Both. I need a whole set of plates, bowls, cups, and saucers."

Emery wrote it down. "Pots and pans?"

"Yes, a few of those too. And some big spoons to stir with. Uncle Homer only left me a cast-iron skillet and one pot! Can you imagine that's all he had?"

"Well, he didn't cook much."

"My menu will have a much better variety."

"I suppose you need staples—flour, sugar, salt, lard."

She nodded. "And some pretty napkins."

Emery couldn't imagine pretty napkins were a priority. "What else do you need for food?"

Miss Taylor stared at him. "I can't think right now. Maybe when I go to the store, I'll remember what else I need."

"Do you have your menu written out?" It seemed odd that she didn't know what her recipes called for.

"Yes, of course. But I don't have it with me right now."

Judd came in carrying a large basket covered by a red-and-white checked cloth and set it on the table in front of them looking quite pleased with himself. "Here's your food, Miss Taylor."

"Why, thank you, Judd." Her Southern drawl took her twice as long to say things, but the effect on Judd was mesmerizing. "Won't you sit down and eat with me?"

Judd jerked off his hat and grabbed a chair, then spotted Emery as if for the first time. "Oh, I'm sorry, Mr. Wright." His face drooped with repentance. "I didn't know you was eatin' too."

Emery stood, waving his hand to allay Judd's fears of inadequacy. "I'm not, Judd." Emery tore off the slip of paper and handed it to Miss Taylor, leaving the pencil on the table. "I was just leaving. You two go ahead."

Judd sat, and Miss Taylor offered a smile. "Thank you for coming by, Mr. Wright. Next time you see this place, it'll look brand-new!"

Emery donned his hat as he headed out the door. "I can't wait to see the transformation."

🌿

Sarah Beth looked at the list while Judd gobbled down his food. What else did she need? She tried to remember what was in the kitchen back on the plantation when she'd go there to talk to

Maudie, their cook. Pepper? Yes, she needed that too. But what else?

"Judd?"

He looked up from the food he was hunched over. "Ma'am?" He squeezed in the word midchew.

"Judd, do you know anything about cooking?"

His eyes widened. "Just a little. Sometimes I help my Granny cook. You don't want me to cook, do you?"

"Silly boy, I'm not asking you to cook. I just wondered if you could think of what I need to buy for the kitchen."

"Eggs?"

She pointed the pencil at him. "Good idea. Where do I get them?"

"Chickens?"

Sarah Beth sighed. "Yes, of course. Chickens. Do you know anyone who has some that I can get eggs from?"

Judd nodded.

"Well?" The conversation was going nowhere.

"Miss Taylor? I bet the cook at the hotel knows what you need for your kitchen."

"Why Judd, that's an excellent idea!" She took a bite of biscuit. Biscuits! She'd serve biscuits and eggs for breakfast. That shouldn't be too hard to do. She'd watched Maudie make them a hundred times. "Tell you what, Judd. Soon as we're finished eating, I'm going to run some errands. First, I'll stop at the mercantile and see what they have. And then maybe I'll go to the hotel and talk to the cook. Can you do me a big favor and stay here while I'm gone?" She batted her eyelashes. "I have something very important for you to do."

"Oh yes, ma'am." Judd drew himself up. "I can do whatever you need."

"Sugar, you're such a blessing!" She pointed to the bar. "Would you find all the glasses back there and wash them for me?" She gave him her most endearing smile. "I want everything here to be so clean, you can eat off the floor!"

"Yes, ma'am. I sure will."

Sarah Beth left most of her food untouched and offered it to Judd, who gladly accepted. She had too much to do to eat right now. She excused herself and hurried to check her appearance in the mirror behind the bar. Goodness! What a sight. If only her room here was ready, she could run upstairs and freshen up. Why, she'd move in this afternoon. Surely the mercantile carried bed linens.

"Judd? One more thing, please."

"Anything, ma'am."

"Would you please make sure my room upstairs is clean and that the mattress has been taken outside and beaten? I think I'll move my things over from the hotel and stay here tonight."

Judd's eyes bugged out. "You sure you want to do that, Miss Taylor? Stay here all by yourself?"

"Why, of course. This is where I'll be living from now on."

"You won't be scared?"

"Now why would I be scared? Do I look like I'm too fragile?"

"Well. . ."

"Never mind. Just take care of it, please."

"Yes, ma'am. Whatever you say, ma'am."

She brushed the dust off her blouse and shook out her skirt, then repinned her hair. Grabbing her bonnet and gloves, she hurried out the door. Now, where did she see that mercantile? Two ladies engrossed in conversation walked past her on the boardwalk. They would know.

"Excuse me, ladies. I'm new in town. Would you please direct me to the mercantile?"

The ladies looked at each other and giggled. One of them pointed to the storefront beside hers. "Why it's right there!"

Heat rushed to her face. "Ha ha. As my daddy used to say, 'If it was a snake, it would've bit me!'"

The other ladies glanced at each other, then gave her a polite smile and continued walking, lowering their heads to talk, no doubt about her. Well, that was fine. Soon they'd be talking about what a wonderful café she had.

Sarah Beth walked next door to the mercantile. The bell on the door rang as she opened it, and the man behind the counter looked up and gave her a huge smile.

"Good day, ma'am. Can I help you find anything?"

She strolled to the counter. "Oh my, yes, you can! I'm Sarah Beth Taylor, and I've just acquired the business next door."

The man straightened. "The saloon? Oh, you must be Homer's niece. He told me he was handing it over to you." The shopkeeper extended his hand. "William Greene. Nice to meet you, Miss Taylor. Forgive me for saying it, but you don't strike me as a saloonkeeper."

Sarah Beth giggled. "You are right, Mr. Greene. I am certainly not a saloonkeeper. I'm turning the saloon into a respectable café."

"You don't say. Well, more power to you. This town could use a nice café. So I suppose you'll be needing some things to accomplish that."

"Yes, I will, and I hope you have what I need."

"I try. Got a little bit of everything."

Sarah Beth handed her list to Mr. Greene.

He looked it over. "Yes, I have these things. Do you know how many of each you need—glasses, plates, and so on?"

How many? She hadn't thought of that. As if reading her mind, he continued.

"How many tables and chairs do you have?"

She counted in her head. "Five tables with four chairs each."

"That's twenty. Will you be serving anyone at the bar?"

"No, sir. Everyone will eat at a table like a civilized person."

He chuckled and looked back down at the list. "Pretty napkins? We've got some napkins over there, but I don't know how 'pretty' they are."

Sarah Beth walked to the shelf he pointed out and riffled through the small stack of linens. "I was hoping for something with a bit more detail."

"We can order them. I have a brand-new catalog here you can look at." He handed Sarah Beth the book, and she flipped to the page with napkins. Selecting one, she pointed it out to Mr. Greene. "These will be perfect."

"Yes, ma'am. I'll order them for you." He glanced back at her list. "I see you have some food supplies listed here. Are you sure you want them right now? When do you expect to open for business?"

"Soon as I can. Maybe next week?"

"I'll see if I can get the napkins by then. But if I were you, I wouldn't get any food until you know you're ready to open. You don't want the rats getting into it."

Rats? They came inside?

"Why, you're so smart to think of that. I'll wait on the food then."

"Since I'm right next door, I can get your purchases to you as soon as they come in."

"That would be so kind of you, Mr. Greene." Sarah Beth scanned the room. "Sir, do you have any bed linens?"

"Why, yes, ma'am, they're right over here." He walked her over to a table with blankets and pillows stacked up. He moved the blankets aside to reveal the sheets beneath them. "Where will you be living, Miss Taylor?"

"Above my establishment like Uncle Homer did."

Mr. Greene's eyes widened, and his mouth fell open. "By yourself, ma'am?"

"Well, I don't have a husband, so yes, by myself. Why does that surprise you?"

"I. . .uh. . .just never knew a woman to live by herself, least not a young woman like yourself."

Alarm raced through Sarah Beth. Was he suggesting she was a woman of loose morals?

"Mr. Greene, are you a God-fearing man?"

"Why, of course I am. Why do you ask?"

"Because I want you to know I'm a God-fearing woman. The good Lord has gotten me through some terrible times the last few years, losing my parents and my home, but He's still looking after me. And I expect He will continue to do so."

The storekeeper's face reddened as he stammered, "Oh yes, ma'am. I'm sure He will."

Another customer came in the door, and Mr. Greene excused

himself to go wait on him. Sarah Beth chose some bedsheets and pillowcases. As she was walking back to the front, a lady came through a door behind the counter. The woman's grayish-brown hair was parted down the middle and pulled tight into a bun, a severe style that matched the stern expression on her face. She stared at Sarah Beth, eyeing her up and down. When Mr. Greene was finished with the other customer, he turned to Sarah Beth. "Sorry for the interruption, Miss Taylor." Noticing the woman who had just joined him at his side, he said, "Miss Taylor, this is my wife, Imogene. Imogene, this is Sarah Beth Taylor. Miss Taylor is Homer Taylor's niece, and she's changing the saloon into a café."

"Nice to meet you, Mrs. Greene." *Kill 'em with kindness, Daddy used to say.*

Mrs. Greene nodded, expressionless, as if her face might break if she moved a muscle in it.

"I'll get together twenty-four plates, cups, saucers, and bowls for you. That'll give you a little extra in case something gets broken. You'll be needing silverware too, I assume?"

"Well, I won't be having people eat with their fingers!" Sarah Beth chuckled, attempting to get a response from Mrs. Greene. "Oh, and I'll need some cooking spoons and a good knife too."

"Yes, ma'am, will do. Did you want to start an account or pay me now?"

Mrs. Greene jerked her head and glared at him.

"I can pay you now. What do I owe you?" After tallying the bill, Mr. Greene showed it to her. She hid a gulp but pulled the money out of her reticule and handed it over. Would her reticule be empty before her café started making money? She wasn't about to take charity from anyone, especially someone as inhospitable as Mrs. Greene.

Mr. Greene took the money and deposited it in his cash register. "I'll bring the things over after a while."

"Thank you so much." She extended her gloved hand. "It's a *pleasure* doing business with you." Facing Mrs. Greene, she said, "I look forward to being neighbors with y'all."

Chapter 4

ood afternoon, Miss Taylor." The hotel clerk grinned as she entered the small lobby. "How are you today?"

"I'm fine, thank you. Could you do me a very big favor, sugar?"

"Yes, ma'am. I'll try to. What do you need?"

"I'd like for someone to please carry my trunk over to my new establishment. I'll be moving in over there."

His mouth fell open. "You're moving to the saloon, ma'am?"

"It's not a saloon anymore. It's a café, and it has suitable living quarters available there." At least they would be suitable when she got through with them. "I'm going to my room to freshen up, but please send someone in a little while to get the trunk."

"Yes, ma'am. Say, is Judd still over at your. . .um, your café?"

"Yes, he is. He's been such a dear and has helped me immensely today. Why, does he need to come back here?"

"Well, he's the one who'd carry your trunk. We haven't seen him since he left here this morning and said he was going to help you."

"I see. Well then, when I go back to the café, I'll send him over." She started toward the stairs, then turned to the hotel restaurant. At the entrance was a large slate board with the day's special.

"Would you like to be seated, ma'am?" An aproned young lady approached.

"Not right now, thank you. But do you have a paper menu I can borrow?"

"Yes, ma'am. Here's one."

Sarah Beth took the menu and headed upstairs to her room. Such a meager selection! She'd offer more variety for her customers. The menu resembled a piece of stationery with the name of the establishment at the top and the categories listed. The day's selections were written in by hand under the categories. She envisioned the name of her own café emblazoned across the top of her menus, "The Southern Charm Café." A thrill of pride triggered her pulse to race. She couldn't wait to open for business!

Sarah Beth rinsed her face and hands in the basin, then threw her mirror and brush into her reticule and glanced around to make sure she'd picked up all her belongings. It would take some work, but she hoped to make her room over the café as comfortable as this one.

She hurried back to the café and found Judd washing glasses in a tub out back. "Hello, Judd. I can take over from here. Would you please go to the hotel for my trunk and bring it back over here?"

He grinned at her. "Yes, ma'am. I'll go right away." He handed her the rag he'd been using. "Oh, I got a surprise for you."

"A surprise? Do tell. Where is it?"

He crooked his finger. "Come see." He went back inside, and she followed him to the bar. Reaching down, he pulled out a brown bottle. "Sarsaparilla! You got some sarsaparilla! I found it when I was looking for glasses."

"I do? Well, that's a nice surprise. How many bottles are there?"

"'Bout twenty or so."

"That should be enough for my opening day." She clapped her hands. "I have a wonderful idea! We can have a celebration when we open and pour glasses of sarsaparilla for our guests."

"Yes, ma'am." He eyed the bottle hungrily.

"Judd, when you get back with my trunk, I'll have a little treat for you!"

"Me?" His face turned red.

"So hurry on." She waved her hand toward the door. "So you can get your treat."

"Yes, ma'am!" He rushed out the door, almost bumping into Mr. Greene carrying a crate. "Oh, sorry, Mr. Greene."

The storekeeper had stepped back to avoid the collision, grasping the crate. His look of irritation left as he entered the café door. "Miss Taylor. Here're your dishes. Where should I put them?"

"Right there on the bar would be good."

He set them down, then blew out a breath and looked around. "The place is looking a lot better already."

"Thank you, Mr. Greene." She walked to the bar and peered into the crate. "Ah, there they are." She pulled out the sheets and pillowcases. Holding them against her chest, she surveyed the room. "You know, I just remembered a few more things I need to make this place pretty. I need tablecloths and curtains. Do you have any?"

"I have a few, but I'll have to check to see if I have enough. But perhaps you'd like to see what they look like first."

The image of his stern-faced wife came to mind. "Well, the curtains should be lace, and the tablecloths should be linen, perhaps with some flowers embroidered on the edges?"

"Ma'am, if you don't mind my asking. . .are you going to serve men too?"

"Why, of course. Why do you ask?"

He shrugged. "I don't know, just sounds like a place for women, what with all the lace and flowers and such."

Sarah Beth frowned. How dare he criticize her ideas? Yet, what if he was right? She needed men to come in too. After all, they were the ones with the money, for the most part. "Perhaps I'll use plain tablecloths, but with pretty napkins. But I definitely want those curtains."

"Yes, ma'am. I'll make sure you get some." He wiped his hands on his shopkeeper's apron. "Well, I guess I better be getting back to the store."

No doubt his wife was counting the minutes until his return.

"Thank you so much, Mr. Greene." She walked him to the door. "You're such a dear to bring my things over. I'm so glad you could carry that heavy box for me. I'm afraid I'm just not that strong."

Mr. Greene's face flushed as he hurried out the door, and Sarah Beth smiled to herself at the good fortune she'd had to find such helpful people in Crinoline Creek. God was surely blessing her with good neighbors, a sign He would bless her new café with success as well.

Judd stumbled in with her trunk. "Thank you, sugar. Will you please take it upstairs for me?" He huffed out a breath then turned toward the stairs. Sarah Beth laid her hand on his arm. "Just a minute. I'll get your surprise."

He set the trunk on the floor, eyebrows lifted. Sarah Beth retrieved a bottle of the sarsaparilla and handed it to him. "This is for your help."

His eyes widened as he took the bottle. He pulled the cork out, then tilting back his head, he gulped it down. He paused to look at her. "This is real good. Thank you, ma'am."

"You are very welcome. I'll have to ask Mr. Greene to order some more for us."

When he finished the bottle, he exhaled a deep sigh then belched. Sarah Beth frowned, and he apologized. She followed him as he carried her trunk upstairs, showing him where to place it in the room. "Thank you. Now I can get busy fixing this area up. You can go on back down and finish putting the clean glasses away, then you can go back to the hotel or home, wherever you're expected."

"Yes, ma'am." Judd left the room, and his heavy footsteps sounded on the stairs.

Sarah Beth unfolded the sheets and made the bed. Then she lifted her trunk lid and pulled out a quilt. As she laid it on the bed, she stroked it with her hand. Three women had worked on the basket quilt—Grandmother, Mother, and herself—working together for hours, cutting, pinning, and sewing the design. Pink calico flowers on green stems grew from baskets made of pink and green. Sarah Beth had felt so grown-up being able to work alongside the other women in the family. Now she was the only one left. Her eyes misted at the memory of times past.

She finished arranging her room, making it as homey as possible with the meager furnishings. But at least she had a bed, a lamp and table, a chair, a chest of drawers, and a washstand, which would do until she could acquire more.

What else did she need to do? She hadn't put away the new dishes Mr. Greene brought over. Her steps seemed unusually loud as she went downstairs, surveying the empty room as she descended. For the first time, she realized how alone she would be that night. Would Mr. Wright come back by when he left the bank? But why should he? He had no other business with her, at least until he became a customer of the café. She pushed aside thoughts of the handsome banker and got to work removing each dish and piece of silverware from the crate, wiping it off, then placing it on a shelf behind the bar. The light dimmed as the afternoon progressed to nighttime and she finished putting away the last piece. There was nothing left to do but lock up and go to her room. She could finish working on her menu upstairs. She'd be uncomfortable sitting at one of the tables downstairs by herself by the lamp, since anyone who passed by could see her through the windows.

Sarah Beth hurried to lock the door, wishing she had shutters to cover the windows. She grabbed the kerosene lamp and lit it, then carried it to the kitchen and made sure the back door was closed and locked as well. The lamp only made the rest of the room darker, and she shuddered as her surroundings became more foreign. Grabbing her skirt with one hand and the lamp with the other, she climbed the stairs to her room and closed the door behind her.

Emery locked up the bank and stared across the street. What was Miss Taylor doing? The sun had fallen behind the buildings, and the street was practically empty, as everyone had gone home for the day. He imagined Miss Taylor relaxing back in her room at the hotel, tired from the effort she'd expended cleaning up the saloon. He chuckled at the way she looked this morning in the oversized apron with dirt on her clothes and her tousled hair. Funny how even with being so disheveled, she was still pretty.

But did she really know what she was doing? Or had she taken on more than she could handle? She didn't lack for enthusiasm, that was for sure. But her request for him to help her with what she needed seemed odd. Seemed like she should've known those things already. He shrugged. Why did he concern himself? It wasn't like he had an interest in the café. She owned the deed free and clear.

He headed toward home, but as he was walking past the hotel, he thought he'd look in the dining room and see if she was there. Just in case she needed him for anything. He entered the front door and walked to the open doorway of the dining room, scanning the patrons seated inside. A waiter approached.

"Can I help you, sir?"

"Yes, is Miss Sarah Beth Taylor in here, or has she already dined?"

"No, sir, she's not here. I heard she moved to the saloon today. She's gonna live there, you know, where Homer did, upstairs."

"Oh, of course. Thank you."

The waiter nodded and walked away. She was already staying in the saloon? The idea didn't sit right with him. Even though it was no longer a saloon, it didn't seem to be suitable arrangements for a young woman. Wasn't she afraid? Most women would be afraid to stay alone in such a place. He had the urge to go stand guard nearby, but that was ridiculous. Apparently, he'd been a soldier too long. He wouldn't argue that fact. But would that life and those memories ever let go of him? Even though he tried to immerse himself in work, battle scenes appeared in his mind without warning. The war had ended for the country, but his own private war still raged.

Sarah Beth strained to see in the dim kerosene light while she wrote out her menu. She would offer some of the things Maudie had cooked back on the plantation. She also wanted to serve some of the items from her favorite café in Savannah. The hotel menu had helped her fill out her list. The Southern Charm Café would have a wonderful menu with delicious pies and cakes for dessert. She yawned and stretched as sleep called her to bed. She got up one more time to make sure her door was closed and locked, but she was so tired, she didn't even care to be afraid.

She turned off the lamp and climbed into bed as moonlight filled the room. As she closed her eyes, she heard a noise. Her eyes popped open. What was that? She listened again. Something was moving in the room. Sleepiness left her as her heart raced. More noise, like rustling, or was it scratching? She sat up slowly as a shadow crossed the floor. Sarah Beth reached for the lamp just in time to glimpse a rat chewing on the leather straps of her trunk.

She let out a scream that scared the rat back to wherever it came from, then she sat up on the bed, shivering. Tears flowed down her face, releasing the exhaustion and fear she'd held inside. Back home, someone would've come to her aid. Father, Mother, Maudie, somebody. But nobody was here for her now. Nobody cared what happened to her anymore.

Chapter 5

Was that a woman's scream? Who was it? Emery ran toward the sound but didn't see anyone outside. He stopped in front of the saloon and looked up. A light shone in the upstairs window. Was Miss Taylor all right?

He banged on the door, imagining all types of troubling scenarios. Had someone broken in? The front door was locked, but someone could've come in the back door. Or what if someone had hidden in there, waiting for her? Or what if some cowboy was looking for the saloon? He kept banging on the door until he saw a light inside moving down the stairs.

"Who is it?" Miss Taylor asked from the other side of the door.

"It's Emery Wright."

The key turned in the door and Miss Taylor opened it, holding a kerosene lamp. She held her ruffled nightgown at the neck with her other hand. Her blond hair hung over her shoulders, and her eyes looked as if she'd been crying.

"Why, Mr. Wright, what are you doing here?" She sniffed and wiped her cheeks with the back of her hand.

"I heard a scream. Was it you?" Emery knew he should avert his eyes, but he couldn't help looking at her.

She nodded. "I'm afraid it was." She lowered her gaze to the floor. "I'm sorry to have bothered you."

"May I ask why you screamed?" She looked so helpless, like a little girl.

"There was a rat in my room." Her gaze traveled to his face, and her lips quivered. "I never had rats in my room before." A tear slid down her cheek.

He couldn't help himself. He took her in his arms and held her. "It's all right. Tomorrow we'll set some traps and get rid of him. . . and any of his friends too."

She stepped back and looked at him. "His friends? There could be more?"

"I don't know, but we'll make sure they leave for good."

"I don't think I can sleep now."

What was he supposed to do? She couldn't very well walk to the hotel in her nightgown.

"Tell you what. Just keep the lamp on all night, and they'll stay away. They only come out at night." He hoped his solution would work.

"Truly?" Her wide eyes implored him to be right.

"Yes, they hate the light."

"All right. I'll keep it burning." She put her hand over her mouth to hide a yawn. "I'm really tired."

"I'm sure you are." He took her hand and patted it between both of his. "You need a good night's sleep. You'll be fine."

She nodded. "Good night."

He tipped his hat. "Good night, Miss Taylor." He stepped back outside as she closed the door, and then he waited for her to turn the key. But she opened it again instead. "Thank you, Mr. Wright." Then she closed the door again and locked it. He watched the light move away and go back up the stairs. *Lord, please keep those rats away so she can sleep.*

Sarah Beth teetered on the chair as she tried to attach the curtains to the window rod. If she were just a little taller. She stretched up on her tiptoes. Where was Judd? Was he coming to help her today?

The door opened and bumped her chair, and she fell, right into Judd's arms! He was as surprised as she was, and his face turned beet red.

"Miss Turner? Whatcha doin'?"

She wiggled out of his arms to stand on the floor. "I'm trying to hang curtains, but I'm just too short. I am so happy to see you!"

Judd offered a shy smile, a blush still pinking his ears. He removed his hat and held it in front of him. "I'm happy to see you too, Miss Turner."

"Well, let's get to work! I want to get all these windows covered."

"Yes, ma'am."

He took over the hanging as she supervised and handed him each curtain.

"Judd, I need a cat."

"You do?"

"Yes, I need a cat to get rid of the rats around here. I'll have you know there was one in my room last night!"

"There was? Did you get him?"

Sarah Beth stepped back with her hand over her chest. "Me? Get him? I think not!"

"You gonna set some mousetraps?"

"Yes, I am. I'll go next door and get some from the mercantile as soon as we finish this. But I still want a cat. Can you find me one?"

"Sure. I know lots of folks with cats who won't mind giving one away."

"Good. Please get me one today."

"Yes, ma'am. You want me to check in your room for holes the rats came in through?"

"Why, bless your heart! That would be such a nice thing for you to do. Why don't you check while I'm next door?" She certainly didn't want to oversee that process.

When they got the last curtain hung, Sarah Beth and Judd stepped back to admire their work. "They sure make the room look purty," Judd said.

Sarah Beth smiled. "They do, don't they? The room needed more than plain old shades. Just you wait until I finish with this place!" She grabbed her reticule. "I'm going to get some more things. Maybe you can find the rats—or a cat while I'm gone."

She strode next door to the mercantile. A wagon waited in front of the store. Inside, a bewhiskered portly man heaved a sack on the counter. "You got my flour, sugar, cornmeal, and salt?" he asked Mr. Greene.

Sarah walked to a display and studied it, trying not to interfere with the men, but listening with rapt attention.

"Yes, Jack. And your lard, pepper, beans, dried apples and peaches, and coffee."

"Did you throw a couple sacks of potatoes on there?"

"Put one. You want two?"

"Yeah, put two. Guess that about does it. Just help me load her up, and I'll be on my way."

"Will do, Jack, and I'll bill the Lazy B."

The two men hauled sacks out to the wagon and tossed them in. When they'd finally finished, Mr. Greene came back in, brushing his hands off.

"Good morning, Mr. Greene."

"Why, good morning, Miss Taylor. Sorry I didn't notice you come in. How are you today?"

"Fresh as a peach, since I got some sleep."

"You sleep okay? We thought we heard some noise coming from your place last night."

"Oh, do you live near here?"

He pointed to the door behind him. "Right back there, and up there." He pointed to the ceiling.

So they'd heard her scream? And didn't come see if she was okay? Well, thank God Mr. Wright was nearby. She'd hate to think what would've happened if she'd been in any real trouble.

"So you really are my neighbors. How nice." She glanced around the store. "Do you have mousetraps, Mr. Greene?"

"I sure do. Right over here. How many do you want?" He pointed and walked her to their location. "Got some rat poison too. Want some of that?"

"I'll take five traps. But I don't think I'll take the poison." She shook her head. "That might be bad for the cat."

"You have a cat?"

"Not yet. But I will." Sarah expected his sullen wife to make an appearance any moment. "Mr. Greene, do you know when my other orders will come in?"

"I telegraphed them, so maybe on the next stage. If not, then the next one." He bagged her mousetraps and handed them to her. "That'll be twenty-five cents."

Sarah Beth handed him the money and took the package. "Mr. Greene, who was that man that just left?"

"Oh, that's Jack. He's the cook out at the Lazy B Ranch."

"He bought a lot of food."

"He cooks for ten or twelve cowboys, and it takes a lot to feed them. Anything else you need today?"

She tapped her finger on her lips. "Let's see, there was something. Oh yes, window shades. I need a couple of those for my room."

"Just happen to have some." Mr. Greene strolled to a shelf and took them down, then returned to the register and laid them on the counter. "That'll cost you another twenty-five cents."

"Would you please make sure I have some of the things that ranch cook ordered for my restaurant as well?"

"Yes, ma'am, but he got a lot of supplies. I hope you'll feed as many customers. When do you want them?"

"Well, today is Saturday, so I'd like to have them first thing Monday morning, please." She paid for the shades, picked them up, and turned to leave just as Mrs. Greene appeared through the door behind him. "Thank you, Mr. Greene. It's so nice to have you close by."

"You're welcome. I'm looking forward to some good meals right next door."

Mrs. Greene glowered at him, although he didn't see her. She crossed her arms and cleared her throat. "You have good meals right here already."

Mr. Greene's face reddened, and he sputtered. "Of course, I don't need to eat at the café, but I know many folks in town that would appreciate it."

Sarah Beth added extra sweetness to her smile. "Oh hello, Mrs. Greene. I didn't see you there."

Mrs. Greene's lips straightened in a tight line, and she didn't reply. Sarah Beth's daddy would say she looked like she could spit nails. Sarah Beth hurried out the door before it came to that.

When she returned to the café, she didn't see Judd right away. Thumps and bumps sounded from upstairs, so she carried her purchases up to her room and found him crawling around on the floor.

"Judd? Have you found the holes yet?"

"Found two, but I'm lookin' for more."

"Good. Here's the traps. Please be a darlin' and set a couple in here and also put two in the kitchen and one behind the bar."

"Yes, ma'am."

"Oh, and if you have time, will you please hang these shades on the windows upstairs for me?"

"Yes, ma'am." He stood up. "When do you want me to get you the cat?"

"When you're finished with those things, please." She walked to the door, then stopped. "You know, I need an icebox to keep things cool. I wonder if I can order one from the mercantile."

"An icebox? I heard of them before but never seen one."

"Are you telling me no one in town has an icebox? We had one at the plantation. How do people keep things cold here?"

"We use a springhouse and put things down in it. My granny has one behind her house."

"Does she live far from here? Would she mind if I used it too?"

"I'm sure she won't mind you using it, and she lives just down the street."

"Would you ask her for me, please? Will you be seeing her soon?"

"I reckon I will. I live with her."

"Oh, I see. Well, I have a couple more errands to run. I'll see you later."

It occurred to her that the hotel could tell her where to get eggs and milk, and maybe they could put her in touch with the farmers they used. She couldn't believe that even the hotel didn't have an icebox. She headed toward the hotel, crossing the street thinking about all the things she had to do. A wagon almost hit her, but the driver jerked the horses away just in time. "Lady, watch where you're going!" Sarah Beth opened her mouth to reply, but a cloud of dust from the horses' hooves and wagon wheels covered her. She rushed the rest of the way across the street trying to avoid another collision.

At the hotel, she stopped at the entrance to the restaurant and waited for the waitress to come over.

"Would you please ask your cook to come out? I need to ask him something."

"Ma'am, the cook is busy right now. Can I ask him for you?"

"Oh, I wanted to ask him where he gets his eggs and butter."

"He gets them from Ben Jones, who has a farm just outside of town." Sarah Beth turned to see the man who'd answered her question, a large, well-dressed man with gray hair and a beard. "Why do you want to know?"

"I'm Sarah Beth Taylor, and I'm going to open a café here in town. And who might you be, sir?" She didn't appreciate the man not introducing himself to her first.

"Pleased to make your acquaintance, Miss Taylor. I'm Sam Roberts, the proprietor of this hotel."

"Nice to meet you, Mr. Roberts." She dipped her head in a partial curtsy. "I'm new in town, so I need to find out where to find supplies for my café. I'm fortunate to be next to the mercantile, but they don't have everything I need."

"So you want to use the same suppliers we use." He tucked his thumbs in his vest pockets and rocked back on his heels.

"Well, sir. I suppose so." Was it really his business where she got her milk and eggs?

"But wouldn't it be bad business for us to help our competition?"

"Your competition? Me?"

"Of course. Your place will take business away from ours. Besides, our supplier might not be able to supply both of us, so one of us might get shorted. And I don't want that to be us."

Sarah Beth's ire threatened to come out, but she bit her tongue. "Oh my goodness! Why, I'd never want that to happen! Don't you worry, I'll find my own supplier." She forced a smile. "It was very nice to meet you, Mr. Roberts."

"The pleasure is mine, Miss Taylor." She hurried out the door. Well, she certainly wouldn't ask him for anything ever again. Who else could she ask? Why, Mr. Wright, of course. He had been so helpful to her and was always pleasant. The memory of last night's incident flashed through her mind, and her face warmed. Why, the man had seen her in her nightgown! She might be embarrassed to see him again. He'd even held her in his arms. Oh my. And she barely knew the man. Mama would be horrified. What must he think of her? To be honest, it had felt pretty good to be in his embrace, even if his intentions weren't romantic. *Sarah Beth Taylor! Why are you thinking like that?* She'd just have to pretend that little scene had never happened. And hopefully, he would too.

Chapter 6

Emery was not going near the saloon today. No doubt Miss Taylor was embarrassed about last night. Besides, he had spent enough time worrying about her. Judd was doing a good job of helping her, and that was the kind of help she needed. Yet his arms had fit so comfortably around her. *No.* He wouldn't allow such thoughts.

Bright sunlight blinded him as he stepped out of the bank and bumped into someone. "Excuse me," he said, pushing his hat brim down to shield his eyes.

"Mr. Wright. We keep running into each other." Sarah Beth Taylor looked up at him, her smile as bright as the sunlight.

"I'm so sorry, Miss Taylor. I truly didn't see you." He tipped his hat.

"Can you see me now?" She tilted her head.

He couldn't help but smile back. "Clearly. How are things going at the sa...café?"

"Shaping up."

"Did you take care of that little problem you had last night?"

She raised her eyebrows. "Oh, the rat. Yes. Judd is putting out some mousetraps for me, then he's going to get me a cat."

"A cat? Well, hopefully, it'll be a good mouser."

"Aren't they all?"

"I guess so. I never actually had a cat before."

Miss Taylor's eyes widened. "You know everybody in town, don't you?"

"I suppose I know most of them. Why?"

"I need to get eggs and milk for the café, and you probably know where I can get them."

"Yes, I know a few farmers. They can probably help you with other things too, like vegetables and such."

"Why, I knew you could help me! I just don't know what I'd do without you!"

Emery glanced away, hoping the heat in his face was the sun and not a blush. "Glad to be of service, ma'am."

"Why don't people here have iceboxes?"

"We don't have any ice. The closest ice plant is in San Antonio, about four hundred miles away. By the time the ice got here, it'd be melted. Maybe someday the railroad will come through and we can get things faster, but I don't know when that might be. So meanwhile, we use springhouses."

"Yes, Judd told me about them. He said I could use his granny's, but I hate to be a bother."

"I'm sure she won't mind. She's a sweet old lady and raised

Judd since he was a baby after his parents died. She's done a good job of it."

"Bless her heart. And his too."

"Well hello, Emery!" Priscilla Morgan sashayed up, her lace parasol held aloft. She batted her eyelashes at him, barely glancing at Miss Taylor. "How are you? I haven't seen you lately. How's your dear mother?"

"Priscilla Morgan, this is Sarah Beth Taylor. She's opening a new café here in town."

Priscilla, who was squeezed into her dress with a shoehorn, towered over the petite Miss Taylor, eyeing her up and down. "So you're the one that's turning that old saloon into a café. I knew your uncle Homer. I think he was sweet on me."

"Nice to meet you, Miss Morgan. Unfortunately, I haven't seen my uncle since I was a little girl. He was very kind to leave me the saloon."

Priscilla chuckled. "Too bad he didn't strike gold first, then he could've left you something valuable."

"Miss Morgan, have you heard the expression 'One man's trash is another man's treasure'? Well, in this case, it's a woman's treasure, and I intend to increase its value even more."

Emery enjoyed the verbal combat between the two women but was afraid it might get ugly, knowing Priscilla. "And so you will," he said to Miss Taylor. Not that she needed defending, as she was doing a good job by herself. Yet he needed to silence Priscilla. He took Miss Taylor's elbow and urged her down the boardwalk. "Now let me show you the rest of town. Good day, Priscilla."

Priscilla stood with her mouth open. Hopefully, she wouldn't swallow a fly. He led Miss Taylor away.

"That an old flame of yours?" She glanced sideways at him.

"No. But she wishes she were."

Miss Taylor grinned. "Why, Mr. Wright! You should be ashamed of yourself."

"Probably. Truth is, Priscilla's been after me ever since I moved to town three years ago."

"I take it you didn't wish to get caught."

"Not by her, no."

"So there is no Mrs. Wright?"

"Yes. My mother."

"Oh, and do you live with her?"

"Yes. She asked me to come out here after the war and take over the bank after Father died. So I did."

"I'd like to meet her sometime. Maybe she can be one of my first customers!"

"She'd like that. There aren't too many places for her to go around here."

"So where are you taking me?"

"What?" He looked down at his hand and realized he still held her by the elbow. Startled, he let go. "I'm sorry. I wasn't thinking. Did you have some place in particular you were going? I didn't mean to kidnap you."

She giggled in a cute, melodious way. "Oh, it was fun being kidnapped that way." She glanced at the buildings on either side of the street. "Why is the bank the only building that's whitewashed?"

"That was my father's doing. He was pretty particular about appearances and thought a bank should look dignified."

"Well, I want my place whitewashed too."

"But you're not the only business in the building. You'd have to convince the mercantile to whitewash their side too."

"Why wouldn't they?"

"They never have, so maybe they have no interest in doing so."

"Can't never could!"

"What does that mean?"

"Daddy used to say that. It means you can't do something if you don't try. So I won't know if the Greenes will allow the building to be whitewashed if I don't ask."

"That makes sense. The building would look rather odd with only half of it painted."

Sarah Beth twisted her lips. "Heaven forbid. I think Mr. Greene would be agreeable." She frowned. "I'm not so sure about his wife though."

"Imogene? Why is that?"

"She hasn't been very friendly to me. In fact, I don't think she likes me at all."

Emery wasn't surprised. Imogene Greene watched her husband like a hawk, and he probably welcomed the sight of pretty Sarah Beth Taylor and her spirited personality. He leaned toward Sarah Beth, putting his hand over her ear. "I'll tell you a secret. Imogene doesn't like many people, especially other women. I think she's got a jealous streak."

"Pfft!" Sarah Beth waved her hand. "You think she's afraid I'll snatch her husband away?"

Emery chuckled. "Something like that."

Sarah Beth leaned into him. "She needn't worry. I don't want him."

He laughed out loud, releasing emotion he'd held confined for too long. What a refreshing feeling it was.

"So, as I was saying. . . I want to whitewash the building, and I also want to hang a new sign. Do you know where I can get one?"

"Of course. We can get one made for you. Guess you want a sign that says 'café' instead of 'saloon.'"

"Well, not just 'café,' but 'The Southern Charm Café.'"

Emery paused and faced her. "Is that what you plan to call it?"

"Why, yes, don't you like the name?"

"Well, I suppose it's all right. It's your café, and you can call it whatever you want to."

"You're not fond of the name though. I can tell. What's wrong with it?"

He watched a cowboy ride by. "I can't say there's anything *wrong* with it." He shrugged. "It just sounds kind of feminine, I guess. Like a tea parlor for ladies. So the ladies in town will probably like the name."

"But the men won't, is that what you mean?"

Emery rubbed a rough spot on the boardwalk with his boot. "Maybe."

"So I should name it something men would like? Such as. . .the Spit and Chow? Does that sound manly enough?"

Emery burst out laughing. "Miss Taylor, you certainly have a way with words. But the sign will just tell them how to find you. The food is what will keep them coming back."

A shadow crossed over Sarah Beth's face, then she straightened her back. "And I shall have the best food in town!"

"Better than the boardinghouse shouldn't be hard. Better than the hotel might be a challenge. Their food is pretty good. And you're going to do all the cooking and serving and everything else by yourself? You're going to be busy."

"It shouldn't be any harder than cooking a meal for a big family, now should it?"

"And you've done that before, have you?"

She quickly glanced away. They were reaching the edge of town and the end of the boardwalk. He pointed to the last building. "There's the butcher shop. I suppose you'll be giving him a lot of business."

"What does he carry?"

Emery frowned and bit his lip. "Meat. Mostly beef."

"Beef? What about chickens?"

"I don't think he handles chickens. Most people raise their own chickens. But I think he has ham."

"Well that's good to know. I don't want to offer just beef."

"Around here, that's what most people eat. There's plenty of cattle in the area."

"Then perhaps I should introduce myself to him."

"Yes, I think that would be a good idea." Emery motioned to the door and opened it for her. Inside, the butcher stood behind the counter in a bloodstained apron. "Dan, I'd like to introduce you to Miss Sarah Beth Taylor. She'll be opening a café in the old saloon. Miss Taylor, this is Dan Davis."

Miss Taylor nodded and smiled, averting her eyes from the hanging carcass behind Dan.

"Welcome to town, Miss Taylor. How soon do you plan to open?"

"Next week. I hope you can supply me with some nice steaks and roasts."

"Yes, ma'am. Just let me know when, and I'll make sure it's fresh."

"That would be appreciated." She nodded and spun around, heading for the door.

Emery nodded to Dan as well, then hurried to open the door for her.

"Is something wrong, Miss Taylor?" he asked when they were outside. Her skin color had paled. "Are you feeling well?"

"I'll be fine. I just didn't care for the odor in there." She inhaled and blew out a breath, glancing toward the outskirts of town where the church sat alone in a pasture. "What a sweet church building! And it's so pretty and white!" She faced Emery. "I suppose you and your mother worship there."

Emery nodded. "Yes, we do. It's Mother's favorite thing to do these days."

"I'd like to go tomorrow. Would y'all mind if I sat with you? I'd feel a little uncomfortable sitting by myself."

"Why, I'll do you one better. How about we collect you on our way there, so you don't have to go alone?"

Sarah Beth's smile brightened her face. "That would be so hospitable of y'all. Do you think your mother would mind?"

"Not at all. I'm sure she'd love to have you join us."

"Then I accept! What time should I be ready?"

"The church service begins at ten o'clock, so we'll stop by around a quarter till. That way, you'll have time to meet some people first."

"Thank you, so much, Mr. Wright." She gazed at the church a few minutes longer, a wistful expression on her face. Then she turned to him. "I should be getting back to the café now and check on Judd's progress."

They were walking back when the stagecoach rumbled into town.

"So you've kept Judd pretty busy, I see. I guess he's happy to make some extra money."

She jerked her head toward him, eyes wide. "What do you mean?"

"You *are* paying him, aren't you?"

Her face flushed. "Well I. . .I. . .not yet. How much should I pay him?"

"Depends on how many hours he's put in. If he works a full day, probably a dollar a day. Half a day, about fifty cents."

"Oh." They walked on in silence until they reached the bank and she stopped. "Thank you for escorting me."

"My pleasure, but I intend to walk you back to the café."

"There's no need. It's right over there." She nodded across the street.

"But I'd like to."

She eyed him with a lifted eyebrow, and they started to step off the sidewalk. Just then three cowboys came around the corner as if they were racing. Emery grabbed Miss Taylor around the waist and pulled her back.

She shook her head, brushing off dust when he let go of her. "Must those cowboys be so reckless?"

"They should be more careful, that's for certain. I guess they're so used to riding the range, they forget how to ride in town."

"I'm surprised no one's been hurt by such carelessness."

"They just got paid for the week, so they're probably anxious to spend their money."

"On what?"

"Frankly, they used to go to the saloon. But there are other places to go, like the mercantile, the blacksmith, to get new shoes for their horses, or the leather shop for new bridles or saddles and such. Some even go to the boardinghouse to buy a bath."

"Too bad my café isn't open. They might enjoy a good meal or something more refined than what they normally get."

"And you think the Southern Charm Café will attract them?"

She stopped walking and put her hands on her hips. "You don't think that name would attract a cowboy."

Emery shook his head. "Nope, I don't."

She tapped her chin. "Hmm. Maybe I'll wait on that sign then and see if I think of another name for the café they'd take a liking to."

"I think that's a good idea."

They'd reached the café, so Emery said goodbye, still uncomfortable leaving her to stay all night there by herself. But she'd survived so far, and hopefully, her mousetraps would work tonight.

"Mrrow!"

"Ow, you little varmint!"

Sarah Beth followed the noise to the kitchen where a massive pale orange cat, back up, stood in the corner, hissing at Judd.

"What on earth is going on, Judd?"

"That dadburn cat scratched the devil out of me!" He pointed to a scratch with blood running down his hand.

"Oh, I'm so sorry."

"Well, there's your cat. I hope he's as mean to the rats as he is to me!"

"Thank you, Judd. I didn't mean to put you out like that." Sarah Beth glanced between the cat and Judd. "Why don't you go out back and wash off the scratch? Just leave him to me."

He raised his eyebrows then shook his head. "You be careful, miss."

When Judd went outside, Sarah Beth took a few short steps toward the cat, then when she got about six feet away, crouched down low and extended her hand. "Come here, kitty." She waited patiently, then spoke again. "Here, kitty, kitty. I won't hurt you." The cat relaxed and watched her as she continued to call. Then it got up and came toward her, meowing and sniffing. "It's all right. We're going to be friends. I'll have to get you some milk." Sarah Beth looked around the room. "We need to make you a bed. I'll see what I have."

Sarah Beth walked out of the room, calling the cat as she went through the café. She glanced over her shoulder and saw the cat creeping several feet behind her. Sarah Beth continued up the stairs to her room with the cat following. If only she had some food to give it. But maybe it was a good thing she didn't so the cat would be hungry tonight. Once in her room, she looked around for something soft. She spied the old cover that had been on the bed lying in the corner. She'd thought to use it for rags, but maybe the cat would like it. Sarah Beth stood still as the cat crept into the room, sniffing around. He investigated every nook of the room, then found the old cover and began pawing it, "making biscuits," as her mother used to say. After a few minutes, the cat curled up in a circle and lay down.

"Well, it looks like you found your new home." She studied the striped cat settled peacefully in its bed. "What will I name you? Hmm? Your light orange color reminds me of Georgia peaches. That's it. Peaches! Your name is Peaches." If only she had some milk to give him. But since she didn't, she'd get some water for it in one of the old chipped bowls she'd found under the bar.

As she went downstairs to fetch it, Judd was coming from the kitchen. "Where'd that cat go? Did it run off?"

"No, Peaches is sleeping quite comfortably in his new bed upstairs."

"Peaches? Sleeping in a bed?" Judd shook his head. "I don't understand cats."

"That's all right. He's going to work out fine. I sure wish I had some milk for him though."

"I can get some from Granny's, if you don't want much."

"That would be wonderful. I'll pay her for it." Sarah Beth reached for her reticule sitting on the counter behind the bar.

He waved his hand. "She won't take it."

"Well, I need to pay you anyway for all your help here. What does the hotel pay you?"

"A dollar a day, but I ain't been there all day since I been helping you."

"Then I'll give you two dollars. That should cover the difference. Does that sound fair?"

"Yes, ma'am. Real fair. I appreciate it."

She handed him the money. "Will you and your granny be in church tomorrow?"

Judd shrugged. "If Granny wants to go. Are you going to be there?"

"I certainly am, and I look forward to meeting your granny."

"Yes, ma'am. I'll tell her. You want me to bring the milk back today or tomorrow?"

"Today, if it's not too much trouble, since tomorrow's Sunday. I don't want you working on Sunday."

"Yes, ma'am." He pocketed the money. "Be right back."

As he left, Sarah Beth fought the battle with worry. If Mr. Wright hadn't mentioned it, she wouldn't have thought to pay Judd. But she wanted to do what was right, even if seeing the money disappear made her wonder how long her funds would last before she made more. She needed to get open soon, but could she really handle everything by herself—serving customers, handling the money, managing the whole business?

After all, she'd never done any of it before, and despite her determination to succeed, she had to admit there was a minor problem. She'd never cooked anything before. Her pulse quickened with fear of failing, of embarrassment. But she could learn. She'd find some recipes and practice, and hopefully, the learning process would be easy and fast. Surely God wanted her to succeed or He wouldn't have laid this opportunity in her lap just when she needed it.

Chapter 7

Sarah Beth liked Mrs. Wright as soon as they met. The silver-haired woman with kind blue eyes and a warm smile made Sarah Beth feel welcome, as if they'd known each other a long time. In fact, the impulse was so strong, Sarah Beth wondered if they'd met somewhere before.

When Mr. Wright and his mother came for her Sunday morning, they were in a buggy. Sarah Beth had expected to walk, but the distance was too much of an exertion for the elderly woman, as Sarah Beth determined when the woman was helped out of the buggy in front of the church. Despite using a cane, Mrs. Wright walked upright, though stiffly, tastefully dressed in a burgundy silk dress and matching hat. Surely those clothes were store-bought, as they were of much higher quality than the homespun clothes the other women wore. Sarah wore her pale blue taffeta with ruffles on the sleeves and tiered down the dress plus a matching bonnet and parasol, one of the few pieces of her wardrobe she'd brought with her.

Mr. Wright led them inside the modest church to a bench Sarah Beth assumed was their regular seat and sat between her and his mother. Sarah Beth tried not to look at Mr. Wright lest she stare. He was impeccably dressed, his hair and mustache perfectly trimmed and combed. Even with the scar on his cheek, he was very attractive. She sensed the stares of the townspeople who no doubt wondered who she was and why she was sitting with Emery Wright and his mother. A quick glance over her shoulder, and she caught the glare of Priscilla Morgan trying to sear a hole in her. Sarah Beth straightened to sit a little higher, lifting her chin, proud to be sitting in the company of the handsome banker.

The congregation was small but large enough for the church. Sarah Beth spotted Judd and his granny, who gave her an endearing smile. Sarah Beth would have to introduce herself. Mr. and Mrs. Greene were there, sitting erect with eyes straight ahead. Why did Mrs. Greene always look angry? Sarah Beth felt sorry for her husband living with such a joyless woman.

Dan Davis was sitting across from Sarah Beth with his wife and three children. He nodded and gave her a big smile, nudging his wife, who glanced over and nodded as well. Sarah Beth didn't see the hotel owner. Of course, hotels were still open for business on Sundays. Thankfully, Sarah Beth would not have to open her café on Sunday and could enjoy worship and a restful afternoon.

After the service, while Sarah Beth met Judd's granny, Mr. Wright helped his mother into the buggy. He waited beside it for Sarah Beth. "Thank you for bringing me," she said to him, "but it's pretty crowded in there with me too, and I don't mind walking home." How strange it felt to call the café "home."

"Mother wants you to join us for dinner. Do you mind, or do you have other plans?"

Other plans? Trying to figure out her menu was utmost, but her stomach rumbled, changing her priorities for the time being.

"I'd very much like to join you. Thank you for asking."

He helped her into the buggy then climbed in beside her. She hadn't thought about how close they were on the way to church because she was more focused on Mrs. Wright. But now, the close contact with him reminded her of the night she'd fallen into his arms, and the warmth of that memory quickened her pulse.

The buggy turned off the main street and pulled up in front of a charming, two-story Victorian white house complete with gingerbread brackets and a picket fence around the small yard. The house was so pretty and welcoming, it seemed to smile. "What a lovely home!" Sarah waved her hand toward flowers growing in the yard. "And such pretty flowers! You must have a green thumb!"

Mrs. Wright smiled as she was aided by her son to disembark. "Thank you. I do enjoy gardening."

Inside the house, Sarah Beth found the same style and charm as the outside of the house. The furniture was well-crafted with rich upholstery and very tasteful, like the woman who lived there. Sarah Beth had not expected such refinement in this little cowboy town.

A rich aroma wafted through the room. "What is that wonderful smell?"

"Chicken and dumplings. They've been on the burner since we left for church, so they should be just right now." Mrs. Wright removed her hat and gloves and hung them on the hall tree by the door. "Please excuse me and I'll go check on our dinner." She walked toward the door in the back of the room, her slow steps aided by her cane.

"May I help you?" Sarah Beth asked, removing her bonnet and gloves. Mr. Wright took them from her and put them on the hall tree as well.

"If you'd like to, certainly." She looked at Mr. Wright. "Please excuse us, Emery."

He motioned for them to go on. "I'll just do a little reading while you ladies handle the meal." He picked up a book on a small table and sat down in a stuffed armchair.

Sarah Beth scanned the tidy kitchen, trying to memorize all she saw in case she needed to get more items for the café's kitchen. A rolling pin, a coffee grinder, a large soup spoon—she'd pick those up tomorrow at the mercantile.

Mrs. Wright lifted the lid on a large pot and stirred the contents. Sarah Beth looked on, inhaling the delicious scent. "Perhaps I'll serve this at my café. Would you mind sharing the recipe with me?"

Her eyebrow lifted, Mrs. Wright said, "It's not too complicated. You've never made chicken and dumplings before?"

"No, ma'am, I haven't. Our cook used to make it though."

"Hmm. Well, I'd be happy to show you how." She looked over her shoulder. "Would you mind setting the table for us? The china and silver are in the cabinet in the dining room. So are the napkins and glasses." She nodded toward the room. "And please ask Emery to come pour this into the tureen for me."

"I'd be happy to." Sarah Beth found the dishes and set the table, marveling at the fine china. The Taylor plantation used to have an excellent collection of china and silver as well. Many guests had the privilege of enjoying fine meals on their dinnerware. Her heart twisted, threatening tears, but she couldn't allow them. Daddy would say, "No use crying over spilt milk." That life was over, and dwelling on it wouldn't bring it back. She straightened her spine, then approached Mr. Wright in the adjoining room. "Excuse me, but your mother needs your services in the kitchen."

He stood and went to the kitchen. Soon, the food was on the table, along with some bread that had been sliced. Mr. Wright assisted the ladies with their chairs before he sat.

"Shall we say grace?" He bowed his head and thanked God for the food, the church service, and the women at the table. "And please bless Miss Taylor's café. Amen."

"This is excellent," Sarah Beth said after the first bite. "Even better than we had at home."

"Thank you. I'm sure yours will be just as good," Mrs. Wright said, holding her spoon aloft.

Sarah Beth glanced down at her food. Was it even possible for her to make something so tasty? She had no idea how to begin. "Then make sure you give me your recipe, so it will be."

"When do you plan to open?"

"I hope sometime next week. I need to make sure I have all my supplies."

"And you know what your menu will be?"

Sarah Beth nodded. "Pretty much. I've been thinking about it a long time. I'm just not sure I can get all the supplies I need here." She put down her spoon and patted her mouth with her napkin. "Tomorrow I'm going to do some experimenting and make sure I'm familiar with the café kitchen. It's not nearly as well set up as yours."

"No, I imagine not. Homer didn't do much cooking. I think he made stew every so often, but I don't know of anything else. At least, from what I heard."

"Did you know him well?"

Mrs. Wright nodded. "He used to come visit me."

"Homer was sweet on Mother."

Mrs. Wright blushed and swatted Mr. Wright with her napkin. "Don't listen to him. Homer was just a good friend. I hope he'll do well in the west."

"I'm sorry I didn't get to thank him in person for giving me the saloon. After all, he's my only living relative." Sarah Beth paused, then recovered. "But I'm glad he saw fit to do something for me."

Mrs. Wright glanced at her son. "Well, we're glad he did too. I must say, I'm glad to see the saloon gone. Too many cowboys rode in on the weekend to get drunk and cause a ruckus. It's much more peaceful now."

"They're probably not very happy it's not in business anymore."

"They aren't," Mr. Wright said. "Now they have to go to another town for their drinks."

Mrs. Wright put a hand over her face. "Oh, I almost forgot the pie!"

"I'll get it," Sarah Beth said. "Where is it?"

"Thank you, dear. It's on top of the cupboard. Would you please bring a knife to cut it too?" She turned to her son. "Emery, please get some saucers out of the cabinet."

Sarah Beth found the pie in the kitchen and a knife nearby and brought them back to the table, setting it in front of Mrs. Wright. The older woman cut ample slices for each saucer and passed them out.

"Oh my, this is wonderful!" Sarah Beth savored the tasty dessert. "Where did you get the cherries?"

"From the mercantile. They come in a can since we don't have fresh ones here."

"I'll have to remember that." Surely pies were easy to make. Weren't they like biscuits? Not that she'd made any of those. "My customers would love it."

"What kind of pies do you like to make?" Mrs. Wright asked.

The piece of pie got stuck in her throat. "Well, I like all of them." She wasn't lying, because she did like all the pies she'd ever tasted. Maybe they wouldn't notice she didn't say she made them.

Mrs. Wright frowned, but didn't reply, and exchanged looks with Mr. Wright.

Having dinner with Mr. Wright and his mother was almost like being with family again, even though it wasn't her family. At least they didn't treat her like an outsider. When they finished the meal, Sarah Beth cleared the table, insisting Mrs. Wright rest. Afterward, they visited in the parlor until it was time for her to leave. Mrs. Wright talked mainly about her late husband and how they came to Crinoline Creek. Emery Wright stayed rather quiet. Why didn't he say anything about himself? When his mother referenced him, he shook his head and cut her a look as if to say he didn't want to be an object of conversation.

Mrs. Wright began to look tired, and Sarah Beth was afraid she was keeping the woman from resting. She stood. "I guess I better get back to the café. I still have plenty to do." At the woman's raised eyebrows, Sarah Beth added, "I need to get to bed early tonight because tomorrow will be a busy day."

Mr. Wright stood as well. "I'll see you back."

Mrs. Wright leaned forward and attempted to stand, but Sarah Beth said, "Please, don't get up. Thank you so much for inviting me into your home. Your hospitality means a great deal to me."

The woman leaned back in her chair. "You're quite welcome, dear. I hope you can come back another time."

"I'd like that." Sarah Beth wanted to kiss Mrs. Wright on the cheek but was afraid the act would be too bold for a non-family member. She smiled instead. "And you must come to my café!"

"I will."

Emery was surprised at how well Mother and Miss Taylor got along. They had been quite comfortable with each other, unusual because Mother had become somewhat of a recluse, and he assumed she didn't care to have any company. But Sarah Beth Taylor had touched her heart with her innocence and sparkle. Maybe they could become friends. That would be good for Mother.

Although she appeared brave to take on the task of running the café by herself, Emery detected a hint of fear and insecurity hidden beneath the surface. He figured she wanted to make people think she was confident and capable, and put up a good pretense. Surely she had doubts about her success. He had his own doubts about it. What experience did she have running a business? Running a plantation was not the same thing. And she had help on the plantation. Was she planning to hire some help? Judd couldn't do it all. He might be good at heavy work and cleaning, but he wasn't a cook or a waitress.

They didn't talk for a few minutes on the way back to the café. Miss Taylor was quieter and more pensive than he'd seen her before, and he didn't want to express his concerns about her business.

"Your mother's a very nice lady." She broke the silence.

"Yes, she is. And she enjoyed your visit today. Other than church, she doesn't get out much anymore."

"Then I should go visit her sometime."

"She'd like that."

He waited for her to unlock the door to the café. "Miss Taylor, if you need any help, please let me know."

She gazed at him as if trying to read his mind. "I will."

But would she? Would she be honest enough to admit she needed more help running the café, or would her pride keep her from asking? He hoped she wouldn't wait too long to realize she couldn't do it all by herself.

Chapter 8

The next day, a stranger came into the bank. His dusty clothes were a bit fancy, with a black vest, string tie, and hat, not the normal attire for a cowboy. A fancy pearl-handled pistol in his holster spelled danger, especially one with that many notches in the handle. Emery came from his office to assess the stranger and be ready for trouble, his own gun hidden beneath his coat.

The man held up a sheet of paper in front of the teller. "You seen this man?"

George looked uncomfortable. "No, sir, can't say as I have."

Emery strode up. "Can I help you, sir?"

The man faced him, gave him a slight tip of his hat and a tight grin. "I'm looking for this man. I've followed him this far, so I think he's around here somewhere."

"May I see that?" Emery took the wanted poster the man handed him.

SONNY CLINTON. WANTED DEAD OR ALIVE.
Horse thief and cattle rustler. Also wanted in the Spring Creek stagecoach robbery. Dangerous. $1000 Reward.

Emery looked up from the poster. "And who might you be?"

"Jack Cash."

"You're a bounty hunter." Emery didn't offer to shake his hand.

"That's right. A good one too." Mr. Cash puffed out his chest and raised his chin in confidence.

"Well, I haven't seen this man either."

"Can you point me to the saloon? I'll ask there."

"Don't have one."

Jack Cash raised his eyebrows. "You don't have a saloon? What kind of town don't have a saloon?"

"This one. We used to have one, but it closed."

"Well, you got a hotel?"

"Yes." He motioned down the street. "It's down that way."

"Guess there's no fun in this town." The bounty hunter grinned.

"Not the type you're looking for."

Cash cut him a dirty look. "How do you know what I'm looking for?"

Emery shrugged. "Just a guess."

Cash touched the brim of his hat, glancing from Emery to George. "Thank you, gents. Be sure to let me know if you see that guy."

"We will."

When he left, Emery and George looked at each other. "Hope he doesn't stay long," George said.

"He probably won't, since we don't have any 'fun' around here."

"What if the outlaw he's looking for shows up? Think we'll have a gunfight?" George seemed excited by the idea.

Emery gave him a sharp glance. "Do you really want that kind of violence to happen here, George? Frankly, I've seen enough in my lifetime already." A flood of memories charged into his mind.

George looked penitent. "No, I guess not."

"I'm going to step out awhile." Emery grabbed his hat and went outside. He shook off a shudder at the reminder of the war. *Lord, I sure hope we won't have bloodshed around here.* As he gazed across the street, the image of Sarah Beth Taylor rattled him. Would she be in any danger if the outlaw came to town? Just to be sure she was safe, he decided to go see how things were going at the café.

Looking through the windows, he didn't see anyone. The door was unlocked, so he went in. Banging and slamming came from the kitchen. He followed the noise and peeked in the door. Miss Taylor stood with her hands on her hips, staring at the stove.

"Are you having a problem?"

She blew out a breath. "I can't make this thing work!"

From the smudges on her face and hands, she'd given it a try.

He took off his jacket and laid it and his hat on the table. "Let me see what I can do." He rolled up his sleeves, opened the oven door to make sure she didn't have something in it, then opened the woodbox, which was empty. "Do you have some wood around here?"

She pointed to a corner. "There's some over there."

He walked over and picked up an armload, then carried it back to the stove and pointed to the open woodbox. She had obviously never started a stove before. "You put wood in here. It helps to use some smaller pieces like kindling to get it going." He laid several pieces of wood in the box until it was almost full. "Now you light it. Do you have any matches?"

"Yes, I use them for the lamps." She hurried out and came back with a tin of matches. Emery struck one and held it in the woodbox until the wood caught fire. He closed the door and brushed off his hands. "It'll take a while to get the stove hot. What do you plan to put in it?"

"Biscuits. I'm going to try a batch and see how they are."

He looked behind him at the worktable where the rolling pin lay beside an open book. "Then you'll need to wait at least forty-five minutes for the oven to get hot enough for biscuits."

"Oh. I didn't know it would take so long."

"Well, at least you don't have a batch ready to go in."

"But I will soon!" She pointed to her rolling pin and recipe book.

"Is that a family recipe book?"

"Oh no, I bought it next door."

"I see." He looked around the kitchen, eyeing the back door. "Where's Judd?"

"He's at the hotel working right now and said he'd be here later. I don't really need him now, anyway, because I'm going to be cooking."

Emery nodded toward the door. "Do you keep that locked?"

She followed his gaze. "Not during the daytime, since I have to go in and out to get water." She tilted her head and eyed him. "Why?"

He shrugged. "I just think it'd be a good idea to keep your doors locked when you're alone—the front door too."

"Mr. Wright, is there something I should know about? You act like a mouse waiting for a hawk to drop out of the sky and pick him up."

"I was just thinking you don't know much about the West and what unsavory characters can come through town."

Miss Taylor crossed her arms. "Are you speaking of any *particular* unsavory characters?"

He blew out a breath. "All right. Today a bounty hunter came into town looking for an outlaw he followed to this area."

Her eyes widened. "An outlaw? My word, and you think he might come in here?"

"I just want you to be very careful. Some of these men are pretty dangerous."

"And that's why you're wearing a gun?" She eyed his holster.

"I always wear it, just in case I need it. You just didn't see it under my coat before."

"At least I don't have to worry with you around, that is, if you're a good shot." She gave him a teasing smile.

"I am." As he'd proven too many times before.

"Maybe I should get a gun too."

"You?"

"I know how to shoot. My daddy taught me how."

"With what? A rifle?"

She lifted her chin. "A shotgun. I can shoot a turkey at twenty yards."

Emery envisioned her facing off with Sonny Clinton holding a shotgun. She wouldn't stand a chance.

Judd walked in and startled both of them. "I got done with my work at the hotel, so I can help you now."

Emery and Miss Taylor glanced at each other.

"I'll be going now that Judd's here."

Judd raised an eyebrow and looked puzzled.

"You run right along. Judd and I can handle ourselves."

Emery had no reason to stay any longer. He wasn't her protector, even though he was drawn to be. He pointed to the rolling pin. "You save me a biscuit, all right?"

Her cheeks turned pink and she offered a demure smile. "I'll be happy to, Mr. Wright."

An outlaw in town? Sarah Beth shuddered. What had he done? Mr. Wright didn't tell her. Was he a killer? She'd acted like she wasn't afraid, but now, the what-ifs popped into her head. She took in the size of Judd, truly thankful for his presence. But what would she do when he left? As soon as she finished making the biscuits, she'd go buy a shotgun. Peaches would take care of the rats, but he was no help with this kind of threat.

She followed the instructions, adding flour, shortening and salt, baking powder and milk. She worked the dough with her hands, trying to blend it all together, but it kept sticking to her hands, so she threw in more flour, pushing on the big lump of dough until her arms were tired. Wasn't this the way Maudie used to do it? She lifted her arm to wipe the perspiration from her brow. When the dough looked smooth to her and wasn't sticking to her hands anymore, she grabbed the rolling pin and started pushing on the dough to flatten it. Getting it to a reasonable thickness, she took a glass and cut out circles in the dough, then laid the circles on a baking pan.

Hot air blasted her when she opened the oven door and slid the sheet inside. How long should they take? She checked the flour-coated recipe book. Ten minutes. Enough time to run next door. She took off her apron and wiped the dough off her hands, then grabbed her reticule and hurried to the mercantile. Mr. Greene turned around from the shelves to look when the bell rang. His mouth dropped open.

"Miss Taylor? Do you need something?"

"Yes, a shotgun. And shells. Do you have them?"

"Why, yes, of course. But who are they for?"

"They're for me." Mr. Greene seemed incredulous. "Haven't you ever known a woman who could shoot?"

"Well, maybe one or two, but I didn't know you could."

"Well, I can." She looked at the clock on the wall. "Can you bring them over? I have to hurry back. Got biscuits in the oven."

"I, um, can't leave the store right now."

"Oh, never mind. I'll send Judd. How much will it be?"

"That'd be forty dollars for the gun, fifty cents for a box of shells."

Sarah Beth gulped. "That expensive?" She looked in her reticule. "Oh, silly me. I didn't bring enough money! Would you mind starting a bill for me like you did for that ranch?" She offered her best smile.

His brow creased, and he glanced over his shoulder at the door to his living quarters. "Why, yes, I can do that for you."

"You're a dear, Mr. Greene."

She hurried back to the café, where an acrid smell hit her nose. Oh my stars. She ran to the kitchen and saw smoke billowing from the oven. When she opened the door, the smoke escaped out into the room. She ran to open the back door. Where was Judd? After waving the smoke away, she saw the blackened biscuits. Sighing, she grabbed a folded rag and pulled the hot pan out, then ran to the back door and tossed them out.

"Ow!" Judd held his hand over his head where the hot biscuit hit him.

"Oh dear, I'm sorry, Judd. I didn't know you were out there."

"Just using the outhouse, ma'am. What was that what hit me in the head?"

"Biscuits. I stayed too long next door and they burned. Now I have to make another batch."

"It sure packed a wallop!" Judd rubbed his head.

She certainly couldn't give one of those to Mr. Wright.

❧ Chapter 9 ❧

*S*arah Beth made five more batches of biscuits before she got them right. She felt like *she* was cooking too, it was so hot in the kitchen. She had to leave the back door open for air. Now she knew why Maudie wore a turban. Sarah Beth considered wearing one too. Making biscuits was much more difficult than she expected. How did Maudie make it look so easy? The last batch had a nice color and consistent size. She should take one of those to Mr. Wright as she promised. Judd had tasted some of the other batches for her, but he had to leave rather abruptly to get back to the hotel.

She went into the dining room, looked in the mirror behind the counter, and gasped. There was no way she would be seen in public in such a mess. She'd have to freshen up. She dragged her feet up the stairs to her room, fatigue setting in from working all day. The sun shone through the window in her room right on Peaches curled up in his bed, where he spent most of the day. Seeing him so comfortable tempted her to fall onto her bed as well. Maybe she'd do that after she delivered the biscuit. She rinsed the flour and dough off her face and rearranged her hair, pinning loose strands back up where they belonged. Glancing down at her clothes, she noticed every place the apron didn't cover had flour or dough on it. And her fingernails. Would she ever get the dough out from under them? Good thing she could cover them with gloves. She splashed a bit of lavender water on her neck and shook off her skirt. There. That would have to do.

She hurried back downstairs and grabbed two biscuits, wrapping them in a handkerchief. Her napkins better be on the next stagecoach. She eyed her new shotgun lying on the counter, the most expensive thing she had bought so far, and hoped she could remember how to use it. After all, it'd been years since she'd last shot one. Maybe she shouldn't leave it there for everyone to see. Mr. Greene had loaded it for her when he brought it over so it'd be ready when she needed to use it. She shuddered. Would she be able to shoot a man? She walked over and put it under the counter out of sight and put the shells right next to it. She glanced around at the empty room, which seemed to get larger after Judd left. She better hurry to the bank before Mr. Wright left and the lengthening shadows darkened the town.

As she grabbed the doorknob and turned it, she remembered she hadn't relocked it after Judd left. She stepped out, then turned to lock the door behind her. When she turned back around, she walked right into a man. Jumping back, she said, "Oh, I'm sorry."

For a split second she thought she'd run into Mr. Wright again, but this man wasn't Mr. Wright.

The man grinned, his teeth barely visible beneath a black bushy mustache, and tipped his black hat. "Well howdy, ma'am." His gaze roved over her like a vulture sighting a carcass and made her want to cover herself with a cloak. She glanced at the white handle of the gun at his side. Was this the bounty hunter? He looked behind her. "You know where I can get a drink around here?"

"No, sir, I don't."

He looked down at the old wooden sign lying next to the door. "Saloon? This place is a saloon?"

"No, it's not. It used to be, but not anymore."

"Well, what is it then?"

"A café." Her hands clutched the biscuits. How could she get the man to leave?

"A café, huh? I don't see anybody eating in there."

"It's fixing to be a café, but it's not open yet."

"Well, maybe it'll open before I leave town and I can try it."

Sarah Beth mustered a polite smile. "If you'll excuse me, I need to go somewhere."

He stepped aside and tipped his hat again as she hurried past. If this unsavory man was the bounty hunter, the man working on this side of the law, how much worse would the outlaw be?

Emery was headed toward the café when he saw Jack Cash talking to Miss Taylor. His gut clenched and an unfamiliar sensation gripped him. Why was Cash talking to her? Was he bothering her? Whatever was going on, he needed to get involved. She had no idea who the man was. Hopefully, she wasn't being as friendly as usual. Someone like Cash could get the wrong idea and take her charm to mean more than innocent sociability.

He strode toward the pair just as she stepped away from Cash. When Miss Taylor saw Emery coming, she walked toward him. As they met, she looked relieved, though shaken. Emery glanced over her head at Cash, who watched her walk away. Cash nodded at him and grinned, then turned and walked the other way.

"Are you all right?" Emery studied her face. "Was he bothering you?"

She shook her head. "He didn't do anything really. It's just the way he looked at me that I didn't care for. He's the bounty hunter you told me about, isn't he?"

"Yes, that's him all right. His name is Jack Cash."

"How long will he be in town?"

"Until he gets his man or gives up looking for him here."

"What will he do if he finds the outlaw?"

"The poster he's carrying says 'dead or alive,' so he doesn't care which way things turn out."

She winced at his words. "My goodness, I hope he doesn't find the man here in Crinoline Creek."

"You and me both." He glanced down at the item in her hands. "What have you got there?"

Glancing down, she seemed surprised to discover she was holding something. "Oh, they're biscuits. These were the best batch I made, and you said you wanted to try one, so I was bringing them to you."

"Why thank you! I'll have them with my supper tonight."

"I made several batches to get them just right."

He noticed flour behind her ear and smiled. "Did Judd try them?"

"Yes, he tasted the other batches and suggested I keep trying. He told me his granny could show me how to make a good biscuit. But I think I've got it figured out now. I'm just sorry he had to leave before I took the last batch out."

"So where are you going now?" Emery wanted to invite her to supper just to keep her safe, but Mother wasn't expecting company.

Her eyebrows puckered. "I suppose I'm going back home. It's going to be dark soon, and frankly, I'm tired."

"Don't forget to lock your doors."

"I won't." Her face brightened. "I bought a shotgun today! So now you won't have to worry about me."

"You really bought a shotgun? Then heaven help the poor man who trespasses on the café."

She tilted her head and pursed her lips. "Are you making fun of me, Mr. Wright?"

"Me? Heaven forbid." He couldn't help but smile though. "Seriously, I hope you don't have to use it, but keep it close by. A warning shot might be all you need to scare off trespassers. Just don't shoot through the wall or you might hit Mr. and Mrs. Greene." He winked at her.

Her face reddened and she started walking back to the cafe. "Good night, Mr. Wright."

"I'll walk you home." At her angry glance, he added, "I want to see that new gun."

In the café, she retrieved the gun from under the counter and showed it to him. "Mr. Greene loaded it for me. But I know how to load it myself."

He turned the gun over in his hand. "Nice shotgun. You got this at the mercantile?"

She nodded. "I didn't realize how expensive guns were."

"They're a pretty important item around here." She raised her eyebrow. "Every farmer or rancher needs a gun to hunt with and protect their livestock from wild animals." He handed it back to her. "Just be careful with it, and don't shoot at every noise you hear."

She put the gun back and placed her hands on her hips. "Mr. Wright, I am disappointed by your lack of faith in my judgment."

"I apologize, ma'am. I didn't mean to offend you."

She stifled a yawn.

"I see you need your rest, so I'll take my leave." He turned to walk to the door, then paused, about to remind her to lock the door behind him. But he bit his tongue. He'd given her enough unwanted advice already. Still, he wished he could keep an eye on the place, at least while there was a threat of unsavory characters around.

When he reached the door, she said, "Why don't you come by tomorrow morning and have breakfast here? I'll make some more biscuits and eggs, and you can be my first customer!"

"You're opening tomorrow?"

"No, but if my napkins arrive tomorrow, I'll open the next day."

"All right, then, I'll see you in the morning." He tipped his hat. "Good night."

Sarah Beth locked the door and pulled the shade when Mr. Wright left, then took a lamp and went upstairs. It wasn't late, but darkness had settled, and she was tired. She didn't have any supper, but she'd nibbled on biscuits all day and wasn't hungry.

When she entered her room, Peaches meowed and stretched, then came over to greet her. "Time for you to go to work," she said as she petted him. She undressed and rinsed off with a clean cloth, then put on her nightgown and fell into bed. Her arms and legs ached from working in the kitchen all day. Maybe she would get used to the labor with practice. She hoped so. A good night's rest was what she needed.

Chapter 10

The sun was just beginning to wake up the town when Sarah Beth went downstairs the next morning. She opened the curtains and ambled toward the kitchen, ready to try out her new coffee grinder and make some coffee. As she stepped into the room, alarm raced through her. The back door was standing wide open.

With a pang of guilt, the truth hit her. She had not only forgotten to *lock* the door, she'd forgotten to close it as well. Anyone could have walked in. She hurried over and closed it, glancing around to see if anything seemed out of place. Come to think of it, she hadn't seen Peaches this morning. Apparently, he'd let himself out. She sure hoped he'd come back. Even the cat's company was better than none.

She got the oven started and made the coffee. It was strong, but she needed its strength. After downing a cup, she began working on the biscuits. Her hands still ached from yesterday's efforts, but she was certain she wouldn't have to make so many batches today. Once she got them in the oven, she went to unlock the front door so Mr. Wright could come in when he arrived.

As she glanced around the room, she noticed something missing. The room was devoid of pictures. But she knew how to fix that. She rushed upstairs and dug through her trunk until she found what she was looking for, then raced back downstairs with the picture, laying it on the counter so she could get to the kitchen before she burned the biscuits again. She'd just pulled them out of the oven when she heard Mr. Wright's voice call out.

"Good morning!" He appeared at the kitchen door, looking as dapper and fresh as ever.

"Good morning. You're just in time." She poured him a cup of coffee. "Why don't you have a seat while I fix your eggs."

"You don't want an audience?"

"Not especially. But it won't take long, and I'll come join you." She nodded to the coffeepot. "Help yourself to some more if you'd like."

"All right, then, I'll go back to the dining room." He paused at the door. "Any intruders last night?"

"Thank God, no." She didn't dare admit she'd left the door open.

Sarah Beth hoped she could get the eggs right. She'd experimented with them yesterday too, with Judd's guidance. She put some lard in the frying pan, cracked a couple of eggs, and dropped them in. Soon the eggs began to brown, so she slid them onto a plate. They didn't look too bad. She added two biscuits and a spoonful of butter to the plate and carried it into the dining room.

Mr. Wright was standing by the counter admiring the picture. "Where'd this come from?"

"I brought it with me. This place needs some pictures." She set the plate down on a table and handed him some silverware.

"It's nice. Who painted it?" Mr. Wright went to the table and sat down while she picked up the picture.

"I did. It's the Cockspur Lighthouse near Savannah. My daddy took me on a steamship ride, and we passed it. It was such a sweet little lighthouse, I just fell in love with it."

"You're very talented." He took a bite of the eggs and sipped some coffee.

"How are the eggs?" She braced herself for his response.

"They're fine." He sipped more coffee then slathered some butter on the biscuit and took a bite.

"Are you sure? And the biscuits?" They weren't quite like Maudie's, but they were the best she'd made so far. She couldn't tell if Mr. Wright enjoyed the food or was just being polite.

"Fine. Good." He pointed to the picture, trying to swallow. "Did you paint any more?"

She nodded. "Yes, but this is the only one I brought with me. The rest wouldn't fit, and this is my favorite. So many good memories in that picture."

"Where do you intend to put it?" He glanced around the room.

"I don't know. Maybe over there on that bare wall."

"You don't want to put it behind the bar so folks will see it right away?"

"I don't know. Hey, what do you think about naming the café the Lighthouse Café instead of the Southern Charm?"

"Now that's a thought." He finished his eggs and a biscuit, leaving the other. Getting up from his chair, he took the picture, walked to the wall, and held it up. "Here?"

She put her chin in her hand. "Hmm. Maybe. What do you think?"

"Let's see how it looks over the bar." He carried the picture to the bar and held it up again.

"I'm not sure. If I name the café the Lighthouse Café, maybe it should be the first thing they see."

His gaze lowered and he frowned. "The shotgun's still here. Didn't you take it upstairs with you to your room last night?"

Heat rushed to her face. "I. . .I forgot."

Thank God the gun was still there.

Emery's chest tightened. What good did it do her if the gun was nowhere near her?

He tried to stay calm. "Better remember next time."

"I will." She lowered her gaze and appeared truly repentant. He wouldn't lecture her on the dangers of a woman alone.

"So what do I owe you for my meal?" He reached into his pocket.

Miss Taylor's eyes widened with surprise. "You're not going to pay me! I invited you to be my guest."

"Next time, then. You have to make money if you want your café to succeed."

"After I perfect a few more things, I'll open. In fact, that's what

I'll be doing today, so you can come back for lunch and try the chicken and dumplings. And I'm going to make a pie too!"

The breakfast biscuits still weighed heavy in his stomach. Hopefully, her chicken and dumplings would be better and the pie would be lighter than the biscuits. Before he could answer, Judd came in carrying a box.

"Granny sent you some things she thought you could use—some of her own canning."

"Well, wasn't that nice of her?"

Judd nodded. "She said she can help you cook if'n you want her to. Granny's a good cook."

From the looks of Judd, Emery had no doubt. Miss Taylor should take him up on his offer.

He said his goodbyes then left for work, hoping she wouldn't expect him back for lunch. He surely had too much work at the bank to leave.

Sarah Beth spent the rest of the day and the next trying recipes, asking Judd to sample everything she made. He said it was all good, but he didn't act like it. Later, Mr. Wright dropped by and sampled her chicken and dumplings too. He also said they were good. Why did she get the feeling he wasn't telling her the truth? Of course they didn't taste like his mother's, but Sarah Beth hadn't had the practice his mother had. Not that she needed his opinion.

The napkins arrived, and the menu was set, at least for the first week. She might change it up a little each week to keep her customers from getting bored. Was she ready to open now? Why should she wait any longer? Judd arrived each day with a box of things his granny sent, from canned beans and peas to pickled okra and blackberry jam. Goodness, the woman was keeping her well stocked.

"Judd, I think we'll open for business tomorrow."

His mouth fell open. "Tomorrow? Are you ready?"

"Of course. I'm going to pick up a ham from the butcher, and we'll have that tomorrow with beans and biscuits and pickled okra." What else? "And maybe I'll make a pie."

Judd's eyes widened. "A pie?"

"Why, yes. Didn't you like that pie I made today? I thought I'd make another."

Judd chewed on his fingernail. Then he turned to her. "What about a sign? Don't you need a sign?"

"Oh, bother. I suppose I do. I'm still not sure what to name it, so for the time being, let's just hang a sign that says 'Café.' Do you know where I can get one?"

He nodded. "I think so."

"Then let's get one right away."

"Yes, ma'am."

Sarah grabbed a rag and started dusting off the furniture with her back to the door, when she heard it open. "Judd? Did you get the sign already?"

"Name's not Judd."

She jerked around and saw the bounty hunter standing in the café.

"Sir, we're not open yet."

"Well, when you gonna be open? Fella needs another place to get grub."

"Actually, we're opening tomorrow."

His crooked grin turned her stomach. "Well, then," he drawled. "I'll be back bright and early tomorrow morning."

The sight of Mr. Wright walking up behind the man was a welcome relief. His frown said he wanted to know why the bounty hunter was there.

"Mr. Cash? Have you some business here?" Mr. Wright stood in the door behind Jack Cash. "Find your man yet?"

Cash spun around. "Why, it's the banker. No, I haven't found him yet." He looked over his shoulder at Sarah Beth. "I was just asking this pretty lady when her café is going to open, and she told me tomorrow."

Mr. Wright's eyebrows lifted, and he glanced at Sarah Beth. "Well, now you know. Good night, Cash."

Mr. Cash shrugged and looked back at Sarah Beth, tipping his hat. "I'll see you tomorrow."

She flinched as he strode out the door.

"Are you really opening tomorrow?"

"Yes. I think I'm ready."

"Are you sure?"

She crossed her arms and lifted her chin. "I have to open sometime. Can't put it off forever."

She wasn't ready. Her cooking needed a lot of improvement. Yet he hadn't had the guts to tell her so. What should he do? Be her only customer? Check that. Be one of her two only customers? He gritted his teeth. Why was Jack Cash still in town anyway?

Emery tried to think of a reason to keep Miss Taylor from opening yet, but she was obviously determined and wasn't willing to change her plans. If only she'd hire someone else to do the cooking. But how could he suggest it?

"Is there anything I can do to help?" He glanced around the room. The chairs and tables were straightened, the dishes stacked behind the bar.

She sauntered over to him and smiled a sweet smile that melted his insides. "You really want to help me, Mr. Wright?"

His collar tightened. "Yes, of course. Anything." Would he regret saying that?

"Then call me Sarah Beth. Every time you say Miss Taylor, it sounds like a child addressing his teacher."

Emery relaxed. "I can do that, especially since you don't remind me of any teachers I've ever had."

"And would it be possible for me to call you by your given name, Emery?"

It sure was getting hot in the room. He cleared his throat. "Emery sounds much better coming from your lips than Mr. Wright."

She blushed and gazed at him with those sparkling blue eyes.

Judd barged in, and the spell was broken. "I got your sign, Miss Taylor." He held up a wooden sign that said CAFÉ.

Emery glanced at her. "Just 'Café'?"

"For now. I can't decide on what to call it. But I have to hang something up so people will know I'm in business."

"I suppose you're right about that."

"You want me to hang this up now, Miss Taylor?"

"Yes, Judd. Please."

Judd went back outside, and Emery found himself caught in Sarah Beth's gaze again. "I better say good night now. After all, I plan to be your first customer tomorrow."

She beamed. "I can't think of anyone else I'd rather have for my first customer." Then she sobered. "But there is something else you can do for me."

"Yes? What is it?"

"You can pray for me and my café."

"I'd be happy to do that."

"Good night, Emery."

"Good night, Sarah Beth."

Chapter 11

Her first day in business. She should be thrilled. But after a restless night, she woke up with a heavy, pounding heart. Her palms were sweaty before she'd even dressed, as if she were about to appear on stage. Which she was, in a sense. But could she pull off this performance?

The sky was barely light outside when she went downstairs, a habit she had almost gotten used to, but the chill of the morning was still inside the café. She shivered and rubbed her arms. Once the stove got going and she started working, she'd forget that chill soon enough. She lit the oven and started the coffee, then glanced down at her hands. Red, rough skin marred her formerly creamy, soft hands. Mother wouldn't be pleased. But who would wear gloves in the kitchen?

Sarah Beth hugged herself against the chilly room, waiting for it to warm up. Was it that much colder outside today? She glanced around and noticed a gap in the back door. It wasn't closed all the way. Hadn't she locked it last night? She'd been so tired, she must've forgotten. She walked over and pulled it shut. When was Judd going to get here? They needed to get an early start, not to mention the fact that she'd like his company right now.

She better go unlock the front door so he could come in. After she unlocked the door, she pulled the shade and watched as the town came alive outside the windows. A noise came from behind her. She spun around but didn't see anything. Must've been Peaches. Soon, Judd came rushing in the door carrying a pie.

"Judd? What is this for?"

"Granny made it. It's a peach pie. She said you could serve it to your customers today."

"How sweet of her." Sarah Beth thought of the sad-looking pie sitting in the pie safe in the kitchen, the pie she had made late yesterday. This one looked so much better. Sarah Beth took the pie from him. "I'll put it on the bar. Anyone who sees it will certainly want a piece!"

Judd looked anxious. "I've got to go work at the hotel first this morning. I'll come back over here as soon as I can."

Sarah Beth was sorry to see him leave for some strange reason. Was she so lonely? Or had she just gotten used to having him around? Maybe she just wanted his support when her customers arrived. She shook her head. She was being silly.

Time to get started on breakfast. She made the biscuit dough and cut it out, then placed the biscuits on the pan and put them in the oven. While they baked, she went to the dining room and opened the rest of the shades and got some light inside the café. Next, she needed to get the ham and bacon from the storage room. She opened the door to the dark room, letting her eyes get accustomed to the dim light. Something moved, and she saw him. A strange man stood in front of her. He lunged forward and grabbed her, clamping his dirty hand over her mouth before she could scream.

"Keep quiet now and you won't get hurt," he rasped into her ear. "I just need some supplies, then I'll be on my way." His stale breath choked her as he spoke close to her face. Was this the man that was wanted, the man the bounty hunter was after? "All right?"

She nodded, despite trembling from fear.

"Hello? Is anybody here?"

Sarah Beth recognized the bounty hunter's voice. What would he do if he knew the outlaw was in here?

"Quiet," the man whispered, his hand so tight she could hardly breathe.

Footsteps sounded from the café.

"Hello? I thought you were open for breakfast today."

The footsteps drew closer.

Emery checked his watch. It was early, but he wanted to be at the café when Sarah Beth opened.

"You leaving already, Emery?" Mother stood in her housecoat. "I was just getting ready to make some coffee."

"Don't bother. I'll get some at the café. Sarah Beth is opening this morning."

"Sarah Beth?" Her eyebrow lifted and a subtle smile appeared.

"Are you referring to Miss Taylor?"

"Yes, ma'am. We agreed to dispense with formalities. Just doesn't seem practical in this part of the country."

"I see. And how early is she opening? It's barely daylight, isn't it?"

"You know, I forgot to ask, but I told her I'd be her first customer, so I want to hurry and make sure I am."

Mother chuckled. "At this hour, I think you will be."

He kissed her on the cheek and headed toward the café.

The air in the storage room was stifling, and sweat popped out on her hairline. If they didn't get out of here, she would suffocate. But Sarah Beth was trying so hard to be quiet, she discovered she was holding her breath.

The man was fidgety, and he kept readjusting his grip on her. Was he afraid or just nervous? Did he have a gun? She hadn't seen one, but things had happened so fast and it was dark, so she couldn't tell for sure.

Steps outside the room continued as the bounty hunter walked around the café. Sarah Beth strained to listen as the footsteps grew more distant. Was he leaving? She didn't know whether she wanted him to or not. Was she better off if there was a gunfight?

What if Emery showed up? Alarm raced through her. If only the man would leave before anyone found him there. She couldn't bear the thought of Emery getting hurt.

Her captor must've noticed the steps had gone away also, because he nudged her to the door so he could peek out. No one was around, so he pushed open the door, keeping her in front of him.

"You got any food here?" he muttered.

"I have to get the biscuits out," she whispered.

He motioned to the stove and let her go. "Get them."

She grabbed a rag and pulled them out, placing them on the table. He snatched several and stuffed them in his pockets.

"Give me some of that coffee."

She found the metal cup she used to scoop flour and poured some in, handing it to him.

He took a swig then motioned her to the back door. "Open it."

"You said if I was quiet, I'd be okay."

"I need insurance. Open it!"

Sarah Beth complied just as loud footsteps sounded from the café. The man threw down the coffee and grabbed her again, holding her in front of him, just as the bounty hunter appeared in the doorway between the dining room and the kitchen.

Emery noticed the shades were already up as he headed toward the café. He could just imagine how eager Sarah Beth must be about her first day in business. He smiled to himself. Had to hand it to her—she was determined.

As he stepped up on the boardwalk, he glanced in the windows. His heart stopped at the scene inside. Jack Cash had his back to the window, gun drawn on a man in the kitchen. Dear God. Clinton must be there. But where was Sarah Beth? A glimpse of blond hair confirmed his fears. She was between the two men. His pulse raced and his military training took over. He had to do something to keep her from getting hurt.

The back door to the kitchen opened into an alley behind the building. If he could just get around there and slip in behind Clinton...

✦

"Clinton! I knew you'd be here. Let go of the little lady and come with me if you want to stay alive." The bounty hunter waved his gun.

"You think I'm gonna trust you? You'd just as soon shoot me and get the reward anyway."

The back door creaked open and a large yellow cat raced in, distracting them all.

Jack Cash accidentally stepped on Peaches's tail, and the cat hollered. Cash stumbled and grabbed the hot stove for balance, burning his hand and dropping his gun as Clinton pushed Sarah Beth away. She ran toward the dining room as the two men wrestled, trying to get Cash's gun.

Should she go get help? No, that would take too long.

Noise at the back door caught her attention. Emery stood there, his gun drawn. He glanced at her then at the men on the floor, taking in the scene.

✦

She was okay, at least for now. "Get out!" Emery said to her, aiming his gun. But he couldn't get a clean shot as the men rolled around. One of them grabbed the gun, and the wrestling continued until a shot went off. The bounty hunter's body stilled, and Clinton pushed him off, holding the gun.

"Drop it." Emery aimed.

"My fight's not with you, mister. Just get out of my way."

"I'm afraid I can't do that," Emery said. "Just throw down the gun."

Clinton acted as if he was going to, then drew and fired at Emery as another shot rang out.

Clinton spun around just as a huge chunk of plaster fell from the ceiling, knocking him to the floor.

Behind him, Sarah Beth stood, shotgun in hand, pointed at the ceiling.

Emery's hand was bleeding as he rushed over to the moaning man and tied his hands.

"Did I kill him?" Sarah Beth whispered.

Emery shook his head then glanced up at the ceiling. "No, but I think your ceiling is injured."

He checked on the bounty hunter. "Still breathing. Looks like he took a shot to the shoulder."

Judd appeared in the doorway, his mouth gaping and eyes wide. "Judd, run get the sheriff. He needs to get these men out of here." Emery winked at Sarah Beth. "We need to clean up the kitchen and get ready for business."

Chapter 12

Emery sipped his coffee with a bandaged hand and eyed the customers coming into the café, which had been open for two weeks.

Sarah Beth greeted each one and showed them to their seats, handing them a menu then taking their orders. She breezed past him to the kitchen where she called out the orders.

When she passed by his table again, he grabbed her wrist. "Can a man get a refill here?" He held up his cup. She grinned and returned with the pot to top off his coffee.

"I heard the bounty hunter left town with his prisoner," Sarah Beth said as she poured.

"Yep. Doc bandaged them both pretty good. Clinton's got quite a lump on his head."

Sarah shrugged, her face turning red.

"Business looks pretty good here at the Cowboy Café."

Beaming, she said, "I never had any doubts."

Emery laughed. "I suppose you were planning to hire extra help all along."

"Why, of course! It's such a blessing that Judd's granny loves to cook, and who knew her sister does too!"

"So you think you'll sell them the café?"

Sarah Beth put her hands on her hips. "Emery Wright, why do you think I would want to sell the café after all the hard work I've put into opening up this place?"

"So you can be a wife." He pulled her onto his lap. "Mine."

"Mr. Wright, is that supposed to be a proposal?"

"Does it count?" He winked at her.

She put her finger to her lips. "Hmm. I'm not sure. It's not really a *proper* proposal."

"Well, goodness knows, I sure don't want you to use a shotgun to make me give you a *proper* proposal."

Sarah Beth giggled and blushed as Emery shoved her off his lap and got down on one knee. He pulled a sparkling ring from his vest pocket and held it out. "Sarah Beth Taylor, I love you with all my heart and hereby offer you a proper proposal for marriage. Will you accept?"

"Sugar, you just got yourself a wife!"

Marilyn Turk

Award-winning author Marilyn Turk calls herself a "literary archaeologist" because she loves to dig up stories hidden in history. Marilyn is excited to be in this collection with her first Western novella. A lighthouse enthusiast, she and her husband have traveled to over 100 lighthouses and even served as volunteer lighthouse caretakers. As a result, lighthouses often show up in her writing. When not writing or climbing lighthouses, Marilyn enjoys gardening, boating, fishing and playing tennis. Connect with her at pathwayheart.com.

Bea Mine

🌿

by Kathleen Y'Barbo

To Annette O'Hare and her amazing team from Writers on the Storm
This book is dedicated to you with much love and appreciation
And to Ellen Tarver, who makes me look like I know what I'm doing

Chapter 1

Georgia, August 1864

"I do believe this is the hottest summer ever endured in Georgia," Bea Wilson muttered under her breath as she dabbed at her temples with her handkerchief and watched yet another long line of soldiers marching past. Behind them, men in cavalry uniforms sat upon horses that looked worse for wear, matching their riders in their lack of enthusiasm for the task at hand.

From the second-floor balcony, she could view most of Jonesboro. Today, as in the years since this dreadful war began, there was nothing to see but despair.

The flowers fought with the heat to remain in bloom, and nearly every store on Main Street bore signs that its owner was either gone to war or greatly reduced in circumstance by that very same conflict.

Rumbles in the distance reminded her and anyone else who still paid attention that war was not a distant thing but rather a real and constant threat here. Rumor held that General Sherman was approaching. If that was true, those who were to oppose him did not look up to the task.

At least not from the balcony of Papa's store.

She would own this store someday, this she knew. Not from anything she'd been told directly, but rather from listening to Mama and Papa's hushed conversations behind closed doors.

Papa insisted she would need a husband like his store manager, Henry Neville, to assume the duties of running things, while Mama felt she could manage just fine whether she was married to that ancient storekeeper or not. Neither had bothered to ask her, and if they had, she would have politely declined.

Oh no, she had other plans. Plans that did not involve living anywhere near Jonesboro, Georgia, or being shackled to a man old enough to be her father. To be certain, she would miss Mama and Papa terribly, but when she got where she was going, she would send for them.

Wherever that was. At present, she hadn't managed to figure out how to leave Jonesboro, but she knew with the power of prayer it could be accomplished.

One of the soldiers looked up and caught Bea watching. His back was straight and proud and his expression insolent as he stared up at her. Dark hair fell in curls beneath his cap, and his lips turned up in a smile.

"Afternoon, ma'am," he called.

"Good afternoon, soldier," she responded, taming her grin. "Have you come to save us?"

"We aim to do just that," he said with a broad smile.

"And how far have you come?" she asked.

"All the way from Texas," he told her with a lift of his cap. "Eighth Texas Cavalry, at your service."

"Thank you, Eighth Texas," she told him. "Georgia is thankful to have you here. Do watch yourself!"

"On the contrary," he told her. "It is our job to watch others, not ourselves. Though my eyes have not yet landed on any prettier vision than you, ma'am."

"Perhaps you will remember me and return so that I might congratulate you on the victory you are surely about to win."

And take me away was thought but disappeared quickly on a wisp of warm breeze.

The soldier reached into his pocket and retrieved a gold pocket watch. "I'm afraid I don't have the time now, but maybe I will find you when this is over."

"Don't you tease me now," she said playfully as a flame lit in her heart. "There's always time."

Maybe he would find her. And maybe when he found her, she would go with him.

The men around him barely looked up at the exchange, such was their apparent level of exhaustion. Bea's heart went out to all of those poor, tired men. Oh, but that one who dared to speak, even to offer a poor attempt at flirting? He seemed to be the exception.

The cavalry kept up their slow but steady pace until the last one disappeared around the corner. Only then did Bea go back inside.

Later that evening, as she lay snug beneath the leaking ceiling of Papa's store where he felt she and Mama would be safer than out at the farmhouse, Bea wondered about that dark-haired man. She allowed a moment's reflection on the smooth lines of his freshly shaved face, on the way his smile tipped up slightly on one side, and on the fact that if he was returning to Texas, perhaps he just might take her with him.

It was ridiculous, of course, to even consider it. But life with a man who looked like the handsome soldier would be much preferred to the alternative facing her here. If only it was possible.

🌿

Captain Gil Hollis held tight to the image of the smiling woman in the pale blue gown, even as preparations for war took precedence. Sherman's men were at arm's length and would soon oppose them.

As one of just a few men in the Eighth Texas with medical training, Gil knew all too well what sort of carnage they would face at the hands of those troops. Better armed, better trained, and better fed, Sherman's army would decimate them unless some sort of miracle occurred.

"Watch yourself" chased him through each day, as did that smile. So unaffected by war. Untouched by all the ugliness around her. That woman on the balcony in Jonesboro, Georgia, became the unexpected reason why he would leave this war with no scars.

He would watch himself. He would go home. He would live. And if it was in his power, every man under his care would live too.

It defied explanation why she had become his touchstone, but as the day came and Sherman's men made their move, Gil set his mind on this task and his heart on living to someday tell that woman how her small and seemingly inconsequential moment of greeting to a weary soldier had made a difference.

Even as the bullets flew around him and he charged into battle, he carried her image. When his horse fell beneath him and Gil was forced to continue on foot, the lady in blue walked with him. Every time he stooped down to offer aid to an ailing soldier, she waited there for him.

It was a sort of madness found only on the battlefield, or so he told himself. *"Watch,"* she told him. And he did.

The first bullet struck him in the shoulder, a sting he barely felt. The second tore a track across his face and then skimmed his neck, scarring him and nearly claiming him for dead but sparing his life by the slightest of distances.

Watch. The word took on another meaning as he fumbled for his weapon. Blood clouded his vision until he could barely see, but something compelled him to set his gun aside to retrieve his father's gold watch from his pocket.

He swiped at the bloody fingerprints marring the glass. Frowning, he blinked to try to see the numbers. To watch the second hand's slow sweep around the dial.

Blood. So much blood. *Must see the watch.* Gil held the watch against his chest just over his heart and rubbed the glass against his uniform in a feeble attempt to remove the blood.

A searing jolt of pain hit him, and he looked down at his right hand. Though he still clutched the watch, blood seeped from a wound in his hand. The hand that had been over his heart. Wincing, he turned the watch over. Where there was once a perfectly smooth surface, there was now an ugly scar.

At his feet, he saw the bullet. The one meant for his heart. The bullet that was stopped because of a watch.

And because of the warning from the girl in the blue dress.

Someday he would tell her that she saved his life. Someday. If he lived through this.

Chapter 2

June 1869

The stagecoach moved on, wheels endlessly rolling along in a rhythm that alternated between taunting Bea and lulling her to sleep. One more mile farther away from San Antonio. One more mile closer to completing her mission.

Her eyes drifting shut, she leaned against the makeshift pillow she'd made of her cloak and thought of what she'd left behind. What she'd been trying to leave behind for years.

Poverty had never suited her, and yet it had been Bea's plight more than once. From her vaguest memories of early years spent with a sickly mother and an absent and very old father to the abrupt move to her aunt Lou's home when both her parents went to be with Jesus, she had learned to adapt.

What her aunt and uncle's accommodations lacked in creature comforts, they made up for with love and laughter. Though her mother had referred to Lou and Ben as Papa's poor relations, Ben ran a general store that was profitable enough to hire help to run it for him.

Help in the form of a man as old as Henry Neville, who fancied himself the perfect husband for Bea.

Bea much preferred their cozy Georgia farmhouse to her mother's tiny room that she left behind. At the farm she had her own room with a curtained bed and soft pillows. She was, in every way, completely spoiled and adored from the moment she arrived.

She quickly became the beloved daughter Lou and Ben never had, and they became Mama and Papa to her. She grew from an awkward child to a young woman in what seemed like a blink of her eye. The family fortunes seemed to grow at the same rate, allowing for a life of comfort and ease in a lushly appointed home.

Then General Sherman's troops arrived on their doorstep and changed everything in a flash of fire and ashes. The farmhouse now gone, the three of them moved into town and lived above the store.

Shelves were nearly bare, but Papa carved a meager living out of what he could manage to sell. More than once, she would catch him slipping an extra loaf of bread into a widow's hands or offering a piece of fruit to a hungry child.

Bea often looked to the doors of the store, half expecting her soldier to walk through them with his gold pocket watch in hand. "It's time, Bea. Let's go," he would say.

But he never came.

Then suddenly one day their fortunes changed, and Bea got her wish to leave Georgia behind, though not through the means she expected. The three of them moved to New Orleans where a lovely establishment was awaiting them on a tree-lined avenue. The shelves were filled to the brim with the most elegant fashions, and clerks were hired to manage things while Papa supervised the building of a grand home on the Rue Royale. This time, the curtained bed was handmade and delivered by the man who carved the delicate flowers and swans on the posts.

Life was good again. Better than good. Their days of poverty were gone. Mama smiled again and Papa would often catch her up in an embrace to dance across the carpets she'd ordered all the way from Europe.

Then Henry Neville showed up not two weeks ago demanding Bea's hand in marriage. She heard rumblings of disagreement between Mr. Neville and Papa, but only from behind closed doors. Threats of calling the authorities were shouted on both sides of the fray, and then silence. She'd nearly jumped out of her skin when Papa's office door flew open and Mr. Neville marched out.

"Not a word to her," Papa shouted from two steps behind his former employee. "Not a word or it's all off."

Mr. Neville glanced her way, his normally kind expression replaced with a predatory look that made her shrink back. "See you in Mexico, sweetheart," he hissed before whirling around to disappear down the corridor toward the back exit.

Papa stormed through the door and then stopped short, obviously only just realizing that Bea was nearby. "What did you hear?"

"Nothing," she'd said, as much to placate Papa as to convince herself it was true. "But I will not marry him."

There had been no response to that statement. At the time, she took that as agreement. She still hoped that to be true.

Bea thought of Papa now as she shifted positions on the unforgiving wooden seat where she was wedged next to a snoring old woman and knocking knees with a man who reminded her far too much of a younger version of Mr. Neville.

The man offered her a leering smile, but Bea ignored him to look out at the ever-changing landscape of Western Texas. Exhaustion tugged at her eyes and attempted to lull her to closing them, but she resisted. The last time she'd slept on a decent bed was back at the Menger Hotel in San Antonio, where she'd conducted an errand for Mama and then stayed for two lovely days until the stage arrived to bring her here.

How she longed for that bed.

No, in truth, she longed for the curtained bed with the swans and flowers carved into the posts in her second-floor bedroom. For mornings spent in conversation with Mama and evenings attending one New Orleans soiree after another.

For the life she left behind, before she became a commodity to be married off rather than a precious child to be coddled and spoiled. And though it made absolutely no sense, she longed to see the soldier again, to hear him tell her he'd come back for her.

A silly thought, of course. But sometimes silly thoughts made everything happening around her easier to endure.

Her gloved hands worried the trim of her sleeve as she thought of what awaited her at her destination. Another relative could surely see to Mama's interest in the land she inherited in Texas. Someone else could claim what Mama suddenly declared was precious family property, and yet Mama insisted she go.

The deed had been sealed in an envelope along with other documents that Mama said would be needed. Mama's instructions were clear: do not open the envelope until she arrived in Crinoline Creek, but do read the documents before she presented them to the authorities there.

Though she called the woman Mama, Lou Wilson was no blood relation of hers, and thus she had no familial claim to this land. Necessity had brought them together, and love bound them up. Thus, Bea would do as she was asked and see to this matter.

Plus, it got her out of a household where tensions were running high and the constant threat of Mr. Neville and Mexico never seemed far away.

"Next stop, Crinoline Creek," the driver called as he strolled down the aisle with his pocket watch in hand.

Bea sighed. Dare she hope that the local hotel had a nice bed with pretty bed curtains?

A soft bed wasn't what he'd hoped for, but Gil Hollis sure was glad he had one. With images of the dead and dying waiting behind his eyelids when he dared to try to sleep, he'd made little use of the accommodations his brother had provided now that he was in charge of the family ranch.

Time spent here in Crinoline Creek had healed him some, but not enough to suit him. Though he'd mustered out of the army some time ago, he'd put off returning home in favor of joining up with several of his buddies from the war to lead wagon trains of settlers out west.

On the trail, no one cared that he'd grown a beard in a poor attempt to hide the scars on his face or that he could only rely on one of his hands to grip a pistol or the reins of a horse. All they cared about was whether he knew where he was going and could get them there safely.

Though he'd never claim he was happy, Gil found his misery eased on the open trail with no one staring and no one caring. Then Ed caught up to him to break the news that Pop was gone and Gil was needed at home.

So he went home. For Ed, and for Pop.

To make up for the time he'd missed, Gil had done just about everything Sheriff Ed Hollis asked him to do, except join him as deputy. For months now, he'd claimed he had far too many chores back at the ranch to consider the offer of strapping on a weapon and helping Ed patrol Crinoline Creek.

It wasn't that he didn't want to take up a gun again. He'd done that plenty since leaving the trail behind, but only to provide food for the table or to rid the land of a beast that meant harm. In fact, he found great pleasure in setting his sights on a target, taking aim, and firing, and great accomplishment in providing a meal for the family who'd loved him even when he was at his worst.

Had the rangers not been disbanded during the war, Gil might have considered returning to their company and keeping Crinoline Creek as his home base. But with that not an option, he'd settled in here and tried to make himself useful at the ranch.

Just two days ago, he'd been approached about taking on another wagon train that was leaving next week. He'd said no, but not without pausing to think about it first. Now he wondered why he'd paused.

He didn't mind the idea of working with his older brother. With their ages so close, they'd practically been raised as twins anyway, so they'd worked alongside one another most of their lives.

No, the thing that bothered Gil most about taking on the responsibilities of the deputy sheriff of Crinoline Creek was that blasted roof. He looked up now and shook his head. Why in the world would anyone sign up for a life of staying indoors and shuffling papers when he could sit on the back of a fine paint pony like Gideon with nothing but the sky overhead?

Pop had understood. He hadn't been tamed by polite society either, although he'd certainly been tamed by Mama. When the fever took her in the second year of the war, Pop was never the same. The tough old man had been able to do just about anything but live without the love of his life.

He'd also understood Gil, it might be argued, better than Gil understood himself. When Winston Hill started looking for a man to join his doctoring practice, Pop had written to Gil to inform him he'd already promised Dr. Hill that Gil would be his partner. To seal the deal, he'd bought a nice plot of land adjacent to the family ranch where Gil could someday bring home a bride and raise his children.

Though he had no fear on the battlefield, Gil was afraid to write back to Pop with news that his doctoring days were over. So he joined the wagon train and told Pop he'd come home someday and do as he asked, just not now.

Now Pop was two months gone and Gil still hadn't spoken with Dr. Hill other than to offer a nod in greeting when they passed one another on the street or at church.

Gil shifted positions to look toward the west. With the sun rising behind him, the Davis Mountains were cast in a familiar purple hue. He'd thought about those purple mountains when his eyes only saw the battlefield. Now that he was here, it seemed wrong to be thinking about the battlefield.

Except for when he slept, Gil had managed to keep his mind moving in a different direction most of the time. Thoughts of the gold watch in his pocket had him standing right in the thick of it all again.

Gil flexed his arm and felt the tendons stretch. He tried once again to curl his fingers into a fist, but the tendons were as tight as the damaged skin that was stretched across one side of his face.

His medical knowledge told him it was possible, but once again his hand refused to cooperate. Still, he would try again tomorrow and every day until his right hand could operate the same as the left.

Rather than continue the direction of his thoughts, Gil reached into his pocket to retrieve the watch. Though the timepiece bore a significant dent to the back of it, the second hand swept around the dial just fine and the mechanism appeared to be doing its job as well as it ever had.

Running his finger over the rough edge of the dent, Gil refused to allow his mind to once again travel back to that day. To that battle.

Instead, he conjured up the lady in blue along with a smile. He'd long ago decided she was some angel delivered to that balcony to send him a message that the Lord meant to keep him alive for a while longer.

The sound of a horse approaching echoed across the distance. Gil slid the watch back into place in his pocket and turned his mount to face the man headed his way.

Ed, of course. No one else would think to look for him here.

Or care to look at all, if the truth were told.

"The answer is no," Gil called across the distance.

"You don't know the question yet," his brother responded as he reined in his gray mare.

"Don't need to. You're the one doing the asking."

It was a conversation old as time between them and yet the words never changed. Neither did the smile it always brought.

"I came to talk to you about that job."

And here it was. The other conversation where the words never changed. For some reason, Ed's ability to chase off a new recruit to the sheriff's office seemed to surprise everyone but Ed.

"No. I will not be your deputy."

"Wasn't asking you to." Ed lifted the brim of his Stetson and swiped at his forehead with his handkerchief. "Got the position filled. New deputy starts today."

Gil gave his brother a sideways look. He'd had three deputies in the last two months and not a one of them had lasted longer than a few weeks.

"Yeah? How long do you think this one's going to stay?"

With a lift of his shoulder, Ed dismissed the question. "Not that you asked, but he's a fellow by the name of Emmett Blair. Said he's aiming to put down roots. He ordered himself a bride and is having her sent here."

"Is that so? All of that and you hired him just today. Impressive. Where'd you meet him?"

Ed put on his defensive expression and shrugged, two signs that whatever he was about to say troubled him despite whatever words to the contrary he was about to offer. "Down at the café."

Gil's laughter startled both horses. He grasped at his reins to keep from being thrown, but Ed wasn't so lucky. His mount tossed him, and he landed on the ground in a cloud of dust.

Now Gil was laughing so hard he was crying. He reached down to help his brother stand.

Ed took his hand and started to climb to his feet. Then he tugged hard and the horizon tilted. Another yank and Ed had managed to haul Gil down onto the dirt with him.

They lay on their backs laughing like schoolchildren instead of the grown men they were. Finally Ed stood and offered Gil a hand up.

He took it, albeit warily. "Miz Mattie is going to have our hides over the extra washing we're going to cause her."

Matilda Walsh had been with the family since before either of the Hollis boys were alive. She'd come west as a nanny when their mother was a child, and the slight woman with an Irish brogue who had outlived two husbands would probably outlive Ed and Gil.

"Since this is your fault, I'm not worried."

Gil dusted off his trousers and picked up his hat where it'd fallen in the dirt. Meanwhile Ed's skittish mare was alternating between helping itself to prairie grass and nervously casting glances over at Ed while flicking her tail.

"I'm not worried either. Miz Mattie always did like me better," Gil said as he watched his brother try to sneak up on his horse.

After several attempts to snatch the reins, Ed paused to look over his shoulder at Gil. "That's not true and you know it."

Gil made a soft clicking sound to call the mare over to him. Immediately she came toward him and allowed him to scratch her between the ears.

"How in tarnation?" Ed said as he took the reins and resumed his spot in the saddle. "She's had it in for me since I traded that bay mare for her last fall."

"Guess she likes me better too," Gil said.

Of course he wouldn't mention the fact that every morning when he went out to feed Gideon he always snuck a treat to the bay. This morning it had been a pair of carrots pulled out of Miz Mattie's garden. Yesterday, he'd brought her a lump of sugar that might have garnered him a lump on the head if Mattie had caught him taking it from her pantry.

Ed gave him that sideways look that meant he was about to deliver news that Gil wouldn't like. "It's a good thing you're so popular. It'll serve you well in your new position."

Gil shook his head. "Oh no you don't. You just told me you have a new deputy, so you can't rope me into taking the job this time."

"Not trying to." He shifted his attention to the horizon and then back at Gil. "And you're right. I've already got a deputy."

His eyes narrowed. "Go on."

"Emmett's going to work out just fine as my deputy, but he doesn't know his head from a hole in the ground in regard to what goes on in this town. I need a man to lead him along until I get back. That's you."

"No, that's you," Gil said. "You're the sheriff."

"I need you to step in temporarily as sheriff."

"No." Gil straightened his hat and walked over to where his horse was waiting. "The people elected you, not me." He paused to look back over his shoulder. "Where are you going, anyway?"

"San Antonio. Got a lead on that mail fraud scheme the feds warned us about. Looks like one of the operatives spent a few nights there recently and may have passed off more fake land grants to a buyer there. I'm going to follow up on that lead."

"San Antonio's not that far, and you've time to whip Deputy

Blair into shape. I'm sure your deputy will do just fine for a few weeks." He patted Gideon and then climbed into the saddle. "So good luck to you both."

Ed remained where he sat, his expression unreadable. "I need you to do this," he finally said. "I can't be in two places at once, and I can't send Blair out there to do this without any training. I'm leaving now. I need to catch up to this suspect before word gets out that I'm coming."

Gil wheeled around to face his brother. "I can't be you, Ed. My right hand is useless for shooting, and nobody in town will look me in the eye because of my scars."

"You shoot better left handed than you ever did right handed. As to your scars, you're wrong. You're just too dead set on believing it that you haven't given anyone a chance."

At least one of those statements was true. Still, Gil kept his silence.

"Please. For Pop."

Three words, and yet they changed everything. "That's not fair."

"Wasn't trying to be fair." Ed paused. "That land Pop bought for you to set up housekeeping on? I always thought something was fishy with that deal, and it turns out I was right. I've got solid proof that the land documents were doctored and that at least two other people were sold the same piece of property."

"I'll do it," he managed. "But I need to know everything."

"All right," Ed said. "The first thing you need to know is that trouble just may be headed to town in the form of that perpetrator who was in San Antonio. The federal agents think she's coming here next based on a telegram she sent to New Orleans. If that's the case, she'll be here on the afternoon stage."

"She?"

"Yes, there's a description in the telegram, but my understanding is she's pretty enough to stand out in a crowd, so you shouldn't have any problem finding her."

"I'll watch for her, then. I assume you've got a description." At Ed's nod, Gil continued. "All right. What else?"

"Well," he said slowly as he clasped his brother's shoulder, "the second thing you need to know is that you're going to make a fine temporary sheriff."

❧ Chapter 3 ❧

*I*f that was her, then trouble wasn't just headed for town. It had arrived.

Gil had been leaning against a post outside the café just long enough to see the stagecoach arrive and its passengers spill out. While most hurried to greet folks who awaited them before the dark clouds overhead turned to rain, this one stood at the door and seemed reluctant to move past the last step. Not what he expected from a woman who'd committed fraud in at least two states, but then he was no lawman, so his opinion was personal and not professional.

From his vantage point, it was easy to look up from beneath the cover of his hat to watch unnoticed as the woman finally decided to complete her arrival in Crinoline Creek. The disgruntled older woman who was threatening to push her out of the way might have quickened the process.

The report from the federal agent in San Antonio had indicated the suspect was of average height with auburn hair and stylish figure. The agent had added that she was pretty. Just how pretty was made clear when she stepped into a beam of sunlight pouring through the holes in the old station's roof.

She was a city girl for certain. Everything about her, from her porcelain complexion to the fan she retrieved, told him she'd come from quality.

But that's exactly what Ed had told him to expect. Her coconspirators were smart, and they were sneaky, but above all, they had plenty of money. The agent in charge back in New Orleans had warned that the criminals had already taken lovesick men and prospective landowners for a tidy sum. With that sort of operation, it was sure they'd have someone pretty fronting it all.

And there she was making a feeble attempt to get someone to haul her bag for her. The woman adjusted her gloves and looked around and then back at poor Jim Beckett.

Jim had been meeting the daily stagecoach almost as long as Crinoline Creek had been a town. The old man was good for greeting the folks and making them feel welcome but couldn't lift a bag without aggravating his sciatica. Thus, what he brought in enthusiasm and cheerfulness, he lacked in size and strength.

Keeping his hat down low, Gil ambled toward the comical scene.

"I'm sorry, ma'am," Jim was saying. "I would love to help you with your bag, but you see, there was this unfortunate incident back before the war where I tried to lift..." He shook his head. "Well, I'll be. Is that you, Sheriff Hollis?"

Gil sighed. Ed had only just left two hours ago but already the word was out about his temporary appointment.

"Need some help, Jim?"

"I do not, but this lovely lady is in need of an escort to the hotel and assistance with her bag. Might that be within your purview?"

Gil suppressed a grin. Old Jim sure had developed a fancy vocabulary in the presence of the lady.

"I'll have the deputy come get the lady's bag." He swung his attention to the woman he'd been told was named Beatrice Wilson. Per the plan he'd cooked up with Ed, Gil turned on the charm. "But I would be pleased to escort the lady."

She looked up at him with an expression that might have melted his heart had he not already decided she was the prettiest con artist he'd ever met. Wide eyes in a shade of pale blue that seemed somehow familiar shimmered with tears.

"Do I know you?"

Not at all the greeting he expected. The truth was he'd felt some recognition upon seeing her. Had to be the fact he'd read her description and been expecting her though.

"I doubt it, ma'am," he said. "Let me help."

"Thank you," she said as she swiped at her cheek with the back of her gloved hand. "But I couldn't possibly leave without my bag. It contains very important documents."

"Here, miss." Jim offered her his handkerchief. "Welcome to our humble town."

Oh, she was good. Poor Jim was practically groveling at her feet. He'd better get her out of here before things got any worse. Best not to arrest her in front of Jim anyway.

Gil put on his best manners and attempted a smile. He could feel the taut scars protest beneath his beard as he managed the unfamiliar expression. "What's your name, ma'am?"

The woman gave only a moment's pause until her eyes landed on his chest and the shiny silver badge Ed had planted there as his last act before leaving town. Slowly her attention returned to Gil's face. Scrutiny rarely bothered him. He understood what a shock his scars were to those who were innocent to the ways of war.

This woman's gaze, her slow attention to the details of his ruined face, bothered him. Too much.

"Beatrice," she finally said. "Beatrice Wilson. Are you certain we haven't met?"

Indeed the woman he'd been warned would arrive. The woman whose arrest warrant was being signed in San Antonio, possibly at this very moment.

"I am."

"And you are?" she asked when she'd finished her scrutiny.

"Hollis," he told her.

"Sheriff Hollis," Jim corrected with a smile.

He shouldered the criminal's bag and gave Jim a withering look before turning his attention to the woman. "Come on, Beatrice Wilson. I'll help you and your bag get to where you need to be."

She followed without question, though Jim did almost ruin the ruse when he shouted a question regarding their direction. Leave it to the old man to notice he'd turned toward the jail instead of the hotel.

"Making a stop at the office first."

"Carry on, then," Jim called.

Miss Wilson picked up her skirts and hurried across the street beside him. When they reached the sheriff's office, he paused long enough to hold the door open for her, then gave silent thanks that she stepped inside without question or comment.

Where was Emmett? Ed said he would be there.

Of course, the newly hired deputy was nowhere to be found. Oh well. He could do this.

Gil dropped his hat and the bag onto the deputy's desk then turned to face the woman. Ed had reminded him not to be swayed by a pretty face, and that reminder served him well at this moment. Because her face was pretty, even before she aimed a smile in his direction.

"I am confused as to why I am here, Sheriff Hollis." She toyed with the ribbons attached to her bonnet as she seemed to take in her surroundings. Without warning, her gaze collided with his. "Though it is quite nice." She paused. "For a jail, that is."

"You don't have any idea why you're here?"

"No, I'm sorry. I don't." She smiled. "Unless this is where land transactions are handled. I do have some business related to that sort of matter."

"What kind of business?"

"Just something my mother has asked me to handle," she said lightly, her gaze never wavering. "A family matter. If you'd like, I can show you the letter of instruction from her. It's in my bag."

"That won't be necessary for now. And no, that is not the type of business we transact here."

She shrugged. "All right, then."

He leaned on the edge of Ed's desk and looked down at the bag beside him then over at her. If she suspected what was about to happen, Miss Wilson gave no indication. Either she was very good at what she did or she was innocent.

But that was not his to decide. All Gil had to do was follow Ed's instructions and arrest her then let the judge make the determination whether she was guilty.

It had seemed so simple when Ed explained it. But now, with the potential prisoner smiling up at him like he hung the moon, nothing seemed to be going as planned.

Ed warned him not to take long in getting her under arrest and into Cell One else she try to talk him out of it or, worse, make a fuss. Because when a woman made a fuss, the menfolk came running, and most of them wouldn't like to see a pretty girl caged up even if she was a wanted criminal.

Better not to have that happen.

The darkening sky and first drops of rain outside cast the room in deep shadows. Miss Wilson stood by the desk, her attention flitting around the office as if taking it all in. He left her there to light the lamps.

That task done, Gil took a deep breath and let it out slowly. He had the advantage of surprise, but once Miss Wilson figured out what he was intent on doing, that advantage would be gone.

Plus, once he made the arrest he could leave the rest to the deputy to handle. Sure, he was temporary sheriff, but Ed would be back soon. In the meantime, Miss Wilson would be fine with minimal supervision.

And from what he'd heard, that's about all the deputy could offer.

"Miss Wilson, there's no easy way to do this, so let's just get it over with. I brought you here because—"

The door flew open and Ed's new deputy tumbled in, bringing

the rain with him. Kicking the door shut, Emmett stumbled, and his hat went one way and his handcuffs the other, landing at Miss Wilson's feet. The smell on Emmett's breath arrived at the desk before he did.

"Am I late?" he managed as he stumbled across the floor and skidded to a stop inches away from Gil's boots.

Gil looked down at the fool and shook his head. "You are," he told him. "But that isn't all. You're also fired and under arrest for public drunkenness."

Reaching down, Gil yanked Emmett to his feet. The deputy swayed backward then overcorrected. Gil caught him by the shoulders, turned him around, and marched him to Cell Two, the one farthest from the office. Removing Emmett's gun from the holster at his waist, Gil closed the door behind him.

"Hey now," Emmett complained as he wrapped his hands around the bars and gave them a shake. "I'm not the one who's supposed to be arrested. She is."

Great.

Miss Wilson's expression went sour. "What is he talking about?"

Gil quickly positioned himself between the pretty lady and the door in case she decided to try to escape. "Beatrice Wilson, in the name of the state of Texas and this county, I am placing you under arrest."

Chapter 4

Mama had warned Bea there might be some opposition to handling the land matter, but this was ridiculous. She mustered up every bit of righteous indignation she could and stared up into the face of the man who was now her enemy.

"You will do no such thing."

The sheriff's expression quickly told her he hadn't expected that response. Nor, apparently, did he know what to say next.

Emboldened, she crossed her arms over her chest and continued. "Step aside and let me take my bag and leave this place. I have done nothing wrong, and if I had, you would have told me."

"Woo hoo," the odious drunk called from his cell. "Got a temper, this one. I sure hope my wife has this kind of fire in her."

"Shut up, Emmett." The sheriff stood his ground, back straight and his hands at his side like a gunfighter ready to draw. A muscle in his bearded jaw moved, but only slightly.

This man was a warrior or had been. The scars that showed on his face did nothing to mar his handsome features, but she doubted he realized that. Though she ought to have been afraid, there was something in his eyes that told her he was more gentle giant than angry lawman. Something in the way he looked down at her that pleaded for her to just do what he asked.

Of course, she wouldn't. Not if it meant facing a jail cell.

"All right," she said sweetly. "If you will not respond, then I am left to believe you have decided you were wrong about me." She took a step toward the desk where her bag had been placed, and her foot landed on something hard.

"Stop right there," he told her. "The charges against you are mail fraud, real estate fraud, participating in organized criminal activity, and, if you're not careful, resisting arrest. And those are just the ones I can remember. Ed will have to tell you the rest of them."

"Who paid you to say that?" she demanded.

He looked as if she had slapped him. "I'm an honest man, Miss Wilson, and I am only doing my job. I don't take payments to sway me one way or the other. Don't make this any more difficult than it already is."

"He ain't doing his job," the prisoner called out. "He's doing Ed's job. That's why I ain't fired. Only Ed can fire me."

"Shut up, Emmett," Sheriff Hollis said again. He spared a glance at the prisoner then returned his attention to Bea. "Miss Wilson, I don't make the laws, I just enforce them."

"Until Ed gets back," the drunk man interjected.

He cleared his throat. "Ignore him. My job is to see that you are held for questioning here in our jail. Whatever I do, I do my best. So you're just going to have to cooperate and go into that jail cell willingly."

Her foot nudged the object beneath her toes. "And if I don't?"

Bea punctuated the question with a smile. Again, he seemed to be caught off guard. If this man was indeed a sheriff with any sort of authority, and she had begun to doubt that, he did not have much experience in arresting people.

Not that she had any experience in being arrested.

"Then I suppose I'll have to put you there myself."

The man in the other jail cell let out a whoop. "That's telling her. Don't let a woman be the boss of you. I know I won't when my sweetie arrives. She's going to know that her husband Emmett is the boss and what the boss says goes."

"That's enough, Emmett," the sheriff said.

The door opened behind the sheriff, and that nice man who met the stagecoach stepped inside. "Need something, Jim?" Sheriff Hollis asked.

"Just checking on the little lady," he said as he looked around the lawman to offer Bea a smile. "Seems like it was taking you a while to escort her over to the hotel, so I figured I'd see if you needed my help."

"We're doing just fine here, Jim." The sheriff kept his gaze steadily on Bea. "Go on back to work."

"Actually, sir." Bea upped her smile and aimed it at the older man. "If you wouldn't mind, I could use some assistance getting my bag to the hotel. Would you be a dear and do that for me?"

"Of course," he said, stepping inside.

"Stay right there, Jim." The sheriff turned around to face him. "She's fine. The bag is fine. Go on now. If you choose not to leave, then you may be joining Emmett in a jail cell."

"What's Emmett doing in the jail cell?"

"That's between me and him," he told the older man. "The question is whether you want to join him."

With the lawman's back turned, Bea quickly knelt down to retrieve the object upon which she had been standing. A moment later, she had hidden it in her pocket.

She also had a plan to get the man to listen to what she had to say.

"There's no need to be that way about it," Jim said. "I was going to tell her I can't lift heavy bags anymore, what with my sciatica and all." He once again looked directly at Bea. "But I can send someone from the hotel down here to fetch whatever you need fetched. And why is Emmett in the jail cell?"

"Jim," Sheriff Hollis said evenly, "go. Now."

"Yessir." He hurried out the door without a backward glance.

The sheriff turned back to Bea. "All right. Enough nonsense. You're under arrest, Miss Wilson. Are you willing to walk peaceably over to that empty cell and step inside?"

"Look out, Gil," the drunk called. "She's got something in her pocket."

Bea froze. "Don't pay any attention to him."

The sheriff's expression now looked every bit as threatening as that question sounded. Bea decided to try to distract him.

"Surely there is another option. I have no idea what mail fraud is, but I expect the accusation regarding land has to do with my mother's property here in the county."

When he merely stared, she continued. "You appear to be a reasonable man. Can't we compromise?"

"Reasonable men don't compromise when it comes to the law, Miss Wilson. I'm just doing my job."

Bea allowed her gaze to travel the length of him, settling finally on those beautiful eyes. Whatever she'd seen before in the way of softness was now gone. In an instant, she realized she'd gone too far.

In one swift move he hauled her into his arms. "Stop this," she shouted as she attempted to squirm out of his grip. "I am not a criminal. If you would just listen to me."

"I'm tired of listening to you. Tell it to the judge."

Without a word, Sheriff Hollis whirled around and headed for the cage next to the one where the odious man named Emmett was now cheering. She could not allow this. Not when good sense would obviously prevail if she could just get his attention.

Before the lawman could react, Bea pulled the handcuffs out of her pocket and slipped one on her captor and the other on herself. Sheriff Hollis yanked his hand away and then wheeled backward onto the cot when Bea tumbled with him.

Yes. Now she had his attention.

"What have you done, woman?" he demanded as he scooted as far away as he could while being attached to her at the wrist.

What indeed? Bea steeled her courage and looked up at the sheriff. "Just something to get your attention because you're being unreasonable. I'm sure your deputy has a key for it, don't you, sir?"

"I do indeed," he said with a leering smile.

"See. He does. Now will you listen to me?"

The sheriff looked past her to the drunk man. "Emmett, give me the key."

Emmett rose then fell back on his cot. On his second attempt, he managed to find his feet and stood. A moment later, on wobbling legs, he retrieved the key from his pocket and held it in his fist.

"Don't think I will." He held the key up and grinned. "Unless you give me my job back, that is."

The sheriff rose and moved toward the door, and Bea had no choice but to go with him. Grabbing the ring of keys off the wall, he jammed one into the lock and turned it.

"You're not getting your job back," he told the drunk man.

They were in the other cell now, Sheriff Hollis first and Bea trailing at arm's length. This close, the man smelled worse than just the liquor he had consumed. She peered from around the sheriff to see the odious man grin.

"You sure?"

"I'm sure," the lawman said. "Now give me the key."

Sheriff Hollis reached for it, and Bea was forced to lunge with him. His elbow caught her bonnet and sent it sideways, covering her eyes.

"Use your other hand," she demanded as she made a poor attempt at straightening her bonnet with her left hand. "Or at least warn me."

The object of her irritation ignored her. Had the drunk man been able to walk properly, he might have slipped past them and escaped as Bea and the sheriff untangled themselves.

Instead, he landed back on the cot with a thud then slumped against the wall. With a chuckle, the prisoner opened his mouth and tossed the key in then swallowed.

Gil stared down at Emmett until the urge to punch the man subsided. Not that he could, given the fact his good hand was shackled to Beatrice Wilson.

Great. Without a word, he turned his back on the former deputy and walked out of the cell.

"Surely there's another key," the woman said as she followed him through no choice of her own. "I mean, who just has one set of keys for the handcuffs, right?"

"Just one per set," Emmett said. "Ain't that right, Gil? That's the way Ed had 'em made."

Gil slammed the cell door and then studied the keys on the ring. If there was another key, Ed had it with him. The brief shower had ended, but raindrops still dripped from the windows.

A plan occurred to him, but it required Miss Wilson to cooperate. He looked down at her and she ignored him. What she couldn't ignore was the fact she was still attached to him at the wrist.

Gil tugged on her arm and led her toward the door.

"Where are we going?" his companion demanded.

"To get these cuffs off," he said.

"Hey now, don't be like that," Emmett called as they walked away. "I didn't mean any harm. I'd have given it to you if I'd been thinking straight. I would've. I swear it."

The fool was still talking when the door closed behind them.

Ed would never talk him into something like this again. Ever. He'd told his brother it was a bad idea, and here he was just a couple of hours into the job of temporary sheriff and his deputy was in the jail cell and his prisoner was attached to his left wrist.

"Howdy, Gil." He glanced behind him and saw one of the Martin twins sweeping the mud off the sidewalk in front of the barbershop.

"Howdy," he said in return.

"Looks like you got a prisoner," the Martin boy said. "She's pretty."

So much for the townsfolk not knowing.

Letting out a long breath, Gil shook his head and turned toward the new blacksmith shop on the other side of the boardinghouse. A tug at his sleeve reminded him he wasn't alone—as if he needed that reminder.

"Where are we going?"

He looked down at Miss Wilson. "To get this situation taken care of," he told her. "Then I'm taking you back to jail."

She looked away. "You're really intent on arresting me? I can prove I have not committed any crimes if you just let me go get my papers from my bag."

Gil refused to be taken in by those blue eyes, by that pretty face. He did, however, slow his pace to match hers when he realized she was struggling to keep up.

"I'm intent on doing the job I agreed to until I am relieved of that duty."

"So you are just the temporary sheriff, like the drunk man said."

"I am," he said. "Ed should be back in a few days, although I will warn you that he's the one who is certain you're guilty, so don't expect to try and convince him otherwise."

"Why? He's never met me. How could he make such a decision?"

"Since I'm not a sheriff by trade, you'll have to ask him when you see him." He paused at the corner to let a wagon go by.

"What are you if you're not a sheriff?" she asked.

He ignored her.

"Hey there, Gil," the driver called.

Gil looked up to see Ben Simmons guiding his wagon around a muddy spot in the road. "Ben," he said in response.

"Looks like you've got yourself a prisoner," Ben called over his shoulder.

Ignoring him, Gil stepped off the sidewalk to cross the road. Two steps later, he realized he'd lost the cooperation of his companion when he felt a tug on his wrist. He turned around to see her still standing on the sidewalk.

"Come on," he told her.

"I'll ruin my shoes in this mud. Isn't there another way to get where we're going that doesn't require me to slosh through this?"

Gil sighed. "Yes, there is, but I'll go ahead and apologize right now because you're not going to like it. Don't guess it'll help you to know that I won't like it either."

She gave him a perturbed look. "I haven't liked much about our interactions since the minute I first spoke with you. I assure you there's nothing you could do that will change my opinion at this point, except perhaps to listen to me defend myself against your ridiculous charges."

"Listening to you is Ed's job."

"I don't know who Ed is, but if I cooperate in helping you get these handcuffs off, maybe you could just look at what I brought with me? If you do, I'm sure you'll see I'm no criminal."

He appeared to be considering the question. "All right. Once we get these off, I'll let you make your case if it'll make you happy, but remember, I'm just temporary. Only Ed can decide whether to press charges. I'll have to hold you in custody until he gets back no matter what. And for the record, Ed is the sheriff."

Her nose wrinkled. "Surely you do not expect me to stay in a cell next to that odious man."

Gil hadn't thought that far ahead. That did put him in a pickle. He'd have to figure that out later. For now, he needed to get the issue of the handcuffs handled. For that, he needed his old friend Ethan Caldwell, a former ranger and the new owner of the blacksmith shop across the street.

Ethan would solve this problem quickly and without anyone in town realizing what happened. The last thing he needed was to be teased about being shackled to a prisoner on his first day as temporary sheriff.

But first he had to get himself and the woman he was chained to across a muddy road. "Are you certain you don't just want to walk across the street like the rest of us?"

Miss Wilson looked around and then back at him. "I do see that others are crossing just fine, but I doubt they purchased their footwear in one of New Orleans' finest establishments. These are too expensive to ruin, Sheriff Hollis."

Gil looked down at the lady's delicate footwear and then back up at her. "I see your point. You look more suited to a party than a walk to the blacksmith's shop."

"Finally you're making sense." She gave him a look that told him exactly how she felt about him. "Just find another way to fix this, please. It seems we are attracting a crowd."

She was right. Several townspeople had joined the Martin boy in front of the barbershop, and a few others were collecting across the street by the boardinghouse and the mercantile.

"If you insist."

He reached down and slung her over his shoulder.

❧ Chapter 5 ❧

*B*ea's world tilted. She stifled a scream as she scrambled to hold on to her bonnet. "What are you doing?"

"Exactly what you asked. I found another way to fix this and am helping you get across without ruining your shoes."

She couldn't exactly argue with that. Still, this was *not* what she meant, nor was it what she expected.

"Be still or we will both end up in the mud."

"This was not what I had planned, Sheriff Hollis, so forgive me for trying to keep my hat on and my dignity intact."

A cheer went up from behind them. Bea glanced back to see a buggy passing by. Two matrons were staring at them with expressions that showed how little they appreciated the sheriff's behavior. The driver and his friend, however, were the source of the noise.

She refused to allow humiliation to take hold. Instead, she offered a smile to the idiots. Soon she would have this whole mistake cleared up and she would be on her way. At least her shoes would not be ruined in the process.

The Hollis fellow headed across the street to deposit her on the sidewalk in front of a freshly painted sign that proclaimed the building to be Caldwell's Blacksmith Shop. Without a word, he led her inside.

The scent of woodsmoke immediately enveloped her. Bea blinked to adjust her eyes to the murky darkness as she tried to stay a step behind the lawman.

"Ethan," he called. "Where are you? I need a favor."

No response.

Bea measured her steps to match the sheriff's but still found herself hurrying to keep up. The farther back into the building he went, the darker it got until she found herself grasping tight to the hand connected to hers.

"Ethan," the temporary lawman shouted again. "Where are you?"

Finally they reached the back of the shop. Sheriff Hollis pressed open a door and stepped out into the alley. Sunlight blinded her, and she stumbled forward to land against her companion's broad back.

He turned to face her. Frustration etched his features. "He's not here."

"No, it seems as though he isn't," she said. "But surely he's got tools that we can use."

The substitute sheriff shook his head. "Nothing that the two of us can manage."

"We could ask for help," she offered.

"I'd rather not let anyone else see the predicament we're in. It's bad enough that we've already caused a scene." He paused. "Come with me."

"Where are you taking me?"

"To my ranch," he said.

She stalled, yanking his arm back. Until now she had been relatively patient with this miscarriage of justice, but she certainly wasn't going to willingly leave this city for some unknown location without raising a fuss. Or at least being better informed.

"Oh no," she told him. "I don't know you, and I certainly don't have any reason to trust that you won't do something untoward or illegal."

He looked down in surprise. "It'd be pretty stupid of me to do either of those things when my brother is the sheriff, now wouldn't it?"

"I suppose," she said slowly.

"And I am not the one who put us in this predicament."

Unfortunately, the truth.

He must have deduced her thoughts, because he continued. "My horse is over at the livery. I'll have a couple of the ranch hands cut the cuffs apart then I'll bring you back to town."

"All right," she said. "But I need my bag."

"It's too much trouble to bring with us by horse," he told her. "The bag will be fine where it is."

"There is vital evidence in that bag that I'm sure the real sheriff and the judge would not want to go missing." She gave him a sideways look. "Are you willing to take that chance?"

A few minutes later, the Hollis fellow had secured a buggy from the curious livery owner. Pulling the buggy to the curb, they darted inside the sheriff's office without any comments from passersby.

Emmett was too busy filling the room with his snores to notice their arrival. He also missed their exit a few minutes later.

Mama hadn't spoken much about the land she owned here or the ancestors who had settled it. Bea found herself wishing she had. The terrain was rugged and yet breathtaking.

Lush golden lands studded with low scrub trees and patches of brilliant green fanned out on either side of the well-worn trail. On the horizon ahead, mountains collided with a cloudless sky so blue that it hurt her eyes to look at it for more than a moment.

Bea took it all in as she tried not to think about the ache in her right arm. She clutched the edges of the seat with her free hand as the buggy jolted over ruts. For some odd reason, the temporary sheriff insisted on using his left hand to hold the reins, leaving her to stretch her arm out at an uncomfortable length.

"Something wrong?" her companion asked.

"Can't you use the other hand?"

Her question seemed to surprise him. Then, swiftly, something else clouded his features. "No" was his abrupt reply.

He returned his attention to the trail ahead. They rode in silence until the trail forked and became narrower. A few minutes later, a cluster of buildings came into view. As they drew closer, Bea could make out a barn and several outbuildings set apart from what appeared to be a sizable main house built into a copse of trees.

To the side of the house, a woman in a yellow dress watched them approach. Even from this distance, Bea could see her regal bearing.

Horses and cattle filled pastures as far as she could see, their abundance surprising her. The buggy stopped at the edge of a pen where several men were attempting to lasso a wild horse.

"I can't promise your shoes are safe here," he told her as he swung her down. "But I will try to avoid the mud."

"Thank you," she said, not ready to be carried again.

He let out a shrill whistle and all activity in the pen ceased. "McCrae and Townes, I've got a project for you."

A tall, rangy man with a hat that made him even taller broke away from the group and headed toward them while a shorter fellow in chaps hurried to catch up. Though both of them eyed Bea suspiciously, neither did so in view of the lawman.

The Hollis fellow barked out orders as he headed for a small outbuilding on the other side of the barn and then paused to open the door. The same smoky smell of the blacksmith's shop tumbled toward her as she allowed herself to be led inside.

"What is this place?" she asked as she looked around at the soot-stained walls and the oversized anvil bolted to a table in the back of the building.

"It is a place where a gentleman ought not take a lady," a woman with a distinct Irish brogue said from behind her.

Bea turned around and spied the woman in the yellow dress heading toward her. Her face showed her to be ageless, though wisps of gray hair mingled with red curled beneath her bonnet.

Though her smile was broad when she looked at Bea, it disappeared when her attention shifted to the men. "Gilbert," she said evenly, "ought you to be here? I thought you'd be taking over for your brother today."

"Miz Mattie," he said, his tone like that of a chastised schoolboy.

"You're right, but I ran into a problem."

Her gaze fell on the handcuffs that linked them and then returned to Bea. This time her expression showed no hint of humor. "I see that you do. And what is your problem's name?"

"I am Beatrice Wilson," she told the woman. "Pleased to meet you."

"Likewise, and you may call me Mattie." She leaned against the doorframe and studied them all. "I am curious how you found yourself in this predicament, Miss Wilson. You don't strike me as the type of woman who would end up in a toolshed chained to a man who ought to know better."

"Well, I—"

"She's in my custody," Gil interrupted before Miss Wilson could offer an explanation.

"I see that," Mattie said. "What I don't understand is why she's attached to you at the wrist."

"It's a long story," he said on an exhale of breath.

"It is my fault. Emmett swallowed the key," Miss Wilson said. "Otherwise this would have all been over in a few minutes. You see, I was just trying to get him to listen to me."

"Did it work?" Mattie asked, as if hearing that a deputy swallowed a handcuff key was completely unremarkable. But then maybe she'd met Emmett.

Miss Wilson shook her head. "Not really."

"Doesn't surprise me. And where is Emmett now?"

"In a holding cell," Gil said as he looked over his shoulder to where Townes and McCrae were huddled up in the corner, likely hoping they would avoid Mattie's wrath. "You two come over here and help me with this."

"What is it you propose to do?" Mattie moved closer as if to inspect the situation. "You don't be putting this young lady in harm's way, now."

If only she knew what this young lady had done. Or what Ed believed she'd done. Still, she had a point.

Gil nodded toward his employees. "Townes, you're going to cover her hand with yours while McCrae cuts the chain. If he gets too close, you're the one who'll lose a finger, not her."

The cowboy gave him a weak smile. "You're joking, right, boss?"

"Sure," he said, though he wasn't completely certain that it couldn't happen. McCrae was chosen because he was the stronger of the two, not because he was any smarter or had any skills that might otherwise make him better qualified.

In fact, Red McCrae was known to be a bit nervous in the company of women. With two of them in this small space, that didn't help the odds of something going wrong.

Gil placed his hand on the anvil and indicated for Miss Wilson to do the same. He stretched the chain as far apart as it would go and then nodded for Townes to protect the woman's hand. "All right, McCrae. Grab the ax. One good blow right in the middle of that chain ought to do the trick."

"Lord a mercy," Mattie said. "You are not going to do it this way. Come here, child."

Gil looked over his shoulder to see which of them was being summoned. Not that it mattered, he realized. Where Bea Wilson went, he had to follow.

Townes stepped back with a grateful expression then wiped the sweat from his brow while McCrae set the ax on the floor at his side. Mattie reached beneath her bonnet and retrieved a hairpin.

"Stand still now." She took Miss Wilson's hand in hers and jabbed the hairpin into the lock. A moment later, the cuff sprang open. "Look at that. Now your turn, Gilbert."

"How did you do that?" he demanded as he watched the woman who'd practically raised him pick the lock on his handcuff.

She smiled but did not respond. Instead, she tucked the hairpin back under her bonnet and linked arms with the criminal. "Come with me, young lady. I've got coffee on up at the house and I suspect you could use a cup."

"That would be lovely," she said.

"Gilbert, you come too." Interesting that this invitation wasn't given nearly as sweetly as the one she offered to Miss Wilson. Still, he followed. He might be hardheaded, but he knew when to listen to his elders.

Especially when that elder was Mattie Walsh.

Gil helped both ladies up into the buggy and headed toward the house. True to her habit, Mattie jumped down on her own as soon as the buggy stopped. Before he allowed Miss Wilson down, however, he waited until Mattie had disappeared inside.

"Don't get any ideas of running off," he told her. "You're still a prisoner and in my custody and will be until Ed gets back and takes over. Understand?"

"I understand that you do not yet see the full picture," she told him as he lifted her to the ground. "But once you listen to me, I'm sure we will get everything cleared up. You may even be interested in buying my property. For now, though, would you please fetch my bag?"

Without a backward glance, Gil's prisoner walked inside the door that had been left open. He shouldered her bag and then thought better of it and put the thing back in the buggy. Better for her not to get too comfortable in the house. She was going back to a jail cell soon as he could manage it.

"Hey, Gil," Red McCrae called from the other side of the pasture as he gestured wildly. "Look over yonder toward town."

Gil turned and spied a narrow plume of dark smoke rising from what surely was the town of Crinoline Creek. "Miz Mattie," he called as he hurried inside. "I've got to go."

He found Miss Wilson and the housekeeper huddled over mugs of coffee at the kitchen table. "What's the fuss?" the older woman demanded. "We just sat down."

"Stay where you are," he told her. "I'm the only one leaving. Looks like there's a fire in town."

"Again?" Mattie said. "You'd best see to it, then. Take the men with you. I reckon you'll need the help, but I hope you won't."

"I'm leaving Red here. Don't let my prisoner talk you into letting her go."

"Where would she go?" Mattie asked. "There's nothing but prairie all around us, and unless I miss my guess, those are not walking shoes she's wearing."

"The quality of her shoes has already been established." Gil shifted his attention to Miss Wilson. "Don't think of trying to make a run for it while I'm gone. Red won't let you." He paused. "And I will have your bag with me. You'll get it back *only* if I find you here when I come back."

Miss Wilson rose and began to protest, but Gil ignored her to turn his back and walk outside. First a drunk deputy and then an argumentative female prisoner. Now a fire.

And this was just his first day.

Chapter 6

"Wait." Bea hurried to follow the lawman outside. He turned to give her a look that ought to have stopped her in her tracks.

It didn't.

"Keep my bag, but just let me get one thing out of it. My mother gave me a letter and told me to read it when I got to Crinoline Creek. I just realized that in all the excitement I forgot to do that."

"A letter." He shook his head. "Look, I need to leave now. I don't have time to hunt for a letter."

"It's right on top," she said. "I promise it's easy to find. I can get it myself if—"

"No." He walked around to where he'd stowed the bag and opened it. Sure enough there was a folded paper with the irritating woman's name written on it. He lifted it up. "This?"

"Yes," she said with a smile that almost did him in. Then she looked up at him and those blue eyes collided with his. Once again an odd recollection of a memory rose up. He ignored it to thrust the paper toward her.

"Miz Mattie," he called. "I'm leaving now. If you're not comfortable watching over a prisoner, I can bring her with me into town."

The Irish woman came to stand in the doorway. "Go on, then. I'll take care of her while you're gone. Do be safe. I'd like both of my lads to come home without injury."

"And I thought it was just Ed you worried about," he said as he swung a long leg up into the buggy and drove away grinning.

"Come, child," she told Bea. "You look famished, but I can fix that."

Mattie Walsh was good company. Somehow with her food and conversation, which ranged from tales of her family back in Ireland to life on the Texas prairie with the Hollis family and their young boys, the Irish woman had settled Bea's nerves and made her almost forget her tenuous situation. So comforting was the older woman's presence that, for the first time in days, Bea felt her eyes closing.

"I've bored you to tears," Mattie declared as she pressed away from the table and stood. "And now perhaps you'll have a rest? There's a room at the end of the hall that'd be perfect for you."

"What would the sheriff say if you let me out of your sight?" She'd said the words in a teasing tone, but Bea did wonder what would happen if the grouchy man that Mattie Walsh referred to as Gilbert came back and found her lounging in a room as if she were a favored guest.

"Oh pish posh," Mattie said with a sweep of her hand. "Gilbert will say nothing to you, and it is doubtful he'd say anything to me either. He's got his hands full right now and doesn't have to know, now does he?"

Bea offered a smile. "If it means anything, I promise not to try and run away." She shrugged. "Where would I go if I did?"

"You do have a point, still I will accept your promise and take you at your word. Now come with me and I will get you settled."

Clutching her mother's letter, Bea followed her hostess down a short hallway that led off the kitchen. She stopped at a door and then opened it with a key. "This ought to do just fine," she said. "Make yourself comfortable until Gilbert returns."

Bea stepped inside and smiled. The room was simply furnished, just a narrow bed and a table that held a candlestick, a pitcher and bowl, and a book entitled *The Prairie Traveler* by Randolph B. Marcy. A plain wooden chair rested next to the table beneath windows that opened onto a sunny pasture beyond, and sunlight spilled into the room.

"I won't lock you in," Mattie told her. "I hope you will not abuse that trust."

She turned around to smile at the older woman. "I made a promise. I will keep it."

With a curt nod, Mattie stepped out of the room and closed the door behind her. Bea settled onto the edge of the bed and sighed. This was not at all the bedchamber she'd been hoping for, but as tired as she was, it would do quite nicely for a nap.

Before she fell asleep, however, she did as her mother told her and opened the letter. Unfolding the paper, Bea read the words Mama had written, and her heart sank.

Should you hear that Papa and I have run off

*somewhere, possibly Mexico, do not believe it. We
would do no such thing unless we took you with us. If
we are gone, it is to our graves, and it will have been
murder at the hands of Henry Neville.*

*Yes, my darling. I have sent you away to Texas to
save your life. The family land in Crinoline Creek was
sold some years ago just after the war to a neighbor. The
money enabled us to move to New Orleans and start
again.*

*Do not come home, Bea, nor let Neville know
where you are, or he will kill you too. Your papa and
I love you very much. Enough to have done things to
keep you in comfort. Enough to keep you from knowing
about these things. And enough to do what I can to
save your life. Yes, I, for Papa does not know.*

*I placed money on deposit at the Crinoline Creek
Bank for you. It is a small sum, but it was all I could
manage and should be sufficient for your needs until
you can establish yourself there. Papa and I hope to survive and join you. If we do not, know that everything
we have ever done was out of love and so that we could
give you the very best. We so very much wanted to
prove your mother wrong.*

The signature was Mama's, but the words seemed so unbeliev-
able that Bea had to read them again.

And then, she folded the letter and set it beside her on the bed
to formulate a plan. Henry Neville would not get away with any of
this. Not as long as she was able to stop him.

And she would.

Bea leaned back against the pillows and stared up at the ceiling. She would rest now but only until the temporary sheriff returned. Then she would make him see that freeing her to return to New Orleans would keep two good people alive.

Yes, she decided as she closed her eyes. Surely after reading Mama's letter, Gilbert Hollis would see things her way.

$$\rlap{\text{\textit{{\tiny ✿}}}}$$

"What in the world, Gilbert?" Mattie exclaimed when she saw him. "You're a mess."

"That'll happen when you go into a burning building to haul out a drunk man who managed to turn over a lamp." He paused to tamp down on the anger that was still simmering. "Ed has picked some idiotic deputies over the past few months, but none of them nearly burned the office down until now."

"Oh no," she said as she hurried him inside. "What of the other buildings? Is the doctor's office still standing?"

"It is, but it'll take some work to get it fixed up. I'll send some of the boys down there in the morning to do what they can there and at the sheriff's office. In the meantime, Doc will just be doing house calls. I'll go back up there later to see if I can set the sheriff's office back to rights to where it is usable again."

"And the deputy?" she said carefully. "Did he survive the fire?"

"The fool ought not to have, but he was so drunk he slept through most of it in his cell. I let the doctor look at him then threw him in the wagon and brought him back here to finish sobering up. Townes is keeping an eye on him."

"Well thank goodness for that. I'm sure Edward will have

something to say about this man's behavior. He won't be employed there long."

"Oh, he had already been fired by me well before the fire happened." He looked around and then returned his attention to Mattie. "Where's the prisoner?"

"She's fine," Mattie said. "I put her in the maid's quarters to rest."

"Alone?" He started off down the hall.

"Yes, alone," she told him. "But she was warned that she shouldn't try and escape. She agreed that she would not."

"Well, wasn't that civilized of her," he said as he threw open the door and then stopped short.

Miss Wilson lay curled up on the narrow bed, an old quilt covered her up to her chin, and her hair tumbled around her on the pillow. On the braided rug beside the bed was a letter that appeared to have fallen from her hand.

"Not much of a threat, that one," Mattie whispered. "She nearly fell asleep in her chair in the kitchen. I figured it was less of a threat to have her sleep in a bed than to have her fall out on my good tablecloth and spill the coffee all over the place."

Rather than respond, he gave the housekeeper a look that told her he still wasn't pleased with her choice to leave the prisoner alone. Of course, Mattie ignored him to walk away without any further comment, leaving him alone with Miss Wilson.

Gil sighed as he leaned against the doorframe. The sheriff's office wouldn't be fit to spend much time in until the smell of smoke cleared out. Though he'd do what he could later today to make that happen, it certainly couldn't house a prisoner tonight, especially one as delicate as this one.

For as he studied her, he could see she was delicate in spite of the spitfire personality she'd shown today. She had, after all, put him in handcuffs just to get his attention. No other woman had done that before.

No man either, for that matter.

He reached down to pick up the letter, and her hand moved. A moment later, she sat up and kicked the quilt aside.

"Go ahead and read it," Miss Wilson said with a yawn. "I planned to show it to you when you—" She shook her head. "You look awful and smell of smoke. I hope the fire wasn't as bad as it looks on you."

"I can thank my brother's former deputy for how I look. After we left, he decided to try and break himself out of the cell. He shook the bars so hard that one of the lamps fell over. Burned most of the empty cell and had started on his when I got there and pulled him out."

"Oh no," she said. "Is he all right?"

"He shouldn't be, but he is." Gil lowered himself onto the old chair and looked down at the letter in his hand. "What is this?"

"It's what I wanted to get out of my bag. The letter from my mother." She shrugged. "She told me to read it before I spoke to anyone about the family property, but I got sidetracked with this being arrested business and never did."

He looked over at her, his heart thudding at the beauty of her. No longer was the irritating woman insisting on her way. Something had changed, not the least of which was her appearance. But then being newly awakened from sleep, she likely had no idea how lovely she looked with her hair tumbling out of its hairpins and the flush of sleep still on her cheeks.

"But you have now?" Gil said, forcing his mind back to the topic at hand.

"I have," she said. "Twice. Because I didn't believe what I was reading the first time." Miss Wilson paused. "I want you to read it. There are things she says that should be read by someone in law enforcement."

"But I'm just the temporary sheriff," he protested. "If your mother has a grudge against someone, it's my brother who needs to handle it."

"Your brother isn't here, Mr. Hollis." Her eyes began pleading with him before she said another word. "Please just read it and judge for yourself," she finally said.

Gil unfolded the letter. When he finished reading he looked up at the prisoner. "What do you figure this means?"

"I think it's plain, don't you? My parents are in danger."

"Why is that?" he asked as he handed the letter to her. "A man doesn't just decide to target people for no reason. What do you figure your parents have done to deserve this kind of threat?"

Miss Wilson set the letter on the quilt beside her. "I think it's not my parents he's angry with. It's me."

"All right," Gil said. "What have you done to make this man so angry? Was he promised a wife who didn't show up? Or maybe he was sold land that didn't belong to the seller?"

"None of those things," she snapped. "He is an awful, vile man, and he's old enough to be my father. He's angry because I refused to marry him."

"I see." Gil shook his head. "I guess I'm just not understanding this, but as pretty as you are, how does you turning down his offer of marriage translate to him threatening your parents and then you?"

He shrugged. "No offense, but I think there's more to it."

"If there is, I don't know about it," she said. "Mr. Neville was a valued employee of my father's at the store back in Georgia. When we moved to New Orleans after the war to buy a new store, he came along and helped there too. Only recently did he begin to act surly, and that was when I put my foot down and told Mama and Papa that I would never marry him."

"If you'd told him yes before and then that yes turned to no, maybe he wasn't too happy with that."

"But that's just the thing," she said. "It was always expected that I would marry him, but no one ever bothered to ask me. They were all too busy working at the store when times were good and then trying to hold things together during the lean years when the war came. I thought when we moved to New Orleans, life would be good again. Then Mr. Neville disappeared. Two weeks ago, he returned. He and Papa argued. Then he made a threat against me."

The idea of a man threatening this woman made his blood boil. "Tell me about that," he managed evenly.

She told him of overhearing a conversation between this Neville fellow and her father and then the threat of Mexico that followed. "Mexico, as in what your mother mentions in the letter."

"Yes, that's what has me worried the most. I don't care what he might do to me, but I do care very much what he does to my parents. They took care of me when no one else would. I cannot let him harm them."

He took note of what she said and pondered it a moment. "What does she mean when she writes that she had to prove your mother wrong? Isn't she your mother?"

"Not exactly," Miss Wilson said. Then she told him the story of how she came to live with Ben Wilson and his wife. "So I suppose what she meant was that my mother used to call Ben Wilson their poor relation. Ironic, considering where my mother was raising me at the time. Maybe that's the reference?"

She tucked a strand of hair behind her ear and looked away as if considering her question. Gil let out a long breath and leaned his head against the wall behind him.

"All I know is that your people have been named in an indictment that involves some pretty nasty dealings. If he got crossways with them, maybe he wasn't happy with the terms of his arrangement with them."

Fire flashed in her eyes. "You're determined to believe that I am a criminal and so are my parents, aren't you?"

❧ Chapter 7 ❧

*G*il's eyes narrowed. "I am determined to do the job I promised my brother I would do. Beyond that, I have not formed an opinion. I just know that you're remanded into the custody of the sheriff of this town until the judge decides what to do with you."

"I understand you're doing what you have to do, but I can't stay here," Miss Wilson said. "I have to save my parents. Don't you understand what this letter says? They could be in serious trouble."

"Or dead," he added then immediately regretted it. "Look," he said more gently. "I see that you're wanting to help them. But I cannot let you go. What I can do is write a letter to whoever is in charge over in New Orleans and have him investigate. Would that help?"

"That could take weeks," she told him. "Something must be done now."

He shrugged. "I'm sorry. I can't do more than that."

She looked down at the letter then back up at him. "All right. Do that. Please," she added.

Her swift change of tone ought to have given him a measure of comfort. Instead, it put him on edge.

"First thing in the morning," he told her. "I'll need the names and addresses of your parents and anything you can tell me about this Neville fellow. I'll send all of that in the letter on the morning stage."

"Thank you." She smiled. "I do appreciate the help."

There was more. He could tell. "But. . . ?"

"Gilbert," Mattie called. "A word with you, please."

He glanced over at the door and then back at Miss Wilson. "Stay right where you are."

When she didn't protest, he left her there to find Mattie waiting for him in the kitchen. "Outside, please," she told him.

Gil followed without question. He'd long ago learned that Miz Mattie made few requests of him, but when she did, she meant for him to do as she asked. Most times he did.

"What're you going to do about the girl?" she asked.

He shook his head. "What do you mean? I did as Ed asked and placed her under arrest. Not much more I can do with her." He paused. "Oh, you mean now that the jail has fire damage. I hadn't given it much thought."

"I have," she told him. "That's why I put her in that room. If she'd wanted to escape, she would have the minute my back was turned. But I do think she's got plans to leave Crinoline Creek."

"And why do you think that?"

"Because I read that letter." She shook her head. "Don't you look at me like that, Gilbert Hollis. I keep up with what goes on around here, and anything to do with that girl is my business too, as long as she is under our roof."

Gil elected not to comment. Instead, he glanced over toward the mountains where the sun had just dipped out of sight, leaving streaks of gold in the sky.

"She needs to be here with us until the jail is fixed," Mattie continued. "And maybe after, because I cannot see a scenario where it would be appropriate for a woman alone to be locked up with a man holding the key."

"Even if she is guilty of a list of crimes?" Gil asked. "Because Ed believes she is."

"Do you?"

"It doesn't matter what I think," he told her. "I have a job to do and I'm going to do it."

"Fair enough, then." Mattie walked back toward the door then stopped and turned around to face him. "It isn't often that Ed has a female prisoner, but when he does, I am given charge of her."

"Fine," Gil said. "Beatrice Wilson is all yours, then."

He turned to walk away and spied Red McCrae coming toward him.

"Where are you going?" Mattie called. "I have dinner on the stove."

"I need a bath and a change of clothes, but first I need to check on the other prisoner. Leave me a plate, please. I'll come in later for it."

"I shouldn't, you know. Your mama and I didn't raise you boys to miss meals."

"But you will." He smiled at the laughter that trailed toward him from the kitchen door. "I always was your favorite."

"Hush and get on with you now," she said with a chuckle just before the door slammed shut.

He caught up to Red near the entrance to the bunkhouse. "The deputy won't go anywhere for a while," he said. "He was getting mouthy, so Townes had to hush him up."

"And how did he do that?" Gil asked.

"Just punched him once. That fellow's got a big mouth but a low tolerance for fighting, I guess."

Gil sighed. His training told him a man down from a punch could have simply passed out or could be dead. It all depended on where the blow hit and how he landed. "I better go check on him."

He found Emmett facedown on a bunk. "Turn him over," he told Red.

When he did, Emmett grinned and then threw a punch that Red easily ducked. "Guess he's all right, boss."

"He's fine." Gil turned his attention to Red. "Let him sleep it off, then take him to the edge of the property and leave him there. He can go where he wants, but he won't be staying here. And if he's smart, he won't stay in Crinoline Creek either."

He left the bunkhouse and walked back toward the house. The sky had darkened to purple around him, and a three-quarter moon was rising over the homestead. Lights had been lit inside, allowing him to see Mattie and Miss Wilson laughing together in the kitchen as they appeared to be fixing their plates for dinner.

The fact that his normally particular housekeeper had taken to the prisoner so quickly ought to have bothered him. But today had been a long day, and tomorrow would be longer.

So he settled for a quick bath in a cold tub of water and a prayer before he fell asleep that the Lord wouldn't give him more than he could handle. And that He would see that Ed returned home much sooner than expected.

He'd only been asleep a short time, or at least it felt that way, when a racket outside woke him up. Throwing on his pants and stepping into his boots, Gil grabbed a clean shirt off the peg and put it on as he hurried outside.

There he found Red and Townes in an argument. "If either of you wants a job tomorrow, you will shut your traps and go back to whatever it was you were doing before you woke me up."

"It's the girl, boss," Townes said. "I saw her running down that way like somebody was chasing her." He gestured toward the west where silver moonlight covered miles of Hollis land before it rose into the mountains. "I hollered, but she didn't even look back."

"I told him he ought to have chased her down," Red offered. "In a situation like that, you don't let the prisoner out of your sight."

"And I said I best not go off alone if she was being chased and there was more than one of them. Plus, we have another prisoner in the bunkhouse who needs to be watched, and I'm the one on guard duty for him right now."

"How were you watching that prisoner if you saw the other one running, you fool?" Red asked him.

"I stepped out for a minute," Townes said. "Besides, Miz Mattie is usually the one who keeps watch on the female prisoners, so I didn't think I ought to interfere."

"That old lady is spry, Townes," Red said, "but do you think she could give chase to a woman half her age? And what would she do if there were men out there who didn't want that girl to be caught? Think, man."

Biting back on the words he wanted to say, Gil took a deep breath and let it out slowly. "That's enough, both of you." He turned to Townes. "How long ago was it?"

"Not more than a few minutes."

"All right, Townes, you go get Gideon and bring him out here. Red, I want you inside the house to be sure it was Miss Wilson who Townes saw. Then I want you to find Miz Mattie and make sure whoever is chasing Miss Wilson, if it is someone chasing her, didn't harm our Mattie in the process."

"Yessir, boss." Red hurried off toward the house just as Townes returned with Gil's horse.

Gil climbed into the saddle and aimed the horse toward the house. "Is Mattie all right, Red?" he called through the open door.

"She is," Red responded as he returned to the door with Mattie, covered in a quilt, her sleeping cap awry, a step behind him. "She was sound asleep and didn't hear a thing. And the girl's room is empty."

Gil turned the horse around and headed off in the direction Townes had seen Miss Wilson go. Gideon was a sure-footed horse, so they made good time across the familiar prairie.

Rather than call her name, Gil kept watch on the horizon. If she was out here, he'd find her. If she wasn't alone, he'd find them all.

⚜

Bea clutched the quilt around her shoulders. She might have been faster without the bulky blanket, but the night air was chilly, and she preferred warmth to speed. There were hours to go before sunrise, so her absence would likely not be noticed until Mattie came to fetch her for breakfast.

Escape had not been her plan. Rather, she wouldn't have minded a good night's sleep in that bed at the ranch house. But he'd found her there and forced her out here into the darkness where nothing looked familiar and everything looked the same.

Though she was certain the man in the mask had not been Henry Neville, she was just as certain that he had been sent by Henry. And that meant that the man who had threatened her life and the lives of her parents was nearby.

The sound of horses' hooves echoed in the distance. She had to hide. But where?

The only cover between here and the mountains was the patches of green she'd seen from the buggy yesterday. What seemed so lush and beautiful then looked bare and pitiful in the silver moonlight, but she dove in beneath the branches anyway.

She curled into the smallest space she could manage, tucking the quilt around her and holding her breath until her breathing slowed. Only then did she allow herself to feel the sting of his slap against her cheek, the pain of the shoulder that he had wrenched out of place, and the blood that dried where her legs had been scratched as she escaped.

Her heart still pounded a furious rhythm, matching the sound of the approaching rider. Abruptly the sound ceased, and silence fell around her. A moment later footsteps approached.

"Come out, Miss Wilson."

She let out the breath she had been holding and lurched out of hiding and into the arms of the temporary sheriff. "I'm so glad you're here," she said. "I thought I was going to die."

He didn't believe her. Even in the pale silver light she could see it on his face.

Then a shot rang out.

He dove for cover and took her with him. Bea's shoulder slammed against the ground, and she cried out in pain.

"Who is that?" he demanded.

"I don't know," she said. "But I'm certain that Henry Neville sent him."

"Don't move," he told her. He rolled away from her and stood. She heard footsteps retreating and then nothing but the night sounds that fell around her.

Finally there was shouting.

"I left her over there," Gil Hollis called. "Miss Wilson? You'd better still be there."

Bea climbed to her feet, wincing with the effort. "I'm here," she said, and then there was a blinding pain at her temple.

The world tilted and she landed on the ground. Someone or something was tugging at her arm.

Then gunfire. Then silence again.

She opened her eyes again to find she was back in the small room at the end of the hall with a different quilt tucked around her and a worried-looking temporary sheriff watching her from the chair. Head in his hands, his body hunched forward as if he'd slept where he sat.

Sunlight hurt her eyes, and she blinked several times as she sat up and swiveled to face him. "What happened?"

"I've been waiting for you to wake up and tell me that." He sat back. "The truth, Miss Wilson."

"The truth is I was taken from this room. I did not choose to leave on my own."

"Go on," he said evenly.

"I awakened to a gag thrust into my mouth. I tried to fight back, but he was too strong. He. . ." She paused to wince at the movement. "He hurt me."

Mr. Hollis sat up straight, his expression clouding. "How did he hurt you?"

"My arm," she said. "Something's wrong with it. And there's a bump on my head, so he probably also. . ." She shrugged. "I don't know why I'm bothering. You haven't believed a thing I've told you since I arrived in Crinoline Creek. Why would you believe I didn't try and escape?"

"Let me look at that shoulder," he said, moving to the edge of the bed to press his palm against the spot where it hurt until she gasped. "Your shoulder needs to be put back in place. I've got medical training, but I can call the doctor out to do it if you prefer."

She looked up into his eyes. "Just do it, please. It hurts."

"It's going to hurt to fix it too."

It did, but she bit back on the scream that she wanted to unleash. When he was done, he returned to his spot on the chair. "See if you can move it better now."

Bea gave him an uncertain look and then made the attempt and found the pain was gone. "You've done it," she told him. "Thank you, Sheriff."

A grin rose, and Bea found herself staring at him. Gilbert Hollis was quite a handsome man when he smiled.

"I'm not the sheriff," he said. "Best you just call me Gil, all right?"

"But you were the sheriff yesterday, temporarily, as I understand."

"I was indeed," he said. "But this morning my brother rode in at first light, so he's back to being sheriff again."

"That's good, I suppose," she said. "I didn't get the idea that you liked the job much."

"No." He ducked his head as he chuckled. "I didn't."

"Then you ought to call me Bea, I suppose. Most everyone does." She flexed her arm and tested her shoulder once more. "What happens now?"

"Some folks would like to talk to you in the parlor. Are you up to it?"

"Why?" She shook her head. "Because of Henry Neville?"

"Partly," he said. "But there's more. I'll help you up if you want, or Mattie can come in and see to you."

Bea shook her head then winced at the pain between her eyes. "Thank you. There's no need to call her." She looked up into his eyes. "I trust you."

And she did. Odd that it was. The man had done nothing but irritate her and accuse her of crimes that she hadn't committed, and yet, he'd saved her life out there when Henry's man was determined to take it.

The smile rose again. Then he sprang into action by offering her his arm and easing her to her feet. She wobbled just once, but he caught her.

"Are you sure you're up to this? You took a pretty hard bump on the head when Blair hit you."

She nodded. "I'll be fine."

Grasping Gil's arm, Bea allowed him to escort her down the hall, through the kitchen, and into a beautiful parlor that looked as if it belonged in an English castle instead of out here on the West Texas prairie. Two men were waiting there, one she recognized as the man Gil had called Red, and the other vaguely resembled Gil.

The men rose when she and Gil walked in. "Gentlemen, this is

Beatrice Wilson," Gil said.

The one who looked like Gil stepped forward. "I'm Ed Hollis, Gil's more handsome older brother."

She smiled in spite of herself. "Pleased to meet you."

"I understand you know Red." Ed looked past Bea to focus on Gil. "Have you told her yet?"

❧ Chapter 8 ❧

*N*ot yet," Gil said. "Come sit down, Bea."

Bea settled onto the rosewood settee covered in blue striped silk and surveyed the room like a queen seated on her throne. He had no idea how she would take the news she was about to receive, but he did know she was tough and would be fine.

He'd figured that out yesterday when she managed to handcuff herself to him just to get his attention. It was confirmed a few minutes ago when he reset her dislocated shoulder without her so much as making a sound. Then there was the bump on her head. Through it all she hadn't complained.

Ed stood and offered Bea a smile.

She gave Ed a look. "Sheriff, I have already explained to Gil that I am not involved in anything illegal."

"I know," Ed offered. "And you can blame me for telling Gil to arrest you."

"I already did," she said evenly. "He did a fine job of following your instructions."

"So I heard." He exchanged a grin with Gil then returned his attention to Bea. "I only got as far as the first stage stop before I met up with a messenger from San Antonio looking to head me off and give me an update. Turns out the person we were looking for wasn't you at all, Miss Wilson."

She slid a look toward Gil then returned her attention to Red and then Ed. "Of course it wasn't."

"Our man had arrived a few days before." Ed paused. "And he'd managed to get himself appointed as the new deputy."

Gil's blood boiled at this even though he'd already heard the story. How Emmett Blair managed to weasel his way into a badge and gun was beyond him. Had the fool not spent his first day on the job getting drunk, he might have accomplished what he was sent to do without anyone being the wiser.

"Great job of picking a deputy, Ed," Gil snapped.

The minute the words were out, he wished he hadn't said them. But the damage was done. Ed looked away, defeated. "I thought if I could pick someone awful, you might give up and come to work with me."

Gil's heart sank. Of course. That explained all the short-term deputies who had not worked out. "Hey, I'm sorry. I shouldn't have said that."

Bea met Gil's gaze. "So the odious drunk man who swallowed the handcuff key is the man you were looking for."

At this Red and Ed looked over at Gil. He pretended not to notice.

Bea continued. "Was he also the man who tried to kidnap me last night?"

"Based on Red's description, we think so," Ed said. "He is no longer a threat, but we don't know who else might be on their way, which is why we need to do something about you."

"Excuse me?" She looked over at Gil. "What is he talking about?"

"He's doing a poor job of telling you that there may be others sent after you, presumably because of something you know about this Neville fellow and his business activities."

"But I don't know anything other than he was the manager at my father's store in Georgia and then, after we moved to New Orleans, he followed us there." She paused. "There is one more thing: his intention since I was young was to marry me when I came of age. Papa knew I would refuse if he asked. I suppose he could have told Neville this. The last thing Neville said to me was when I saw him in the hallway outside Papa's office. He told me he would see me in Mexico."

Something inside him flamed. Anger, yes, but something more. Something he'd rather not examine too closely. Gil's fists curled.

"Maybe you know something and don't realize it," Ed offered.

She shrugged. "Truly, I only know what was in my mother's letter."

"Even so," Gil said, calming his temper. "You're no longer safe in Crinoline Creek, Bea. Neville knows you're here. I've come up with a plan, but you may not like it."

"Where are my parents?" she demanded. "I want no part of any plan that doesn't keep them safe too."

Ed looked down at his boots. "The messenger tells me the police in New Orleans believe Neville killed them. I'm sorry, ma'am."

"They *believe* it? Can they not say for certain?" she demanded.

"At this time they cannot," he told her, "but they are missing, and their home showed signs of a struggle before it was set on fire. It is assumed they did not survive this struggle."

She turned her blue eyes, now shimmering with tears, on Gil. "Did you know this?"

"No. I was not told any of this." He gave Ed a look, but his brother ignored him.

Bea returned her attention to Gil, her backbone ramrod straight and her face drained of its color. A lone tear traced its way down her cheek.

"All right," she said slowly. "I will do whatever it takes to catch anyone associated with Henry Neville. Tell me about this plan."

"You're coming with me, Bea," Gil said. "We leave in four days. Until then, you're going to be guarded night and day. You're no longer a prisoner here, but it would be best if you didn't leave the ranch for now."

Out of the corner of his eye, Gil caught Red watching closely. He'd have an opinion for sure, but Gil had no plans to ask what that was.

"Should I bother to ask where we're going in four days?"

Gil looked down at her. "Does it matter?"

"I suppose not," she said. "Just one more thing. Is the deputy still in jail?"

"He's in the Crinoline Creek cemetery," Ed said. "Anyone else who tries to harm you will suffer the same fate."

"Thank you," she told him before glancing over at Gil. "What does a lady wear where we're going? I've already determined I have the wrong shoes for Crinoline Creek."

Gil chuckled despite the gravity of the situation. "You'd best talk to Miz Mattie. She will have better advice on that than any of us would."

Ed nodded. "You're considered a valuable witness, so we will take care of whatever needs you have. Gil will be the one escorting you and keeping you safe, but we will all be praying for your safety while we find the ones who are responsible."

The next morning, Mattie ushered Bea from the kitchen and refused to allow her to help. "You're a guest in this house," the dear lady told her. "I'll not have you underfoot while I'm working, though I am most grateful for your offer."

Denied the opportunity to push her grief aside in favor of domestic labor, Bea retrieved the book from her bedchamber, wandered outside, and settled onto a rocker on the far end of the porch. Though she tried to read, Bea found little distraction in a chapter explaining how to cure a rattlesnake bite.

She turned the page and then closed the book. All she could think of was home. Of her parents. When she'd thought of these things last night, she'd cried.

Today the situation made her angry.

How dare Henry Neville take her family away? And for what reason?

She longed to find the man who harmed her family and see that he was brought to justice. Or, depending on the moment, bring justice on him herself.

The screen door opened and then closed again. Bea glanced over expecting to see Mattie standing there. Instead, it was Gil.

She'd seen him out in the far pasture before breakfast and wondered how early he'd risen in order to watch the sunrise from the back of a bucking horse. He'd fallen a few times and climbed back on until finally the horse gave up and let him stay in the saddle.

It had been fun to watch him. And impressive. A city girl, she had never given thought to how a horse might be tamed, just that horses were useful for getting around.

Gil had washed off the dust of the corral and appeared to have scrubbed up nicely. The ends of his hair curled against his neck, and his freshly pressed shirt showed no evidence of his previous scuffle with the horse.

Hat in his hand, Gil appeared not to know what to say. "Busy?" he finally asked her.

"Not at all. I offered to help Mattie, but she shooed me out of her kitchen. Something about being a guest and her not wanting me underfoot."

He chuckled. "Don't take offense. Miz Mattie isn't one to share her kitchen with anyone except to feed him." He paused. "Or her."

"I understand. My mother was the same way." Her lip quivered at the mention of Mama, but she bit it until the moment passed. "Are you on your way somewhere?"

"Town," he said as he shifted his hat from one hand to the other. "Some of the hands are working on cleaning up after the fire. Thought I'd make myself useful."

He appeared to have finished what he intended to say, and yet he continued to stand there looking at her. "Was there something else?"

"I just noticed what you're reading. Are you finding it interesting?"

"I did try, but I'm having trouble concentrating. I may not have picked the most interesting chapter."

He moved closer but stopped shy of the rocker next to hers. "Which one are you reading?"

"Curing rattlesnake bites," she told him.

"Ignore that chapter." Gil shrugged. "In my experience, there are better ways to treat a bite than what is suggested in that book."

"What is your experience, exactly?" She nodded to the chair. "You can join me, you know."

Though he looked reluctant, Gil settled beside her. "I've got medical training."

"You say that like it's something bad." Bea shrugged. "I'm certainly glad you knew what to do when my shoulder needed fixing."

"I'm glad I was able to do that." He looked down at his right hand, which was slightly curled. "I'd thought I would come back here and take up with the local doctor. My father wrote to me that he needed the help, and I figured I'd be the one to help him."

"But you didn't do that."

"I couldn't." He looked up at her. "I was injured in battle. You might have noticed."

Bea shook her head. "What do you mean?"

He gave her a look she couldn't quite decipher. "The scars, Bea. They're pretty obvious."

"What scars?"

Gil's eyes narrowed. "Don't patronize me. I've been told I ought to be glad that the bullet only grazed my face because it could have been much worse, but I know what I see in the mirror. Then there's my right hand. It's useless for most everything because I can't grip with it."

"Gil," she said gently. "I don't know what you see in the mirror, but I see a man who went to war and came home alive. Neither of the things you've just mentioned kept you from repairing my shoulder. I'm not saying you should consider doctoring. Only you can decide that. But I am saying that it is possible that the things you think are obvious flaws are things that the rest of us hardly notice. You are still a healer."

His gaze went to her eyes. "So are you, Bea."

She smiled and reached across the distance between them to pat his hand. "I'm just telling the truth, Doc."

"I'm not sure whether I like being called that," he admitted.

Those blue eyes twinkled. "I don't believe I asked whether you liked it or not."

"I see." He stuck his hat on his head and leaned forward but did not stand. "Are you always this honest with people you don't know?"

"It's funny, but I feel like I know you."

Gil stood and put on his hat. With a nod and a grin, he walked away.

❧ Chapter 9 ❧

Three days later Bea stood on the porch of the Hollis ranch house and bid Mattie Walsh goodbye. Though she still hadn't asked where she and Gil would be going, she assumed it would be back to New Orleans or perhaps some other big city where she could hide in plain sight. Mattie had certainly provided her with clothes that would look at home there, although Bea had noticed Mattie's tastes were much plainer than her own.

Thus, when Red met them with a wagon loaded with items that made it appear as if they were going on a long journey, she was confused. "How are we going to fit all of that onto the stage?" she asked him.

"You didn't tell her yet, did you?" Red asked Gil.

"She didn't ask yet" was his response. "But I guess it's time to tell her all the same. So, Bea, you and I are joining up with a wagon train heading west."

"A what?" She shook her head. "You're joking."

"Nope."

"Why?" she managed.

"Because it's the best way to get you away from here without attracting too much attention, and it's the safest way to travel with you, given that we won't run into too many folks out on the prairie, which is ideal." He held up his hand as if anticipating her protest. "A few of my army buddies are leading the train. They've been informed about why you're there. We went through war together, and I've worked alongside them for several years since then. I trust these men with our lives."

"All right," she said. "I suppose that does make sense."

"Ed and his posse of volunteers are hoping to round up the rest of the gang quickly. The plan is we aim to ride with the wagon train as far as El Paso then make our way back by stage on the San Antonio–El Paso Road."

She gave him a skeptical look. "How far is that?"

Gil grinned as he lifted her into the wagon and then loped around to climb up and take the reins from Red. "About two hundred miles to El Paso."

Two hundred miles of riding on the hard wooden seat of a covered wagon during the day and sleeping in the back of one at night. Not at all what she expected.

"I see."

Red wedged himself into the back of the wagon and nodded to Gil. "Time to go," Gil told Bea.

"Just one more question," she said as Gil held the reins in his hand. "I assume there is some kind of cover story that I will have to know about myself. I mean, I can hardly tell the others on the wagon train that I am Beatrice Wilson from New Orleans and I'm fleeing the man who killed my parents for no apparent reason."

"No," he said thoughtfully. "Your cover story is simple. You'll still be Bea. That's a common enough name. But adding Wilson to it makes it too dangerous. So the plan that Ed and the government man came up with is that you'd take my name." He slid her a sideways look. "You'll be Bea Hollis." He paused, his ears reddening. "Because you'll be pretending to be my wife."

Gil waited for the reaction he knew he deserved. Telling her that at the last minute wasn't fair. He'd had three days to prepare her, but then he hadn't prepared himself either.

His excuse, which he stuck by, was that Bea had been so deep in grief for the parents she feared she'd lost that he couldn't put another thing on her to worry about. It was a good excuse, and a poor one, and Gil knew it.

Maybe if he'd told her they were going to have to play husband and wife, she might have been distracted from her grief enough to give him trouble instead. Had Gil considered that three days ago, he might have told her.

For as much as he hated it when a woman gave him grief, he wouldn't have minded as much if it was Bea Wilson.

Bea turned those blue eyes on him. Just as he expected, she wasn't pleased. "So I'm to be married for two hundred miles."

"Or less," he offered.

Bea smiled, but the humor did not quite reach her eyes.

"Well, we can always hope."

At that, Gil elected to say nothing further. Instead, he snapped the reins and set the wagon in motion.

Red, however, laughed out loud. "Now that's the best thing I've heard all day. Wait until I tell the boys back at the ranch."

"You can't tell anyone, Red," Gil reminded him. "We don't know who to trust and who not to trust."

The ranch hand sobered. "I guess that's the truth, isn't it. Sort of makes a man wonder whether he's been laying his head at night in a bunkhouse where a snake is sleeping too."

"If there's a snake in the bunkhouse, he will be found," Gil said.

"And once he's found I'm going to get to tell the tale of the new Mrs. Hollis?"

Gil glanced at him over his shoulder, hoping his employee understood his mood from the look he gave him. "I'll let you decide if you think it's worth telling, Red."

"Oh, it is."

Once they arrived at the meeting place, Gil made short work of finding the wagon that would be their home for the next few weeks. Or rather, Bea's home.

While Red helped him unload, Bea sat in the wagon and appeared to be surveying the scene taking place around her. Several dozen prairie schooners had circled up and were in the process of being readied for the trail ahead. Some had come from far away and others from nearby.

"Hey, Cap, is that you?"

Gil looked over in the direction from which the call had come and spied Rafe Simpson heading his way. Rafe's face was the first one he'd seen when he opened his eyes in the hospital. Big and burly, he gave the impression of an angry bear when he was riled. What few realized, however, was he was never truly riled.

They shook hands and then Rafe grinned. "I knew I'd get you back out here again. Where's the wife? I want to meet her."

He led Rafe over to Bea and made the introductions. "Pleased to meet you, Mrs. Hollis," he said, obviously making sure to say it loud enough for anyone who might be listening to hear. "Your husband and I go way back," he added. "We served together all the way to Jonesboro and back."

"You were in Jonesboro?" She looked over at Gil, studying him intently. "Were you with the Eighth Cavalry?"

Gil frowned. "How did you know?"

"I didn't." Her expression went wistful. "But I was there the day they marched in. The Texas Eighth, I mean. I will never forget it."

Now it was Gil's turn to stare at her.

"Nor will we," Rafe said. "But that's the past." He nodded toward the wagons. "And that there is the future. We'll get these folks headed west by sunup tomorrow. You two going to be ready to head out by then?"

"I'm ready now," Bea said, though she continued to study Gil as if she were seeing him for the first time.

"Well, all right then." Rafe grinned at Gil again. "I'll leave you two to get settled."

"Mr. Simpson?" Bea called. "Just one question."

"What's that?"

"Well," she said with a smile, "I was just wondering what the plan was for keeping all of us settlers safe at night. Will you have men standing guard?"

Rafe exchanged glances with Gil. He had no idea where Bea was going with this line of questioning, so he offered a shrug in case Rafe believed he had some insight.

"Yes, ma'am. We will have men posted all around the camp every night. Men will take turns standing watch."

"Excellent." She looked down at Gil from the wagon seat. "I'm sure you will want to take the first watch tonight. And every night for the next two hundred miles."

"Now, honey," he said with a wink that he hoped would also serve as a warning. "Don't tease Rafe like that. He's going to believe you're serious."

Bea's response was a smile. That was enough. Gil smiled back and then helped her down. He paused a moment before releasing her.

Their eyes collided and something shifted between them. Bea looked away first.

"Hey, Cap, we're going to need some help over here after all," Rafe called. "Get your wife settled then come see me, if you don't mind."

He did mind. Right then, he did not want to be anywhere but right here with Bea Wilson trying to figure out what had just happened. Trying to wonder why the Lord had placed another woman who was at Jonesboro in his arms.

She looked up at him with those pretty blue eyes. Surely she wasn't the same one. Surely the angel who had saved him on the battlefield wasn't the flesh-and-blood woman standing right there in front of him.

As soon as the thought occurred, he pushed it away. The possibility was so remote, it shouldn't even be considered.

❧ Chapter 10 ❧

*G*o," Bea told him, heat rising in her cheeks. "Red can unload the wagon. I'll see that he puts things away."

"You do that," Gil said. "I won't be long."

"Take your time. We'll be fine," Bea said.

But the thumping of her heart told her she would not be fine. Whatever it was that passed between her and Gil a moment ago had scared her out of her wits. She barely knew this man and yet she turned to watch him walk away as if she'd be counting the minutes until he returned.

Then there was his connection to the Eighth Texas. To Jonesboro. And to that promise made by a soldier who likely went off to die in that battle like so many brave young men did.

Perhaps Gil knew him. She could never ask, of course,

because she knew nothing about the soldier who had haunted her thoughts all these years beyond the fact he carried a gold pocket watch.

Out of the corner of her eye, she spotted Red watching them. Squaring her shoulders, Bea put on a neutral expression and turned her attention toward the piles of boxes in the wagon.

"Let's get this moved over to whichever of these is going to be ours for the next two hundred miles, shall we?"

Red grinned. "It's that one over there. You just stay out of the way and I'll handle it."

True to his word, Red McCrae made short work of transferring all the supplies into the Conestoga wagon that would be Bea's temporary home. "You have to arrange things where the wagon isn't off balance," he told her. "But you need to leave room right there in the middle for sleeping."

"Yes, well, room for one is all we will need," she snapped.

"Yes, ma'am," he said, clearly embarrassed.

"And Red," she added, her expression somber. "I believe if you consider things, you will find that the story isn't worth telling after all."

Surprise registered on his face and then, slowly, he nodded. "Yes, ma'am. I reckon you're right about that. I do apologize."

"Apology accepted," she said. "Now it looks like we're done here, but perhaps you will want to check with Gil before you leave?"

He muttered a swift agreement and hurried to join the circle of men who appeared intent on figuring out something of great importance. Or at least that's how they appeared from where Bea stood.

The rest of the afternoon and evening passed in a flurry of activity. While Gil stayed busy helping others prepare for tomorrow morning's departure, Bea spent the remainder of her time meeting the strangers who would become her traveling companions on the trail out west.

By the time the evening meal was finished and the lamps all over the camp were being extinguished, she'd had her fill of smiling. In fact, the last thing she felt like doing was smiling.

All she could think of, now that the rush of the day had given way to the quiet of the night, was the possibility that she would never see her parents again.

Or her home. Or, though it was the least of all her losses, the lovely bed with the swans that Mama had ordered for her.

Mama.

"Oh Mama." The words fell out on a breath and lingered like the fog on a New Orleans morning as she climbed into the back of the wagon and drew the quilt up to her chin.

She must have slept, for the next time she opened her eyes the night was black as pitch and an awful racket was rumbling near the canvas flap at the back of the wagon. Bea tossed the quilt aside and peered out the flap to find the source of the noise was her temporary husband. Apparently with his guard duties completed, Gil had taken up a spot just beneath the tent flap at the end of the wagon and was sound asleep leaning against the wheel.

All around them, similar sounds rose from other wagons. Though she had no experience with such things, Bea was left to assume that the male of the species were given to snoring loudly.

"Gil," she whispered, hoping she could capture his attention long enough to get him to cease the nighttime male chorus. When he did not respond, she tried again. Once again, she failed.

Leaning closer, her grip on the wagon precarious at best, Bea extended her hand in hopes of poking the snoring man but came up a few inches shy of reaching him. Trying once more, she leaned farther forward and managed to come very close to pressing her index finger against his shoulder.

If she just stretched a tiny bit more, she could reach him. So she did. Her finger grazed his sleeve and touched his shoulder.

Then she tumbled head over heels out of the wagon.

Bea stifled a cry as she landed on the grass next to Gil. Her temporary husband jumped to his feet, his pistol in hand.

"Don't shoot," she whispered as she settled her skirts around her and leaned back against the wagon. "I just fell out."

Gil let out a long breath and lowered his weapon. Even in the moonlight she could see his expression of disbelief.

"You did what?"

"Shhh," she urged him. "Keep your voice down."

"Are you all right?" He looked around and then let out another long breath. "Do you have any idea how close you were to getting shot?"

"Sit back down," she said. "You didn't and I'm fine."

"Let me look at your shoulder," he said. "You may have dislocated it again. How's that bump on your head?"

"It's fine," she insisted. "I'm fine. The only thing I hurt was my pride."

He holstered the pistol and then returned to the spot where he'd been sleeping. He slid her a sideways look.

"Want to tell me how you fell out?"

"More like why I fell out," she said. "You were snoring."

Gil laughed. "I'm not the only one."

"Yes, but those other men aren't sleeping at the opening to my tent," she said.

"No." He swiveled to face her. "I meant you, Bea."

"Me?" She shook her head. "Don't be ridiculous. A lady does not snore."

"Suit yourself," he said.

"Quiet down over there," someone called from a nearby wagon. "Some of us are trying to sleep."

Bea frowned. "Will we be in such close quarters the whole time we're with these people?"

He looked around and then back at Bea. "Closer sometimes. When the wagons are circled for safety, the neighbors can be close enough to touch."

She groaned then allowed a companionable silence to fall between them as she searched for constellations in the murky sky overhead. The night smelled of rain, and the wisps of clouds that slid past confirmed it.

"Bea," Gil finally said. "You can't just surprise me like that, all right? I was a soldier too long. When someone comes up behind me or touches me when I'm sleeping, my instincts kick in. And my instinct is that I am being attacked and need to defend myself."

"I'll try to remember that."

Lightning zigzagged across the sky just as the first plops of rain landed around them, sending Bea to her feet. "Looks like this conversation is over."

"All right," he said. "Try not to snore when you go back to sleep.

It might wake me up."

"Don't be ridiculous," she told him as the patter of rain drummed against the canvas roof. "You can't stay out there in the rain. Don't you have a dry place you can go? Like over with your army buddies?"

"They're outside like me," he said. "Go to sleep. I'm fine."

"You're sure?"

He gave her a look and she climbed inside. Still, she remained by the tent flap. Another streak of lightning split the sky.

"All right, Gil," she said. "Enough of this. Come on in the wagon."

He looked up from under the brim of his hat, swiping at the raindrops that dripped there. "Just go to sleep," he told her.

"I can't. Not knowing you're out there in the storm. Please make it easy on both of us."

Gil shook his head. "I don't suppose anyone has accused you of being stubborn before." Thunder rumbled as he climbed to his feet. "Fine, but I don't know how we will both fit in there."

She scooted to the back of the wagon and tucked her feet under her then moved the quilt over to her side. "Easy. I'll sit up over here, and you can sit over there. Put those boxes between us to divide our spaces. If neither of us is going to sleep well, we might as well sleep dry."

He frowned but did as she asked. After a few minutes he had wedged himself on the other side of three stacked crates and appeared to be trying to get comfortable there.

"Would a blanket help?" she asked him after a few minutes. "I think there's another quilt in the trunk behind you."

He lit the lantern next to him then maneuvered himself around until he could reach into the trunk. The first thing he pulled out was not a quilt.

It was her old blue dress.

Chapter 11

Gil's hand curled around the swath of blue linen. His thoughts scattered and then focused again. To a hot day in August and a pretty girl waving from a balcony.

To Bea Wilson.

Slowly, as if time had been suspended, he turned toward her. And he looked at her. Truly studied her.

Yes, there were the blue eyes. The smile.

"It was you," she said before he could. "You found me."

"Eighth Texas Cavalry at your service," he said softly, calling up the memory of riding on that horse and looking up at that balcony.

Of how young he'd felt. How alive, even though he was facing what he knew was an almost certain death.

"Thank you, Eighth Texas," she whispered, tears filling her eyes.

"Georgia is thankful to have you here. Do watch yourself!"

Watch yourself.

Gil clutched the blue linen to his chest, leaning now against the barrier of crates that separated him from the woman he'd really never forgotten. With his free hand, he reached into his pocket and retrieved his watch.

Could she see the scars there? He couldn't tell.

"On the contrary," he told her. "It is our job to watch others, not ourselves. Though my eyes have not yet landed on any prettier vision than you, ma'am."

She shifted positions. Her eyes and her focus were now on the watch.

"Perhaps you will remember me and return so that I might congratulate you on the victory you are surely about to win." Her gaze lifted to collide with his. "And take me away."

He shook his head. "I don't remember you saying that last part, Bea."

"I didn't," she managed. "But I should have."

"You saved my life on the battlefield," he told her. "I've always wanted to find you and tell you that."

Bea swiped at her eyes with the corner of the quilt. "How could I have done that?"

Gil returned the dress to the trunk and swiveled back to face her. "You told me to watch myself, remember?"

"Of course," she said.

He told her what happened on the battlefield and then traced the scars in the gold with his index finger. "That one, where the bullet hit deepest, it would have killed me. It was right over my heart."

At her gasp, Gil looked up at her. "But I watched." He shrugged.

"I know. It sounds crazy. But you've never left me since that day. You've always been here in my heart and in my mind."

"Oh Gil, all this time I held you close too. Every man I met since then has been compared to that handsome soldier who rode by my balcony on that hot August day. Every one of them."

Handsome soldier. Something inside him swayed. "I'm not that man, Bea."

"So you've said." She leaned over the crates to trace the scar that cut across his cheek. Then she smiled as she gave his beard a quick but gentle tug. "No, you're not. I think you're even more handsome now. Though I do wonder what's under there."

His heart soared. "Bea, I—"

A shot rang out, and Gil froze. "Stay right here," he told Bea. "That might be nothing, but it might also be what we've been trying to avoid."

"Neville."

"I hope not," he said as he checked his weapon then returned it to his holster.

"Gil, watch yourself." She pressed her hand to his cheek. "We only just found each other."

"I'll be back for you. You protected me, now let me protect you." He leaned over to give her a quick kiss and then doused the lantern. "Stay out of sight and hide if anyone comes near the wagon."

🌿

Just when she thought Gil might not return, he climbed into the back of the wagon. It was all Bea could do not to launch herself at him.

"Was it him?"

He shook his head. "Just a couple of idiots blowing off steam. Rafe's explained to them that they'll be heading back home instead of coming with us. I think they're packing up now."

She nodded. "Speaking of going home. . ."

"What about it?" He closed the curtain flap.

"I was thinking while you were gone." Bea chose her words carefully. "I know a lot of planning went into keeping me safe for the next few weeks, but I just can't do it."

He looked down at his hands and then back at Bea. "I should have told you about the pretend marriage scheme when I first heard about it so you could be prepared. We don't have to keep up that pretense. There's probably another way to handle this. Let's put our heads together and figure something out."

"No," she told him. "I mean that I can't run away. I want to go home. To New Orleans."

Bea expected Gil to argue. Instead, he studied her intently. "I understand. I'm not a fan of running either. But I can't see putting you in that kind of danger, Bea. I just found you. I don't want to lose you. It's out of the question. The answer is no."

She shook her head. "I don't want to lose you either, but I have to find out for myself what happened to my parents. Everything they did was for me. I need to do this for them."

"And you can." He paused. "But not yet. I plan to keep you safe, and that means staying right where you are."

"Well, I do appreciate that plan," she told him. "But I am no longer willing to participate."

He gave her a sideways look. "Bea."

Bea held up both hands in response. "No, Gil. I am not going to willingly ride off on some wagon train going west when my parents could very well be alive in the opposite direction. I can't do it." She paused. "I won't do it."

Gil chuckled. "Is that a threat?"

"It's a promise." She squared her shoulders and met his even gaze. "If you insist on taking me west, I will escape the first chance I get. I'll find a way to get to New Orleans, whether it is with or without you."

"You wouldn't," he told her, though she could tell he wasn't as sure of that answer as he had been.

"I would. You're a sound sleeper, Gil. You can't stay awake twenty-four hours a day for the next fourteen days." She paused to let that sink in. "The minute you fall asleep, I will be gone. You know I'm telling the truth."

He did. She could see it on his face. His very handsome, ever so serious face.

"All right," he finally said.

Bea grinned. "I knew you would see the wisdom in my plan."

"I won't debate you on that, but *wisdom* is not the word I would use. Bottom line is that I'm not letting you out of my sight, Bea Wilson." He paused. "But we can talk more about that later. I'll go let Rafe know we're turning our wagon east instead of west."

The men must have argued, because Gil returned to the wagon in a worse humor than he'd had when he left. "We'll head out at daybreak. Don't think of doing anything other than getting your sleep in before then."

"I won't," she said. "I assume your friends weren't happy with the news?"

"No comment," he told her as he settled back down with his gun at the ready. "Good night, Bea."

"This is the right thing to do," she said. "Thank you for agreeing."

No response.

"I can't just hide out here." She paused. "You wouldn't if it were your parents, would you?"

Silence.

Bea made a face. He ignored her to stare out into the darkness.

"Fine," she said. "Good night, Gil."

Snapping the curtains shut, Bea tried to sleep but found it impossible. She shifted positions a dozen times and then sat up and shook her head. This would never do. Instead, she grabbed her quilt and climbed out of the wagon.

"Bea, I warned you," Gil snapped.

"Hush," she told him as she settled down beside him. "You told me to go to sleep, but you didn't say where."

Gil looked as if he might argue. Instead, he shook his head and said nothing.

He ought to have made her take herself right back up into the wagon and sleep there. It would have been safer, and she was certainly easier to protect when she was hidden away inside the wagon.

But when the stubborn woman settled down next to him all wrapped up in that quilt, he was done for. She smelled like sunshine and lilacs, and he didn't complain a bit when she fell asleep and ended up with her head resting on his shoulder.

An hour or so later, something woke her up. She shifted positions and straightened. "Gil," she whispered.

He thought about ignoring her so she'd go back to sleep, but he couldn't help but respond. "Yeah?"

She looked up. "When you were in the war, were you ever afraid you would never see your home again?"

Gil's gut clenched. "Every day," he told her. "But I did what I needed to do. It's what kept me alive."

Bea reached out and touched his sleeve. Then she adjusted her quilt and closed her eyes. It didn't take long for his shoulder to become her pillow again.

Rafe wandered by a few hours later on patrol, but, true to their friendship, he looked the other way and pretended not to notice that Bea was snuggled there. This morning, however, with the sun not yet up but the time nearing to set off, his buddy would be around soon to check on them.

Gil preferred that they slip out quietly under cover of darkness rather than have to make explanations. Thus, he grudgingly nudged his sleeping companion. "Wake up, sleepyhead. It's almost time to leave."

Her lashes fluttered, but her eyes remained closed. He tried again. This time she sat bolt upright, her arms struggling against the quilt until she gradually came fully awake.

"Oh," she said as she swiped at an errant strand of hair. "It's already time?"

"Yes. We'll be leaving soon," he told her. "See to your needs now. There might not be another opportunity for a while."

Bea stumbled out of the tangle of blankets and then paused. For a second, he thought she might say something else. Then she straightened her skirts and walked off into the darkness. Though he owed Bea her privacy, everything in him wanted to keep her in sight. He didn't breathe well until she returned and climbed onto the seat beside him.

Gil slid her a sideways look. "You sure about this? I can't guarantee your safety when it's just the two of us out there without the protection of the others."

"The truth?"

He nodded.

"I'm afraid," she told him. "But it's what I need to do."

"All right, then." He looked over at her. "One more thing. Until I get you back to the ranch, what I say goes out there. All right?"

"I want to go home, not to the ranch."

"First the ranch," he said firmly. "Then I get you home. One step at a time."

Her eyes blazed. "I didn't agree to that."

"Bea," he said gently. "We're on the same side. I want Neville caught, and I want to find your parents alive. At the ranch I can get backup so we aren't traveling alone. It's a long way from West Texas to New Orleans. So will you do as you've promised and let me take the lead on this? If not, I need to know right now."

She nodded, although reluctantly. Before she could change her mind, Gil eased the wagon out of its spot and guided the horses around to turn them in the direction of home—his home.

Rafe rode up beside him, his rifle across the saddle horn. They exchanged nods and then parted. By the time the sun rose, he and Bea were well on the road toward Crinoline Creek. At this rate, they would see the ranch's border in no time.

"I suppose your brother will be surprised to see us," she said, breaking the comfortable silence between them.

Gil grinned. "He might be, but Red will never let me hear the end of it."

She matched his smile. "Why is that?"

"He loves to give me a hard time. He always has."

"You know," she said slowly, "I sort of envy the life you have, Gil."

"You do?" He shook his head. "Why?"

"You've got a family at the ranch who love you. Mattie couldn't stop telling me how wonderful you are, and it's obvious how much your brother cares for you."

"It is?" He winked. "I guess I like him all right. But tell me more of how wonderful I am."

"Stop it." She giggled. "That is between Mattie and me, and she would not be pleased if I repeated any of it."

"You better watch out for her. She's been trying to marry Ed and me off for years."

"What's wrong with marriage?" she asked.

"Nothing, in theory." He scanned the horizon and then returned his attention to Bea. "I believe when the Lord puts a man and woman together, there's nothing better. But the man ought to be able to take care of his woman."

"Well, that is true." She paused. "So why haven't you married before now, Gil?"

"You're joking." He shook his head. "That's not a question a woman generally asks a man."

"Well," she said matter-of-factly, "I'm asking now. And don't tell me you cannot support a wife, Doc."

"I'm no doctor," he managed through gritted teeth. "Doctors need full use of both hands."

"Gil, look at your hands."

He did. Sure enough, he'd become so interested in the conversation that he hadn't realized he'd shifted the reins from his left hand to his right. He shifted back and then held up his hand and flexed his fingers.

It worked. All his fingers curled properly.

It was a miracle. His heart soared.

Thank You, Lord.

He looked over at Bea and found her crying. Immediately he pulled back on the reins. "What's wrong?"

"Nothing," she said. "Everything is so very right. Look at you." She gave him a sweeping glance and then returned her attention to his eyes. "Now you can go and be a doctor, Gil. That's wonderful."

He reached over to pull her into his arms. "Bea," he whispered against the top of her head.

After a minute he released her. She met his gaze. Words failed. Words that might have let her know what he was feeling, and not just about taking up doctoring again. Words that might have asked her right then to be his wife.

A gunshot echoed off in the distance, startling the horses. The moment was over. Whether that was a man hunting a meal for his family or an outlaw taking aim, it was a sound he could not ignore. Not when this wagon held the woman he loved.

Yes, loved.

And wanted to marry.

Gil sighed. *You sure picked a bad time to have me realize this, Lord.*

He nodded toward the ranch, as much to change the topic as to explain his next move. "We're close to home now. I'm going to run the horses for all they're worth and get us there quick as I can. That gunshot probably didn't come from anywhere near the ranch, but I need to know that for certain, so hold on tight."

Bea braced herself just in time for the wagon to jolt forward. Gil was an expert horseman, but at the pace they were going, the horses wouldn't last long.

Up ahead she spied what had to be the ranch house and out-buildings of the Hollis ranch. As they neared the gate, Bea couldn't see that anything was out of order. Rather, it all seemed very quiet. Instead of men working the cattle or in the paddock with the horses, the place seemed to be abandoned.

Gil pulled the wagon to a halt outside the house. "Climb into the back of the wagon, find your pistol, and wait for my signal," he said softly. "And remember, if there's trouble brewing, the last thing we need to be doing is sitting out exposed like this."

She nodded and slipped into the back of the wagon. There she found the weapon she'd left in her sleeping spot. "Got it," she answered.

He stuck his head into the back of the wagon. "No matter what, be prepared to shoot whoever comes in here after you."

"Unless it's you," she said.

"Well, yes."

"Gil," she said. "Watch yourself."

He grinned and patted his shirt pocket. Then he was gone, his footsteps leading away from the wagon, though she couldn't tell whether he was heading toward the house or one of the outbuildings.

Her heart beat a furious rhythm, and she longed to escape the confines of the wagon. Instead, she sat very still and did as Gil asked.

A shot rang out. And another. Then there was shouting. Two men. One was Gil.

The other was Neville.

"No," she whispered as a third shot sang past the wagon.

Then the curtain on the back of the wagon opened and the man who had haunted her life for far too long appeared. "Hello, Bea," he said as she took aim. "I thought I would find you here hiding. Come on out. You don't want to harm the one man who ever loved you."

"There's no love between us," she snapped. "Tell me what you've done with my parents. I know you're far too much of a coward to shoot them."

He laughed.

"I'm only going to ask once more, Neville. Tell me what you've done with my parents."

"I've made a lot of money with them," he said. "Not that your stupid father figured it out until it was far too late for him to do anything about it. I'm sure they'll both hang for the crimes that I committed, but that won't matter when you and I are in Mexico. I've built a villa for you there. Come with me now. It's the wise thing to do."

"No," she said evenly. "The wise thing to do is to stop you now before you hurt anyone else."

"You won't."

Bea pulled back on the hammer. She would.

The curtain behind her opened, and a flash of light slid over her head, followed by the deafening sound of a gun discharging. Neville fell backward, and the curtain closed behind him.

Bea scrambled around to see Gil. Blood decorated his temple and splattered his shirt, but otherwise he seemed fine. "Are you all right?" he demanded.

She grasped his wrist. "I am, but you've been shot."

"No time to explain," he told her. "Stay put while I go make sure Neville is dead."

A moment later, Gil opened the wagon's back curtain and held out his arms to her. She quickly climbed toward him and then, averting her eyes from the man lying on the ground, fell into his arms.

Gil carried her up the steps and inside. "You can all come out now," he called.

As Bea landed on her feet, she spied her mother racing toward her down the hall. "Mama!"

Only a second behind her was Papa, who gathered them all into an embrace. Mattie hurried to join them.

"Why are you here?" she asked Papa.

"We got a telegram inviting us to join you here. Of course we made our plans to do that, but we only got as far as San Antonio. The man we were to meet was not there. So it took some time to arrange travel from there to here."

Papa paused to release the women from his embrace. "We only just arrived in Crinoline Creek this morning. When your mother and I went to the sheriff's office, we found that it had been burned. There were a number of men working there, all of whom are ranch hands for this ranch. A fellow named Red told us if we would wait, this kind lady would be bringing lunch to them and we could ride back with her." He grinned at Mattie. "What we didn't know then is that she very possibly saved our lives."

Gil stepped into view. "Miz Mattie knew something wasn't right when she came back, so she pulled the buggy around back and sent your parents into the root cellar and she went with them. Since Ed and I built the entrance to be hard to find on purpose, it worked out that Neville couldn't figure where they were hiding. I surprised him poking around the house. He got the first shot off, but his aim was bad."

Bea went to him and slid his hair back to reveal a scratch on his temple. She reached into her pocket to retrieve a handkerchief and then held it to the wound just as a racket sounded in the front of the house.

The sheriff and half the men in Crinoline Creek were shouting as they rode toward the house. Gil shook his head.

A moment later, Sheriff Hollis rushed inside. "Too late, Ed. Neville's dead. Oh, and these are the Wilsons. As you can see, they're alive."

He surveyed the room and then returned his attention to Gil. "I see that. You want to tell me what happened?"

Mattie spoke up first, followed by Mama and Papa. Everyone was talking except her and Gil. Then the sheriff whistled and the room went silent.

"One at a time. Miz Mattie, I'll take your statement first. Mr. and Mrs. Wilson, I'm glad to see you here alive and well. We've been taking care of your daughter and praying for your safe return."

Papa stepped forward and reached to shake the sheriff's hand.

"No, sir," the lawman said. "The credit goes to my brother, Gilbert Hollis. He's the true hero here for watching over your daughter." He paused. "And unless I miss my guess, I would say he's also the one who dispatched Neville."

"That he is," Mattie exclaimed. "I heard it all, though I admit I ought to have been down in the cellar with these fine folks."

Her father shifted positions and held out his hand to Gil. "Is that true, son?"

"I did what any man would do," he said to Papa.

"Thank you," he told Gil. "I owe you a debt that will never be adequately repaid. Please know my door is always open to you should you find yourself in New Orleans."

"I will remember that, sir."

Papa looked over at Bea. "Daughter, I have waited far too long to say this, but get your things. Your mother and I are taking you home."

"Now?" she asked.

He nodded. "The sooner the better. There is a stage leaving Crinoline Creek in just over an hour. We must be on it."

"Dear," Mama said gently, "it would be quite rude to presume on these nice folks and then leave so abruptly."

"You've not presumed upon us at all," the sheriff said. "I understand that your family is reunited and should be back home. Gil, don't you agree?"

Bea held her breath, hoping for the soldier who would be a doctor to speak. To say something, anything, that would keep her here with him. Instead, he looked beyond her to Ed and nodded.

"Good. Then I will let you do the honor of driving them to town while I wrap up the crime scene here. First, however, I need the statements. Miz Mattie," he called. "You first, and keep it brief."

Bea took advantage of the distraction to step out onto the porch. She wandered as far as the rocker and settled there. Her thoughts scattered and refused to form.

Then the door opened and Gil appeared. He closed the distance between them and knelt in front of her. Her heart rose. Now he would say the words.

"Bea," he said as he took her hand in his. "I'll never forget you."

With that, her heart shattered. She rose, leaving him kneeling there. "That's it?" she demanded. "You'll never forget me?"

He stood and said nothing for far longer than she expected. Then, slowly, he shook his head. "No, there's just one more thing."

He pulled her into his arms and kissed her. As quickly as the moment arrived, it was gone, and so was Gil, leaving her to stand there not knowing whether to be angry at his impertinence or disappointed that he hadn't kissed her sooner.

On the way into town, Gil gave no evidence of what had transpired between them. Even as he bade them goodbye at the stage stop, he kept quiet. As the stage rolled out of Crinoline Creek, Bea could not stop the flow of tears.

✿

Bea sat on the balcony of her second-floor bedroom and looked up at the stars. She was home again. In New Orleans where she belonged. She'd had several weeks to settle back into life here. Then why did she feel so out of place?

Just on the other side of the door was her beloved bed with the carved swans and the feather mattress. But rather than sleep, she remained in place looking up at the sky and wishing the stars of West Texas were the ones she saw overhead.

The memory of those stars, of that man, of that kiss threatened, but she pushed it away. Though she'd cried enough tears to fill the Mississippi River past flood stage, they still came so easily. Would she ever forget Gilbert Hollis?

Probably not.

A rustling sound echoed in the courtyard, followed by someone calling her name.

She went to the edge of the balcony and looked down.

The man she had shed all of those tears over was right there just below her, and he was seated on the back of a beautiful horse that she recognized from the ranch. Her heart soared as she took in his handsome face, now free of the beard that had hidden it before.

"Gil, what are you doing here? And why are you on that horse?"

"I'm doing what I promised to do back in Jonesboro. I'm here to take you with me."

Her heart soared. "Take me where?"

"To the first parson willing to marry us," he said. "We can add that to what we tell your parents in the morning, because I would like to tell them you're coming back to Crinoline Creek to be a doctor's wife." His smile faltered slightly. "Bea? Answer me."

"You haven't asked me anything," she said, her heart singing.

He shook his head. "I guess I haven't. All right, then. I told you way back when we were leaving the wagon train that a man had to be able to take care of a wife before taking one. Well, you might have thought I hadn't given any recollection to that kiss on the porch, but I have. Every waking moment and more than a few nights while I was dreaming."

"I'm not disagreeing with any of that," she said through her grin, "but you still haven't asked me anything."

"Bea Wilson, I've taken over as the town doctor in Crinoline Creek and am looking for some input into that house I am building on my own land adjacent to Hollis Ranch."

"Again. . ."

He laughed. "I know. This isn't familiar territory, but I'm getting to the point. Bea Wilson, will you come away with me and be my bride?"

"Doc Hollis," she said as she picked up her skirts and headed for the stairs leading down to the courtyard, "I thought you'd never ask."

❧ Author's Note ❧

The Rest of the Story

$\mathcal{A}$s a writer of historical novels, I love incorporating actual history into my plots. As with most books, the research behind the story generally involves much more information than would ever actually appear in the story. In truth, I could easily spend all my time researching and not get any writing done at all!

Because I am a history nerd, I love sharing some of that mountain of research I collected with my readers. The following are just a few of the facts I uncovered during the writing of this novel. I hope these tidbits of history will cause you to go searching for the rest of the story.

Here are just a few of the interesting things I've discovered during the writing of *Bea Mine*:

When the story opens, Gil is riding into Jonesboro, Georgia, with the Texas Eighth Cavalry. This was an actual group made up of former Texas Rangers who joined the war effort when Texas seceded from the Union. General Sherman's troops routed the Confederate troops in the Battle of Jonesboro, which began on August 31, 1864. This battle had heavy casualties on both sides and led to Atlanta falling into Union hands.

Fort Davis is an actual fort that has had multiple uses over the years. Located at the foot of the Davis Mountains, the fort was opened in 1854 as a post to protect travelers, mail coaches, and freight wagons making their way out west.

The Prairie Traveler by Randolph B. Marcy, US Army Captain, is a real book that was published in 1859 by the United States War Department. Its actual title is quite long: *The Prairie Traveler, a Hand-book for Overland Expeditions with Maps, Illustrations, and Itineraries of the Principal Routes Between the Mississippi and the Pacific*. The book is a treasure trove of information for settlers planning to leave city life behind and set out by wagon trail to their new homes out west. Everything from routes to wagon maintenance to shelter and provisions is included. I found a new copy of this book, now published by Applewood Books, in a museum shop in Park City, Utah, and had to have it. If you enjoy reading or writing books set in the Old West, this reference book is a must-have.

The San Antonio–El Paso Road was an actual road that ran between San Antonio and El Paso. It started out as a trail blazed by Texas Rangers and became a heavily traveled route for merchants and pioneers heading west and for the delivery of mail. Stages also used the route, as did soldiers before and during the Civil War.

Kathleen Y'Barbo

Kathleen Y'Barbo is a multiple Carol Award and RITA nominee and bestselling author of more than one hundred books with over two million copies of her books in print in the US and abroad. A tenth-generation Texan and certified paralegal, she is a member of the Texas Bar Association Paralegal Division, Texas A&M Association of Former Students and the Texas A&M Women Former Students (Aggie Women), Texas Historical Society, Novelists Inc., and American Christian Fiction Writers. She would also be a member of the Daughters of the American Republic, Daughters of the Republic of Texas and a few others if she would just remember to fill out the paperwork that Great Aunt Mary Beth has sent her more than once.

When she's not spinning modern day tales about her wacky Southern relatives, Kathleen inserts an ancestor or two into her historical and mystery novels as well. Recent book releases include bestselling *The Pirate Bride* set in 1700s New Orleans and Galveston, its sequel *The Alamo Bride* set in 1836 Texas, which feature a few well-placed folks from history and a family tale of adventure on the high seas and on the coast of Texas. She also writes (mostly) relative-free cozy mystery novels for Guideposts Books.

Kathleen and her hero in combat boots husband have their own surprise love story that unfolded on social media a few years back. They make their home just north of Houston, Texas and are the parents and in-laws of a blended family of Texans, Okies, and one very adorable Londoner.

To find out more about Kathleen or connect with her through social media, check out her website at www.kathleenybarbo.com.

JOIN US ONLINE!

Christian Fiction for Women

Christian Fiction for Women is your online home for the latest in Christian fiction.

Check us out online for:

- Giveaways
- Recipes
- Info about Upcoming Releases
- Book Trailers
- News and More!

Find Christian Fiction for Women at Your Favorite Social Media Site:

Search "Christian Fiction for Women"

@fictionforwomen